BLOODLINES:

Clan

Mae Tanner

Table of Contents

Inheritance
Lylathin Lake: Autumn Y1015

Lord Sulwin Grimwolf lay on the bed, watching the woman as she dressed. "I have a proposition for you."

She turned to face him, her blouse half on. "Yes?"

"My wife is barren and I need an heir. Would you be willing to become my mistress and bear one for me?"

She laughed. "Ain't you got any housemaids willing to serve you that way?"

He curled his lip. "I want my heir to favor me. Most of my followers are dark. I suppose it's possible I could find one among them to bear me a tow-headed child. Some of my guards even have red hair. You're blonde, though. With you, I'd have a guarantee of a blond heir. Besides, ain't you an Irclaw bastard? You've got the mouth. If I got an heir from you, it would be high clan."

She shrugged. "I suppose I could be a clan bastard. Ma never said who my da was. I doubt she knows. I enjoy my life, though. Do you truly expect me to be faithful to you for any amount of time?"

"It would only be until you've borne a child. Once you've done that, you can do as you please. I'll pay well. I should have done this years ago, but I kept hoping Barza would carry at least one child to term."

She raised a brow. "And I wouldn't have to raise the brat?"

"Well, I'd hope you'd at least nurse it until I can find a wet nurse. After that, sure, you can just leave it with me."

She bit her lip, her brow creased. "You said you'd pay well. How much is 'well'?"

"Five hundred marks plus your clothes and living expenses until the child is weaned or I get it a wet nurse, your choice. I'll also provide you with clothes fit for a clanswoman."

She sat on the bed by his side. "Make it a thousand marks and you've got a deal."

He nodded. "Agreed." He pulled her in for a kiss. "While we're at it, I should know the name of my heir's ma so I can have it added to the clan records. What is it?"

"My name is Chianne."

***

Winter Y1016

Sulwin entered Chianne's room and stood, watching her nurse her baby.

He held out his arms. "Let me have a look."

She handed the infant over. "You have a daughter. I named her Serrin."

He examined the child and frowned. "Gray eyes? I want my heir to look like me. *I* have *blue* eyes."

She scowled at him. "*My* eyes are gray. Are you trying to weasel out of our deal? You only cared about hair color before. The brat's a blonde. That was all you asked for."

He grunted. "It's fine. Do you want your marks now or when you leave?"

"I'll take them *now*, if you don't mind. Have you found a wet nurse for the brat yet? I'd like to go back home. I'm tired of being cooped up. You didn't tell me you were going to keep me locked in your suite when I agreed to this. I want to see the sky again. I want a different man in my bed."

He laughed. "I had to be sure *I* was the child's da." He pulled a sack out of his satchel and tossed it to her. "Here. There are a few extra marks for the inconvenience. It shouldn't take long to get Serrin a wet nurse. You may leave any time you please."

"It'll take me a few days to recover from giving birth. I can

2

nurse her until then."

He nodded and handed the child back. "It's been a pleasure doing business with you."

***

Spring Y1022

"How is she?"

The healer bowed. "I'm sorry, my Lord, but she's fading."

Sulwin sat beside his wife's bed and took her hand, leaning over to kiss her brow.

Barza opened her eyes and gazed up into his face. "I'm sorry I was such a disappointing wife for you," she whispered.

He stroked her hair. "You were a *fine* wife."

"I couldn't give you an heir "

He traced her lips with a fingertip. "I managed. Serrin will suffice. She even has Irclaw blood. Her ma's an Irclaw bastard."

Barza laughed. Her laughter turned into a fit of coughing. Sulwin lifted her off the pillow until her breathing eased, then laid her back down.

She reached up and stroked his cheek. "You chose that woman because she's my kin? How romantic."

"If *you* couldn't give me an heir, I wanted the woman who did to at least *look* like you."

"You forget I saw her. She looks *nothing* like me. She's young and beautiful, Irclaw mouth or no. I'm old and wrinkled."

"The only difference between the two of you is your eyes."

"My mirror tells me different."

"Your mirror lies."

"Flatterer." She sighed. "I'm tired Sul. So very tired."

"Rest. I'll stay by your side."

She closed her eyes.

***

Sulwin entered the nursery and stood, leaning against the doorjamb, watching his daughter eat breakfast. The nursemaid caught sight of him and took Serrin by the shoulders, turning her towards him.

"Look Serrin, there's your da."

The child ran to him, and he picked her up.

"Da! Whatcha got for me?"

Serrin's as avaricious as her ma. "Nothing today. I just came to see how you're doing."

"Sir?" the nursemaid asked. "How's mistress?"

"She died early this morning."

The nursemaid lowered her head. "I'm so sorry, sir."

"She's no longer in pain."

"Yes, sir, and she lived a full life, even if she never had children of her own."

"There is that." I need to get away from the keep. Go some place I won't see her ghost everywhere I look. I need to go somewhere no one knew her.

* * *

Sulwin led a team of workers to the transport docks. He pointed at the shore. "Build me a ship. I want to explore the seas."

The foreman nodded. "Yes, sir."

Over the following weeks, Sulwin kept close track of the workers' progress. When he wasn't at the docks, watching the ship's construction, he was in conference with his seneschal.

"I'll be leaving you in command. See that Serrin receives the proper training for her future role as Lady of the house."

Rilva nodded. "Yes sir. I'll care for her as if she were *my* child. When do you think you'll return?"

He shrugged. "That's in the hands of the gods."

The day came when the ship was seaworthy and well stocked with supplies. Sulwin boarded with a squad of guards. Rilva brought Serrin to bid him farewell on the deck.

"Sir? The keep won't feel right without you."

"I need to clear my mind. A sea voyage will do that. Take care of my daughter."

"Yes sir. I'll see that she's cared for as befits her station in life."

"I'll see you tomorrow, da," Serrin said.

He picked her up. "I'll be gone much longer than that." He kissed her cheek and handed her to Rilva.

"Come Serrin," Rilva said. "We need to go back to shore."

"Bring me back a present, da!" Serrin called to him as

Rilva carried her off the ship.

***

Lylathin Lake: Summer Y1027

The ship sailed in to the harbor and the crew tied it to the dock. Sulwin ordered a pair of his guards to set out for the keep and bring back horses. He had chairs placed on the deck of the ship for himself and his bride.

"Since they're on foot, it'll take the guards a couple of days to get to the keep. We'll have to stay on the ship until they return with horses."

Nemed nodded. "It's very warm." She took her coat off and hung it on the back of her chair.

"The climate here is milder than your home. Summer's warmer and winter ain't as harsh."

She pointed at the transport docks. "What's that?"

He glanced in the direction she'd pointed. "It's unimportant. You don't need to worry yourself about that."

Lines appeared between her brows.

He leaned back in his chair with a sigh. "It feels good to be back in a more temperate climate."

Three days later, Rilva arrived with horses and a carriage.

She bowed to Sulwin. "Welcome home, sir. The guards told us you've taken a new bride." She waved at the carriage. "I thought the two of you might like to ride home in comfort."

Nemed smiled at the other woman, her glacier blue eyes crinkling at the corners. "Thank you. I appreciate that."

Sulwin escorted his bride to the carriage and helped her into it, turning to Rilva before entering himself. "We were married according to *her* people's customs before returning here, but I want a true clan wedding. I don't want there to be *any* question regarding the legitimacy of our marriage. Please arrange for that."

She nodded. "Yes sir. What's her full name?"

"Nemed Starblossom."

"Very well, sir. I'll arrange for a herald to announce the wedding."

When they arrived at the keep, Sulwin brought Nemed to the family suite. He glanced towards the door to the room where Barza had spent her last days before leading the way to the master bedroom.

Nemed paused by the bedroom door to look around the sitting room. She pointed at a picture of a blonde woman holding a bouquet of roses hanging on the wall by the door to the hallway. "Who's that?"

He hesitated a moment. "That was Barza Irclaw Grimwolf, my late wife. I had the picture painted shortly after our marriage. I'll have a picture painted of you to hang on the other side of the door."

She nodded and entered the bedroom.

***

Autumn Y1027

"*Must* your bastard live in our family suite?"

Sulwin frowned at his wife. "She's my heir unless *you* give me one. Barza accepted her presence in the suite, and she was my wife when Serrin was born. If *any* had cause for jealousy towards the child, *she* did. My arrangement with Serrin's ma was strictly business. She's a doxy who lives at the Irclaw tavern. I ain't so much as spoken to the woman since Serrin was a baby."

"The brat's been coming into our room and taking my things."

"I'll have a talk with her nursemaid."

"That ain't enough. Serrin's a sneak. Sila ain't able to keep track of her all the time."

He sighed. "I'll have a lockbox made for you. You can keep your valuables in there. You can keep a key safe from a child, can't you?"

"I'd prefer she moved out of our suite. A lockbox is a temporary solution. I suppose it'll do for now, though."

***

Spring Y1028

Sulwin bowed to his guests. "Welcome, welcome." He gestured towards the youth the couple had with them. "Is this the boy?"

The man nodded. "Yes, this is Edreal, our eldest."

"Come and meet my daughter." He led the way to the

family suite.

Nemed was in the sitting room, sorting colored ribbons.

Sulwin kissed his wife on the cheek. "Is Serrin in her room?"

She nodded. "I believe Sila is giving her lessons at the moment." She raised a brow at the couple and their son. "Who are our guests?"

"Kirtu and Dracna Rastag, with their son Edreal. We've been discussing marriage prospects for Serrin once she's old enough."

A crease appeared between Nemed's brows. "You're arranging a marriage for your bastard while she's still a child?"

Kirtu laughed. "We're considering it. Of course, it's contingent on Serrin remaining Lord Sulwin's heir."

"I see."

Sulwin tapped on the door to Serrin's room, and Sila emerged.

"Could you bring Serrin out? I have some guests I want her to meet."

The nursemaid nodded. "Yes, sir."

That night, when Sulwin retired to bed, he found his wife sitting naked on their bed as she brushed her pale gold hair.

"You have no intention of siring a legitimate heir. *Do* you?"

He frowned at her. "If it happens, it happens. I ain't *trying* to avoid it."

"*Ain't* you? We sleep in the same bed, but you ain't touched me since our wedding day. It'll *never* happen if you don't do *your* part. Or are you too old? Do you expect me to take a lover and pass another man's bastard off as your get?"

"No."

She set her brush aside and extended her hand towards him. "Then come. Perform your husbandly duties. At least *try* to sire an heir with me."

***

Summer Y1028

Sulwin handed his guest a drink. "My wife is pregnant. It seems Serrin will cease to be my heir come winter."

Kirtu took a sip. "Perhaps the child will be a daughter. We can still connect our clans."

"It's a wide age gap. Edreal would be a man grown by the time my new heir is old enough to wed. Can you guarantee he'd be willing to wait that long before he marries?"

"I have younger sons."

"Very well. We'll plan on that."

***

Winter Y1028

The midwife emerged from the birthing room. "My Lord? You have a son."

Sulwin frowned. "I'd planned on a daughter."

The woman shrugged. "The gods decided differently."

He stood. "Well, if I have a son, I'll adjust my plans." He walked into the room where his wife sat on the bed, nursing her child.

"What's the boy's name?"

"I've named him Hulos."

"Give him over and let me look at him."

She offered her son to Sulwin, and the baby started crying.

He wrinkled his nose. "Fussy thing, ain't he?"

"He was nursing. You get cranky yourself if you're interrupted during a meal."

"What's this bruise on his back?"

Lines appeared between her brows. "It ain't a bruise. It's a birthmark. I have one just like it on *my* back. You've seen it. Do you have *nothing* good to say about your son?"

He handed the baby back to her. "He seems healthy enough. I'd planned on a daughter, though. Kirtu and I spoke of a betrothal between your child and one of his younger sons."

The creases between her brows deepened. "There's plenty of time before we need to think of a spouse for him. He ain't even a day old yet."

"I'll be seventy-one in a couple months. I need to ensure the future of the clan before I die."

"And I am but twenty. I can serve as his regent if necessary. There's plenty of time."

***

"Do you have any daughters?"

Kirtu shook his head. "All I have are sons. I suppose I could ask around the clan to see if one of my kin has a daughter, though."

Sulwin shook his head. "No. Your ma was my late wife's sister. I want to connect our clans through *your* line."

"Well, my wife is pregnant. Perhaps she'll bear a girl this time."

Sulwin grunted. "I'll make an offering. If your wife bears a daughter, I'll take it as a sign the gods' favor a connection between our clans."

***

Summer Y1029

"My Lord. A messenger brought a letter from house Rastag."

Sulwin opened the letter and scanned its contents. He set it down and bowed his head, his hands clasped.

Nemed looked up from her plate. "What's the news?"

"Dracna has borne a daughter. She named her Miawa." He rose from the table. "I need to make an offering to the gods. They've favored me this day. I *will* connect house Grimwolf to Rastag. We'll hold the wedding fourteen years from now."

"Are you seriously planning Hulos's marriage while he's an infant?"

"Of course. I'm an old man. I need to ensure the succession while I'm still able."

***

Winter Y1035

"It's time to assign companions for you, boy."

Hulos cocked an eye towards where his father sat at the head of the table. "Companions?"

Sulwin nodded. "You're seven now. It's time you started taking an active part in the clan. In order for you to do that, you need companions." He motioned with his hand and four men stepped forward. "I've chosen these guards to serve."

Nemed frowned. "Surely his companions should be around

his own age! In house Starblossom, the heir's companions serve as friends and playmates during childhood."

"Hulos needs to learn how to be Lord of the house as quickly as possible. I'm an old man. He'll ascend while still young." He turned back to Hulos. "From now on, you're to sit in when I hold court. You'll accompany me when I make my inspections in the summer. You'll spend the rest of your time taking lessons. In the morning, you'll go to the practice grounds and join the children of the guard in weapons' training. In the afternoon, you'll study the scholarly arts with a tutor."

"I don't recall you organizing your bastard's days like this before Hulos was born!"

"Rilva organizes Serrin's schedule. A girl has different needs than a boy. I can assure you, however, that Serrin's days are just as full as Hulos's will be. She's still part of the succession, after all. She needs to know how to rule too."

"Yet she *still* finds time to come into our bedroom and steal things."

Sulwin frowned. "Ain't you keeping your things in that lockbox I had made for you?"

"It ain't big enough to hold all my clothes. I can barely fit my jewelry and cosmetics into it. We've discussed this many times before. I want her *out* of our suite!"

He slammed his hand on the table. "*Enough*! Serrin is *still* my daughter. She's in the succession after Hulos. She'll remain in her room. Our bedroom door has a lock on it. I'll have a key made for you. We'll keep the door locked from now on."

* * *

Hulos surveyed the other children lined up for weapons' practice. One boy smiled at him and waved. His spirits brightened, and he waved back. Perhaps weapons' training wouldn't be terrible.

The instructor chose partners for each of the children. The instructor paired him with another boy, and it soon became clear that he was woefully outclassed. Try as he might, he couldn't match the other boy's speed and skill. The instructor came and watched them sparring for a bit.

"Ulson, take it easy on master Hulos. He's younger than you and ain't used to this yet. When you're partnered with a weaker opponent, your job is to teach. Once he's up to speed, then you can start testing your limits. Remember when *you* were new?"

"Yes, sir, master Burzock."

When practice was over, the children went to the washroom to bathe. Ulson invited Hulos to join him and his friends to play during their free time.

Hulos shook his head. "I can't. Da has me taking lessons after lunch."

"Well, if you ever get any free time, come join us. We get free time every afternoon and have lots of fun."

After lunch, his father introduced him to his tutor, a woman named Tharula. Tharula had him go over harvest and tribute records, showing him the relationship between a homestead's increase, its running costs, and the tribute it was required to pay. At first, the lessons confused him and made his head spin.

I wish I could spend afternoons with my friends from weapons' practice.

As time passed, one day blended into the next. The only time there was any variety was on court days and holidays. Court took priority over his regular instruction. Once court was over for the day, his father grilled him on the petitions and crimes brought before the court.

***

Summer Y1043

"Come to the audience chamber after lunch, Hulos."

"Is it court today? Ain't it too soon for that? You just held court yesterday."

Sulwin shook his head. "No, it ain't court today. You're getting married. Your bride will arrive this afternoon."

Nemed scowled at her husband. "You're really going through with this, ain't you? Hulos is only fourteen. He's much too young for marriage."

"Miawa is the same age. If her family considers her old enough, then Hulos is too. I *must* secure the succession. Kirtu and his family will be here this afternoon. The marriage *will* take place."

"It's ok ma. I don't mind getting married. Ciarus and Dulgo like to brag about the women they tup. If I get married, I'll have something to brag about, too."

"Who are Ciarus and Dulgo?"

"Two of my friends from weapons' practice. We talk in the washroom as we're cleaning up before lunch."

Sulwin laughed. "No doubt they're the type your ma thinks would have made better companions than the men I assigned."

"How old are Ciarus and Dulgo?"

"Um, I think Ciarus is twenty-one, and Dulgo is twenty."

"Ain't they a little old to be your friends?"

"Well, Ciarus is Aybrim's brother and Dulgo is Ulson's. Aybrim and Ulson are my friends, too."

"How old are they?"

"Aybrim and Ulson are both fifteen."

"Do you have any other friends?"

"Grukor. He's seventeen."

"Why are all your friends older than you?"

Hulos shrugged. "Ulson is my weapons' practice partner. He introduced me to the others."

Sulwin stood. "If you're done interrogating the boy, we need to prepare for the wedding ceremony."

***

Hulos eyed his bride. She had a serious expression on her face as the ceremony progressed and their lives were bound. Her golden blonde hair and bright blue eyes pleased him. None of his friends could have lovers as pretty as Miawa. He glanced at his half-sister, who was sitting by his father, and smirked. Serrin's mouth was too wide for beauty; she looked like the woman in the painting on the other side of the door from the one of his mother in the family sitting room. Miawa had a pert little mouth.

After the ceremony, his father pulled him to one side to explain what he needed to do in the nuptial bed while Miawa's mother did the same for her. Their parents then escorted the two of them to their room.

The next day, as Hulos and his friends were washing up, he bragged about his wife; how pretty she was and how good she was in bed. He had a grin on his face throughout lunch, but it faded when the meal was over.

I thought once I was married, da would give me more freedom, but everything's the same except now I have a wife in my bed.

He dragged his feet all the way to the schoolroom, where he had his lesson in scholarly pursuits.

Tharula sighed as he walked into the room. "You need to arrive for your lesson promptly."

"I already know all about how tribute is determined. What *else* do I need to learn from you?"

She set a stack of papers on the table in front of him. "There are always exceptions. You need to learn them."

Hulos hunched his shoulders as he picked up the first page. If I ever have a son, I ain't going to force him to spend so much time studying. Weapons' practice is fine, but surely I don't need to read so much! I'll let him choose his own companions, too.

***

Winter Solstice Y1043

Hulos blocked his partner's attack with his sword. "Hah! Thought I couldn't win, didn't you?"

Ulson laughed. "Guess it's time to stop coddling you." He increased the pace of his blows.

Hulos tried to keep up, but in the end, had to admit defeat. His friend threw an arm around his shoulder as they headed to the washroom.

"You're almost as good as me. I beat you, but it was a challenge."

Hulos grinned. "Yeah, sure. Admit it. We're equal in skill."

"I *do* have a slight edge."

Grukor snapped a towel at Ulson. "Only cause Hulos is tupping his wife every night." He jerked a thumb at Ciarus. "He's always slower the days after a night of romance."

"Well, if *that's* Hulos's excuse, it's a good one."

Hulos shook his head. "Mia wasn't feeling well last night, so I let her rest. I hope she ain't sick."

Dulgo nudged him, chuckling. "Maybe it's something

else."

Hulos furrowed his brow. "What do you mean by *that*?"

"You ain't married to a guardswoman."

"What does *that* have to do with anything?"

"You keeping track of your wife's menses?"

Hulos frowned. "No. Why should I?"

Ciarus laughed. "Oh ho! You think our little lordling's got a bun in the oven?"

Dulgo shrugged. "He's been tupping her long enough, and I doubt either of them's been taking precautions."

Hulos stared at his friends. "You mean... maybe I'll be the first of us to be a da?"

Dulgo snorted, flexing his muscles. "*I'm* already a da. I tupped Sulsi when she was trying for a baby. Little Shade's my daughter."

Ciarus shook his head. "No, she ain't. *I* tupped Sulsi *too*. Shade's *my* daughter! You think you could sire a redhead with those black locks of yours?"

Aybrim snorted. "Half the guardsmen tupped Sulsi. Some of them tupped her more than once. *Neither* of you are even in the running. She only took you two into her bed out of pity."

The two young men grabbed Aybrim and dumped him in a tub full of dirty water while their friends giggled.

When Hulos went into the dining room for lunch, he eyed his wife thoughtfully. Miawa didn't *look* any different. Just in case, he filled a plate from the sideboard with the finest Solstice delicacies and brought it to her. She smiled at him.

***

Late Spring Y1044

Hulos stomped through the hallway. The midwife was with Miawa and he wanted to be there with her when she gave birth, but his father had insisted he go to his classes.

You'd think, of all times, the birth of my first child would be a reason for me to be excused from going to class. Even ma thought they should allow me to at least stay in the waiting room. Not da though. Never da!

Serrin called after him. He stopped, turning to face her.

"I'll come let you know what happens as soon as the midwife tells us the news."

He smiled at her. "Thanks." *Ma don't like Serrin, but I think she's just jealous. Serrin ain't taken any of my things. I don't think she's ever really taken any of ma's things either. I think ma just says that because she don't want Serrin in the family suite.*

He was sitting at his desk, reading the record of some obscure case Tharula had handed him, when Serrin slipped into the room. She knelt by his side.

"You have a son. Miawa named him Norris."

He grinned at her. "Thanks."

After she left, he couldn't concentrate on his lessons. His thoughts kept straying to his son. He whispered the words to himself. "My son. My son, Norris."

That night, when he returned to his room, he found his wife seated in a comfortable chair and nursing their new son. He knelt by her side.

"May I see him?"

She offered him the baby. "Be careful."

Carefully, he took his son in his arms and examined him, counting the tiny fingers and toes. "He's perfect." Hulos took a peek at Norris's back. "He even has my birthmark." He grinned at his wife as he returned the baby to her. "You've done well."

***

Summer Solstice Y1044

"Hulos!"

He disengaged from his sparring partner and looked towards the side of the field, where Serrin sat on a horse.

"What is it?"

"Da has special guests for the Solstice feast today. You're to dress up for lunch."

"Thanks."

She turned her mount and headed back towards the keep.

When they went to the washhouse, Ciarus wrapped an arm around his neck. "Your sister sure looks fine. I don't suppose you'd care to introduce me?"

"How would I go about doing that? You don't serve in the dining hall and she don't usually come out to the practice field."

"Tell her I'll be in the stables after the feast today." He flexed his muscles. "Tell her I'm the tall, blond one. I saw her looking at me."

Hulos shrugged. "I'll tell her. She probably won't come, though."

"We'll see."

His da's special guests were Hulos's father- and mother-in-law. He fetched a plate of special delicacies for Miawa while she sat with her parents and showed off their baby. He stopped beside his sister and dutifully passed on his friend's message.

She eyed him for a moment, then gave a curt nod. "Thanks."

"I told him you probably won't go, but he insisted I tell you."

"The blond, right?"

He nodded.

"I'll think about it."

***

Spring Y1045

"There's an execution after breakfast today. Everyone is to be there before you go about your normal activities." Sulwin's cheeks were flushed, and his brow was deeply furrowed.

Hulos started. "An execution? You ain't sentenced anyone to death in court. At least I ain't been called to attend a court where you condemned anyone to death."

"This is a special case. I need to make an example." Sulwin rubbed his left arm, his nostrils flared.

When they'd finished eating, they filed out into the courtyard. Serrin sat in a chair by Sulwin's seat, weeping. She hadn't been at breakfast. Tied to the whipping post was Ciarus. Hulos gasped.

"Da, *no*! That's one of my *friends*!"

Sulwin turned to him. "I caught him tupping your sister in the barn last night. The punishment for that is death." He sat in his chair and motioned for the execution to begin.

"No!" Hulos shouted. "Don't do it!" He knelt beside his father. "Please da, not my friend!"

Sulwin stood and shook his fist in the air. "Get *on* with it!"

He gasped and grabbed his arm, slumping to his knees, his mouth working.

Nemed was at his side immediately. "Someone fetch a healer. His Lordship is ill."

The executioner turned to face them. "Shall I continue with the execution?"

Hulos shook his head. "No, release him."

Healers came and bundled Sulwin off to his room. The rest of the family sat in the sitting room, waiting. Nemed turned on Serrin; her cheeks flushed bright red.

"You've *killed* him. You've killed your da with your whoring. Get out of my *sight!*"

Serrin ran to her room and shut the door.

An hour later, the head healer came out of the room with slumped shoulders.

Nemed stood. "Is he?"

The healer shook her head. "I'm sorry. There was nothing we could do."

Nemed's head drooped. She turned to Hulos. "I wish to return to my people. Please grant me this boon."

Hulos blinked. "What?"

"Your da is dead. You are Lord now."

He looked at the door to his parents' room. "But…"

Nemed touched his arm. "They pulled the ship that brought me here out of the sea and put it in dry dock. It should still be there. Please order it made ready to sail and give me a crew for it. I want to go home."

He nodded numbly.

Not knowing what else to do, he headed for the courtyard, stopping to stare at the whipping post.

"Hulos?"

He turned. Ciarus stood a few yards away with a bundle in his arms.

"I'm sorry."

"Da died."

Ciarus nodded. "I heard." He hung his head. "You know I can't stay. Thank you for ordering me released."

"You're my friend. You've been my friend since I started weapons' practice. Do you *really* have to go?"

Ciarus nodded. "My presence would be a problem for you.

It's *my* fault your da's dead. I can't even stay anywhere near the lake."

"Ma's taking a ship back to her people."

He laughed. "Are you suggesting I go *with* her? Do you really think she'd welcome *me* as part of her crew?"

Hulos sighed. "No. You're probably right."

"I think I'll head south along the river that runs out of the lake. See what I can find that way."

Hulos hugged him. "I'll miss you. Take a horse and be careful."

"Watch over Serrin for me, will you?"

Hulos nodded, his brow furrowed. I'll watch over her all right. I'll keep very close watch on her. She ain't going to cost me any more of my friends.

His eyes burned as he walked with his friend to get a horse from the stables and watched him ride out the gate.

Ciarus paused before passing through the opening. "Cheer up. Maybe I'll find a beautiful heiress somewhere and become her trophy husband."

Hulos had to laugh. "If you ever come back this way, my gate will be open."

"I'll keep that in mind." He urged his horse forward and was gone.

Back in the family suite, Hulos found his mother pounding on the door to Serrin's room.

"What are you doing?"

She turned. "You can't allow her to stay in this room. She's responsible for your da's death. I thought I'd get her moving."

He shook his head. "She's staying in there. I want her where I can keep my eye on her. She ain't leaving the suite again, not even to eat."

"Are you sure?"

He nodded. "She cost me one friend. I ain't giving her an opportunity to cost me another."

"Very well. In the meantime, you need to move into the master bedroom. Come. We'll get you settled in your new quarters."

The ship proved to be in good shape and was ready to sail a week after they laid Sulwin to rest in the keep graveyard.

Hulos saw his mother off at the keep gates.

"Are you sure you don't want to stay at the keep with me?"

She shook her head. "I can't remain." She handed him a lockbox and a key. "Here, I don't think I'll need this anymore. You take care of yourself."

"I will."

That night, at the dinner table, he glanced around at his new honor guard and sighed. It didn't feel right to be short one of his friends.

Dulgo nudged him in the side, leaning over to whisper in his ear. "Want to go to the Shanty Town tavern tonight? It's Solstice Eve and there'll be a party. We can all drink toasts to Ciarus's health and wish him luck."

Hulos straightened. That was right. He didn't have every minute of his life plotted out anymore. "Yeah. I never got to go to Shanty Town before. It'll be good to drink a toast to Ciarus's health. We can wish him luck finding a beautiful heiress to make him her trophy husband."

Grukor grinned at him. "*That's* the spirit!"

***

Lylathin Lake: Summer Solstice Y1045

Serrin opened her door and surveyed the sitting room. Miawa was screeching at Hulos and his new honor guard. Hulos lay on a couch, holding his nose. Blood seeped through his fingers and covered his mouth and chin. His honor guard stood around, looking like idiots.

"I ain't sleeping with a *drunkard*!" Miawa stormed into the master bedroom and emerged with her baby. "*You* can put him to bed. I'll be sleeping in one of the *other* rooms." She tried to open a door out of the sitting room, but found it locked. Fuming, she took the ring of suite keys from Hulos, found the key to the door, and unlocked it. "I'll be in *here* until he sobers up."

Hulos's honor guard tried to get him on his feet, but they were all falling down drunk. Sighing, Serrin went over and took her brother's arm.

"I'll tend his injury and put him to bed. You lot go to your own quarters."

"Yes'm." They stumbled out of the room.

As she helped Hulos off the couch, he kissed her cheek, smearing a trace of blood on her face.

"Mia," he muttered.

Great. He thinks I'm his wife. "Come on, little brother. Let's get you to bed."

She hauled him into his room.

***

Hulos awoke alone in his bed. He sat up with a groan. His head swam, his nose throbbed, and he felt sick. The light coming in through the windows hurt his eyes.

"Mia?"

Minutes passed. Hulos dragged himself out of bed and over to the wardrobe to dress. He peered at himself in the mirror over Miawa's dresser. He had a bandaged nose and bruised face. When he emerged from the bedroom, a door on the far side of the sitting room opened and Miawa came out with Norris in her arms.

"What were you doing in *there*?"

She sniffed. "I ain't sleeping with a drunk. You can come in to me here when you're sober, but I'll be sleeping in *this* room from now on."

"Da kept that door locked."

"And I *un*locked it. This is a woman's room. It's almost as big as the master bedroom. It'll suit me just fine."

He stumbled over and looked inside. The room looked like a rose garden. Painted roses covered the walls. A wardrobe with roses carved on it sat against one wall. Even the window curtains and the quilt on the bed had roses embroidered on them.

"There are clothes for a woman in the wardrobe and cosmetics on the dresser. The clothes are old-fashioned and the cosmetics probably ain't good but otherwise it's perfect for me. You can have the master bedroom for yourself. I'll be in *here*."

He sighed. "Fine. You can have this room."

She eyed him with her lip curled. "Are you going to be sick all day? It's Solstice. You're supposed to preside over the feast."

He clutched his hair. "I'll be up to it. Let's head to breakfast."

As he opened the door out of the suite, Serrin emerged into the sitting room.

"Are you going to allow me to attend the feast?"

He glared at her. "I'll have a feast plate brought in to you. You ain't leaving the suite."

She stood, eying him for a moment, before she retreated inside her room, shutting the door behind her.

***

Summer Y1045

"Your sister's pregnant."

Hulos glanced at his wife. "*Is* she now?"

She sniffed. "No doubt it's that guard's brat. The one your da was going to execute."

He turned back to his plate. "No doubt."

"You should kill it when it's born."

He glared at her. "If it's Ciarus's child, then Serrin will have made up, in part, for bringing about his banishment. He's *still* my friend. His bastard will be welcome in my home. I may even relax the restrictions I've put on her." *How did I ever find this shrew attractive? If it weren't for Norris, I'd send her back to her clan.*

"Are you planning on getting drunk again tonight?"

"That sounds like a *wonderful* idea!" He turned to address Ulson. "You feel up to getting drunk tonight?"

His friend grinned at him. "Sure."

He looked around at his other friends. "How about the rest of you?"

Ascension
Lylathin Lake: Winter Y1045

Miawa stormed into her husband's audience chamber with her son on her hip, dragging Serrin behind her. Serrin desperately held onto *her* baby while she struggled against the steel grip on her wrist. Miawa's lips thinned and her eyes narrowed as she caught sight of Hulos seated on his throne. A pair of commoners stood before him. Ignoring them, she stepped directly in front of the dais and shoved Serrin forward. Serrin stumbled and fell to her knees, still trying to protect the infant she cradled in her arms.

"I've brought your doxy before you."

Hulos stood. "That's my bastard half-sister, not a doxy."

Miawa curled her lip in a sneer. "Oh? If she's your sister and not your doxy, then why has she born you a son?" She pointed at the newborn babe in the other woman's arms.

Serrin knelt on the floor, clutching her baby and weeping.

"Are you saying you vished her? Because if she ain't your mistress then you must have *vished* her. Your own *sister*!"

She stalked over to a desk that sat before the dais and set her son on it, looking around the room at those assembled. "Either way, I have something to say." She pointed at the toddler sitting on the desk. "This is not my son. He is not the babe I nursed at my breast. He is not the little boy whose small

22

hurts I kiss away." Her face twisted. "He will never be a youth I wish to see grow into a man. I am not his mother. I am a Rastag and I will *never* be the mother of the child of a man who would sire a bastard with his own *sister*." She turned on her heel and left the room.

The little boy burst into tears.

"Bitch!" Hulos shouted after her. He turned his attention to Serrin. "Did you tell my wife that I sired your bastard? I thought Ciarus planted the seed."

"It was you," Serrin whispered. "You vished me."

"I didn't *hear* you," he shouted. "*What* did you say?"

Serrin stood. "You vished me," she said clearly. "Drogan is *your* son."

"You keep saying I vished you. Strange that I don't remember even *bedding* you, let alone *vishing* you."

"You were *drunk* that night," she replied sullenly. "You never remember the things you do when you're drunk."

"How convenient, and you told this tale to my wife?"

"I didn't *have* to. She knew Drogan was your son just from looking at him. He has the same birthmark you do. The one you got from your ma."

He stalked over to stand in front of her. "Are you *sure* of that?"

She spat at him, holding the baby out. "Yes! See? *My* bastard is *yours* as well."

He pulled the child from her arms and, after examining him, handed him to one of his guards. Then, turning back towards his half-sister, he drew his sword and stabbed her through the heart.

He wiped his sword off on her clothes. "Well then, *bitch*, I guess that makes him my *heir* and *you* won't be *able* to disown *him*." He addressed his guards, pointing at his sister's corpse. "Dispose of that trash and one of you find a wet nurse for my new heir."

He turned to the young commoner couple that stood clutching each other and staring wide eyed at the body at his feet. "You two want to marry, do you?"

The pair looked up at him and nodded.

"Yes," the man whispered.

Hulos pointed at the tiny child that sat wailing on the desk.

"Raise the boy as if he was your own and you have my permission."

The woman swallowed visibly, then walked over and picked up the child, soothing his cries. "What's his name?"

"His name is Norris." Lord Grimwolf removed his clan mask, revealing pale blue, bloodshot eyes and tousled blond hair. "Court is over for the day. Everyone leave."

***

Lylathin Lake: Summer Y1062

Shade laughed up at Norris. "Do your parents know you're here with me? Or do they think you're keeping watch over the sheep?"

He kissed her. "Kadan can watch the sheep by himself for a bit." He smiled. "I'd much rather watch *you*."

"And what are your intentions, good sir?"

"Only the most dishonorable!"

She giggled. "In that case. I want a demonstration!"

"Glad to oblige." He lay on the grass by her side and pulled her into his arms.

"Norris! Shade!" Kadan shouted a short time later. "Ware!"

"What is it?" Norris called to his brother.

"Da's coming! You better get over here before he sees what you two are doing or you'll be getting a hiding."

Norris stood. "Damn! You want to stick around and face him?"

Shade straightened her clothes and shook her head. "I'd better go. Your da don't like me coming around and corrupting his innocent son."

"Want to meet at the tavern tomorrow night? There's going to be a dance. We can have some fun without da fussing at us."

She sighed, shaking her head. "Can't. I could meet you there tonight, but I'm on duty tomorrow night."

"I'll sneak out and meet you tonight after the sheep are in the fold, then."

They kissed each other goodbye, and he returned to the sheep while she mounted her horse and headed towards Shanty Town.

***

Drogan frowned. "But *why* do I have to get married? You always say women are bitches. I don't want to be tied to a bitch. I don't understand why you're making me *do* this!"

"Some things are necessary evils. You need a wife so you can get heirs. The clan needs to extend the line of succession."

"Can't I just sire some bastards on the serving wenches? That would be a lot easier."

Hulos shook his head. "It's always better to have legitimate heirs. That's especially important for *you* since you're a bastard yourself. I've arranged a solid match for you. I know there's gossip, but the Splitskulls are tolerable stock. Quia is five years older than you, but she should give you healthy heirs. Now come meet your bride."

Drogan sighed and followed his father to the audience chamber where the wedding was to take place. As he stepped to Quia's side in front of the priest, he glanced at her. Their eyes met, and she glared at him.

She don't look any happier than me.

After the ceremony, the newlyweds retired to his room in the family suite and he undressed. She sat on the bed, her lips pressed firmly together.

He frowned at her. "Ain't you going to take your clothes off? We're supposed to 'unite' so the marriage is complete."

She sneered at him but undressed and lay on the bed with her legs spread apart. "Get it over with."

He frowned as he joined her on the bed. Da's right, women are bitches and my new wife is the lead bitch. I wish I hadn't had to get married. I don't understand why da was so insistent I marry her. Da's never made me do anything I didn't want to do before.

***

Shade was sitting at a table in the tavern when Norris joined her. "Howdy stranger. Buy a girl a drink?"

He kissed her tenderly and smiled. "I'd be happy to. Unfortunately, tending the family sheep don't pay well." He spread his hands.

She grinned. "Well, in *that* case. *I'll* buy *you* a drink! Guard duty pays *very* well."

Several drinks later, she helped him to his feet. "I've arranged a room for the night," she murmured in his ear. "Care to join me?"

"Sure." He sighed, staggering a bit as he stood. "Always happy to coo-cooperate with a member of my Lord's guard."

Much later, as they lay sleeping in each other's arms, the door to the room Shade had rented burst open, startling them awake as it slammed against the wall. They sat up on the bed and stared at Rafin, who stood in the doorway, glaring at them. The innkeeper stood behind him, wringing his hands.

"Get up and get dressed!" he ordered Norris. He scowled at Shade. "What do you think you're doing, getting my son drunk and taking him into your bed?"

Norris's cheeks flushed as he scrambled into his clothes. "We *love* each other, da."

Rafin snorted. "She's older than you are, boy. She's taking advantage of you. You're a toy to her. She'll grow tired of you one day and break your heart. She'll drop you the instant she finds some other youth that strikes her fancy. It ain't as if she'd ever consider settling down and *marrying* you."

Shade's eyes narrowed. "But I *would*! I'm willing to go with Norris to Lord Grimwolf on his next court day, so we can request permission."

Rafin sneered at her. "I'll believe *that* when it happens." He grabbed Norris by the ear and dragged him out of the room. "You're coming home *now*, boy."

* * *

Drogan woke first and looked at his wife. *I should make the best of my marriage.* He leaned over to where she was sleeping to give her a kiss. She started awake, glared at him, then wiped her face where he'd kissed her.

"They may have forced me to marry you, and I may have to spread my legs for you, but I will *not* accept kisses from you. Keep your filthy lips to *yourself*!"

He glared back at her. "What is your *problem*? Did you have a lover they forced you to abandon? Is *that* why you're such a bitch?"

Her lips curled into a sneer. "No. I simply have no desire to have any more to do with a son of inbred vishing than

26

absolutely necessary."

His jaw dropped. "What are you *talking* about?"

She turned her shoulder to him. "*Everyone* knows your da vished your ma, and that she was his bastard half-sister. I feel unclean just being in the same *room* as you."

He flushed. "That ain't true!"

She snorted. "Ask your *da*. His wife was so incensed when she found out she disowned your brother and returned to her family's keep."

"I *will* ask him!" he shouted. He got out of bed and dressed quickly before stalking out of the room.

Drogan found his father sitting on a balcony, staring towards the land north of the keep. "Is it true? Did you vish my ma and was she your sister?"

Hulos started. "Who told you *that* tale?"

"My *wife*! She told me *your* wife disowned your previous heir, too."

His father sighed and rubbed his forehead. "It's true that your ma was my sister. As for whether I got you by vishing her; that I can't say. Apparently, I was drunk that night. The only reason I know you're mine is by your birthmark."

"You were drunk? I don't believe it! You drink nothing stronger than water. And what's this about a birthmark?"

Hulos nodded. "I drank heavily when I first ascended. Da died when I was just sixteen. He'd never let me do anything and never gave me any privacy, so when I suddenly became Lord of the clan, I went wild." He pointed at a small scar on his nose. "I got *this* while in a drunken stupor. I ain't touched a drop since my wife disowned your brother, though. As for the birthmark, it's on the back of your left shoulder. Ain't anyone noticed it when you were washing up after weapons' practice?"

Drogan hunched his shoulders. "I do my bathing in the family suite."

Hulos sighed as he stripped to his waist and showed Drogan his back. "You can't see your own, but you can see mine."

"A family birthmark? If she was your sister, wouldn't I have gotten it from my *ma* then?"

"Not quite a *family* birthmark." Hulos put his shirt back

on. "*I* inherited it from *my* ma. Since *your* ma and I shared our da but had different mas, you could only have gotten it from me."

"And this brother of mine that your wife disowned? What happened to *him*?"

"I gave him to a commoner couple who asked permission to wed. They promised to raise him as if he were their own. He knows nothing of his heritage. Nor will he. What good would it do to tell him? He could inherit nothing."

Drogan frowned. "If you could somehow restore him to his place as your heir, would you do it?"

"There's no point in dwelling on what can never be."

"*Would* you though? If it *were* possible?"

"Of course. I take no pleasure in knowing that one of my sons is a motherless bastard. That can never happen, though. Even my wife couldn't reverse what she did that day."

***

Lord Hulos Grimwolf sighed. Court was boring. Today was no exception. Several couples had come before him to ask for permission to wed. He granted permission automatically and signaled for the next couple to come forward. It was a red-haired woman dressed as a guard and a blond youth who looked like some kind of farmer. He eyed them thoughtfully through his mask.

"Are you looking to marry a *farm boy*?"

She nodded. "We love each other."

"If you want to marry, shouldn't you choose another guard as your mate? Farm folk ain't known for producing offspring worthy to join my guard."

"I don't care." She tossed her head. "Whether they end up as farm folk or guards, I want *him* to sire any children I have." She wrapped her arm around the youth's waist and hugged him.

"You realize you'd be marrying below your station? Not to mention you don't need to *marry* for him to sire your children."

She nodded. "We love each other, and marriage is important to his family."

He turned to the youth. "Do you really love her or do you

just want the better life you'd be able to afford on the pay of one of my guards?"

"I *love* her. I want to marry her so da won't scold when we want to spend time together."

He sighed. "Very well. What are your names?"

"My name is Shade," the woman replied.

"My name is Norris," the youth said.

Hulos froze where he sat. "Norris? Are your parents Rafin and Tisha?"

The boy nodded. "Yes, sir. We keep sheep for you. Our homestead is north of the keep. Da's been headman two years now."

Hulos's mouth went dry. "Are you happy with your life, boy?"

Norris nodded, a slight frown on his face. "Yes sir, and I'll be even *more* happy if I can marry Shade."

Hulos closed his eyes. *Thank the gods no one can see my face behind my mask.* "Permission granted. I hope you two enjoy a long and happy life."

The pair beamed at him. "Thank you, sir," they replied in unison, exchanging a kiss as they left the chamber.

***

At the wedding, Shade introduced her mother to her new in-laws. "Ma, these are Norris's parents. Tisha, Rafin, this is my ma, Sulsi."

Sulsi smiled as Shade left to speak with another guest. "But I *know* you. I believe I was present when you made your request for permission to wed." She glanced at where Norris was being congratulated by the other workers from the compound, his golden mane standing out among all the black or brown-haired folks. "So, Norris is your *son*?"

Tisha lifted her chin. "*Yes*. He's our eldest and has been a wonderful son and a good brother to his siblings."

Sulsi's smile widened. "I'm pleased that *some* women know a good thing when they see one. He's worthy of my daughter."

Rafin smiled at Sulsi nervously. "Is Shade's da here with you?"

Sulsi chuckled. "There ain't enough room here to host all

the potential candidates for *that* position. When I decided I wanted a child, I looked over my fellow guards and, once I received permission, bedded as many of them as fit my criteria. Even *I* couldn't tell which of them planted the fruitful seed. Almost all the guards regard her as kin, and over half of the *male* guards think she might be their daughter. I named her 'Shade' for a reason."

* * *

Autumn Y1062

"I've got a surprise for you. Close your eyes and come with me." Norris led Shade along a graveled path away from his parents' home, eventually stopping. "Ok. You can look now."

She opened her eyes and stared. "A house?"

He nodded. "Lord Grimwolf ordered it built just for *us!*"

"He didn't do this for your sister when *she* got married. Did he?"

"No, but then Nevia didn't marry a member of his personal guard."

"You sure you ain't a clan bastard? I mean, you even *look* different from the rest of your family. You're blond, and everyone else in your family has dark hair."

He laughed, shaking his head. "Don't be silly. If I were a clan bastard, do you *really* think my da would've have left me to grow up on a *sheep farm*?" He led her inside the house. "Come see. It's built just like my parents' home. The kitchen is in the back." He pointed at a passage in the wall. "And there are *five* bedrooms upstairs. I hope you don't mind, but I invited Nevia and Ricco to move in with us. With five bedrooms, there's one room for them and another for us. Then, when we have children, we have a room for the sons, another for the daughters, and we'll still have an extra room for whatever we want to use it for."

Shade smiled at him. "I think it's a *wonderful* idea for you to invite your sister and her husband to live with us. They'll provide you company when I'm on duty."

He smiled back at her. "I'm glad you don't mind. Nevia told me she thinks she's pregnant and they ain't happy living with Ricco's family. How soon do you think we can start having children of our own?"

"I need to get permission from Captain Dinsil and so far, he's refused. He don't want me on the sidelines carrying a shepherd's brat." She wrinkled her nose. "*His* words, not mine. I've been asking ever since our wedding."

He hugged her. "Well, all we can do is keep asking. In the meantime..."

He led her outdoors and pointed at the ground underneath the two windows in the front of their new home. "I'm prepping the soil here. I'll plant roses in the spring. This place needs to be beautiful for you. When you see roses, you'll know you're home."

*** *

Drogan frowned at his father. "I want a separate bedroom from my wife. I'll tup her, but I don't want to sleep in the same bed with her anymore."

"Very well. I'll have a full suite constructed so you and Quia can have separate rooms."

Drogan hunched his shoulders. "I also suspect she's barren. I wish there was some way I could get rid of her."

"Unfortunately, the only way out for you is if she were to die, and if she died by any means other than natural, we'd have her clan at our throats. *I'm* still married to Miawa, even though I ain't so much as spoken to her in years."

"Why don't you have an assassin take her out?"

"And *then* what? Take another wife? You realize, don't you, that if I took a new wife and sired children on her, that *you* would no longer be my heir?"

"Just be done with women altogether!"

Hulos laughed. "I can do *that* **without** sending an assassin after my wife. You don't see her around *here*, do you? And we need women in order to keep the clan alive."

"I wish we didn't."

*** *

Winter Solstice Y1062

Shade bit her lip as she waited for her turn to request a Solstice boon from Lord Grimwolf. She was taking a major chance going over Captain Dinsil's head, not to mention that if

Lord Grimwolf refused her, the answer would not only be final, it would be for all time... but she'd asked each month since her wedding, only to be turned down. She watched as her Lord refused the last boon asked. It was *her* turn now. She licked suddenly dry lips, stepped forward, and bowed.

"What is your request?" Hulos asked.

"My Lord. My husband and I wish to be given permission to bear a child." She glanced towards where Captain Dinsil sat on one side of the room. "Each month since we wed, I've asked permission from the captain of the guard, only to be refused."

Hulos sighed. "Why ain't your husband here to support you in this request?"

Shade's cheeks burned, and she hung her head. "I know you often refuse solstice boons. I couldn't bring myself to build his hopes up when there's a high risk that you might not grant my desire."

"Your request is not unreasonable. You may take one year away from your duties to try for a child."

Shade beamed at him. "Thank you, my Lord! My husband will be *so* pleased. I'm sure our efforts will be fruitful."

***

Once the festivities were over, Drogan followed his father to the family's personal quarters. "Da, why did that woman ask for permission to try for a baby? Couldn't she just get pregnant from being with her husband?"

Hulos glanced at his son and sighed. "She's one of my guards. Female guards must request permission before they get pregnant. Failure to get that permission is a punishable offence and the life of the child would be forfeit. The guards take steps to prevent that."

Drogan frowned. "Are the steps the guards take to avoid pregnancy available for *any* woman to use?"

"I suppose. They'd have to know of them first, though."

That night, when Drogan went in to his wife, he closed his eyes and pretended to himself that her smooth, brown braids were flaming curls, cut short around a beaming face, smiling with pure joy at the thought of becoming a mother.

***

Shade handed Norris a box. "Happy Solstice lover."

"A gift? I didn't get *you* one."

She laughed. "You don't need to. This gift is for *both* of us."

A slight crease between his brows, he opened the box. "Powder?"

She took the box from his hands and cast the contents into the fireplace, where the powder went up in flames. "Yes!" she whispered in his ear. "It's the powder that prevents me from getting pregnant."

His eyes lit up. "You got permission?"

"I got permission." She pulled him down with her onto the sheepskin rug in front of the fireplace. "Lord Grimwolf *himself* gave me the boon of a year away from my duties so we can try for a baby."

***

Spring Y1063

Drogan smiled as he explored his new quarters. It had taken long enough before they were ready for him and Quia to move in. There was a sitting room with an exit to the hallway. He had a spacious bedroom, his wife a slightly smaller one. There was a private bathing chamber, and there were two additional rooms for him to use as he saw fit. For the first time since his marriage, he'd be able to sleep in peace. Even better, *he* had keys to *all* the rooms.

I can lock Quia in her own room if I want to, and only I could release her. I can't keep her locked up all the time, of course. The servants will deliver trays of food without question, but da would ask about her if he don't see her once in a while. I can do it as a punishment, though.

***

Summer Y1063

Norris had made benches to set on either side of the windows of their home. Shade sat on one and smiled as the scent of the roses wafted over her, her hand resting happily on the hard swelling at her waist. Norris and Ricco were out with the sheep while she and Nevia tended to the home. Not that *she* was of much use in a domestic capacity, which was why Nevia had sent her outside while she prepared the mid-day meal in the kitchen.

Nevia cried out from inside the house, "Shade!"

Hurrying inside, she found her sister-in-law sitting in a puddle on the kitchen floor. "What happened?"

Nevia gave a gasp of pain. "I think the baby's coming! Go get ma!"

Shade ran out of the house and down the path towards the house where Rafin and Tisha lived with their younger children.

***

The bear sniffed the air. Its small eyes peered through the trees at the open land where a flock of sheep was grazing. It had been trailing a receptive sow for the last few days, but food was always welcome. It charged the sheep and, with a swift blow from one powerful paw, killed one of them. The rest of the flock fled, bleating. As it settled down to eat, a loud boom filled the air, and it felt a sharp sting on one of its shoulders. It lifted its head and saw a human standing a short distance away. It rose to its hind legs and roared. There was another boom and another sting. The bear charged at the human, slamming into it and biting at its head. There was one last boom as the bear crushed the human's skull with its jaws.

***

Shade looked up from where she sat beside the bed, where Nevia lay nursing her newborn son. Kadan stood in the door. His eyes were red and there was blood on his clothes.

She started in alarm. "What's happened?"

Kadan sniffed. "It's da. There was a bear got after the sheep." He wiped his eyes. "We brought him home. Norris and Ricco are sitting with him."

Tisha gasped. "Is... is he?"

Kadan shook his head. "Bear almost bit his head off. Ripped him up good too." His chin lifted. "Da took the bear out, though. When we found them, it was dead. Norris says we should wrap da in the bear's skin when we bury him."

Tisha knelt on the floor and began wailing.

***

Drogan rode beside Hulos as they passed through the keep gates. It was time to do an inspection tour of the clan homesteads and set the tribute each would be required to pay this year. They headed south first, planning to make a clockwise circuit, ending back at the keep. His spirits were high. He smiled up at the sun shining in the bright sky. It was good to get out of the keep, away from his shrew of a wife... and the farmers often prepared special treats for them to taste while they were in the compounds.

The inspections went as they normally did until they reached the sheep farm at the northern border near the forest. Hulos led them inside the compound and to a two-story house where they pulled up. A woman wearing a baby pack came out of a garden by the side of the building, followed by a boy carrying a basketful of vegetables.

The woman bowed. "My Lord. Are you here for inspection?"

Hulos nodded. "I am indeed. Please send for your headman so I can receive his reports."

The woman turned and took the basket from the boy. "Navry, go fetch Norris."

The boy nodded and ran off.

Hulos raised a brow. "'Norris?' Ain't your headman named Rafin?"

"He *was*, my Lord," the woman replied, winging her hands. "There was an accident last month, and it killed my husband. Our son, Norris, has taken his position as headman."

"I'm sorry to hear that. Rafin was a good man." He turned to his guards and gestured towards her burden. "Carry that basket for her."

When Norris arrived, the inspection party sat in the front room of the large home where the woman lived; eating small cakes the woman had brought them. Drogan raised a brow when he saw the man. Norris had long, golden blond hair and blue eyes. Everyone else he'd seen on the farm either had black or dark brown hair and brown eyes.

Norris bowed to Hulos. "My Lord."

Hulos nodded in return. "Tisha told us about your da's death last month. Have you been able to prepare the report properly or will you need more time?"

"I helped da with his duties and he taught me all I need to know. I have the report prepared."

After they'd completed dealing with the business at hand, Hulos asked about the accident that had taken Rafin's life.

"It was a bear. Da took a flock near the edge of the forest and a bear came out and killed a sheep. Da shot it and it killed him."

"Do you need us to hunt it down?"

Norris shook his head, his chin high. "Da killed the bear, even as it killed him."

"You killed the bear?" Drogan asked. "What happened to the hide?"

Norris turned towards him. "We wrapped da in it to bury him with the bear's skull at his feet."

Drogan frowned. "You should have tanned the hide to give as part of your yearly tribute."

"Drogan!" Hulos snapped. "A man *died*. Show some respect." He turned towards Norris. "Please forgive my son. You had every right to use the bear's hide for your da's shroud."

Later that day, when they returned to the keep, Drogan confronted his father. "That was *him*, wasn't it?" he demanded as soon as they could speak privately. "*That's* why you didn't punish that man for not presenting you with the bear's hide as part of the tribute."

Hulos frowned. "The bear was not part of the harvest. If they'd needed us to hunt it down, I would have kept the hide, but since *they* killed the beast *themselves,* they had the right to use it in any way they saw fit."

"You didn't answer my question. That *was* him, wasn't it?"

"That was who?"

Drogan sputtered. "You *know* what I mean, that blond man on the sheep farm among all those dark-haired folk. That was my brother that your wife disowned. *Wasn't it?*"

Hulos sighed. "Yes, but it has nothing to do with whether they had a right to do as they chose with the bear hide."

"*Sure* it don't." Drogan stormed out of the room.

***

Early Autumn Y1063

Shade smiled tiredly up at Norris. "You have a daughter."

He leaned over and kissed her, then turned his attention to the baby nursing at her breast.

"Hello, sweetheart." He gently caressed the top of her tiny head. "Are you going to be a fighter like your ma?"

Shade chuckled. "It's a little early to tell *that*. Maybe she'll be a shepherd like her da."

"Well, it looks like she has red hair like her ma, and whatever she ends up becoming, she's a welcome addition to our home."

***

Summer Solstice Y1067

Drogan walked into his wife's room just as she was completing the final touches to her wardrobe for the summer Solstice celebration.

"Strip and spread your legs," he commanded vindictively.

She scowled but complied. As he mounted her, she gave him a hostile look. "Just how long do you intend to continue with this futile endeavor? You can't get me pregnant. You're sterile."

"We'll see about *that*."

She sighed and turned her head. "What are *you* staring at?" she snapped. "Ain't you ever seen a man rutting before?"

Drogan glanced over his shoulder to see who she was addressing. A young maid stood in the door to Quia's room, staring at them with her mouth open and eyes wide. The girl's dusky cheeks flushed darker still.

"No, ma'am." She lowered her head and turned away.

"Then come, sit and watch." Quia's voice dripped with malice. "Watch as my husband tries futilely to get me pregnant." She gestured towards a chair near the bed.

The girl gaped at the chair. "Please, *no* ma'am. I'll just go out and come back when he's left."

Quia turned back to Drogan with a sneer. "See? Even a little mouse knows you're less than a man."

The maid was mocking him *too* now? He'd show *her*!

Drogan leaped off the bed and grabbed the girl, ripping her skirt off as he threw her to the floor. When he'd finished with her, he stood. She stared up at him with wide, tear-filled eyes. He scowled; there was blood on her thighs.

"You're bleeding? Are you on your menses?"

"No." She whimpered. "I was a maiden."

For a moment, his shoulders stooped, and he turned away, his cheeks burning as shame washed over him. Then a realization struck him and he turned to glare at Quia. "Bitch!"

Quia laughed. "Did you *really* think house Splitskull would hand one of our maidens over to one such as *you*? Truth be told, I've *proven* my fertility. After our wedding, you asked if they'd forced me to give up a lover. I hadn't. I've never been with a man I couldn't replace with another, but I have a daughter that my clan forced me to leave for others to raise… and the tip of one of her little fingers is worth more than your entire damned clan!" Her eyes darted away from his face. "Oh, look," she pointed at the maid who was trying to slip out of the room while they talked, "the little mouse is fleeing."

Drogan turned and pounced on the girl. "Where do you think *you're* going?" He grabbed her by the arm.

She wept as she struggled against him. "Please? I want my ma."

Quia sat on the bed with her legs crossed and mocked the girl. "Poor little mouse. What are you going to do with her now that you've caught her?"

Drogan glared at her for a moment as he wondered that himself, then turned and dragged the girl out of his wife's room and over to the door of one of the extra rooms he hadn't found a use for since they'd first moved into the suite. He pulled out his keys and unlocked the door. It had been so long since they'd moved in, he'd forgotten what was inside. They'd set the room up as a nursery, with a crib under the window, a larger bed on the left, and a fireplace on the right.

"Perfect!" He shoved the girl inside and locked the door behind her. He turned back to his wife. "We'll *see* if I'm sterile. Commoners breed like rabbits. If I can't get an heir out of *you*, I'll get one out of *her*."

***

"Excuse me, sir," a hesitant voice asked.

Drogan turned. A woman he didn't know was standing at his side, looking up at him. "Yes?"

"I'm looking for my daughter, Tekla. She come to work as a maid here last month. I was told she's serving your wife. She said she'd come visit on her free time, but she ain't come. It's been a month and she ain't come once."

"Uh, Tekla, you say?"

The woman nodded. "Yes. She's fifteen. Just started work last month."

He frowned as if in thought. He hadn't considered that the girl might have relatives who'd come looking for her.

"Ah, yes, I remember. My wife had a new maid. I'm afraid she ran off, though. She only served for a week before she just vanished. No one's seen her since." He shook his head. "The last I know of her, she was with some man. I remember my wife telling me she'd scolded the girl about it."

The woman frowned. "That don't sound like my Tekla. She's a good girl."

"Perhaps I have her confused with another maid then. My wife is a harsh mistress, and it seems to me she's constantly getting new maids. They never seem to satisfy her. It's even possible your daughter never served as one of my wife's maids. I can't rightly tell you any of their names. I doubt my wife could either, and I don't know where any of them might have gone after my wife discarded them."

The woman's jaw dropped. "Your wife discards her maids?"

He nodded. "I'm afraid so. If my wife discarded your daughter, would it have embarrassed her? Would she not seek you out and let you know what happened?"

The woman sighed, turning to go. "That's possible. My poor Tekla."

Once the woman had left, Drogan mopped his brow. He didn't think Quia would volunteer anything about what he'd done with the maid to anyone, but he didn't want to take a chance that someone might ask her directly, and he was sure it would displease his father to learn of his plans for the girl if he were to find out.

***

Autumn Y1067

Drogan sneered at his wife. "I'm sterile, am I? There's no question but that the girl's pregnant now. She's showing, and we both know *I'm* the only man she's ever been with."

Quia sniffed. "If that's true, she'll no doubt lose the brat. Keeping her locked up that way can't be good for a breeding woman. Even if she carries it to term, I'd bet it's deformed."

Drogan glared at her, then stalked over to the room where he kept Tekla confined and unlocked the door. He stood in the opening, checking out the conditions inside. The girl was filthy, and the room smelled bad. He stepped forward, swearing, and grabbed her arm, dragging her out of the room and into the bathing room.

He pointed at the bathing tub. "Wash yourself."

Once she was clean enough to satisfy him, he locked her in the other unused room while he himself cleaned out the room where he'd been keeping her, even stripping the bed and replacing the bedding. When he brought her back to the now clean room, he informed her she was to keep it clean *herself* from now on.

***

Late Winter Y1067

Drogan stared through the window at the dreary landscape outside. *It's time for winter to end.* The year was almost over and spring Equinox would be here soon. He'd go check on Tekla. He smiled to himself as he unlocked the door.

No one knows what I'm doing with the girl but Quia, and she seems to find it amusing. Good thing my suite's so far from da's suite. It'd piss him off if he knew.

He opened the door to the girl's room and found her laying on the floor in labor. As he watched, the infant slid out onto the floor, and Tekla lay still for a moment, gasping. He walked over to pick the baby up and it started wailing. He examined it. It was a boy. He looked at the back of his left shoulder. The birthmark was there. It wasn't as visible against the baby's darker skin as it had been on his father when he'd seen what the mark looked like, but it was there. He glanced down at

Tekla and watched as she gave a last convulsion, expelling what looked like a slab of meat onto the floor.

He stepped back, curling his lip. "Clean this mess up. When you're done with that, I'll take you to the bathing room so you can clean yourself."

She looked up at the infant he held and held her arms out. "My baby! Give me my baby!"

***

Summer Y1069

Shade approached Captain Dinsil. Her daughter was now six. It was time to ask for permission to have another child. Kalida showed signs of taking after her and should become a fine warrior. Norris deserved a child to follow in *his* footsteps. When she finished making her request, Dinsil sat, looking at her coolly.

"Lord Grimwolf said the request was not unreasonable the last time I asked."

He sighed. "Permission granted. However, you're to continue with your duties as long as you're able and you're to return to duty as soon as you can after the birth. You won't get any extra free time for this one."

She smiled at him. "Thank you, sir."

He frowned at her. "Don't ask again. Two is enough shepherd's brats for you to bring into the world."

***

Drogan scowled as he rode north in the early dawn. He'd ditched his companions and snuck a horse out of the stables. When Tekla had gotten pregnant again so soon after having the boy, he'd been pleased. He'd continued being pleased until he'd seen the result. This time, she'd given him a daughter. The girl didn't even have the birthmark. When he'd seen that, he'd smashed the baby against the stones of the fireplace in a fit of fury. Now he had a tiny corpse to dispose of. He found a patch of trees on the edge of a meadow and dismounted.

He'd just finished filling in the tiny grave when he heard sheep bleating. He looked out of the copse and saw the golden head of his disowned brother. His scowl deepened as he watched the man settle down to watch the flock graze on the grass. He stood there watching for nearly a quarter of an hour and was about to leave when he spotted a rider approaching from the south. A crease formed between his brows as he stayed to see who it was.

Once the rider was close enough, he saw a woman dressed as a guard. Norris didn't spot her until she was almost on top of him. When he saw her, he rose to his feet.

"Shade!" he shouted. "I didn't expect you today. I thought you were on duty."

She swung off her horse and removed her helmet, revealing short, flame-red curls. This was the woman Drogan had seen at the winter Solstice celebration years before who'd begged for permission to have a baby. The one he'd fantasized about ever since. He now had a name to pair with her face.

"I traded days with ma. I wanted to surprise you." She reached into her saddlebags, pulled something out and showed it to him. Then, with a flick of her wrist, she sent a spray of something to the wind.

"He said 'yes'?"

She nodded. "He said 'yes'!" She threw both of her hands up and tossed a container and its lid away.

Norris wrapped his arms around her to give her a kiss, but she pulled away and began unfastening his pants.

Moments later, they'd strewn their clothes across the grass and were making enthusiastic love. From where he stood, hidden in the clump of trees, Drogan stared.

This is how coupling should be. Not the way I've experienced it with either my wife or mistress. Quia just lies like a block of wood with her legs spread and Tekla curls up in a ball, so I have to beat her until she submits. It looks like Shade enjoys coupling and Norris is getting more pleasure than I get from either Quia or Tekla.

His fists clenched and his vision dimmed as fury rose within him.

Norris might not be da's heir, and he might live as a simple shepherd, but he clearly has a better love life than I do.

***

Winter Solstice Y1069

Drogan sat to one side of the room, sulkily watching the

Solstice boon seekers enter his father's audience chamber. The boons sought were, mostly, the usual; private homes, marks to spend at the Irclaw tavern in Shanty Town, expensive booze, horses or other livestock. Hulos granted or refused to grant the boons almost at random. The current boon seeker was a worker assigned to tend cattle at a homestead southeast of the keep.

The man bowed down and pulled three wolf furs from a sack. "My Lord, I offer these furs as a sweetener in hopes you'll look favorably upon my request." He spread the furs on the floor in front of the dais. "I killed these wolves as they were preying on the stock I tend."

Hulos rose and came down to examine the furs. "These are fine indeed." He gestured for one of his guards to take the furs away. "What boon do you seek?"

"I wish permission to split from my homestead and build a new one in the north, near the forest. I have several of my fellow workers interested in joining me in this endeavor."

Hulos chuckled. "And if I refuse your boon?"

The man bowed again. "Then I would simply return to my usual duties, my Lord. I know full well that boons depend on your whim. The furs are a gift. Consider them tribute if you wish, not a bribe."

Hulos laughed out loud. "Well said. I grant your boon."

Drogan scowled.

If da can consider the wolf furs as tribute, then the bear hide Norris squandered should have been as well. Da's wife may have forced him to give his original heir away to commoners, but it's clear which of us is the favored son.

***

Early Summer Y1070

Drogan followed his father as they made the rounds of the homesteads. They'd have a new one to visit this year. When they reached the sheep farm, a worker directed them down a path from the two-story house.

"Norris is at his own home today," the woman who greeted them said. "His wife just gave birth to a son and they're taking time to welcome their new child."

When they arrived at the house in question, Drogan felt his

blood boiling. It had surprised him that Norris wasn't living in the old headman's house, but when Norris's home came into sight, he understood all too well. This house also had an upper floor and, besides that, a wall of blooming rose bushes surrounded the building. Shade sat on a bench in front of the house, nursing an infant, a tender smile on her face. Norris sat, cross-legged, on the ground in front of her with a small, red-haired girl on his lap. As the inspection party rode up, he stood, lifting the child onto his shoulder and bowed his greeting.

"My Lord. You come at a propitious time. My wife only gave birth three days ago." He gestured towards Shade.

Hulos dismounted and walked over to Shade, gesturing towards the babe in her arms. "May I?"

She smiled at him. "You honor me, my Lord."

As Hulos picked up the infant, Drogan spotted the birthmark, standing out clearly against the pale skin on the back of the child's left shoulder.

Hulos smiled at the baby. "A *fine* boy. What's his name?"

"His name is Tavar, my Lord."

As he returned Tavar to his mother, Hulos looked at the girl. "And who is *this*?"

Norris smiled proudly. "This is Kalida, our daughter."

Hulos offered the girl his hand, and she reached out and shook it. "You have a fine family. And a beautiful home." He nodded towards the rose bushes.

Norris beamed. "I planted the roses for my wife. They've prospered."

Hulos chuckled. "Perhaps I should have you come tend the gardens at my keep. The roses I have there don't grow near as well."

"It's the sheep manure. We can send some with our tribute if you like. Roses seem to love it."

"I would appreciate that. And it is the year's reports that I'm here for, so I can determine just how much tribute you need to send."

Drogan's rage burned hotter when they arrived at the new homestead northwest of the sheep farm. There were no non-essential touches such as rose bushes *here*. None of the homes the workers of this homestead had built were even fit for his father to enter. The headman said they planned to specialize in raising beef cattle. After examining the reports, Hulos ordered them to send a half-dozen steers as their tribute.

When they'd completed the inspections and returned to the keep, Drogan questioned his father's decisions that day. "Norris promised to send you *manure*, and you act as if it were a precious gift, yet those cattlemen gave you fine wolf pelts at Solstice, and you demand a hefty tribute from them for their new homestead."

"Didn't you see how lush the roses are at his home? I want my own roses to grow as well as his. As for the cattlemen, their homestead needs more breeding stock and fewer steers. Having them send steers as tribute will allow the breeding stock they have to flourish."

Drogan fumed. "Why do you allow roses to be gown on a commoner's homestead, anyway? They ain't got any use for them. Roses ain't crops. And why do they have a second two-story house in their compound?"

Hulos frowned. "Are you *jealous*? Of a *commoner's* house?"

"*No*! It just seems he has the best of what a commoner *could* have. He's got a better wife than I do, though. If I *had* to marry, why couldn't it have been to a woman like *her*?"

Hulos sighed. "I wish I *hadn't* arranged a marriage for you. I wish I'd allowed you to find your own wife. A woman you could love the way Norris clearly loves *his* wife."

"Why *did* you arrange a marriage for me?"

Hulos shrugged. "It seemed the thing to do. My da arranged *my* marriage. I was only fourteen when we married, but I was happy enough with her. At least at first." He sighed again. "It's pretty clear now that your wife is barren. You might as well take a mistress so you can get some bastards."

Drogan blinked. "I have."

Hulos smiled. "Really? Why didn't you tell me this before?"

"You said I need legitimate heirs."

"Well, it would've been best for you to get heirs from your wife, but if you can't, you have no choice but to look elsewhere. The succession must continue and the clan has dwindled dangerously. How are things going with the mistress?"

"She's already given me a son."

"That's good news. What's the boy's name?"

Drogan felt sweat start between his shoulder blades. "She ain't told me his name. I don't get to see them often and the boy only just started walking."

Hulos frowned. "Ask her. A man should know his son's name. And bring him by so I can meet him. I'd love to see my grandson."

"Uh, I'll ask. She don't like to let the boy out of her sight though. I don't think she'd let me bring him here to see you."

"Bring her along then. Your mistress would hold a position of honor here. And since your wife is barren, she must realize you'd *have* to take a mistress."

"I'll see if she'll come," Drogan muttered.

When his father had suggested he take a mistress, he'd thought it would be a good idea to tell him about Tekla and the boy, but doing that had only made matters worse. He could use the excuse that she didn't want to let the boy out of her sight to avoid bringing the brat to meet his father, but what excuse could he make to avoid bringing the bitch herself?

***

Shade sat nursing Tavar as she watched Norris show Kalida papers on which he'd made some marks. "What are you doing?"

He glanced at her with a raised brow. "I'm teaching her how to read. What did you *think* I was doing?"

"Teaching her to read? Why would she need to know *that*?"

He laughed. "It's a useful skill. My siblings and I use it to leave messages for each other on pieces of bark. We have places out on the meadows and around the compound where we can hide notes. It's also required for the position of headman."

"Well, she shows signs she'll follow in *my* footsteps," Shade said, lifting her chin. "She won't need to read for that. *I* don't know how to read."

"You don't?" He raised a brow. "So you ain't read any of the letters I've left you?"

Shade blushed as she shook her head. "No. Were they important?"

He smiled at her. "Do you still have them?"

She nodded. "I like the pictures you draw on them, especially the roses."

"Go get them and I'll read them to you. I'm sure you'll like what the writing says even more."

***

Drogan glared at Tekla. "What's the boy's name?"

She shrank from him, shaking her head.

He stepped closer to her and ripped the child from her arms. "I'll take him away."

She sprawled at his feet and clutched his pants leg, reaching up towards her son. "Please."

"Tell me his name!"

"Kip." She whimpered. "His name is Kip."

Drogan frowned. That didn't sound like a name suitable for a clan Lord. At least it would be easy enough to remember. He eyed Tekla icily.

I can use the boy to make her do what I want! I wish I'd realized that before. "You be a good doxy and I'll let you keep him," he told her silkily. "No more curling up in a ball. When I tell you to do something, you *do* it, and you do it the *first* time I tell you. Understand?"

She nodded.

He smiled at her viciously. "Good, then here's what I want you to do for me right now…"

***

Hulos smiled at his son. "Have you seen your mistress recently?"

Drogan nodded. "I visited her yesterday. My son's name is Kip." He shrugged. "Not a name I would have thought fitting for my heir, but *she's* the one who named him."

Hulos laughed. "Commoners can have odd fancies when they name their children. Where are you keeping them? I'd still like to see them."

"She's in Shanty Town." It was a lie, but Drogan figured it was a good one. "I offered to have her move to the keep, but she's afraid of Quia. I can't say as I blame her. She's also bothered that I can't marry her, so she don't want to meet *you* either."

"Well, see if she'll at least let you bring Kip here. I'd still like to meet my grandson."

Drogan shrugged. "She's adamant about not being separated from him. Maybe when he's older, or perhaps once she's had another baby."

Hulos nodded. "I can wait for that. Be sure to let me know when it happens."

***

Spring Y1071

Drogan's mood was black. Ever since he'd realized he could use threats against the boy, Tekla had been more cooperative, but once again, she'd given him a daughter. This one had the birthmark, and he'd almost let her keep it, but then Quia had asked about the brat and, when he told her it was a daughter, she'd laughed.

"Just watch. The boy will die and you'll have a *daughter* for your heir."

He hadn't been able to stomach that thought and had gone back into Tekla's room and killed the new brat. "No more *daughters*," he'd snarled at the bitch. "You're to give me *sons* from now on. Understand?"

It had been trickier getting *this* brat out of the keep with no one noticing, but he'd managed it. He'd need to figure something out for the future, just in case he needed to dispose of another brat. He rode towards the same clump of trees where he'd buried the first one, wondering if he'd see Shade and Norris there again.

***

Shade smiled at her husband and pointed at a word written on the note he'd left on her pillow. "That means 'love'," she proudly informed him.

He grinned at her. "Do you know what the rest of it says?"

"Uh." She frowned in concentration, staring at the writing, and finally pointed at another word. "There's my name." She looked up at him. "Read it to me?"

He sat on the couch in the front room of their home, pulled

her onto his lap, and pointed at each word as he read his love letter to her.

***

Drogan's mood was no better as he rode back to the keep. There'd been sheep brought to graze near his hiding place where he'd buried the brat, but a pair of boys had been herding them, not Norris, and there'd been no sign of Shade. In his mind, he imagined them together, and when he reached his quarters again, he immediately entered Tekla's room and ordered her to do the things he thought Shade would do for Norris. When the bitch whined about the baby, he once again threatened to take the boy away, too.

He was locking the door to Tekla's room, when Quia came out of her chamber.

"I'm tired of having to be mindful when maids are in here working. Maybe I should talk to your da about your doxy."

He frowned at her, then looked back at the door he'd just locked. "There's no reason *she* can't still do the maid work. I'll just keep the door to the hall locked when she's out of her room. Then it won't matter about maids."

***

Autumn Y1071

"Look da!" Kalida cried, holding up the practice sword Shade had given her. "Look what ma gived me for my birthday!"

Norris smiled at his daughter. "Do you like it better than *my* gift?"

The girl looked at the notebook he'd given her, then back to the sword. "I like them both, but I like them different."

Both Shade and Norris laughed.

"Good answer."

Kalida brought the notebook over to Shade. "Look ma. It has all the letters with pictures of things that start with those letters. Da wrote it and made all the pictures himself. I can help you learn to read good as da and me."

"Oh?" Shade raised a brow. "So, both your presents are for you and me to share?"

Kalida nodded. "We can do lots together."

"You need something to do with your da, then. What can you do with him?"

"I can help da with the roses! I don't *need* a gift to do *that*."

***

Shade helped Norris adjust the pack so it fit comfortably, then stood back and laughed. "Are you *sure* about this?"

"If a ma can wear one of these while she does *her* chores, so can a da. Besides, it ain't as if Tavar were still nursing. It'll be fine, and Nevia has her own children to tend. I can't keep asking her to take care of ours as well. She does enough in our home as it is. Where'll you be taking Kalida?"

"There's a practice field just south of the keep on the shore of the lake. We take the children of the guard there for training. We'll be meeting ma and some of the other guards who are training *their* children. On days when I'm on duty, either ma or my friend Nene will come get her, but today, I have free time, so I'll be able to start her training myself."

He kissed her. "I'll see you at the noon meal, then."

She bit her lip as she mounted her horse. "Norris? Do you ever regret marrying a guard instead of a woman who could stay at home and care for your house? One who could give you as many babies as she pleased?"

He shook his head. "If I'd done that, I'd have missed out on having *you* in my life." He picked Kalida up and handed her to Shade. "Do well at weapons' practice."

"I will da."

***

Winter Solstice Y1071

Norris fidgeted as he waited in line. He'd never sought a Solstice boon before and knew how frivolous the one he intended to request was. He watched and listened as others made requests that seemed to him very reasonable, only to be refused. As the line grew shorter, he concluded Lord Hulos granted or refused the boons at random. His Lordship might well be rolling a die to determine whether he would grant or refuse each request.

Norris almost left before his turn because he knew a

petitioner could never again request a boon his Lordship had refused. When his turn came, he swallowed hard, stepped forward, and bowed.

"What is your request?" Hulos asked.

Norris gulped. "My Lord, my daughter is in training to become a guard. As a guard, my wife has a horse to ride. When my wife takes our daughter to the practice field, the child must ride before her on the saddle. I was wondering if, perhaps, there might be an undersized horse I could have to give my daughter to ride by herself. One that you would otherwise have no use for?" He closed his eyes and held his breath as he waited for the answer.

"Hmm," Hulos said. "Small horses for children now?"

"Yes, my Lord. That was my thought."

"It sounds... an interesting concept. I'll have my herds searched for undersized horses and send them all to you. Breed them and see what you can do with such animals. The children of your compound can ride them freely."

Norris gasped. "Thank you, my Lord." He'd never dreamed Lord Hulos would give him such a bounty when he'd made his request. At most, he'd hoped to be given a single, scrawny pony.

***

Drogan practically exploded when next he spoke privately with his father. "Why are you giving him a herd of *horses*? Even *one* would be more than he deserves!"

Hulos frowned. "The animals I'll be sending him are ones that are normally culled. I have no use for them myself and am curious about how his idea works. Perhaps he can find a greater purpose for small horses than as mounts for children."

"Admit it. If any but *him* had asked such a boon, you would've refused."

Hulos sighed. "Perhaps that may have played some small part in my decision. It is such a *little* thing I can do for him after all."

***

Winter Y1071

Kalida was watching for Norris when he arrived at the

house for the midday meal. "Da!" she yelled. "Come see what's in the corral!"

"What is it?"

"Come see! Come see!" She grabbed his arm and pulled him to the small corral where Shade kept her mount when she was at the compound.

Inside the corral were six yearlings. A grizzled stranger stood beside it, looking in at the animals. When Norris reached his side, he nodded.

"If I might make a suggestion?"

"Certainly," Norris replied.

The man pointed at a bay colt with a blaze down its face. "See that colt there?"

Norris nodded.

"That's the best of the lot. Use that one as your stud when you breed them. Geld any other colts you get." He paused a moment. "We normally cull horses this small. That's why none of them are ready to ride. These are all yearlings and you'll want them to be at least two before you break them and don't breed the fillies until they're three or four. I'll likely bring more when we find them, but this is all we have now."

Norris lifted Kalida up to sit on the corral railing. "What do you think, sweetie? Which one do you want for your own?"

Kalida pointed at the colt the horseman had told Norris to use for his stud. "That one."

The horseman laughed. "No, young miss. If your da follows my advice, he'll keep that one whole. Stallions don't make suitable mounts. You'll want a mare or a gelding to ride."

The girl hesitated a moment, then pointed at a chestnut filly. "Then that one."

The man smiled. "You've got a good eye, young miss." He turned back to Norris, extending his hand. "I'm Ulfan, his Lordship's head horseman. We'll likely see each other frequently from now on. If you have questions, let me know."

Norris reached out to shake Ulfan's hand. "I'll keep that in mind. I'm Norris and this is my daughter Kalida."

Ulfan peered at the pack on Norris's back. "And who is this young tyke?" He pointed at the baby.

"My son, Tavar."

***

"What are those horses in the corral?" Shade asked as she entered the front room of the house.

"Lord Hulos gave them to me."

"You realize, don't you, that even for yearlings, they're all undersized?"

Norris nodded. "They're for the children to ride. Lord Hulos told me to try my hand at breeding them. He'll be sending me his culls from now on."

Shade shook her head. "Well, I guess they *would* be suitable mounts for children. If you're going to breed them, though, be sure not to let your stud anywhere near Lord Hulos's own herds."

"The stud won't ever leave the compound."

***

Autumn Y1072

"Drink it!" Quia said.

"Drink what?" Drogan asked silkily from behind her.

With a gasp, she whirled around. "I fixed the little mouse something to make her more amenable. She's been reluctant to do as she's told lately."

His eyes shifted to Tekla's face. He stepped forward and took the glass from his unwilling mistress's hand and sniffed it.

"How long has my wife been giving you this?"

Tekla looked down. "She been making me drink it since you told me to do for her. I don't like it. It tastes bad."

He sniffed it again, then touched his tongue to it. It tasted bitter. "It's poison. Don't drink it anymore. Don't eat or drink *anything* she gives you. Most important, give nothing from *her* hands to the boy." He walked to the window, opened it, and tossed the contents of the glass outside. "Did you think I'd suspect nothing and you could get away with giving that to her?" He looked around the room. "You have a supply of it here somewhere, don't you?"

The whites of her eyes showed as Tekla stared at Quia.

Quia sniffed. "It *ain't* poison. Look all you like, you won't find anything."

"Won't I?"

He prowled around the room, searching. He came to the vanity where Quia kept her cosmetics and looked through those. "Ah," he said as he opened a box that contained a grayish-white powder. He sniffed it and nodded. "This will be it then." He smiled viciously at his wife as he carried the box to the fireplace and dumped its contents onto the fire, where the powder went up in flames.

"That," Quia said, "was my face powder."

He glared at her. "Well, you can go without cosmetics." He gathered the rest of the containers from the vanity and dumping the contents of each into the fire. "It ain't as if you were trying to look *pretty* for anyone here, *is* it?"

***

Winter Y1072

Drogan smiled as he unlocked the door to his quarters. Ever since he'd caught Quia trying to make Tekla drink whatever it was in that glass, he'd kept both women confined to his suite. Now Tekla was pregnant again. What he found even more delicious was that he was sure Quia was pregnant as well. He'd suspected the powder he'd found among Quia's cosmetics was something that would prevent a woman from conceiving, and considered this confirmation of his suspicions. As he stepped inside, he heard a moan coming from Quia's bedroom. He frowned and went to the door to look inside. His wife lay half dressed on her bed, blood flowing from between her legs and forming a puddle on the bedding. He stood in shock for a moment, then locked Tekla and the boy in their room. Only when he was sure his secret was safe from discovery did he go to fetch a healer.

Hours later, he sat with his father. Hulos placed a hand on his shoulder.

"I'm sorry, son. It's a shame your wife would finally get pregnant after all these years, only to lose the baby. The healer says Quia will recover. It's unfortunate that the healers could only save her life at the cost of her fertility. I don't suppose your mistress will consider coming to the keep now?"

Drogan shook his head. "*She's* pregnant again and is acting broody. I don't want to do anything that might upset her. Especially after what happened with my wife."

Hulos nodded. "I understand, but it's good news that your mistress is pregnant. I hope her pregnancy goes better than Quia's did. Do you think she'll consider letting you bring Kip to meet me?"

It took Drogan a moment to remember that Kip was the boy's name. He shook his head. "No. My mistress's last pregnancy ended in a stillbirth. I don't want to risk doing *anything* that might upset her. The boy seems to be my only seed that's prospered."

After his father left and no one was around that might overhear their conversation, he went into Quia's room and stood by her bed, glaring down at her. Her eyes fluttered open, and she looked up at him.

"You *did* something, *didn't* you? Somehow, you killed your own unborn child and now you can never bear another."

She smiled weakly. "I nearly died. Why would I harm *myself*?" She turned her head back and forth on the pillow. "No, your seed was at fault."

"The other bitch has no problem carrying my seed to term."

Quia waved a hand. "Your little mouse is a commoner. There's nothing of *you* in her brats. Her commoner blood overcomes your clan blood. Just look at them. Little brown brats, every one. Mud babies." Her eyes closed.

"The boy has my *eyes*, and my *birthmark*!"

A faint snore wafted up from the bed.

* * *

Hulos arranged for Quia to return to stay with her family while she recovered from her miscarriage and subsequent surgery. She'd asked, and he'd felt it was the least he could do. He hoped she'd return in a happier state of mind.

If Drogan's mistress fears his wife, perhaps she'll be willing to visit while Quia's away from the keep. I want to meet Kip. The boy's my only grandchild I ain't even seen. Maybe I should've taken a mistress myself and sired a few other bastards, so I'd have more than Drogan to carry on the succession.

* * *

Spring Y1073

"Listen!" Shade said. "I can read your letter!"

Norris smiled. "Can you now?"

She nodded and patted the couch cushion beside her. "Come sit and I'll read it to you."

He settled beside her and wrapped his arm around her shoulders.

She pointed at each word as she read them. "My… dear… dearest… Shade… I… love… you…" She stumbled a little over the longer words in the letter, but read all of them.

He kissed her. "Very good! Soon you'll be able to read them as easily as I write them."

She sighed and leaned against him. "Thank you for teaching me how wonderful reading can be. I'll treasure your letters all my life."

"Well, I intend to write you a new one every time I have a sheet of paper I can spare. Are you sure you'll have the space to store them all?"

"I'll *make* space if I have to!" She wrapped her arms around his neck and pulled him down on top of her. They'd just gotten involved in their lovemaking when tiny hands patted their heads.

"Da!" Tavar crowed.

Shade wrinkled her nose at her son. "Go play with Aunty Nevia. Your da is spending time with ma."

The toddler held his hands towards Norris. "Da! Bick me! Bick me!"

Norris sat up, glancing at Shade with a twinkle in his eye. "I guess we need to be in our room with the door locked if we want to be alone together."

Tavar crawled onto his lap. "Da!" he exclaimed as he wrapped his arms around his father's neck.

***

Drogan grabbed Tekla and rubbed his hand over her swollen belly, puffing out his chest and smiling. She whimpered slightly at his touch. He slapped her face.

"You be a *good* doxy, or I'll take the boy away."

"You leave ma alone!" Kip cried, running over and kicking him.

Drogan felt his cheeks flush, and he slapped the brat away, knocking him hard against the wall, where the boy lay, stunned. Tekla struggled to get away from him. He shook her.

"I can kill *him* too! Instead of just taking him away, I can simply kill him. You ain't the only doxy around, either. I can get another one if you prove too much trouble."

Tears coursed down her cheeks. "Please," she mumbled. "Please."

He shoved her away from him. "Oh, go ahead. Check and see if the brat's hurt."

She stumbled a little, then caught her balance and went to her son's side.

***

Summer Y1073

Kalida rode the chestnut mare to the front of the house. "Ma! Da! Look! I can ride my horse now. She does tricks too. Ulfan showed me how to make her bow." She tapped the mare on her chest with a straight branch she'd cut from a tree and the mare bent one foreleg and 'bowed'.

Shade laughed. "Very good. You can ride her to weapons' training today. Are you ready to go?"

Kalida nodded and waved at Norris and Tavar, who were standing in the doorway. Norris set Tavar on his shoulder and they both waved back.

***

Drogan fumed as he dug yet another tiny grave in the small copse. Was the bitch *ever* going to give him another son? Once again, her spawn hadn't even had the birthmark. He'd just finished filling in the hole when he heard hoofbeats coming his way. He looked out of his hiding place and saw a pair of riders heading south. The smaller rider was on a horse little more than half the size of the other. This must be Norris's brat on a horse their father had given him. His blood boiled and red haze blurred his vision. He stood in his hiding place and watched as they rode by.

When he returned to the keep, he locked the brat in the unused room, then beat Tekla thoroughly before taking her as roughly as he could. When he was done, he ordered her to clean him, threatening to take the boy away if she didn't do what he demanded. As she complied, he watched her through slitted eyes and thought of other degrading things he could force her to do.

***

Hulos sat at the head of the dining table and glanced over at Drogan. "How's your mistress doing? Is there any chance she'd let you bring Kip here to meet me?"

Drogan gave him a startled look, then shook his head. "I'm afraid she had another stillbirth. She's very upset and won't let the boy out of her sight. I think she's afraid she'll lose *him*, too."

Hulos sighed. "I wish she'd agree to come herself. That would solve the issue. With your wife out of the keep, this would be an ideal time."

"No. She feels embarrassed that we can't marry. She says the keep servants will call her a doxy and she couldn't bear that."

"Will I *ever* get to meet my grandson?"

***

Autumn Y1073

Drogan greeted his wife as she entered their quarters. She looked stronger than she had when she'd left, but still had a sour expression on her face.

"Why did you even bother returning? There's no question you're barren now, so there's no point to you even *being* here."

She eyed him coldly. "They didn't give me a choice. My family still desires a connection with your clan."

***

Summer Y1074

Tavar followed close behind his father as Norris showed Lord Hulos the year's records. In his tiny fists, he held a piece of bark and a stick. Hulos glanced down at him, scratching at the bark with the stick, and smiled.

"What are you doing?"

Tavar looked up at him with a serious expression. "I witing. Like da do."

"Your da writes reports for me," Hulos said, lifting the sheaf of papers Norris had handed him. "Is that what *you're* doing?"

The little boy looked at the papers in Lord Hulos's hand, then at his piece of bark, then back at the sheaf of papers. He blinked his eyes, sniffing as he nodded.

"Here." He held up his piece of bark, his voice trembling. "Take *my* weport too!"

Almost reverently, Hulos accepted the piece of bark. "Thank you, young master. This will go into my treasury with your da's report."

Tavar beamed at him. "I wite good weport, jus like da."

Hulos glanced over at Norris. "You should give the boy some paper to write on."

Norris sighed. "We don't have enough extra paper to spare, but we have plenty of bark. Tavar is happy enough to use that."

"I'll send you some extra paper for him. Such an ethic deserves to be encouraged."

* * *

Drogan didn't even bother confronting his father about the paper for Norris's brat. He was sure there'd be some lame excuse or another why it wasn't a great favor to grant. Instead, he went to his quarters and forced Tekla to do the most degrading things he could think of right in front of the boy. He was careful not to hit her. The boy would attack him if he *hit* Tekla, but if she seemed to do the things he ordered of her own free will, the brat would just glare at him.

* * *

Norris stared at the package that Lord Hulos had sent to his home while he was out with the sheep. It had come with a note from his Lordship himself, which read, "Please see that your boy has all the paper he needs and make what use you please of the rest." The package contained enough paper for Tavar to have all he could want, with enough left over for Norris to write Shade a new love letter every day for years to come.

***

Summer Y1075

As Hulos set out on his inspection rounds, he sighed. Drogan had asked to be excused this year. Perhaps he should arrange for something the two of them could do together. Something that would make his son feel proud. He'd done his best to indulge Drogan over the years. His own father had regulated the smallest minutia of his life and hadn't allowed him any room to breathe. He didn't want his son to feel so confined.

When he reached the sheep farm, his mood lightened. Norris's family always had that effect on him. When Norris handed him the year's report, Tavar was standing by with some papers in his tiny hands and proudly handed him a 'report' of his own. He accepted it gravely and was discussing the experiment Norris was doing with the undersized horses when Tavar gave a cry of dismay.

"Oh no!"

Hulos turned back to the boy. "What's wrong?"

The child looked up at him with tears in his eyes. "I dint give you my weport. I give you my wetter for ma!" This was clearly a tragedy of epic proportions.

He looked at the paper Tavar had handed him. The boy had covered it with childish scribbles and some crude drawings. "Why, so you did." He offered the paper back. "It's a very nice letter indeed."

Tavar beamed at him and exchanged another page for the one he'd handed him by mistake. The other paper was more serious in tone, with no drawings to highlight the scribbles.

"Do you write letters to your ma often?"

The boy nodded. "Jus like da."

Hulos glanced over at Norris, who was staring at his son with an alarmed expression on his face.

"Does your da write a lot of letters to your ma?" he asked idly.

The child nodded. "They sit and weed them. Then they kiss and go in their woom and shut the door and won't wet me in." He said the last in an aggrieved tone.

"They read the letters together? Do you know what the

letters say?"

Tavar nodded. "They say I wuv you and you have pity eyes and you have pity b…"

His face aflame, Norris scooped his son up and tickled him. "Lord Hulos don't want to hear about my letters to your ma."

Tavar giggled. "Yes, he *do*. He *asst*!"

Hulos felt a wave of longing sweep over him and sighed at what could have been. "The letters sound lovely. They make me wish *I* had someone to write letters to."

Tavar looked at him with wide eyes, then took his pencil and scribbled something on the page Hulos had handed back. "There!" The boy offered it to him again. "Now it a wetter for *you* and you don't be sad. I wite another wetter for ma."

When Hulos returned to the keep, he took the pages Tavar had given him and carefully wrote the date and what each paper was on the back, where the information wouldn't mar the side the boy had written on. He then pulled his personal strongbox out from under his bed and placed the items inside, setting the piece of bark Tavar had given him the year before on top to hold them in place.

***

Hulos led the way to his audience chamber. "I've asked Alith to paint a picture of the two of us. It'll hang in the dining hall. I should've had this done years ago."

Perhaps this will make Drogan happier. He's been so sour lately.

When they reached the chamber, Alith instructed Lord Hulos to sit on his throne on the dais and for Drogan to stand beside the seat, his arm across the back. He quickly sketched the composition of the intended scene on his canvas before painting them in.

"I'll just get your faces and general poses done today. Then I can work on filling in the rest with no need to bother you further."

***

Winter Y1075

Drogan sat watching the Solstice boon seekers

absentmindedly. Tekla had birthed yet another girl, and he needed to figure some way to dispose of the body. The ground had frozen too hard for him to bury it. At least he'd been smart enough not to tell his father about *this* pregnancy. He doubted the man would continue being fooled with tales of stillbirths, and every time he said anything about the bitch or her brat to him, he'd ask again to see the boy.

I should never have mentioned them to him.

Early on the morning after the holiday, Drogan slipped out of the clan stronghold without his companions and rode north. He'd take the baby's body deep into the forest and dump it there. He rode past the sheep farm and reached the trees. This was still too close. It would be possible for someone to come across the tiny corpse if he left it here. He skirted the edge of the forest and headed towards the cattle ranch. He'd enter the forest past that compound and travel for an hour through the trees before he dumped the body.

***

The great cat sniffed the air. A human was too close to its den. Keeping downwind, it slunk through the trees and brush to see what the human was doing. The human sat on the back of a moving horse. The beast had eaten horse before and liked the taste. It licked its lips as it peered through the bushes. The horse stopped, and the human made a sudden motion. Something landed on the ground a short distance from the cat's hiding place. The horse turned and started back the way it had come. The cat smelled fresh blood. Once the horse had vanished with the human, it crept out into the open, pausing after each step, and investigated the object that had landed so close. It smelled like human, but it also smelled like food. The cat licked it, then took a bite. It was delicious. The animal had tasted nothing like this before. It ate the tiny body and looked around for more, licking up every drop of blood from the snowy ground. Once it had eaten all there was, it followed the tracks of the horse. Surely, if a human could provide it with such delicious food once, it could do so again.

***

Late Spring Y1076

Hulos sat in his audience chamber holding court. A man entered and spoke to the folk who were waiting in line. He frowned behind his mask when those who'd already been in line each allowed the man to take their place. Hulos had barely finished dealing with the current petitioner when the newcomer reached the head of the line. He recognized the man. It was the headman for the compound furthest north from the keep. The one who'd requested a Solstice boon for permission to start a new homestead. Hulos motioned the man to come forward, and he moved onto the floor before the dais, where he fell to his knees.

"My Lord," he said wearily. "A beast has come out of the forest and is preying on the workers at my homestead. It's killed four children, two men and a woman. We dare not leave the safety of our compound. We need your help to kill it."

* * *

Kip sat on the floor of what he thought of as *his* room. His da had been in a hurry today, shoving him inside and shutting the door quickly behind him. He didn't remember hearing the lock click. He looked at the door; thinking about the situation for a moment. Then he stood, walked over to it, and wiggled the knob. It turned in his hand and he was free. He'd never been in any of the other rooms in the suite unless his da had a tight hold on his wrist.

He walked into the sitting room and looked around. The door to his ma's room was open, but the door to the bathing room was closed. Only one of the other three doors was open, and he didn't know where *any* of those led. Kip tried the doorknobs on the shut doors, but they wouldn't open. He wandered over to the open door and heard his ma talking. He peeked through the door into the room.

"Please." His ma stood, hands clasped before her as she pleaded with the other woman he sometimes caught sight of when he was being dragged to either the bathing room or his room. "You hate him too. Tell Lord Hulos about what your husband's doing to me. Tell him about Kip. You can *stop* this! Please? You *must* stop this!"

"Why *should* I? Your fate is all I have to amuse myself with in this forsaken hellhole of a keep. If I told Lord Hulos, he'd only take you and your boy away from here. *I'd* still be Drogan's wife. *I'd* still have to stay. It ain't as if Lord Hulos would have his heir executed. I've told you this before, but you can't seem to get your little mouse mind to understand *my* situation."

His ma sank to her knees in front of the other woman, weeping and repeating the word, "Please," over and over.

The woman gave an exaggerated sigh and rolled her eyes. Then she pointed at him. "Oh look. Drogan forgot to lock your brat up for the day. Why don't you go see if maybe he forgot to lock the outer door, too?"

His ma looked towards where he stood by the door to the room and gasped. She jumped to her feet and ran to him, took him in her arms, and backed away from the other woman, pulling him into the sitting room.

"Don't you touch my Kip!"

The other woman followed them into the sitting room. "Oh, I ain't going to harm your brat. I never tried to hurt *you,* either."

"You gave me poison!"

"It wasn't poison. Drogan lied when he told you it was."

His ma sniffed. "Then what *was* it?"

The woman sighed and sat on a chair in the room. "It was just a little something to prevent you from getting pregnant again. Drogan can't kill your babies if you ain't *having* any, can he?"

"You're lying."

"You didn't get pregnant while I was *giving* it to you, did you? You didn't get pregnant again until after you stopped taking it."

His ma eyed the woman. "You were gone for nearly a year. Did you get any more?"

The other woman shook her head. "I no longer need to take it myself. Why should I bother getting more *now*? I'd been willing to share what I had with you, but I ain't going to the trouble of getting more if it's no longer something that's useful to *me*."

***

Hulos led the hunting party north. He stopped by the sheep

farm before continuing on to the cattle ranch and warned them about the man-eater. The sheep farm was too close to the cattle ranch for his peace of mind. The beast would doubtless move on to the easier target if all the people at the cattle ranch stayed in their compound.

When the hunting party reached the ranch, the people gathered before them, staring at Lord Hulos with pale faces. The beast had killed the children first, carrying their bodies off.

"At first we thought the three boys had run off somewhere, as boys sometimes do," the headman said. "Then it killed a woman and a girl. The woman survived long enough to tell us what happened. It carried the girl off into the forest. We tried to hunt it ourselves, but it killed two of the men that went out. That was when we realized we needed your help."

Hulos frowned at the headman. "How long has it been since the first attack?"

The man hung his head. "The first boy went missing in midwinter, but we didn't know for sure about the beast until six weeks ago, when it killed the woman and the girl."

"You should have come to me *then*! Spring is nearly over and it will soon be Solstice. It'll be harder to spot the beast in the lush months of summer."

"I realize that my Lord, and will accept my punishment for my failings as a headman."

"Your punishment will have to wait until *after* we've killed the beast. Once the man-eater is dead, you're to come to the keep and take your lashes. My ruling is five lashes for each life lost after you knew about the beast. Ten lashes in all."

The headman nodded. "That's more than fair, my Lord."

***

Drogan returned to the keep. He'd left Quia, Tekla, and the boy locked in his quarters, and the hunt was going to take longer than originally thought. Since there was no way for those locked in his rooms to get food for themselves, he didn't dare stay out with his father and the other hunters for more than a few days. He'd pleaded the need to reassure his wife and mistress. His father had granted him permission to return. He fumed at the injustice of the situation. He *enjoyed* hunting.

The bitches better show their appreciation for his losing out on his sport in order to tend to their needs.

When he arrived at the keep, he found all three loose in the sitting room. They'd been without food during the three days he'd been out, but had access to water from the bathing room. Quia bitched at him like the shrew she was, but they all ate the food he'd brought to the suite. After they finished eating, he ordered Tekla to show him her gratitude for his generosity in not leaving them to starve.

***

Early Summer Y1076

"We've tracked the beast into the forest several times, my Lord," Digen said. "The dogs keep losing the scent in the same area. We think the beast must have a lair somewhere past there."

Hulos sighed. "It killed another herdsman early this morning. Did the fool think our presence meant he was safe?"

The dog handler shrugged. "One never knows with homestead workers, my Lord, and these originally came from a homestead closer to Shanty Town so they ain't really familiar with the dangers of the forest."

"They'd best learn then."

***

Guns at the ready, the hunters formed a line and advanced past the spot in the forest where the dogs kept losing the man-eater's trail. Eventually, part of the line emerged into a clearing and a dog alerted, baying at a downed tree. For the first time, Hulos saw the animal he'd been hunting as it leaped off the trunk of the fallen forest giant and attacked a guard in the front. He lifted his gun and shot. His bullet hit its mark, and the beast dropped dead.

As the hunters gathered round the corpse of the great cat, admiring the dappled hide, Digen spotted a cub sitting at the entrance of a tunnel beneath the downed tree's root ball.

"Cubs!" he cried, raising his gun and shooting it.

A quick search of the tunnel under the tree's roots revealed a second cub. They killed that one too and skinned all three animals before heading home. If the cubs had tasted human flesh, they'd become man-eaters, too.

After assuring the cattlemen that they were now safe, the successful hunters headed on to the sheep farm, where Hulos gave the good news to Norris, his family, and *their* workers, too. Norris admired the hide of the great cat.

Hulos stroked the soft fur. "I'm going to have it made into a cloak."

***

The cub crawled out of the bushes, crying. It had chased after a butterfly earlier and been frightened when loud booms had come from the direction of the den, but it was hungry now and wanted its mother. When it reached the clearing around the fallen tree, it smelled human and blood, together with its mother and littermates. After sniffing around, it found something that smelled of its mother, but there was no soft, warm fur, no milk filled teats, only meat and blood. After crying some more, hunger took over, and the cub ate, feasting on its mother's last gift. The contents of the abdomen were the easiest for it to eat, so the cub fed there first. As it ate, it found some half-digested meat that differed from its mother's flesh, meat that was more delicious than anything else it had eaten.

***

Hulos wore his new fur cloak when he did his inspection tour of the compounds. When he reached the sheep farm, Norris had his report ready. Tavar also had a 'report' for him. After handing the page over, the boy offered him a second piece of paper.

"I wrote this letter special for you," he said proudly. "I give ma *her* letter this morning. Ma and Lida go to guard practice."

Hulos examined the pages. Tavar was learning the alphabet now, and instead of illegible scribbles, there were a series of random words… so badly misspelled, there was no telling what the boy had intended them to be.

"A fine report and letter, young master. I shall file the report in my treasury with the others. And I shall place your letter with my correspondence."

Tavar beamed up at him.

When Hulos returned to the keep, he again labeled the

pages on the back with the date and what each was before placing them with the others in the strongbox that he kept under his bed.

***

Autumn Y1076

The cub pounced on the mouse, but it escaped. The carcasses of its mother and littermates had provided it with enough food to last a couple weeks, but its circumstances had now reduced it to eating mice when it could catch them. Another adult had moved into its mother's territory and chased it away. It was too young to hold a territory of its own, so it wandered south, staying close to the familiar safety of the forest. A sound startled it and it hid in a clump of bushes. A bleating flock of strange animals moved into its field of vision and began eating the grass. It licked its lips, but the animals were too big and there were too many of them for it to risk trying to kill one. Then the scent of human came on the breeze and it started drooling. This was the source of the meat it had found inside its mother's stomach. Its eyes half closed, and it began kneading as it drank in the wonderful scent of that delicious food.

***

Drogan frowned to himself. Tekla was pregnant again. The bitch better give him another son this time, or he'd beat her senseless. He was growing tired of the way she spawned girl after girl. He wondered if perhaps he should find a different mistress. One he could show his father. The old man was pressuring him more and more about bringing the boy to see him. Drogan regretted ever telling him the boy existed. He should have taken the brat away from his mother before he'd learned to talk. He could never let his father meet him now.

He entered his quarters, locking the door behind him once he was inside. Ever since the hunt for the man-eater, he'd allowed the boy to roam through the rooms while Tekla attended to her duties for Quia. The brat was sitting on the couch now, glaring at him while his mother cleaned the room. It was shocking to see gray eyes so like his own, looking out at him from that dusky face.

***
Late Winter Y1076

The cub was getting better at hunting. It had now killed and devoured several fawns whose mothers had abandoned them when they'd gone into heat that autumn. This was more satisfying than eating mice. It still craved the meat it tasted when it had eaten the contents of its mother's stomach, though. The meat from the fawns had strengthened it, but it had been awhile since it had killed the last one and it was hungry again. Perhaps it could find a small human, one that wouldn't be too difficult to bring down. It headed back towards the place it had come across the human with the flock of strange animals. If one had come there, perhaps another might as well. It drooled at the thought of the delicious meat.

***

A member of Hulos's honor guard came and stood by his side as he sat at his table for the evening meal, clearing his throat to discretely attract his attention.

He looked up at the guard, recognizing Grukor. "Yes?"

"My Lord," Grukor said softly. "The headman from one of your homesteads has come to the keep seeking an audience with you."

Hulos frowned. If a headman had come seeking him outside a court day, the situation must be serious. He excused himself from the table and rose to follow Grukor.

Grukor led him to the entry to the keep, where he saw Norris kneeling with his head bowed just inside the door. Norris's wife, Shade, was on one knee beside him. He strode up to stand in front of the younger man.

"Why have you come?" He spoke more sharply than he'd intended.

Norris looked up at him with a strained expression. "My Lord," he said hoarsely. "Please forgive me for disturbing you at this time of day, but we've suffered a loss and need your help."

Hulos felt dread strike his heart. "Tell me what happened."

Norris swallowed. "My brother Hane took a flock of wethers west of the compound this morning. With spring so close, he thought he could find some early grass. He didn't return when we brought the sheep into the fold for the night, so a band of us went out looking for him. We found his flock scattered and his body half covered by vegetation. A beast had killed and partially eaten him. I made sure there was no one else missing and ordered everyone to stay in the compound, then came directly here."

"Did you ride?"

Norris shook his head and gestured towards Shade. "My wife is on duty tonight and the horses at the compound are all too small to bear my weight."

"You *walked* here? *Alone*?"

He nodded. "I couldn't risk anyone else and felt you needed to be told as soon as possible." Tears welled up in his eyes. "The beast didn't even *touch* any of the sheep. We gathered the entire flock of wethers and brought them home. Hane was my youngest brother, only a year older than my daughter."

Hulos touched his shoulder. "Have you eaten your evening meal yet?"

Norris shook his head.

"Then come, join me at my table."

"I need to get back to the compound."

Hulos shook his head. "Nonsense! You will stay the night and return with me when I lead the hunting party. Now come, join me at table."

"I ain't fit to dine with my Lord," Norris protested. "If you insist I stay the night, I can eat in the kitchen."

"*I* am Lord here," Hulos said imperiously. "If I say you will dine at my table, you will dine at my table. Now *come*." He extended his hand towards Norris.

* * *

Drogan sat toying with his food. Tekla was due almost any day now, and he wondered if she'd finally give him a second son or if she'd curse him with another daughter. He was so lost in thought, he'd barely noticed when a guard had come to the table and led his father away. When he heard Hulos returning, he looked up absently, only to freeze. Norris was with his father and the servants set a place for him at the table.

This was the last straw. Drogan trembled as his pulse quickened and his vision dimmed. He fought to maintain control. His father mustn't discover his objection to Norris joining them for their meal. He paid no attention to the explanation given for the shepherd's invitation to his Lord's table and left as soon as he could manage an excuse. As he retreated to his quarters, he contemplated the best way to kill Norris.

***

Hulos led the hunting party towards the sheep farm. He'd given Shade a week of free time so she could be with her husband for his brother's funeral. They traveled first to the site where they'd found Hane's remains so the dog handlers could set the dogs on the scent. The dogs couldn't follow the trail more than a few feet, though. The odor of the sheep was too strong. He sighed and consigned himself to a long hunt.

***

Early Spring Y1077

Spring Equinox came and went, but no one at the sheep farm felt like celebrating the New Year. They'd found no sign of the man-eater and the hunters formed small bands that patrolled around the area where they'd found Hane, searching for the beast. The sheep farm was close enough to the keep that Lord Hulos and his son Drogan retired there at night, returning each morning to continue the hunt.

***

When the cub returned to where it had killed the human, its cache was missing. Frustrated, it searched for another human to kill. All the humans it saw were in large groups perched on the backs of horses. These were too dangerous for it to risk attacking. At the edge of the forest, it hid, watching them. It drooled at the scent of the delicious meat, but it wouldn't be able to make the kill on any of them. It watched now as a group of humans riding horses came near its hiding place. The breeze wafted a faint but familiar scent to its hiding place and it lifted its head. It hadn't smelled that scent in a long time, but it recognized it immediately. Its mother was out there. The scent came from the riders who were nearing its hiding place. It peered at them and saw dappled fur on the back of one. It recognized the pattern. Its mother was on top of the human. If its mother was there, it must be safe to attack. Its mother would protect it. Clearly, the cub's mother intended for it to join her in attacking the human she'd marked as prey. The horse with that rider passed the cub's hiding place, and it leaped onto the human, knocking it off the horse, which bolted. The cub sank its teeth into the back of the human's neck in a killing blow and bit down. It didn't hear the blast of the gun that killed it.

***

Shade kissed Norris as they exited their home. "Life must go on, so I'm taking Kalida for weapons' training. I'll see you at noon."

"She's been schooling Burk and Mora on what you've been teaching her."

"Well, it's good practice, and even shepherds can find it useful to know how to fight." Shade sighed. "I hope Lord Drogan proves as good a Lord as Hulos was."

"He *is* the old Lord's son. I'm sure he'll live up to his da's legacy and he killed the beast that killed Hane."

***

Drogan sat by the bier. He'd kept watch through the night alongside his father's honor guard. As the light of dawn shone through the windows, he glanced at the skin of the beast that had killed his father. His followers expected him to wrap Hulos's body in it when they buried him, but the great cat's fur was beautiful and he'd much rather keep it in his quarters as a memento.

Damn them all. I'm Lord of the clan now. I'll keep the fur for myself if I want to. The beast damaged da's cloak in the attack, but it's the same type of fur. We can bury him in that.

His quirt swung from his wrist as he rose. He hadn't changed clothes since they'd brought Hulos home and he still wore his riding garb. He hadn't been back to his quarters, let alone gone in to Tekla since the hunt ended so tragically. She might have had the brat by now. He'd check on her before deciding what he'd do next.

When he opened the door to her room, he saw Tekla sitting on the bed nursing a new baby. "Is it a son?"

She shrank from him, and he felt his rage rising. Another daughter? Drogan ripped the child from her arms and confirmed that it was indeed the fifth girl she'd given him. He walked towards the fireplace while she screamed and babbled about the brat. He glared back at her just before he swung the infant against the stones of the fireplace.

"Your *job* is to give me *sons*!" he bellowed.

"No!" the boy yelled, launching himself at Drogan's arm and wrapping himself around both it and the baby. "Don't hurt her!"

Drogan dropped the baby on the floor where the brat lay, squalling, and grabbed the boy. He'd left him with his mother for far too long. With one hand, he took his belt off and strapped it around the boy's wrists. He paused a moment, then spotted a nail on the support beam of one wall. He hooked the belt on it so the boy's feet dangled above the floor.

"Watch and learn, boy," he growled at the child as he turned back towards the fireplace, only to find the bitch had grabbed the baby and was now crouching over it in the far corner of the room. He stomped over to her and again ripped the infant from her arms.

Tekla grabbed at his leg, begging and weeping, but he kicked her off him and swung the child against the stones of the fireplace.

"Your *job*," he shouted, "is to give me *sons*!"

He didn't stop until the infant dangled, limp and lifeless from his hand, at which point he dropped it. He'd deal with it later, *after* he'd shown the bitch her place. When he finished with Tekla, he turned to the boy, who was struggling futilely against the belt.

"You need to learn too, boy," he snarled, as he turned his son so he was facing the wall. He ripped the boy's shirt off and, taking the quirt into his hand, whipped him.

He continued the whipping for a few minutes after the boy stopped screaming. For a moment, he was afraid he'd killed the child, but a quick examination showed that the brat was still breathing. He lifted the boy's body off the wall and dumped him on the bed with his mother.

"I've left him in here with you too long. When I return, I'll take him away. I'll teach him the proper way to behave, but I have something *else* I need to do first."

As he locked the door to the room where he kept Tekla, he saw Quia seated on a couch in the sitting room. He glared at her.

"*I'm* Lord now. I have a task to do, but once I've finished that, it'll be *your* turn."

He locked the main door to their suite as he left. His wife wouldn't escape her fate while he was out, but he didn't have time to deal with her now.

Drogan led a squad of guards north. He'd deliberately chosen younger male guards. He didn't want any hysterics over what he planned to do and didn't trust older guards to obey the orders he planned to give. When they reached the sheep farm, he first headed to Norris's house and ordered the roses razed and burned. Now that *he* was Lord, he wouldn't allow commoners to have frivolous plantings around their homes. It was shearing season, so he knew where his prey would be.

When they arrived at the shearing pens, he spotted Norris's golden head. A miniature version of the man shadowed him, copying everything he did as the workers harvested the wool. His rage increased at the sight. Norris's son wanted to be like his father while his *own* son rebelled against him. He ordered his guards to grab Norris and bring the man over to stand in front of him.

Norris appeared confused. He asked what was wrong. In response, Drogan ordered the guards to secure him, then walked around behind the object of his hatred. He cut Norris's shirt and coat off, then took his dagger to his brother's back, cutting around where the birthmark was so he could remove it. Norris gave a cry of pain and writhed in the guards' grip as the blade bit into him. As Drogan was cutting, Norris's spawn attacked him.

"Leave da alone!" the child screamed, kicking and hitting him with tiny feet and fists.

Drogan knocked the boy to the ground and, pulling his gun, shot him. He was tired of being attacked by brats, first his own son, now Norris's. Norris tore himself from the grip of the stunned guards and gathered the brat into his arms.

"*Why?*" he screamed. "What have we done to *deserve* this?"

Looking around, Drogan noticed that the sheep farmers were glaring at him and gripping their shepherd's crooks tightly. He grimaced. It'd be better to finish what he had planned in the keep itself. He ordered his guards to grab Norris once more and headed back to the keep.

***

Shade arrived home to a still and silent compound. Frowning, she led the way to their house and stared, stunned by the loss of her roses.

"Ma?" Kalida asked. "What happened?"

"I don't know, sweetheart," she replied, dismounting from her horse and heading inside.

Several people were sitting in the front room, weeping quietly.

She looked around. "What happened?"

One pointed at the stairs that went to the second floor. "They shot Tavar. He's in the spare bedroom upstairs."

Shade ran up the stairs, her heart in her throat. How could this have happened? Who had shot her son? When she reached the room, she saw Tavar lying on the bed, tossing feverishly and calling for his father. She knelt by the side of the bed and caressed his brow.

"Shh," she whispered. "Ma's here."

"Ma," he whimpered. "Where's da?"

She looked around the room, noting that Norris was absent. Tisha stood by the head of the bed, weeping.

"Tisha? Where's Norris?"

Tisha looked at her through tear-filled eyes. "They came and took him away, the new Lord and his guards. Lord Drogan cut on his back first, and Tavar tried to stop him. That's when he shot him. Then they left, taking Norris away with them."

Shade stared at her mother-in-law for a moment, then turned to her daughter. "Kalida, you stay here with your brother. I'm going to go get your da."

***

When Shade reached the keep, she found the main

courtyard filled with people staring silently at what their new Lord was doing. Drogan stood on the platform beside the whipping post, wielding a scourge. The victim of the flagellation hung limp in his bonds. She'd know that golden mane anywhere. She fought her way to the front of the silent crowd, but just as she reached the platform, Drogan dropped the whip, stepped forward, and slit Norris's throat with a dagger.

She leaped onto the platform and slammed her sword against the ropes binding her husband's wrists, dropping the weapon so she could catch his body. She knew at once that he was dead, but wasn't sure if it had been the slash across his throat that killed him or if he'd already been dead from the whipping.

Tears streaming down her face, she looked up at Drogan. "*Why?*"

He spat in Norris's face. "I *won't* have a motherless bastard serving me." He threw a scrap of skin at her.

Without conscious thought, Shade found her sword back in her hand. She rose and plunged the blade deep into Drogan's body.

"And *I* will not *serve* a Lord who would destroy my family for a *whim!*" she screamed.

He dropped at her feet and she continued stabbing the weapon into him until the blade caught on his ribs. Her rage spent, she returned to Norris and gathered his body in her arms. As she mourned her loss, she paid no attention to the commotion that broke out.

Much later, a gentle touch on her shoulder brought Shade back to the present. She looked up at her mother's worried face.

"Take him home," the older woman breathed. "His family will want him buried with kin."

Shade looked around numbly. Guards surrounded the platform where Drogan had executed Norris, all facing outward. Captain Dinsil lay on the ground outside the circle of guards, blood staining his clothes, the bodies of a few other guards around him.

"What happened?"

Her mother eyed Dinsil's body, her lip curled in a sneer.

"He thought he could take leadership of the clan, but most chose *you*. I recommend you discard any that have survived who supported his bid to take over."

"'Discard'?" Shade shook her head. "I don't understand."

"You killed the seated Lord of the clan. He has no heir. The clan is now *yours* to do with as you please. I pledge my allegiance to you, as do all these others." She gestured at the guards that surrounded them. "You are Lady Shade now. You need to choose a clan name and symbol."

One of the other guards stepped forward. "My Lady. Please allow us to transport him home for you."

Shade nodded, and several guards stepped forward to pick Norris up. As they carried him away, she spotted the scrap of skin Drogan had thrown at her. Numbly, she picked it up. She didn't realize what it was at first. She smoothed it out, frowning at it. Then it hit her. There, in the center of the piece, was the birthmark from the back of Norris's left shoulder. Drogan had skinned her husband's back before whipping him. Shade's fist clenched around the scrap of skin.

"Bastard!" she screamed at the corpse, kicking it again and again.

The guards waited patiently until her fit of anger passed.

Shade's chin lifted, and she looked around at the guards who supported her. She pointed at Drogan. "I want him stripped. Mount his naked corpse on the wall by the keep gate until the crows have picked his bones bare. I want those bones ground into powder and cast into the cesspit. I want every *trace* of his existence removed from the records of the house." She spat on Drogan's body. "I don't want his name used again. If there are any serving the clan who have the same name, they must change it or leave."

"My Lady," one guard said, "Lord Hulos still lies in state in the audience chamber. What shall we do with *him*?"

"Lord Hulos was a good Lord. We'll bury him in state, as we planned before Drogan despoiled his legacy."

As they loaded Norris's body onto a cart for transport to the sheep farm, five guards approached Shade and knelt before her.

"My Lady," their leader said. "We submit to your judgment."

She looked at the men and sighed. "What have you done that I should judge you?"

The leader of the five bowed his head. "We accompanied... Drogan... when he went to the sheep farm to take your husband. While we were there, we obeyed his orders. We make no excuses. We are all equally culpable."

Shade looked more closely at the men, noting now that they were all unarmed. "You expect me to order you executed, don't you?"

He nodded.

"Is this all of you who were there?"

He shook his head. "The others sided with Dinsil. They died during the fight."

"I see," she said coldly. "Which among you held my husband's arms as you took him? Which tied him to the whipping post?"

The man shook his head again. "We make no excuses. Regardless of who did what, we are *all* equally culpable."

Shade closed her eyes for a moment and drew a deep breath. If it hadn't been *her* family, she would probably have obeyed the orders herself. Opening her eyes, she looked at the men again. She knew them. She knew their families and loved ones. They had served together for years.

"Fifty lashes each."

The men nodded and turned to walk to the whipping post for their punishment.

* * *

Shade raced ahead of the cart on the fastest horse from the stable. There was nothing more she could do for Norris, but her son had still been alive when she'd left for the keep. When she reached the house, she slid off her horse and raced inside, stumbling up the stairs as fast as she could. She found the healer assigned to the compound sitting on the floor outside the room.

She eyed the man with her heart in her throat. "Is he?"

The healer shook his head. "Not yet, but it won't be long. I'm sorry. There was nothing I could do for him other than make him more comfortable."

She entered the room and crouched by the bed. Tavar's

eyes were closed, and he was breathing shallowly. Gently, she stroked his forehead.

His eyes flicked open. "Da?" His voice was so faint it was barely audible.

"It's ma, baby," she murmured.

He whimpered. "I want da."

"He's coming, sweetheart. He'll be here soon and you can be together."

He smiled at her, gave a little sigh, and lay still.

Shade knelt on the floor, wailing as Tisha had when the bear killed Rafin.

* * *

Shade walked around the house dry eyed, staring blindly at the destruction of the roses Norris had planted for her. She had no tears left to weep. She reached the back of the house and froze. A single, ragged bush with a solitary blossom had survived the destruction. She knelt beside it, staring at it with her heart in her mouth. It was a bi-colored rose, with a deep yellow heart and red edges on the petals.

"'When you see roses, you'll know you're home,'" she whispered.

"Ma!" Kalida called from the front of the house.

"Coming," she called back, heading in that direction. When she reached the front, she saw the cart with Norris's body pulling up. She looked down at her daughter. "Go get Tavar."

Kalida frowned, but went inside to do as she'd been told. When she got back, she stopped in the doorway, holding her brother in her arms.

"Where's da? You told Tavar he could be with da."

"He's in the cart. Put Tavar beside him. We'll bury them together."

Kalida stared at her. "No!" she screamed. "You went to get da. You told Tavar he was coming."

"I was too late. We lost them both today. Put your brother with his da."

Weeping, Kalida went to the back of the cart and looked inside. The guards had wrapped Norris in linens. Sobbing, she laid her brother beside him. Shade came beside her and wrapped her arms around her.

Kalida looked up at her mother. "If I'd been home, I would have stopped them. Da and Tavar would still be here."

Shade shook her head. "He would have just killed you, too. I'd have nothing left of your da."

Tisha came up and hugged them both. "Was there even a reason?"

"Drogan said some nonsense about not wanting a motherless bastard serving him."

"No!" Tisha cried. "I don't care *what* that woman said. *I* was Norris's ma, and he was our *son*. If *that* was Drogan's reason for this, I won't serve *him*!" She pulled her belt knife and cut her clan symbol off her coat, throwing it on the ground and grinding it under her heel.

"You don't have to. I killed him. The clan belongs to *me* now."

Tisha looked at her daughter-in-law, hope shining in her eyes. "What's your clan name and symbol?"

Shade thought about that lone, ragged rose bush behind the house. "Duskrose. I'll call my clan Duskrose. The symbol will be a rose with three leaves and two teardrops. Our clan colors will be red and yellow."

***

Shade insisted that the guards prepare the bodies for burial. She wanted them arranged with Norris's arms wrapped around his son and didn't want any of her husband's family to see what Drogan had done to him. She was grateful they thought this was an honor the guards were showing them.

That night, after the burial, she retired one last time to the room she'd shared with Norris. There, on her pillow, she found a letter. He must have written and placed it there before he'd headed to the shearing pens. As she picked it up, she wept once more.

When she prepared to leave the next morning, she asked Tisha and her surviving children to come to the keep and live there with her. Only Nevia and her husband Ricco accepted the invitation. The others wanted to continue keeping the sheep.

"Kadan can be headman now," Tisha said. "He knows

what to do."

Tisha had gotten everyone in the compound who could sew to work on the new clan symbol during the night, and there were enough by the time Shade left for the keep, that those who were going back with her were each able to replace their shoulder patches.

When they reached the keep gates, Sulsi met them. She smiled at the sight of the new clan symbols. "What's the clan name?"

Shade looked down at her from the back of her horse. "Duskrose."

Sulsi nodded. "It's a good name. Most new clans choose something that sounds ferocious." She offered Shade a ring of keys. "We found these when we were stripping Drogan. I thought you might find a use for them." She waved a hand at an older man standing by her side. "This is Aelan. He can show you around the parts of the keep you're less familiar with."

Aelan took them first to Lord Hulos's quarters. "I recommend you go through everything before you decide what to do with any of his Lordship's things. There may be items you want to keep for yourselves." He pointed to a ring of keys hanging from a hook by the door. "You should be able to open any lock you find in here with one of those."

"I'm sure we won't need any of his *clothing*."

"As you please."

Eventually, they reached Drogan's rooms. He'd locked the door. Shade pulled out the key ring her mother had given her and jangled it.

"I'm guessing one of *these* fits *this* lock." She tried each key and the fourth one fit. She unlocked the door.

As they entered a sitting room, a door to one side opened, and a woman stepped out. "It's about *time*! Just how long did you…?"

She caught sight of them and froze. "Who are *you*?"

Shade stepped forward. "I'm Lady Shade Duskrose, the new clan leader here. Who are you?"

"Allow me to introduce mistress Quia," Aelan interjected smoothly. "She was Drogan's wife."

Quia frowned. "'Was'?"

"I am afraid you're a widow, ma'am."

Quia's response to this was to laugh. She ripped off her coat, threw it on the floor, and ground it under her foot. "In that case, I'm a Splitskull. Please return me to my clan."

"You're free to leave," Shade told her. Adding as Quia turned to reenter the room she'd come out of, "In the clothes you're wearing. You're to leave any other items house Grimwolf provided you with behind."

Quia hesitated for a moment, then shrugged. "Very well." She walked out the door.

Shade held up the keys again. "Well, let's see which of these keys goes to which door. We know which key unlocks the door to the hall."

They circled the sitting room, finding keys to each door in turn. One key unlocked what had clearly been Drogan's room. A second went to the room Quia had emerged from. The third fit the lock on the bathing room. When they opened the next door, however, the sickly sweet odor of decay wafted out.

Shade motioned for the others to stand back and entered with sword drawn. Kalida ignored her mother's direction and followed a step behind. The room had been set up as a nursery, with a crib under the window, a larger bed on the left, and a fireplace on the right. Crouching on the bed were a woman and a small boy, both dressed in rags and staring at Shade with wide eyes.

It was Kalida who discovered the source of the stench. "Ma!" she cried, pointing at the fireplace. "A baby!"

Shade sidestepped over and glanced down. The crushed skull on the tiny corpse told her all she needed to know.

"What happened here?" she demanded of the woman on the bed.

"He killed her," the woman croaked, her voice a harsh rasp. "He killed my baby girl." She gripped the living child in her arms tighter.

Shade sheathed her weapon and stepped closer. The other woman shrank back. "It's ok. I won't hurt you. Who *are* you?"

The woman swallowed. "I'm Tekla and this is my son, Kip."

"Why are you in here?"

"He locked us in."

"Who did? Who locked you in here?"

Kip glared up at her with stormy gray eyes. "My da. My da keeps us locked in here."

Shade stared at the pair as the horror of the situation hit her fully. "*Why*?"

"Because he wants sons and his wife won't give him any children," Tekla replied bitterly. "He killed my daughters. He killed every one of them." She drew a sobbing breath. "He only wants sons."

"Come with me," Shade said gently, extending a hand towards Tekla. "I killed him. He can't hurt you anymore and you can leave here. You're safe now."

When Shade led Tekla out of the room, Aelan eyed her and Kip narrowly.

"You should kill the boy, and probably Drogan's doxy as well."

As Tekla shrank back, clutching her son, Shade turned on the man.

"There've been *enough* innocents killed. I won't add to their number."

He shrugged. "Your choice, but know that the boy could be a threat to your hold on the clan. *Any* Grimwolf would be."

* * *

Sulsi offered to take Tekla and Kip and find rooms for them. Shade then turned to Nevia and Ricco. "I think we've seen everything in the keep now. Did you see any rooms you'd like as your own?"

Nevia looked down and spoke hesitantly. "These rooms here, where Drogan lived, look like they'd make a good place for us. There are enough rooms for Ricco and me and all our children. We can clean them up and make them our own."

"Very well. You may keep anything you find in here for your own use. We need to bury Tekla's baby before you move in, though."

Nevia nodded. "Of course."

"We can take care of that," Ricco added.

* * *

Shade sent Aelan off to his own quarters. She wouldn't

need him anymore.

"Ok," she said to Kalida. "Let's go get started dealing with Lord Hulos's rooms. That's where *I* plan to live."

As they were heading back to Lord Hulos's old quarters, a man approached them.

"My Lady. I am Alith, the clan artist. I need to know what you want done with the paintings that currently hang on the walls of the keep."

Shade looked at him coolly. "Destroy any of Drogan. I don't care what you do with the others."

Alith nodded, bowing. "Very well. I'll store them in my quarters. You may change your mind about them later."

"I doubt I will," Shade replied dryly as she continued on towards Lord Hulos's old rooms, preparing herself to go through his belongings.

When they got to the Lord's chambers, Shade took the ring of keys off the hook by the door. "Ready to see what *these* keys go to?"

Kalida nodded. "Am I going to sleep here with you?"

"Unless there's another room you like better. There should be enough rooms in here for us both. It looks like they have the same layout as Drogan's quarters."

They found locks for all but one key. They searched and searched but couldn't find another lock. Finally, Shade led the way into the master bedroom.

"We'll look for that last lock later. Right now, the bedding needs to be changed." She sighed. "I ain't sleeping on Lord Hulos's used linens."

As they piled the used bedding by the door, Kalida spotted something under the bed.

"Ma!" she cried, pointing. "What's that?"

Shade knelt beside the bed and peered underneath. "It appears to be a strongbox." She pulled it out from its hiding place. "I guess we found what that last key goes to."

"Do you think it's treasure?"

Shade smiled tiredly at her daughter. "He kept it hidden under his bed. It must have been something important to him." She unlocked the box and lifted the lid. At the sight of the contents, she frowned.

Kalida reached in and took out a piece of bark. "Why

would he keep *this* locked up in a secret place? This is just trash."

Shade picked up the first paper that had been beneath the piece of bark and examined it. Childish scribbles covered one side, but on the back, she saw something written in a firm hand. She closed her eyes briefly. That couldn't *possibly* say what she thought it said. She handed the page to Kalida and pointed at the writing on the back.

"What does that say?"

"It says 'Tavar's second report' and a date." Kalida looked up at Shade. "The date is two years ago."

Shade picked up the second paper. "And this?"

"It says, 'Tavar's letter. The boy was going to give it to his ma but gave it to me instead.' It has the same date as the report."

Shade pulled out the last two pieces of paper. The writing on the front of these looked familiar to her. She pressed her hand over her mouth. "What do these say on the back?" she asked faintly as she handed them to her daughter.

"This one says, 'Tavar's third report.' It's dated last year. The other one says, 'Tavar's second letter. He wrote this one just for me. He said he'd already given one to his ma that morning.' And it has the same date as the third report."

Shade knew what the piece of bark must be. Reverently, she picked it up. "This must be Tavar's *first* report. Remember? He used to use a stick and pretend to write on pieces of bark before Lord Hulos sent your da that big stack of paper three years ago, but why would Lord Hulos have preserved keepsakes of your brother?"

"Maybe he wished *da* was his son instead of Drogan and that Tavar was his grandson."

Shade frowned as something her mother-in-law had said came to her mind. "What woman?" she muttered. She rose to her feet. "You stay here. I need to talk to your grandma." She headed out of the suite.

She'd just reached the door to the courtyard when Sulsi came up to her. She could see her mother wanted to speak but asked to be excused. "I need to ask Tisha something and I want to ask while it's fresh in my mind."

"What do you need to ask her?"

"When I told her what Drogan said was his reason for killing Norris, she said something about not caring what some woman said. I need to know what she meant by that."

Sulsi's eyes widened. "Don't. If you make her tell you, you'll only hurt her."

Shade's eyes narrowed. "*You* know what she meant?"

Sulsi nodded. "I was there when the woman Tisha was talking about said what she said. It's an old wound. Please don't reopen it."

"*You* tell me then."

Sulsi looked around. "All right, but not out here. Some place private."

Shade took her mother's arm and led the way to a conference room. "This should be private enough. What's the big secret?"

Sulsi sighed and sat in a chair. "This happened a long time ago. Tisha and Rafin had come before Lord Hulos to ask permission to wed. They were the last to come before him in court that day." She bit her lip.

Shade tapped her foot. "And?"

"They'd just given him their names and were waiting for him to give permission. He never refused a request to marry."

"I think he almost refused when Norris and I went before him," Shade said dryly.

Sulsi shrugged. "Most of the time, he just automatically gave permission. Anyway, before he could give his permission that day, his wife came into the room, dragging his bastard half-sister. It was quite a scandal. There are clans today that still talk about it."

"What was the scandal?"

"Lord Hulos had gotten a bastard on his half-sister while in a drunken stupor. She claimed he vished her, but I have my suspicions about that."

"Drogan?"

"Drogan."

"So what does any of this have to do with Tisha and Rafin?"

Sulsi sighed. "The wife had brought her *own* son into the room with her and she disowned him in front of us all. Lord Hulos told Tisha and Rafin he'd grant their petition to wed on the condition that they take the boy and raise him as if he were their own."

"Norris," Shade breathed.

Sulsi nodded. "Norris."

Shade was suddenly angry. "Why didn't he keep Norris *here*?"

"He was a motherless bastard. If he'd stayed here, he'd have been an object of scorn. He couldn't inherit anything. He would have just been an outsider looking in at something he could never be a part of. With Tisha and Rafin, he had a home. He had a family that loved him. He became the headman of a compound. And Lord Hulos did what he could to make life as good for him as possible. Did you never wonder why Lord Hulos always came through any time you or Norris needed anything?"

"How many know of this?"

Sulsi shrugged. "I think it's common knowledge among the clans about Drogan and what Hulos's wife did. Why do you think Drogan married a Splitskull? No other clan would give one of their daughters to a son of inbreeding. Few know what became of Norris after his ma disowned him, or even his name. It's an old scandal. Most that still talk about it probably think Lord Hulos had Norris killed."

She glanced towards the door. "I ain't the only guard that knows all. Lord Hulos's honor guards *definitely* know. I'm sure for those who know that it played a part in their decision to side with *you* instead of Dinsil. That, and since none of the guards know which of them is your da, they all consider you family, and, well, 'family before clan,' and all that. Drogan didn't take *that* into account."

"Speaking of Hulos's honor guards, *they* were what I wanted to speak to you about. They wanted me to ask you if you'd be willing to accept them as your own honor guards." Sulsi smiled wryly. "One of them thinks he's your da."

* * *

Shade led her daughter to the keep garden and sat on a stone bench to look at the roses. "We need to get you companions. Friends and playmates that can help guard you as you grow to adulthood. Is there anyone you know that you'd like as your companion?"

Kalida looked at the ground. "How many do I get?"

"As many as you want. You need at least four, though."

"Can Burk and Mora be my companions?"

Shade nodded. "They'll need to go to weapons' practice with you, but they can be your companions. Now you need at least two more."

"Kip. Can he be one? I know he ain't much older than Tavar was, but he never got to have a friend before... locked up like that with his ma."

Shade hugged her daughter. "That's a wonderful idea, sweetie. I'm sure he'll be happy to be your companion." She hesitated a moment. "There's something else I think we should do about Kip."

"What's that?"

"You know he's Drogan's son, don't you?"

Kalida nodded. "That ain't *his* fault, though."

"No," Shade agreed. "It ain't. But it means he would've been the next Lord if I hadn't killed Drogan and taken over the clan."

"You ain't going to kill him like Aelan suggested! *Are* you?"

Shade shook her head. "I have something else in mind. I think we should make him part of our line of succession."

Kalida wrinkled her brow. "What's that?"

"Well, you know you're *my* heir, right?"

Kalida nodded.

"If we make Kip part of our line of succession, then he'd be *your* heir. What do you think about that? And of course, there's your da's family."

"I think I'd like that. I can pretend Kip is my cousin, too. Just like Burk and Mora."

"I'm glad you like the idea. Now we need at least one more companion for you. Can you think of anyone, or should I just assign a guard to you?"

"Well," Kalida said slowly, "there's a girl from practice. Her da died when you killed Drogan, and no one will talk to her anymore."

Shade frowned. "Why not?"

"Her da was Captain Dinsil."

"Are you sure you want Dinsil's daughter as your companion?"

Kalida nodded. "I feel sorry for her. Her ma died when she was little and she don't have any family now."

"What's her name?"

"Her name is Jenna."

"All right. I'll get Jenna from the guard crèche and bring her to live with us in our suite so she can be your fourth companion. If you find any other friends you want as companions, we can add them later."

* * *

Shade rode out to the sheep farm to speak to Tisha and those of her children who'd remained behind. She didn't want her new clan to be reduced to the state to which Grimwolf had fallen, and she needed to have a full line of succession to prevent that. She intended to offer to have Norris's family added to the line. When she mentioned this to Tisha, though, her mother-in-law shook her head.

"We're simple shepherds," the older woman said. "We have no place in ruling a clan. Leave us here on the farm. It wouldn't be fitting for us to be tied to the keep."

"Besides," Kadan added. "You're Lady, but Norris was never Lord. Kin of your own blood should fill those positions."

Shade sighed. "Nevia and Ricco agreed to let me include *their* children in the line of succession."

"They're living in the keep with you," Tisha pointed out. "They should be enough. The rest of us can stay here and tend to our sheep and crops. No." She shook her head. "We are where we belong. If you want to extend the succession, you're still young enough to take a new husband or a lover and get more children of your own."

Shade closed her eyes. "No. If I can't have Norris, I'll have *no* man."

Tisha reached out and pressed her hand. "My dear, I understand, but we can't help you with this. We're shepherds. We ain't clan and we don't want to be."

Shade sat, brooding for a moment. "Very well. While I'm here, though, I need to talk to you about Norris and Tavar's

CLAN

grave."

"You ain't moving it?" Tisha asked, her eyes widening. "Are you?"

"No," Shade reassured her. "But I want something done with it. I've arranged for a stone to be carved for them. It should arrive soon. I also want roses planted on and around it. How's the last rose that survived behind our house doing? Could you transplant it?"

* * *

Lylathin Lake: Summer Y1077

Shade sat in her audience chamber watching the envoy from house Rastag. A blonde woman who looked vaguely familiar stood at the back of the group, peering around the room as if she was searching for something. This was the last clan to come meet with her. Some had sought a marriage between one of their sons and Kalida, but she wasn't about to deny her daughter the joy of marriage to a man she loved. So far, however, house Rastag hadn't made this suggestion. Since they'd traveled a long distance and it was now evening, she offered to allow them to stay overnight to rest up before making the return journey.

The next morning, after breakfast, Shade went into the gardens to spend time among the roses. As she strode silently along the path, she spotted someone moving with purpose towards the keep graveyard. Her brow creased as she followed. It was the blonde Rastag woman she'd noticed the day before. The woman stopped at Hulos's grave and stood, looking down at it. Shade settled her clan mask firmly on her head and walked over to the stranger.

"Did you find what you were looking for?"

Up close, she could see fine lines on the woman's face and strands of gray among the gold of her mane.

The woman started and looked at her. "I didn't expect to find *his* grave treated with such honor."

Shade shrugged. "He was the last decent Lord before I took the clan."

The woman sneered. "*Decent*? A man who'd bed his own *sister*?"

90

Shade ground her teeth. "Whatever follies he may have committed in his youth, he was a good Lord to us."

The woman shrugged. "I wasn't looking for *his* grave, anyway. I was looking for his son's grave. He was a proud man. He'd have buried the boy with honor."

"Drogan *has* no grave," Shade said coldly. "I fed him to crows, then had his bones ground to dust and dumped into the cesspit."

"His *son*. Not the bastard he got on his sister."

Shade stiffened. "I don't know what you're talking about."

"Perhaps he hid it in some corner of the yard." The woman looked around. "Are there any unmarked graves? He certainly wouldn't have kept the boy around to be a source of mockery. He was a proud man, after all."

"Who *are* you and what exactly is it you're looking for?"

The woman's chin lifted. "I am Miawa Rastag... Grimwolf. I am Hulos's widow, and I'm looking for the grave of my husband's son."

Shade's eyes narrowed. "Are you looking for the grave of *your* son?"

"I have no son."

"Then I can't help you. Hulos is the last Grimwolf buried here. There are no unmarked graves." Shade pointed at an older grave near the wall, one with only a small marker. "They buried his sister there. All the other clan graves here are much older than hers."

Miawa looked around. "Then what did he do with his son? What happened to the boy?"

"If he wasn't *your* son, you don't need to know."

Her head turned, and she looked sharply at Shade. "But *you* know. Don't you?"

"I'm clan leader here. I know *all* the secrets. You *abandoned* him. You don't deserve to know his fate."

"I'm right in thinking he's dead, though. *Ain't* I?"

Shade shrugged. "You may think what you like," she replied coldly as she turned on her heel and walked away.

***

Autumn Y1077

Shade sat on the throne on the dais, ready to hold court.

The novelty of the procedure had palled on her in the months since she'd become clan leader. As she looked out at the petitioners, she noticed a group of serving maids at the head of the line that appeared to be together and couldn't help but feel this boded ill. Their leader stepped forward and confirmed her suspicion.

"My Lady," the woman said. "Something needs to be done about Tekla."

"Why? What's the problem?"

"She can't do any work. She screams at night. Her screams disturb our sleep. No one but her son can touch her or she screams even more. There's no place she could go in the keep where she wouldn't be a problem. We've borne all we can of her."

Shade closed her eyes and took a deep breath. "I'll see what I can do."

"Thank you, my Lady," the group's spokeswoman said.

***

Shade had Tekla brought to a conference room so she could speak to her privately. "I'm sorry, Tekla, but the other servants are complaining. They say you scream at night and keep them from their sleep. They have other complaints, but that's the most serious. We need to find a solution."

Tekla looked down. "I'll move to Shanty Town. I won't bother anyone there."

"You could move onto a homestead."

Tekla shook her head. "I'd be as big a problem there as I am here. No, I belong in Shanty Town with the beggars."

"What about Kip? He's one of Kalida's companions now. It would be inconvenient for him to move to Shanty Town."

"Kip must stay here." Tekla lifted her eyes and looked directly at Shade. "Only... can he come visit me? When he can spare the time?"

"Of course." Shade pressed her hand. "Shanty Town ain't that far from the keep. He can visit you whenever he has free time."

***

Winter Y1077

Kip wandered the halls of the keep. Since his ma moved to Shanty Town, he had time in the evening after the last meal of the day when he had nothing else to do. Ahead of him he saw light shining out of a half-open door. He hadn't explored this part of the keep before. Curious, he approached and peeked inside. A man sat before a large canvas panel on a wooden frame, applying a brush to its surface. Kip stopped in the doorway and stood for several minutes, watching.

Finally, his curiosity got the better of him. "What are you doing?"

The man looked up from his work. "I'm painting, young master. Come and see." He gestured for Kip to come stand by his side.

Kip slowly entered the room and went to look at the canvas. Depicted on the panel was Shade, seated on the audience chamber throne, with Kalida standing by her side.

He stared. "You *made* this?"

The man nodded. "I'm Alith, the clan artist. I painted many of the pictures you see in this room."

He gestured around and Kip saw stacks of canvas-covered frames on all four walls, leaning with the painted side towards the wall. Kip walked over and looked at one picture. It was a blonde woman with a wide mouth wearing odd clothes and holding a bouquet of roses.

"That's a Grimwolf clanswoman from a couple of generations ago. I didn't paint that one. You may look at the others. I still have work to do on *this* painting. Lady Duskrose wants it hung in the dining hall where a Grimwolf painting hung before she ascended."

Kip explored further. In a back corner, he found a damaged painting. It had a broken frame and someone had slashed half the picture to ribbons. It looked like there'd been another figure in the picture at one time. All that remained was a man seated on the audience chamber throne with the arm of another figure resting along the throne's back. Kip knew that face. There were some things wrong about it. The eyes were blue, not gray, the hair had silver strands among the gold, the man looked older than he should, and there was a blemish on the nose that could represent a small scar he didn't remember, but he was sure this was his da. He picked the damaged picture up and carried it to where Alith sat working on the painting of the current clan leader and her daughter.

"What's this?"

Alith looked up from his work. "Why, that's old Lord Grimwolf, young master. I couldn't quite bring myself to throw it away when Lady Duskrose took the clan."

Kip regarded the painted face. "He looks sad." He'd never thought of his da as being sad, but there was no mistaking the melancholy expression in the pale blue eyes of the painted figure.

"That he was. He was a sad, sad man. *I* blame his wife."

Kip remembered his ma begging Quia to tell someone about them when his da was holding them prisoner and nodded. He could understand how being married to one such as her could make a man sad. Not that it excused what his da had done to his ma.

"Can I have it? Since it's broken and all."

The artist tensed for a moment. "Well, even broken, it's a large painting. I suppose I could cut the canvas down to just his Lordship's head and shoulders and reframe it though. Then you'd have a portrait instead of a full body piece."

"I'd like that. Thank you."

Alith smiled at him. "Thank *you*, young master. I'll be glad to know the work I put into that painting won't go completely to waste."

* * *

Alith whistled as he cut the painting down to turn it into a portrait of Lord Hulos. It pleased him that the boy appreciated the work he'd put into the painting and he saw no harm in allowing Kip to have a picture of the old Lord to keep. Once he had the canvas cut down and reframed, he eyed it thoughtfully. He'd paint out Drogan's arm from where it rested on the top of the throne behind his Lordship's head before he gave it to the boy. No need to leave *that* in.

Escalation
Homelands: Spring Y1042

Korander looked towards where his father sat at the head of the dining table. "Papa, I want to marry."

Saerthan raised a snowy brow. "You'll have to wait awhile. The bride I've arranged for you is still rather young."

Korander blinked. "You've picked a bride for me? I was hoping to marry someone of my *own* choosing."

His father shook his head. "Really? Do you have someone in mind?"

Korander nodded. "I want to marry Davia."

Saerthan's brows furrowed. "Davia? Davia who? I know of no clanswoman named Davia."

"She ain't clan." Korander gulped. "She fixes mama's hair and helps her dress."

Saerthan's frown deepened. "You wish to marry a *commoner*? And one who is a *house servant*?"

Korander nodded. "She's pregnant with my child, and I love her."

Saerthan chuckled. "You don't need to marry a woman simply because you've planted a seed in her. It's acceptable for you to sire bastards. Clansmen don't marry their mistresses just because they've become pregnant."

"But I love her and want *her* child to be my heir!"

95

"Enough!" Saerthan slammed his hand on the table. "You may have this Davia as your mistress, but you *will* marry Sythda Firain."

Korander shook his head. "No! If I can't marry Davia, I won't marry at all."

"Are you defying me?"

Korander firmed his chin. "Yes."

Saerthan motioned to his guards. "Take him to the whipping post and prepare him for punishment, then wait for me there. *No one* will defy me. Not even my son."

***

Korander struggled against the bonds that tied him to the whipping post, but the guards who'd bound him had done so many times before, and the ropes held fast. The sun beat down on his bare body, and he could feel his fair skin burning under its rays. Suddenly, Davia called to him.

"Kor!"

He turned his head. His father held Davia by the arm and stood beside the seat where he sat to watch punishments administered.

"Do you *still* defy me?" his father called down to him.

Fear for his lover chilled him to the core. "What are you going to do?"

Saerthan shook the girl's arm. "If you don't agree to marry Sythda Firain, I'll have your mistress executed."

Korander struggled harder against the ropes that bound him to the post. "No! Please? Do what you must to me, but don't harm *her*."

"Will you marry the Firain girl as I desire?"

Korander sobbed, sagging against the post. "Yes."

"Very well. You still defied me, however, so you need to pay the price for that." His father turned towards the executioner. "Give him twenty-five lashes and don't spare him. Son or no son, he must pay the full price for his defiance."

As the scourge came down on his back, his father spoke again. "Know this boy, any *further* defiance, and I won't give you the *option* of keeping your mistress."

***

Korander lay on his stomach while Davia tended to his back.

"I never expected your pa to give permission for us to marry. I'm content to be your beloved mistress."

He hissed as the cream she applied to his back eased the pain from his whipping. "I had to try. At least papa said the bride he chose for me ain't ready for marriage yet. Perhaps we can still do something. Maybe we can run away somewhere."

"He's ordered you locked in your room. How could we run away?"

"I'll *think* of something."

* * *

"You're to dress and come with us," the guard said.

Korander looked up from where he lay, face down, on his bed. His back still ached from the whipping. "I ain't recovered from my punishment."

"The healers bandaged your back," the guard replied. "If you served as a guard, you'd have had to dress and return to duty within a few days. It's been a week. You can wear clothing. Come, his Lordship awaits."

With a sigh, Korander got out of bed and put on clean clothing. He'd leave his clan coat off. *This* bit of defiance was small enough even his father should allow it and the coat would be heavy on his still tender back. The guards brought him to the keep audience chamber, which was decorated for a wedding. His mother and siblings sat towards the front of the room with a group of strangers wearing the blue and white Firain symbol. A blonde girl wearing a wedding wreath stood in front of the priest.

His father came to him and placed a wedding wreath on his head.

"I thought you said the bride you'd chosen for me was still too young."

Saerthan smiled at him. "I spoke with her parents," he gestured towards the strangers seated beside his mother and siblings, "and we've agreed to advance the wedding. She's young, yes, but not so young that marriage is out of the question." He motioned towards where the commoners stood. "I've had your mistress brought to attend the wedding. She needn't continue serving as a maid if she's giving you bastards."

Korander looked where his father had pointed. Davia stood beside the rope that separated the commoners from the higher status guests, surrounded by guards. She wore a party dress suitable for a clanswoman. Someone had braided festive jewels into her dark tresses. She stared directly at him, her blue eyes wide and her pupils dilated. He swallowed hard, chill filling his heart.

"Thank you," he whispered.

"Good boy," his father cried jovially, patting him gently on his shoulder. "Now come, meet your bride."

***

When they went to the nuptial bed, Korander consummated the marriage, but he wasn't gentle about it. The pain in his back made him savage, and he knew he'd hurt *her*. Afterwards, he turned his back on his new wife as she wept behind him.

The next morning, when he got up to use the chamber pot, she sat on the bed, staring at him. He glared at her.

"What are *you* looking at?"

"Your back," she whispered.

He paused. "You want to see my back? Very well, I'll *show* you my back." He reached back and ripped at the bandages that still covered his healing stripes. He couldn't reach them all, and the ones he *could* reach dangled from the others.

His wife got up and helped pull the bandages off. When she saw what was underneath, she gasped.

"I didn't want to marry you. This is the punishment papa ordered for my defiance."

The girl swallowed audibly. "I'll put new bandages on. Lay on the bed, please."

He eyed her coldly for a moment before he complied. She found the cream that needed to be applied first and pressed the bandages on top of it, her hands tender as she worked. Between his rage and the fresh dressing, he blocked the pain.

When she finished tending to his back and they'd both dressed, he grabbed her wrist and dragged her out of his room.

As he'd suspected, the guards were no longer stationed at the door now that he was married to the bride of his father's choosing. He made his way to Davia's room. He'd show his new wife where her place was in his life, and that was *not* in his heart. In the doorway, he released her and stalked over to where Davia sat, doing needlework. He placed his hand on his mistress's shoulder and turned to face his new wife.

"This is Davia, my mistress," he informed Sythda coldly. "She's the woman who holds my heart. My father ordered to sire children with you, so I will, but Davia holds the greatest importance in my life."

Sythda stared at Davia with wide eyes and Davia stared back. Slowly, Sythda walked to the chair where the older woman sat and knelt by her side.

"Without harmony, there is unhappiness. Harmony can live with love, but not with hatred, resentment, or jealousy. Since my husband loves you, then I must, too." She peered up into Davia's face. "I'm the youngest of nine and have eight brothers. I've always wanted a sister. Will you be my heart-sister?" She offered her hand to the other woman.

Davia smiled at the girl and accepted her hand. "I would *love* to be your heart-sister." She glanced up at Korander. "I approve of your wife. Of all the women your papa could have chosen for you, he chose my heart-sister." She leaned forward and kissed Sythda on the cheek. "How old are you, my dear?"

Sythda smiled shyly back at her. "I'm thirteen."

Davia set her sewing aside and pulled the girl into her arms. "So young to have wed." She sighed, hugging her. "Kor, you must be very gentle with her."

Korander stared at the two women and the ice that had formed around his heart melted. He knelt and pulled both of them into a hug.

"I will. If she's your heart-sister, then I must love her too."

***

Homelands: Late Spring - Summer Solstice
Y1059

Lirin followed her father into the keep, her dark eyes wide as she stared at the Solstice decorations. They stopped in the entry and her father turned to her.

"What do you think?"

She smiled at him. "It's beautiful! I wish we could *live* here."

He laughed. "I'm afraid we can't. We're just here for the holiday. The holding won't run itself. We can stay for the summer though, if you like."

"*Could* we? I'd *love* that."

Servants showed them to their quarters.

On Solstice morn, Lirin was up at dawn. She flung open the window in her room and watched the sunrise. The keep was still in the early morning light as the longest day of the year began. She brushed her long dark hair and braided it into a coronet on top of her head.

At noon, her father brought her to where the festivities were being held.

"Your uncle promised to provide you with an escort during our stay. I have business to deal with while we're here and won't be able to attend to your needs."

She nodded. "Yes, papa." *I hope my escort ain't some old biddy.*

They filled plates at the feast table and her father led the way to where his brother sat. There, he put his arm around her. "Here's Lirin."

Her uncle rose, bowing, and gestured towards a darkly handsome youth who stood at attention behind him. "This is my son, Tollot. I thought he'd be a good choice to watch over her during your stay at the keep."

Lirin beamed at the boy. "Hello." *This is* much *better than an old biddy*!

He bowed. "Hello."

When they finished eating, her father kissed her cheek. "Why don't you two youngsters go off and have fun at the celebration? I'm sure you'll enjoy the games more without us old folk getting in the way."

"You ain't *that* old papa."

He laughed, patting her shoulder. "Go on. Enjoy yourselves."

As they headed towards the courtyard, Lirin glanced up at Tollot. "What do you want to do?"

He peered down at her. "I'm just supposed to watch you. We can do what *you* want to do."

"Well, what *is* there to do? Papa mentioned games."

He nodded, pointing across the courtyard. "The children are playing games over there."

"What do young people who ain't children do?" Must papa continue thinking of me as a child? I'm fourteen! I'm a woman now.

He shrugged. "There are dances."

She peeked up at him through her lashes. "Would *you* like to dance?"

"I'm a bastard. I ain't supposed to dance with clan. You can dance with someone else, though. My job is to watch over you."

She frowned. "That don't seem fair. Don't *you* get to celebrate Solstice?"

"I'm supposed to keep watch on you."

She bit her lip. "Is there an empty room where we can hear the dance music?"

"What do you have in mind?"

"If no one *sees* us dancing, you can dance with me."

***

Late Autumn Y1060

Sythda smiled. "So, we *both* want to go to the Solstice party at house Browarg."

Korander frowned at his wife. "We don't have transport rights to the Browarg docks, so we'd have to go overland. The route to Browarg keep goes out into the wastes. Not to mention we'd have to pass close to the Torust enclave."

"We can ride in a carriage," Davia suggested. "And Sythda told me we could reach it in just an hour or two. That ain't all *that* far. We can both handle riding in a carriage for a couple of hours."

"And we trust you to keep us safe from any Torust folk that might try to bother us," Sythda added, reaching up and stroking his cheek. "Please, husband mine. Take us to the party."

Davia nodded. "I've never been outside the enclave in my life. I would *love* to see the wastes." She stood on her toes and kissed his cheek.

He sighed. "How did you even *hear* of this party?"

Sythda laughed. "One of my brothers married a Browarg. *He* told me about it. Since they're connected to my house, he could get invitations for all of us to attend. We can spend the night and return home via transport the morning after the party."

"What if there's a storm?"

"I talked to old Nes. He has a weather wise ache, and *he* says it'll be clear for at least three days," Davia replied.

He sighed. "How can I say 'no' with the two of you ganging up on me?"

Both of the women he loved more than he could say enveloped him in hugs.

"Thank you, dear," they said in chorus.

***

Winter Solstice Y1060

"Can we come to the party too, papa?" Serelaf asked.

Korander turned. His two eldest sons stood in front of the keep door, watching the closed carriage their mothers were boarding.

"I don't know. My wife will have to approve, but even if you can't attend the party, you can still ride along with the guards. The guards should have a celebration of their own."

The two youths grinned and raced to the stables for mounts.

The journey was uneventful until they were close to the border of the Torust enclave. Just as they were about to enter the wastes to pass around the hostile clan's territory, a band of riders swirled around the party, whooping and shouting. One rider threw an explosive onto the driver's seat, knocking him off his perch into the snow. The explosion spooked the carriage horses, and they raced out into the wastes, pulling the vehicle behind them. Then, as quickly as the attackers had come, they were gone.

As the guards hesitated over whether to chase after their attackers or the carriage, Serelaf dug his spurs into his horse's sides and raced after the careening vehicle that held his parents and heart-aunt, his brother Rothas, hard on his heels.

Inside the carriage, the occupants clung to each other as it violently bounced and swayed back and forth, knocking them against first one side, then the other. The horses raced in a straight line until they reached the edge of a ravine, where they crashed into a boulder. The carriage broke free of the traces and rolled down the side of the ravine until it came to rest at the bottom, upside down.

The two boys were still trying to get one of the carriage doors open when the guards arrived.

***

Zavi eyed herself in the mirror and sighed. *Time for a haircut.* She fetched a pair of scissors and trimmed her sandy brown hair. Once she'd clipped it short enough that no enemy could grab it in combat, she wrinkled her nose at her reflection. The tusk-like lower canines she'd inherited from her father jutted over her upper lip as she grimaced. *I miss you, ma.*

She retreated to her bunk, and sat, staring at her feet as she sharpened her sword.

Akaha opened the barracks door and stuck her head inside. "Zavi, what are you doing in *here*? It's Solstice! You should celebrate the holiday with the rest of us!"

Zavi glanced up at her friend. "I was thinking about ma." She wiped her nose on her sleeve. "She'd be so proud they've appointed me squad leader."

Akaha sat on the bunk and put her arm around Zavi's shoulders. "I'm sorry. I forgot they killed your ma in the attack."

Zavi leaned against Akaha, sobbing. "All my family's gone now. I'm the only one left."

"We'll get them. The clan won't allow the attack to go unpunished. They'll *pay* for what they did, however long it takes. We'll kill them all."

***

Early Winter Y1060

Korander opened his eyes and stared at the ceiling. He frowned. Something was wrong. He tried to sit up and fell back with a gasp of pain.

"Papa?"

He tried to reply, but couldn't get words out.

Serelaf's face came into his view. The boy's eyes were red and swollen, but he smiled as he looked into his father's face.

"You're awake!"

He closed his eyes and took a deep breath, then tried to speak again. "What happened?" His voice was a hoarse croak.

"There was an accident. You've been unconscious for nearly a week. We were afraid we'd lose you, too."

"'Too'?" His eyes flew open and his heart thudded in his chest. "Where are your mama and my wife?"

Tears welled up in Serelaf's eyes. "They died in the crash. We sent two of the guards to fetch help. Mama had her baby while we were waiting for them to return, but died before they got back." He sniffed. "Aunt Sythda was dead when we pulled her out of the carriage. When the guards came back with a healer, she cut the baby out of her. It was a boy, but he was dead too."

Korander shook his head. "No!"

"It was Torust that caused the accident. We all saw the symbols on their coats. They killed mama, Aunt Sythda, and Sythda's baby."

As he lay weeping over his loss, something about his son's words didn't quite add up.

"You said your mama had *her* baby? What happened to it?"

"It's a girl. Mama died before she could name her. We found a wet nurse for her. She seems healthy."

"We'll call her Davia after her mama." He swallowed. "Torust will *pay* for this."

"Grandpapa said he'll call for a clan war if *you* die, but he won't do it for a wife, a mistress, or a baby that already had several older full siblings. He said Aunt Sythda had already served her purpose, that the baby ain't needed for the succession, and that mama was unimportant."

Korander clenched his fists. "Papa's an old man. If *he* won't call for a clan war over your mama, your aunt, or your brother, then *I* will when he dies. I *swear* it."

***

Early Spring Y1061

Tollot smiled as Lirin greeted him at the dining hall door. "It's been so long. I didn't think I'd ever see you again. You never came back to the keep, and I didn't see you when we arrived at the holding."

She glanced at her father. "Shh. We'll talk later. Meet me in the garden after dinner."

He nodded, bowing as he left her side to take his place at the low table.

When he reached the garden, he found her seated on a bench beside the pond, tossing food pellets into the water for the fish. He took her in his arms and kissed her.

"I missed you so much. It's been nearly two years. I thought for sure you'd be married by now "

She hugged him, resting her head on his chest. "I won't *ever* be married. Not if I can't marry *you*."

He laughed shakily. "How can you be so *sure*? You're full clan. You have no choice in who you marry."

"Have you forgotten what we did that summer? No clansman would want me after that."

"But... no one knows."

She pulled away from him to pick a basket up off the ground and set it on the bench. "Oh, they know all right. They just don't know it was *you*." She took a bundle out of the basket and turned back a flap of cloth, revealing the face of a sleeping baby. "Meet your son."

He stared at the child in her arms; the color draining from his face. "My *son*?"

She nodded.

"They'll execute me. You're full clan, I'm just a bastard."

"Papa's afraid to send word to the keep that our son even exists and *I* ain't about to tell anyone that *you* planted the seed." She sat on the bench cuddling the baby.

He knelt beside her. "You know there's nothing I want more than to marry you, but..."

She nodded. "I know. They'd never allow it. It's ok." She gripped his hand. "I'm willing to settle for meeting in secret whenever the opportunity arises. How long will you be here?"

He kissed the baby's cheek. "My assignment is to hunt

bandit. Our scouts tracked them to the northern wastes. There may be multiple camps. We don't know how long it'll take to drive them from the region. I'll be heading out once the scouts have found a target."

She put the baby back in the basket and set it on the ground. "Then let's make the most of the time we have." She rested her head on his shoulder.

He cast a worried look at the basket. "What if he wakes up?"

"I gave him a drop to keep him quiet. He'll sleep for at least an hour."

He frowned. "Ain't that dangerous? Whatever you gave him could hurt him."

"I'll only do it this once. I promise I won't make a habit of it, but I had to show him to you and this was the only way I could be sure he wouldn't wake up and start crying while we're together."

***

Lirin left the table and headed towards the dining-room door.

"Lirin?"

She turned. "Yes, papa?"

He smiled at her. "Would you like to take weapons' training?"

Her eyes lit up. "Oh, *may* I?"

He nodded. "Since the guards who'll be hunting bandits are staying here in our holding, there'll be training sessions every day. The guards will train any of the holding workers who are interested. I thought you could join them. You never know when you might need to defend yourself. I should probably have had you start when you were a child, but it's never too late to learn."

She ran to the head of the table and threw her arms around him, kissing his cheek. "Thank you, papa!"

***

Zavi made her way to where the squad leaders were gathering around the captain of the newly organized company. "Sir, I'm squad leader Zavi. My squad is ready to go."

"Are all the squad leaders here now?"

One of the other squad leaders nodded. "Yes sir. Now that Zavi's joined us, we're all here."

She frowned. "Sir? If I may ask, how *old* are you?"

He sighed. "I'm eighteen."

She raised a brow. "And they gave you command of an entire *company*? I thought *I* was young to be given command of a *squad*, but I'm older than you."

He looked her up and down, taking in her wiry frame and coarse features. "You know this is as much a training mission as anything else, right? Besides, you don't look *that* much older than me."

She shrugged. "*I* ain't the one in charge of the company."

Another squad leader laughed. "Master Tollot's a clan bastard. They *always* give bastards more authority at an earlier age than common guards. Get used to it."

"Right then." Tollot spread a map on the command table so all the squad leaders could see it. "The scouts have discovered several bandit camps in the wastes." He pointed at a spot on the map. "Our current target is located here. We'll go due north from the holding to this location." He pointed at another spot on the map that was well within the wastes. "We'll then split into our respective squads. Your squad's scouts will act as guides to our final destination. We'll surround the camp and attack." He moved his finger to where he'd said their target was located.

Zavi frowned. "Wouldn't it be quicker to go in a straight line from the holding to the camp?" She traced a direct route on the map with her finger.

Tollot hooded his eyes. "It would, *if* we wanted to cross hostile territory. Now, I don't know about *you*, but personally, I'd rather *not* risk having to fight both bandits and a hostile clan's guards."

Zavi's cheeks burned.

He smirked at her, his dark eyes gleaming. "One benefit of me being a clan bastard is that I've attended war councils as part of papa's entourage and have information common guards don't have access to, not even squad leaders."

A squad leader who'd served with her mother patted Zavi on the shoulder. "Zavi's new to her position. Give her time. She'll learn quickly. They didn't promote her to squad leader for nothing."

Tollot examined Zavi through narrowed eyes. "This operation will either make or break you. Since they chose you for this, you must have shown potential. Live up to that potential and you'll go far."

Zavi ducked her head. "I'll do my best, sir."

***

Mid-Spring Y1061

Korander eyed his father coldly. "Do you have any objection to my taking a second wife of my own choosing?"

Saerthan shrugged. "That depends. Are you once again thinking of marrying a commoner?"

Korander shook his head. "I've contacted house Eldragon. There's a daughter of the house in their clan who's of eligible age and they're interested in a connection to us."

The old man cackled. "In that case, you have my full approval. I would never have dared seek to connect our clan to their house myself. They have a terrible reputation." He wagged his head. "*Some* would say an *evil* reputation."

"I'm aware of their reputation. It's *why* I sought them out. *You* may not wage war on Torust, but with the backing of Eldragon, *I* will."

Saerthan cackled again. "You *do* that, boy. I've done my duty towards the clan. You can do what you want with it once I'm dead and gone."

***

"Can I take my sister with me?" Lenoma asked.

Her father frowned. "Which one?"

"Lassie. I love her and I'd miss her if I couldn't take her with me. She's been my playmate since she was born."

He smiled. "Of course you can, sweetheart. Take *any* of the clan bastards you want. You're going to marry a future clan Lord. Your status will increase and you'll need to show that to the world."

Lenoma's mother put an arm around her. "You'll be able to have babies of your own too, dear. You won't have to pretend anymore."

The girl's eyes lit up. "Can I have *lots* of babies?"

Her mother nodded. "As many as you want."

"Your husband-to-be already has several children," her father added. "He had a wife and mistress who were both killed last Solstice and they'd each given him several children before they died. Other women's children ain't as good as your own, of course, but you can practice being a mama with them. His youngest bastard is still a baby, born just before its mama died."

Lenoma's blue eyes sparkled. "Do you think he'll let me help care for it?"

Her mother smiled. "I'm sure he will. Though once you have a baby of your own, you'll want to concentrate on *it* instead."

"So," her father said. "Are you ready to get married now?"

Lenoma nodded. "Yes. As long as I can take Lassie with me and have lots of babies."

"We need to take a transport to his enclave for the wedding," her mother told her. "Since he's heir to his clan, he has to marry there."

* * *

Korander greeted his future in-laws at the keep entrance. When he saw the girl who exited their carriage first, he had a moment of panic. She looked *way* too young. He didn't want another child bride. The girl turned and assisted an older girl to emerge, and he felt his breathing ease. Both girls had bright red hair, but the second girl was almost as tall as he was and wore a shimmering blue dress with black trim. Since she was wearing his clan colors, *she* must be the girl they'd promised him. Introductions proved this to be true, and he smiled at her as he set the marriage wreath on her head.

"Come," he told her. "The audience chamber is this way."

"I hope you don't mind that Lasria will join your household too," his future father-in-law said. "Lenoma couldn't bear to part with her."

Korander shook his head. "I don't mind at all. A spouse needs friends in a new home. My first wife became heart-sisters with my mistress. I'm sure she'd have been very unhappy if she hadn't been able to make that bond. I no longer have a mistress, so it's good for Lenoma to bring someone to keep her company."

Lenoma looked over at him. "Papa says you have a bastard that's still a baby. I love babies. Can I help take care of it?"

He smiled warmly at her. "Davia still needs her wet nurse, but I'm sure the nurse will be happy to let you help her take care of my daughter. I have fifteen children altogether, eight by my late wife and seven by my mistress."

Lenoma smiled back at him. "I hope to have several children myself. As much as I love helping care for other women's babies, I really want some of my own. I hope I can give you at least as many children as your last wife did."

He patted her hand. "You can have as many or as few as you wish."

When they entered the audience chamber, Rothas and Serelaf greeted them. Lenoma stared at the two youths. When Korander told her they were his eldest sons, her face puckered.

"Don't you have any *little* children?"

"I do," Korander assured her. "But Sere and Rothas are my firsts. Sere is my first bastard and Rothas is my heir. All the rest of my children are younger."

"Oh," she said.

"Lenoma, dear," her mother told her. "Women don't have all their babies at once. Of *course,* they're going to be different ages."

"Are you ready to get married now?" her father asked.

She nodded, and they proceeded to their places.

*   *   *

After the ceremony was over, Korander led his new bride to the nuptial bed. "Are you ready for this?"

"Yes!" She smiled, stripped off her clothes, and hopped into the bed. "We have to couple before I can get pregnant."

This bedding differed from what had happened with Sythda. Lenoma entered love making with enthusiasm. She was a little startled when he took her maidenhead, but he apologized for that and explained to her it would only hurt that one time. Once he'd finished, he cradled her in his arms and prepared to sleep.

"Am I pregnant now?" she murmured in his ear.

He chuckled. "You could be. Or it could take months

before you get pregnant. The seed don't always take."

"How often do you need to bed me before I get pregnant?"

"I don't know. I never kept track of how often I made love to Sythda or Davia."

"So, how will I know when I'm pregnant?"

He sighed, thinking back on what had happened whenever his wife or mistress had conceived. "You'll probably feel tired, you'll need to pee a lot, your clothes will feel tight, you may get sick, and, of course, your menses won't come. That last one is the most important sign. You may think they're just late, only you'll be pregnant."

"Oh. My menses last came two weeks ago. I guess I need to keep careful track of them."

He patted her hand. "You do that. I need to sleep now and so do you." He gave her a kiss. "Good night." Dear gods, is she simple? *Sythda seemed more intelligent and mature than her when we were first wed, and Lenoma was much older than Sythda had been.*

***

Lirin made a face as she drained the glass. "Bleah. That stuff tastes horrible. It seems to get worse with each mouthful."

The healer shrugged. "It's medicine, mistress. It's *supposed* to taste bad. That way, you know it's working. The medicine ensures your menses will be light and you won't have any downtime because of female troubles."

"How much longer will I need to take it?"

"You need to take it as long as you're taking weapons' training. You're in good company. *All* the female guards take it." The healer packed up her supplies.

Lirin gave a short laugh. "If I'd known I'd have to drink nasty tasting medicine every day, I wouldn't have agreed to papa's offer. I wouldn't mind so much if I could go out on patrols with the guards." *When papa offered to let me take weapons' training, I thought for* sure *I'd be able to go out with patrols. Maybe even* Tollot's *patrol.*

"Master has your best interests in mind."

***

When Lenoma awoke, she found her new husband laying

on his stomach, still asleep, his snow-white hair covering his face. She'd felt ridges on his back the night before as they were consummating their marriage and was curious about them. Carefully, she worked the covers off him, revealing his torso. She gasped at the sight. A mass of scars covered his back. The sound she'd made woke him, and he lifted his head, pushed his hair out of his face, and looked at her.

"What happened to your back?"

He sighed. "Papa punished me for defying him once. Call me a coward if you like, but I ain't dared defy him since. I even sought his permission before I asked for you to be my bride and I'm delaying my war on house Torust until he's dead lest he see *that* as defiance."

She nodded. "Papa told me you want our help with a clan war and that's why I was to marry you." She stroked his back with her fingertips. "Does this still hurt?"

He smiled. "No. It healed a long time ago."

"Oh." She pressed down hard with her full hand and rubbed the scars that marred his back. "What did your papa do to you to make scars like this?"

"He had me whipped."

She blinked. "Whipping can cause *scars*?"

"Yes. *Anything* that breaks the skin can cause a scar."

"But papa whips *us* when we misbehave and the most it ever does is leave red marks that fade after a short time. He only whipped *me* once, though. Then he said that was the wrong punishment for me. After that one time, if I was really naughty, he'd whip Lassie instead of me and she don't like it, so I try not to be bad."

Korander's jaw dropped, but then he smiled at her kindly. "What does your papa use for that, and how many times does he hit with it?"

"He keeps the whip he uses in his room. The most he's ever hit any of us, though, was when my brother Galar did something *terrible*. He actually made Galar take his shirt off that time, so the whip hit his skin, and he hit him ten times."

"I have a small whip that I use when my own children disobey too, but when my papa had *me* whipped, he had me tied naked to a post in the courtyard for a couple hours first, and I have very fair skin, so the sun burned me. Then the executioner used a scourge instead of a simple whip and he hit me twenty-five times. The worst I've heard anyone else get was when they caught some on duty sentries pleasuring themselves with whores while slum folk raided the storehouse they were supposed to be guarding. They each got fifteen lashes and papa has since made a rule forbidding our sentries from ever having congress with whores while on duty."

She frowned. "What's a scourge?"

"It's a whip with several lashes. Each lash has bits of metal woven into it, so they bite into the flesh when the whip strikes. You can kill someone with one."

Her eyes widened. "And he did this to his *heir*?"

He nodded. "I have five younger siblings, so if the scourging had killed me, there was a replacement ready."

"Your scars are pretty. May I paint a picture of your back?"

He frowned. "Why would you want to do that?"

"Because it's part of who you are and you're a beautiful man."

He shrugged. "I guess so then. Do you paint a lot?"

She nodded. "If I'm sad, I paint something sad. If I'm happy, I paint something happy. I'm going to want to paint lots of pictures of you and your children, especially the little ones. Babies always make me happy."

He smiled at her. "I'd like that. I don't have many pictures of my children."

"Well, I'm an excellent painter, if I say so myself. After I paint your back, I want to paint you together with *all* your children."

"Well, you can do that later. Right now, we need to get dressed for breakfast. You can meet the rest of my children, then I'll take you to meet papa."

"Why wasn't he with your mama at our wedding?"

"He's an old man now. He rarely leaves his room. I hope he dies soon."

"So you can go to war?"

He nodded. "We'll be preparing while we wait for him to die, but we can't actually do much else until then."

At the breakfast table, Korander formally introduced her to all his children. They even brought the baby to the table, and she cooed with delight over her husband's bastard daughter. She could tell which of the younger ones had been Korander's wife's children and which had come from his mistress by the color of their hair. His bastards all had black hair and his wife's children were all blonds. Most of them started going gray around puberty, though, and the oldest of those had pure white hair like their father.

All the children seemed to like her, with the sole exception of Rothas, who was rather standoffish. He was close to her own age, though, so she felt *he* didn't really matter. Four-year-old Maya actually called her mama, which filled her with delight, and she hugged the little girl tenderly as Rothas frowned at them.

After breakfast, Korander took her to meet his father. The old man sat in his sitting room, brooding over something.

"Papa," her husband said. "This is my new wife, Lenoma."

The old man turned his head and peered at her. "Come here, girl," he said in a cracked voice.

She walked over to stand beside his chair. "Hello."

He looked her up and down. "Tall one, ain't you?"

She nodded. "Both my parents are tall and all my siblings are, too."

He looked her up and down again and sneered. "You ain't got much of a figure, though. Too narrow top to bottom." He pointed at her hips. "That there's going to give you problems. A woman should have wide hips."

"I didn't marry her for her figure," Korander said dryly.

The old man cackled. "Maybe you *should* have, boy. I checked out the Firain girl's figure before I chose her for your first wife. A woman needs wide hips or she ain't no good." He shook his head, a distant look in his eyes. "No good at all." He waved his arm at them. "Now go away, both of you. You tire me."

As Korander led her away from his father's room, Lenoma sniffed. "He's a nasty old man. Why would it matter if I don't have wide hips?"

Her husband patted her hand. "It's ok. Just ignore him. He should die soon anyway."

"It can't come soon enough for me! I hate him."

Korander nodded. "I hate him too."

***

Lirin caught sight of Tollot standing on the edge of the training field, watching as she practiced her stances. She finished the set and walked over to him.

"Hello."

He smiled at her. "You're doing well."

She scowled. "I wish papa would let me put my training into practice."

He surveyed the guards on the field, pointing at a pair sparring nearby. "Are you up to that yet?"

She glanced over; her scowl deepening. "None of them will take me on. They just tell me to practice my stances."

He chose a practice sword from the weapons' rack and hefted it. "I can spar with you if you like."

She grinned, moving into a sparring ring. "Great! Let's go at it then."

He draped his coat on the end of the weapons' rack and joined her in the ring. "Ready?"

She nodded.

***

Spring – Summer Y1061

Over the following weeks, Lenoma's new life fell into a pattern. In the morning, before they dressed for breakfast, she worked on the painting she was doing of her husband's back. She had him lie naked and face down on their bed, then positioned him and arranged the covers. Once everything was the way she wanted it, she would paint for half an hour in the early morning light.

After she'd finished painting, they'd go down to breakfast. Then he'd head off to deal with whatever occupied his time during the day and she'd pretend to be his children's mama. More of his younger children started calling her 'mama' like Maya had, and this filled her heart with joy.

The first time she was sick in the morning, she ran to the calendar she'd set up to keep track of her menses and rejoiced to see they were due. She had some spotting over the next few days though, so she went to the infirmary and spoke to a healer, just to be sure she wasn't starting her menses after all.

The healer told her that some spotting was common during pregnancy and not to worry about it, so she went blithely on with her day-to-day activities.

During the next month, the spotting got worse, but since the healer had told her spotting was common in pregnant women, she didn't worry about it. By this time, she was sure she was pregnant. Besides the spotting, she had all the symptoms Korander had told her about.

Shortly after her pregnancy showed, she had cramps. At first, she thought this was nothing to worry about, as she'd often had cramps even before she'd become pregnant. When she went to bed at night, she caressed the small growing swelling at her waist and whispered how much she loved it.

Then, one day, after the midday meal, the cramps got worse and wouldn't stop. Worried that something might be wrong; she went to the infirmary and told the healers. They immediately bundled her off to an examination room.

***

Early Summer Y1061

The progress Korander had made in his preparations for the coming war satisfied him. Both the Firain and Eldragon houses were prepared and waiting for him to give the word. He had to be more careful about preparing his own clan, though. He could work on defenses and guard training, but he couldn't go to a slum and recruit additional troops. That step would have to wait until after his father died. He entered the main door to the keep, looking forward to his wife's cheerful babble about her pregnancy.

"Sir!" a servant called. "You need to come to the infirmary right away. There was a problem with mistress Lenoma."

When a healer led him to the room where his wife lay, he found her curled in a ball on the bed, weeping. He sat beside her and caressed her shoulder.

"Are you all right?"

She threw herself into his arms. "I lost my baby! I thought everything was normal because the healer told me spotting is common during a pregnancy, and I thought the cramps were too, because I get cramps a lot, but I was wrong and now my baby's *dead*."

116

He stroked her back, trying to soothe her. "It's ok. We can try again, and the next time, we'll have the healers keep watch over you as soon as we know you're pregnant. The healers can do things to help. You can have another baby."

She snuffled, gazing at him with tear-filled eyes as snot dripped down her chin. "I can?"

He nodded. "Women have miscarriages all the time. It don't mean you can't have another baby."

She pulled at his arm. "Let's start *now*."

He laughed, shaking his head. "You need to recover first." He kissed her gently on the cheek. "We can start trying again once you're all healed from the miscarriage."

She sighed. "Ok, but I want to get pregnant again *real* soon."

* * *

Lirin rested her head on Tollot's chest. "How much longer do you think they'll station you here?"

He wrapped his arms around her. "I hope to be here until the end of summer. The scouts found several bandit camps in the northern wastes. At the very least, I'll be here until we've cleaned them all out."

"I wish you could be here permanently. Perhaps you could ask to be assigned to the holding as one of our guards, or even ask for your base of operations here to be made permanent."

"Papa likes to keep me near him as much as possible, and since he's assigned to work with the guards, he has to spend most of *his* time at the keep. He ain't happy about my current assignment. If he were the heir, he'd have nixed it. I'm his only son and he ain't got a wife to occupy himself with." He kissed the top of her head.

She sighed. "You're missing out on your *own* son's milestones. You missed the entire first year of his life. He'll be walking soon. He's started pulling himself upright. I suppose I should be grateful they've assigned you to hunt bandits. If it weren't for the bandits, the gods know how long it would've been before we saw each other again."

"Or if."

She nodded. "Or if."

* * *

117

Mid-Summer Y1061

"I've been thinking while you were in the infirmary, and decided I want to learn to be a healer."

Lenoma started, turning to stare at Lasria. "Why?"

"If I was a healer and knew about what should happen and what shouldn't, I would have known something was wrong *before* you lost your baby."

Lenoma hugged the younger girl and kissed her on the cheek. "What a wonderful idea! Let's ask Kor if he'll let you do that."

When the two girls broached the request to Lenoma's husband, he shrugged.

"Sure. If your sister wants to be a healer, she can. I'll tell our chief physician to arrange for her training."

"*Thank* you," Lenoma said. "Once Lassie knows everything, she can be my personal physician."

He chuckled. "It'll take many years of training before she can act as a physician and she'll never know *everything*, but in the meantime, she *can* be your personal nurse if you ever have to go to the infirmary again."

Lenoma touched his arm. "The doctor said I can move back to your bed and we can start trying for a baby again."

"All right, we can start on that tonight." He kissed her gently.

She pouted. "I was hoping we could go to our room and start right *now*. I don't want to wait until tonight."

He sighed. "I have things I need to do."

She made puppy eyes at him. "Please?"

"Don't you and your sister want to spend some time together now that you're out of the infirmary?"

"She can go start her training. *I* want to get pregnant again."

He looked at her for a full minute, then gave another sigh. "All right, but it'll have to be quick. I have a job I need to do."

Beaming, she grabbed his arm and pulled him to their bedchamber.

***

Serelaf sat beside Lasria at the dining table. "Hi."

She looked up from her breakfast. "Hi."

118

"I'm supposed to take you to start your healer training today."

She smiled. "I was wondering when I'd be able to start that. I can't wait until I can be Leni's doctor."

"You love your sister very much, don't you?"

She nodded. "All Leni ever wants to do is paint or play like she's a mama. Some others in our clan like to hurt the bastards." She showed him a scar on her arm. "One of our brothers burned me once, and she got *mad* at him. She told him I'm *her* playmate and if he wanted to burn a bastard, he should get his own."

He stared at her. "Why did he do *that*?"

She shrugged. "He wanted to know how it would look and smell but didn't want to burn himself. I like how *your* clan treats bastards better than mine, and I'm so glad Leni brought me here with her when she married your papa."

"You and me *both*," he muttered, shaking his head. "How old are you, anyway? I don't think anyone told us."

"I'll be fourteen in early autumn."

He smiled at her. "*Will* you now?"

She nodded.

"My birthday's in early autumn too, but I'll be nineteen."

***

Zavi crouched behind the rocks, studying the layout of the bandit camp. A scout assigned to her squad crept to her side, his beast padding silently behind him.

"This camp has access to fertile soil. It's how they're able to keep the horses they stole from our patrols."

She turned and stared at him. "Where?"

He pointed. "See that crack in the wall?"

She nodded.

"It's a path. It leads to a plateau where grass grows. I think they have gardens there too. There are other paths to the plateau, but that one goes into their camp."

Her eyes narrowed. "Are there squads positioned to prevent the bandits from using those other paths to escape?"

He shrugged.

"Find out, please."

He nodded and slipped away.

Twenty minutes later, he was at her side again. "The captain stationed squads at two of the routes off the plateau."

"How many routes are there?"

"Besides the one that goes down to the camp? I found three."

She looked around. "Are we really needed *here*?"

The man grinned at her, shaking his head.

She motioned for the rest of her squad to come closer. "Bring us to that unguarded path."

***

Korander eyed the wall, frowning. "I think we'd be more secure if this wall was thick enough sentries could patrol along the top."

Moze shrugged. "It's a good sized wall. Do you have any idea how much material it would take to make the whole thing wide enough for sentries to patrol along the top? It took generations to build the walls we have now and enclaves ain't always walled. There are places where anyone can just walk right out of the waste onto fertile soil without realizing they're in some clan's holding."

"So, what can we do to make this area more secure? It's too close to the Torust enclave and will probably be one of their first targets when we go to war."

"I think you should just accept that they'll breach the walls of the eastern holdings early on and build up your offensive capabilities. This war will be over who hits hardest, not who has the best defenses."

"I'd feel more confident with stronger defenses. I've been trying to trade for a pack of urfren, but the only clans I've found that have any and will trade with me have asked for more than I can pay."

Moze nodded. "Urfren would certainly improve security. What price do they want?"

Korander made a face. "They want fertile land. Papa would never allow me to trade away any of our holdings, and I ain't sure I'd want to give any up myself. Not even for urfren."

The other man shook his head. "Best put them out of your mind, then. As nice as it would be to have some, that's a price you can't afford. Besides, it takes years for a pack to mature to where you can depend on them. We have dogs. Perhaps they'll be good enough."

"All we have are hunting and farm dogs, and we ain't trained any of them to guard."

* * *

"You said you'd be here until the end of summer."

Tollot sighed. "Yadrac discovered an escape route none of the other scouts found and alerted the squad leader he's assigned to. She blocked it off. Because of this, we caught the bandit leader. This is a *good* thing. Losing their leader demoralized the remaining bandits. The scouts report that their other camps are all abandoned. I put off declaring the mission over as long as I could, but the guards under my command *know* there're no more bandits for us to hunt. When we return to the keep, I'm going to recommend bonuses for both Yadrac and squad leader Zavi."

"Will I *ever* see you again?"

He lifted her chin and kissed her. "We spent two years apart after our summer together. We survived being separated then, we can survive it this time. No matter how long this separation lasts, I'll be *back* one day. Remember that."

Lirin took a pair of scissors from her satchel and cut a lock of her hair. "Here," she said, handing it to him. "Keep this to remember me."

He accepted the hair, twisting it into a ring, then bent his head. "Take a strand of mine so you have something of me too."

* * *

Late Summer Y1061

Serelaf smiled at Lasria. He'd been spending much of his time with her in the weeks since she'd started training to be a healer and enjoyed her company. He'd learned a bit about the craft himself since then because she'd gotten into the habit of asking him to help her with her lessons.

"So, what's today's lesson?"

"Anatomy. Will you help me with it? I need to memorize the names of different body parts."

"Sure. How do I do that?"

"You'll need to be naked. That way, I can see all your parts."

He blinked. "Are you *sure* about that?"

She nodded. "My teacher had pictures, but I don't have those to practice with. Leni will let me practice the woman parts on her, so I need a man to practice the man parts on and see how a man's and a woman's other parts are different."

He shrugged. He wasn't sure this was a good idea. "I *guess* that'll be ok."

She smiled. "Good. We'll do this in my bedroom. That way, you can lie on the bed and be comfortable while I examine you."

When they reached her bedroom, she first had him lay on his stomach while she explored his back. Her touch felt pleasant. Then she had him turn over and started going over the parts on his front. He found it amusing until she reached his crotch.

"Um, don't touch me there."

She tilted her head. "Why not?"

"You're too young to be playing with that part of a man's anatomy."

She laughed, leaning over him. "Don't be silly. I've played with a man's parts before. I've done it *lots* of times. For months until Leni married your papa and we came here, my brother Galar tupped me at least once a week."

"What? That's wrong! Your own *brother*?"

"It ain't like he vished me. He asked first and promised he wouldn't hurt me... and I was curious, so I said we could try once, but then I liked it."

He shook his head. "None of that makes it any better."

"Papa said it's ok as long as I'm taking preventive, but that if I had Galar's baby it would have to be killed."

"No. Preventive or not, it still ain't ok for your brother to tup you."

"Because you think I'm too young?"

"No," he said, nearly gagging. "Because he's your *brother*."

She climbed onto the bed with him and his eyes widened as he saw she'd stripped down to her blouse while he'd been lying on his stomach.

"I miss being tupped." She pulled her blouse off, tossing it across the room as she settled herself on top of him. "Leni thought her husband would make me his mistress and we could both have his babies, but he ain't even *looked* at me. I like *you* better anyway."

He swallowed hard. He felt trapped. With her on top of him, he'd have to push her off to get away from her. He didn't think he could do that.

"You *are* too young, though. You should wait until you're older before you even *think* of being with a man."

"I heard your papa's first wife was thirteen when they married." She traced a line on his chest with one of her fingers. "I'm almost fourteen now. Anyway, I'm still taking preventive, so no one will know if we don't tell them."

She kissed him tenderly on the lips and he lost all restraint.

Afterwards, he cursed himself. "We shouldn't have done that. Papa would have me whipped if he knew."

She laughed, snuggling against him. "Then we won't *tell* him. It was nice. You do it better than Galar does." She kissed him again.

He told himself it wouldn't happen again, but it did. As summer progressed towards autumn, it happened more and more often. Each time he told himself that was the last time and each time he was wrong. He tried consoling himself with how happy it made Lasria, but still knew in his heart that what they were doing was wrong. His father would be extremely angry if he found out. He thought of avoiding her, but if he did that, he was sure people would wonder why, and he didn't want anyone to know what they'd been doing. The guilt was eating him up, but he couldn't stop. Whenever he looked into her green eyes, he felt like he was drowning. Finally, the day came that he looked at himself in the mirror and didn't like what he saw there. He was having trouble sleeping and his eyes were bloodshot.

If my hair hadn't already turned white, I'm sure I'd go gray from the stress.

He closed his eyes and hung his head. He couldn't keep doing this.

***

"Papa," Serelaf said from behind him as he was leaving the dining hall.

Korander turned. "Yes?"

His son looked at the floor. "I need to tell you something." He gulped. "I've been doing something I know is wrong."

He sighed. "What have you been doing?"

Serelaf glanced at Korander's companions. "Could I tell you in private?"

Korander grit his teeth. Whatever this was, it was serious, or at least the boy thought it was. He took his son by the arm and hauled him to a conference room. He told his companions to guard the door, then pulled Serelaf inside and shut it.

"All right, we're private. What have you been doing?"

Serelaf swallowed hard, looking at the floor. "Lasria and I are lovers."

"'Lasria'," he repeated blankly.

"Your wife's bastard sister," Serelaf said helpfully.

"I *know* who she is," Korander thundered. "What I *don't* know is why my son would *do* such a thing. Do you have any idea how *old* she is?"

Serelaf winced. "She'll be fourteen next month."

"And you think that makes it ok for you to be bedding her?"

He hunched his shoulders. "I tried to tell her she's too young, but she said Aunt Sythda was only thirteen when *you* married *her*."

"*She* said that?"

The boy nodded. "I keep trying to stop because I know it's wrong, but she's always so happy when I make love to her." He swallowed audibly. "She says she's taking preventive."

"That don't make this any better."

"That's what *I* told *her* when she said her brother had been bedding her before you married her sister."

Korander sat down heavily in one of the room's chairs. "How did this all start?"

"I've been helping her with her studies. She wanted me to help her memorize the names of body parts. I thought it would be ok." He gave his father a pained stare.

"Go on," Korander said, frowning.

Serelaf hung his head. "We went to her room, and she had me lie on her bed so she could touch each part as she memorized the names. Then she got on the bed and kissed me." He sent his father a darting gaze. "I couldn't stop."

"And what made you decide to confess?"

"I looked at myself in the mirror this morning and didn't like what I saw there."

"At least you have a sense of shame." Korander stood and walked to the door, where he asked one of his companions to fetch Lasria.

When Lasria entered the room, she looked from one man to the other, then went straight to Serelaf, wrapped her arms around him, and glared at Korander.

"You are *not* to have him whipped."

He regarded her for a moment and sighed. "And *here* we have the guilty party. You seduced my son."

She lifted her chin, her green eyes glittering. "Yes, I did. And don't *you* go telling me I'm too young. I know *all* about your first wife."

"Consider this an impromptu court," he said dryly. "The two of you are to stop coupling. Preventive or no, you *are* too young."

Lasria stomped her foot. "I am *not!*"

"I ain't finished. If the two of you can show the self-control to stay out of each other's beds until Lasria is fifteen, I'll give you permission to marry, assuming you want to. Once you're married, you can do what you like."

Serelaf's eyes lit up. "Lassie?"

She stared at Korander, dumbstruck for a moment. "And if we can't?"

"Then I'll send Sere off to a distant section of the enclave and you'll never see him again."

"It'll only be a little over a year," Serelaf pleaded.

"If you're willing to let us marry, why can't we get married *now*?"

Korander chuckled. "You may change your minds after a year, and I consider fifteen to be a more tenable age for a bride than thirteen. Papa didn't give me the option to wait when I married Sythda. If he *had*, I would have waited. Besides, this *is* a punishment. If you'd come to me before you two coupled,

I might have given permission for you to wed when you're fourteen."

"All right," she said, scowling. "I'll wait if I can marry him." Her eyes flashed. "But once we're married, we're never to be separated."

"You won't be. I promise."

***

Lirin exited the manor house and headed to the practice grounds. Before she left the manor itself, she stopped by the kennels and tossed some biscuits to the animals inside, reaching over the fence to scratch one of them behind the ears before continuing on to her destination. A few of the manor guards were sparring when she arrived. She sighed. With Tollot gone, there was no longer anyone willing to spar with her. She picked a training weapon from the weapons' rack and practiced her stances.

***

Autumn Equinox Y1061

Lenoma sat, surveying the people celebrating the autumn Equinox. Lasria was dancing with Serelaf. Her sister had told her that Korander had promised the two of them could marry if they didn't couple for a year. She was pleased that Korander would let her sister get married, but she didn't understand why he thought what they'd been doing was wrong. It wasn't as if Lasria had still been a maiden and she *knew* her husband had taken a mistress himself. Maybe it was because Serelaf was a bastard. Yes, that must be it. The rules must be different for *him*. This made sense to her. After all, the rules were different for her and her sisters than they were for her brothers and the rules for her bastard sisters were different still, so maybe all the rules for bastards differed from what they were for full clan. Both the waiting and the marriage itself must be because Serelaf was a bastard.

She lost interest in her sister's love life and sighed. Her husband had been off somewhere for a week now and her menses had started that morning, right on time. He didn't enjoy bedding her when she was on her menses, so she guessed he could stay away until they were over. She wondered how he was progressing with his plans for the war. That nasty old man was still alive and they couldn't start the war until he was dead. Why didn't Korander just poison his father and get him out of the way? It wasn't as if anyone would punish him for that. Once his father was dead, *Korander* would be Lord of the clan.

Maybe it was because he was still afraid after the punishment his father had given him. The scars on his back told her the damage must have been glorious. She didn't think he enjoyed being hurt. She wished she could have seen it when the wounds were fresh. When their little brother had burned Lasria, her sister had shown her the wound every day while it healed. She'd been mad at him, of course. How *dare* he think he could hurt her favorite bastard without even asking permission? Not that she would've given him permission. *Lasria* hated being hurt. Galar had known better. *He'd* gotten her permission before he'd bedded Lasria and her sister had agreed to it. They'd even allowed her to watch while they did it. Both she and her sister had been curious about coupling, and since *she* was supposed to be a maiden when she married, it'd had to be Lasria that Galar tupped.

She wished someone had told her what to expect the first time, though. Not that her husband would have let her enjoy it properly. He'd actually apologized for hurting her and while she enjoyed coupling, his lovemaking was always gentle. He'd even refused to bed her at all while she was still tender after her miscarriage. Surely if she'd been married within the clan, it would've been different. She decided her husband was a strange man.

***

Early Autumn Y1061

"You're back!"

Tollot nodded, glancing around warily. "I'm leaving on patrol in the morning. The patrol's just a precautionary measure to make sure the bandits are truly gone. I went over papa's head in order to be sent here. This is the last time I can use the bandits as an excuse, though."

"Then let's make the most of it." Lirin took his hand and gave it a tug. "There's an unused guest room on the second floor. No one will disturb us there."

***

The results of his stay at house Firain satisfied Korander. His first wife's family had an extensive artisan workshop and their engineers had developed a marvelous engine that he could use to break down the walls surrounding the Torust holdings. He'd brought several of the engines home. His father couldn't object to him storing them in their enclave.

He stored the wall breakers as close to Torust territory as possible, then headed home to his wife.

He had to smile at the delight Lenoma showed when he walked into their bedroom. She was such an innocent woman-child.

"What wonderful timing," she cried. "My menses just ended yesterday. Come to bed with me."

***

Korander stood in his wife's sitting room, staring at the picture she'd painted of his back. In the picture, he lay on their bed, naked and on his stomach, with his face turned away from the viewer and the covers not quite up to his waist, so all the scars were visible. He found the image disturbing. The feel it gave him was almost if the damage was still fresh and painful. Lenoma came to his side and put her arm around him.

"Ain't it beautiful?" Her arm tightened in a hug. "You're *such* a beautiful man."

He hugged her back. "You're a talented painter." He didn't want to ruin her pleasure in her work by saying anything negative about it, but couldn't bring himself to say it was beautiful. It amazed him she could find beauty in his scars, though he supposed she was someone who could find beauty in anything.

***

Mid-Autumn Y1061

"So, a promotion, eh? Are you going out to celebrate?"

Zavi shook her head. "Promotions don't bring my family back."

"You should request permission to have a baby. That

would give you family. Since you're now the captain of a company, Captain Marda should give permission."

Zavi snorted. "Maybe if I had a lover standing by ready to plant the seed."

"You've taken lovers."

"Oh sure, but they ain't exactly fighting over me. Every lover I've had acted as if *he* were doing *me* a favor. *No,* thank you." She jutted out her lower jaw.

Akaha wrinkled her forehead. "Ain't there *anyone* you're interesting in taking to your bed?"

"Not one I'd want to have a child with."

"So, what do you want in a man you'd be willing to have a child with?"

Zavi shrugged. "Oh, I don't know. I'm sure I'll know him when I see him, though."

"Anything you like in particular? I could help look for him."

"Well, I *am* partial to facial scars. A scarred man is less likely to be full of himself."

Akaha laughed. "I'll keep my eye out for a scarred man, then."

"He needs more depth to him than just a scar. He also needs to have a tragic past. Oh, and he has to be inexperienced with women." A smile played about her lips, and she hooked one of her tusks over her upper lip. "*I* want to be the one who teaches *him* about lovemaking."

"Well, if you're going for the impossible, you must definitely hold out for a clansman."

Zavi tossed her head, a twinkle in her green eyes. "Maybe a bastard. Clansmen are too soft. I want a man who can handle hard living."

"I'll make an offering to the gods and pray that you find your impossible man."

***

Late Autumn Y1061

Lenoma checked her calendar. *Yes!* Her menses were late. For the next couple weeks, she kept her fingers crossed, but aside from other symptoms of pregnancy, all that happened was some spotting. She headed to the infirmary and told the healers that she thought she was pregnant again. They immediately had her move into an infirmary room where they could keep close watch over her. Lasria came with her and they brought a second bed into the room so her sister could sleep there and be her personal nurse.

The primary physician for the house came to her room to speak to her. "Given the course of your first pregnancy, you're to keep us informed of *every* symptom you experience, no matter how minor you think it might be."

She nodded. "I understand. I don't want to risk losing *this* baby."

***

Winter Solstice Y1061 – Late Spring Y1062

The healers gave Lenoma permission to attend the winter Solstice celebration, but warned her not to exert herself. She sat at the table with her sister, watching the others dancing and having fun. Serelaf came and pulled Lasria off to the dance floor twice, but her sister wouldn't leave her side more than that.

A few weeks after Solstice, she had heavy spotting. Dutifully, she reported this to the healers. They examined her stained garments, then ordered her to lie flat on her bed.

"Some spotting is natural and even to be expected," the primary physician informed her, "but this is excessive. It looks as if the baby may tear loose. This must be what happened the first time. The baby tore loose and your body expelled it."

Her throat closed up at those words, and she obeyed the healer's orders. The position made the nausea that accompanied her pregnancy tricky to deal with, but she wasn't about to risk her baby. Over the following months, she lay flat on the bed, watching as her belly swelled with new life. Her sister was at her side round the clock, and her husband came to see her daily. She was so bored with being bed bound and unable to paint that she asked him about his efforts to prepare for the coming war, and he told her a little. He seemed surprised at some questions she asked him.

Near midnight on the eve of the summer Solstice, intense cramps awakened her. Terrified that she was about to lose *this* baby too, she shouted at her sister to fetch the healers.

***
Summer Solstice Y1062

Lasria sat glaring at the door to the room where the healers had taken Lenoma. They'd refused to allow her inside. When she'd insisted that she was her sister's personal nurse, they'd told her that this was beyond her training and she'd have to accept that. Korander, his mother, and some of his siblings and older children had come and were in the room with her. Serelaf sat with his arms around her. Korander paced the floor, and the others in the room just sat and waited.

Dawn came, and the Solstice sun shone in through the windows when the doctor came to the room. Blood covered the doctor's gown. Lasria had never seen so much blood from a birth before.

"You have a healthy son," the doctor told Korander.

"And my wife?"

The doctor sighed. "She couldn't give birth naturally. We had to cut her open to get the baby out. She's in serious condition, but she should live. This time."

Korander's brows drew together. "'*This* time'?"

"Another pregnancy could kill her."

Korander shut his eyes for a moment, then looked at the doctor again. "See to it, that can never happen. I'd rather have a barren wife than a dead one. She'll have to be content with *this* child."

The doctor nodded and left the room.

Lasria stared wide eyed at her sister's husband, then pulled out of Serelaf's arms, ran over, and pummeled him with her fists, tears streaming down her face.

"No! Call him back. Tell him you changed your mind. Leni wants *lots* of babies. You can't take that away from her."

Korander grabbed her wrists. "She can't have *any* babies if she's dead."

Serelaf came up behind her and wrapped her in his arms. She turned and buried her face against his chest, sobbing.

"But Leni... Leni wants *lots* of babies."

***
Early Summer Y1062

Lenoma opened her eyes slowly. Someone was crying nearby. She turned her head and saw her sister kneeling by her bed, sobbing into the covers. Her heart pounding in her breast, she reached down and felt herself. The immense belly she'd developed over the last several months was gone, and her abdomen was tender and painful.

"My baby!" she cried, sitting up.

Lasria lifted her head off the bed and sniffed, choking back a sob. "He's in the crib."

Her chest tingled and her heartbeat felt sluggish. "Is there something wrong with him?"

Her sister shook her head.

She glared at Lasria. "Then why are you *crying*?"

"You can't ever have any *more* babies. The doctor told Kor it would kill you, and he said he'd rather have a barren wife than a dead one."

She closed her eyes for a moment, as the world seemed to spin around her. Then she looked at her sister again. "But I have a son?"

Lasria nodded. "A wet nurse came and gave him his first feeding."

"Bring him to me."

Her sister stood and walked to a crib, where she picked up a bundle. Lenoma heard a mewling sound and her heart swelled in her breast. Lasria handed her the newborn.

"The doctor says he's healthy, and Kor said you'll have to be content with him."

Lenoma gasped as she examined him. "He's so *tiny*."

Fine, red-gold fuzz covered his head. He opened vivid blue eyes and gave a miniscule yawn.

She kissed him. "He's *beautiful*."

She offered him a breast, and he suckled halfheartedly.

"I'll name him Sequinne and we'll call him Quinn for short." She looked at Lasria. "And if I can't have any more babies, then he'll have all the love I would have given his siblings."

"You don't mind that, the doctor…?"

She shook her head. "I *do* mind, but I don't think I could have borne losing another baby, so perhaps it's for the best. Little Quinn here will have to be enough."

"The doctor *said* he's healthy," Lasria said, brightening.

Both sisters were cooing over the baby when Korander came into the room to check on his wife.

***

Lenoma lay on her bed with her eyes closed, luxuriating in the pain from her incision. The healers had given her medication for the pain, but she'd refused to take it, telling them she was afraid it might get into her milk and hurt her baby. They'd shaken their heads, but had given in to her wishes, only leaving a container with the pills on the table by her bed so they'd be there if she changed her mind.

That wasn't the real reason she'd refused to take the medication, of course, but she'd learned long before that many people found her pleasure unsettling. Her family understood that she enjoyed being in pain, but of all of them, only Lasria truly understood how she could love and feel protective of babies, while still taking pleasure from being in pain. Right now, her sister had gone to her lessons on being a healer and her baby was sleeping so she could relax and enjoy herself.

The door opened, and footsteps crossed the floor. She kept her eyes closed and pretended to be asleep. Then Sequinne started fussing. Her eyes flew open, and she sat up. A white-haired man stood at the changing table with his back to her.

"What are you doing?"

He peered over his shoulder at her. It was her father-in-law.

"I'm just changing his nappy. I came down to see my new grandson."

"Bring him to me."

The old man finished what he was doing and brought the child over, sitting beside the bed as she took her baby from him. He cackled.

"I told you them narrow hips would be a problem. Good thing you had a boy. A girl might have gotten your hips. Women need wide hips or they ain't no good."

"What are you talking about?"

"You couldn't birth natural. There's a reason a man likes wide hips on a woman. A man wants a woman who can give him babies. Wide hips make for an easy birth."

She stared at him. "If I didn't have narrow hips, I could have had more babies?"

He nodded. "You got bad breeding somewhere."

"But both my parents are Eldragons!"

He laughed. "That just makes it worse. I make sure all *my* kin marry outside the clan. There's no inbreeding in house Moraven."

She lifted her chin. "First cousins *ain't* inbreeding."

He laughed again. "Sure it is. Just not as bad as when the kinship is closer than that." He patted her hand. "Well, I've seen the boy, so it's time I went back to my room."

* * *

"We're worried about you, especially now your papa's new wife has a son."

Rothas aimed his gun at the target and took a shot. "What do you mean?"

His Uncle Dasver sighed and leaned against a post, reloading his own gun. "Eldragon has an evil reputation. We're worried they might send assassins to kill you and your full siblings, so your new brother becomes your papa's heir."

His Uncle Foshi nodded. "Something needs to be done to keep you safe."

"At least she can't have a second brat," Dasver muttered. "If she could have more babies, your danger would be even greater."

Rothas frowned. "Quinn ain't a brat. He's my brother, and I hope you ain't suggesting I do anything to hurt *him*."

"No, no." Foshi made a soothing motion with his hands. "Nothing like that."

"We've been going around to slums and recruiting extra troops to prepare for the war against Torust," Dasver said. "Some we've taken on ain't from around here. They came from someplace in the south and they told us about a clan down there that's even more powerful than Eldragon."

"What we think you should do," Foshi added, "is head south, *find* that clan, and take a wife."

"You can tell your papa and grandpapa that you're doing it to get a connection to another powerful clan. Tell your papa they'll help with the war when your grandpapa dies."

Foshi nodded. "Yeah, no need to tell your papa about our fears. Your grandpapa might understand, but your papa wouldn't."

Rothas frowned. "What's the name of this clan?"

"It's house Argul. The recruits that told us about them are afraid of them. Seems Argul destroyed their clan."

***

"But I want to help more with the war than I *have* been," Rothas protested, "and I know you don't love Lenoma."

Korander sighed. "While that's true, I had love with your mama and Davia."

"You only loved mama because she was Aunt Davia's heart-sister. If *you* can come to love a wife you hadn't wanted to marry, *I* can do the same thing."

His father smiled wryly. "So you don't want to marry this unknown girl, after all?"

He sputtered. "You know what I *meant*. I'll have the advantage of having chosen my new wife for myself, too. I won't have to depend on being lucky like you were."

Korander sighed. "Your grandpapa would have to approve, and knowing *him*, he probably already has a wife picked out for you."

"I'll go ask him now. The worst he can do is say 'no'."

***

Rothas approached his grandfather's room with trepidation. He knew all about how the old man had had his father whipped and had always been afraid of him. He stopped at the door, standing between the guards stationed there for a long moment before he worked up the courage to knock.

"Come," called a voice from inside the room.

He swallowed hard, then stepped inside. "Hello grandpapa."

Saerthan sat in his chair and eyed his grandson. "What do you want, boy? Out with it."

"I want to get married."

The old man leaned back in his chair. "Is that so?"

Rothas nodded. "Papa said I need your approval."

"Do you have someone in mind, or are you willing to have *me* choose your bride?"

"I've heard of a powerful clan in the south, one that's stronger than Eldragon. I want to connect our clan to them."

Saerthan's eyes narrowed. "*Do* you, now? Why not strengthen our ties to Eldragon and marry one of *their* daughters like your papa did?"

Rothas's eyes flashed. "We have too many Eldragons here as it is. Sere is going to marry an Eldragon bastard."

The old man burst out laughing. "Ah. I see what you're playing at now. In that case, you not only have my approval, you have my blessing. I wish you well in your quest. Just be sure to pick a healthy wife with good wide hips. We don't want another skinny thing like Lenoma, who can barely have even one baby. Now come give your old grandpapa a hug."

He held out his arms, and Rothas reluctantly embraced him.

***

Early to Mid-Summer Y1062

Rothas set out with a full squad of guards at his back. There was no way to know how far he'd have to travel before he found the Argul enclave, but he knew it must be fairly distant since he'd never heard of the clan before. He traveled south until he came upon an enclave that sported a symbol he didn't recognize. He stopped at the gate of one of their holdings and asked the guards on duty, but they hadn't heard of Argul either, so he continued south.

Since guards stationed at different holdings might know things others didn't; he stopped and asked at a new gate each day. He'd traveled south for over a month before he came across anyone that knew the name. When he asked there if they'd heard of Argul, the guards eyed each other, then asked him why he wanted to know. Their reaction made him suspicious, so he told them an allied clan had recruited someone from a slum who'd mentioned the clan, and he was curious.

"Well," the guards said, "you should stay away from them. Your curiosity could get you killed, if not worse."

He nodded. "The recruit I talked to seemed afraid of the clan. I'm traveling in the direction he said their enclave is supposed to be found on clan business though, and don't know their symbol. I wasn't able to ask the recruit to show me before I left."

The gate guards were more than willing to make a sketch for him when he told them that. He examined it. The symbol was... unsettling... but he'd already come so far he wasn't willing to give up. Besides, Eldragon had a terrible reputation, so if Argul did too, all the better.

Two weeks later, he finally came across a gate with the Argul symbol. The actual design was even more unsettling than the sketch the guard had drawn for him. It half covered a second symbol that he couldn't quite make out. He almost turned back as the guards he'd questioned had advised, but after coming this far, he felt he should at least try. Warily, he approached the gate.

***
Mid-Summer Y1062

Lirin stood by her father's side as he greeted their visitors. Her uncle lifted her hand and kissed her knuckles.

"This *can't* be my niece. She's grown so much!"

Her father laughed, placing his arm around her shoulders. "It is indeed." He nodded towards where Tollot stood, like a shadow of his father, at the back of the group. "Your boy there has become quite the man. You should have been here when he took out the bandits that had been raiding the holding."

"I wish I could have been here for that, but they needed me at the keep. I'm too busy to come for simple visits, and I'm only here now because I have business to discuss with you."

"Well, come to my office, then. Lirin can show Tollot your rooms while we talk."

Lirin curtsied. "Come this way Tollot."

She led him to the rooms where he and his father were to stay.

"How long will you be staying this time?"

His eyes flicked towards the servants who were unpacking the trunks. "I don't know. Papa ain't told me what business he has here."

"May I offer you some refreshment in the sitting room or does uncle expect you to remain in your chambers until he's done speaking to papa?"

"Give me a minute to shed my coat and I can come."

Lirin stepped out of the room and stood by the door, her pulse racing. When he emerged, she linked arms with him and led the way to a sitting room.

"With papa here, we have to be extra careful," he whispered in her ear. "He's sharper than he looks and if he ever found out about us, he wouldn't hesitate to order my execution himself."

She nodded soberly.

* * *

A guard coughed. "My Lady, you have a visitor."

Lady Olva Argul turned and eyed the man. "*Do* I now? Who has come and why are they here?"

"It's a youth who says his name is Rothas Moraven. He approached the gate of a Falynx holding closest to our northern border near the bridge to Lyber. He's only said that he wishes an audience with the clan leader. There's a squad of guards with him."

"Moraven? I'm not familiar with the clan. I'll see him in my audience chamber. Bring him there in fifteen minutes."

The guard nodded and bowed. "Yes, my Lady."

Olva fetched her clan mask and made her way with her honor guard to the audience chamber where she settled on her throne. When her guards brought the young man before her, she eyed him thoughtfully. He was a pretty youth, with striking blue eyes, pale skin, and snow-white hair. His clothing was fine and spoke of wealth.

"I am Lady Olva Argul. What business do you have with me?"

The boy swallowed visibly and looked around with darting eyes. "My name is Rothas Moraven. I'm the clan heir after my papa. I've heard that your house is powerful and wish to make a connection."

Behind her mask, Olva raised a brow. "You're seeking a wife?"

He nodded. "Yes, my Lady."

"And you wish to find her in *my* enclave?"

He nodded again. "Yes."

"Has no one told you of my clan's reputation? It's rare

indeed that any approach *our* house in search of a spouse. There've been times we've had to resort to forced mergers and even inbreeding in order to properly maintain the succession."

"I've heard whispers. As I traveled here, someone advised me to avoid your clan."

"Yet you still came. Why is that?"

"Because papa has taken a wife of a clan that has a *similar* reputation and my maternal kin warned me that *her* clan might seek to eliminate me and my siblings so *her* child would become heir."

A similar reputation indeed. She rubbed her fingers over the sigils carved on the arm of her throne. "Why would your papa risk his children that way? If his new wife's kin have a reputation such as that, surely he knows this is a danger."

"We need their aid in a clan war."

She nodded knowingly. "Ah. So you've sought us out for more reasons than simple fear for your life."

"Yes. Your aid would also be welcome in the war."

"I'll have to think about your proposal. You'll be my guest while I consider it. There are clanswomen who might be suitable."

"My grandpapa told me to choose a wife with wide hips. I need a wife who can provide me with many children."

She frowned behind her mask, her fingers going still. "Picky, ain't you?"

He regarded her with furrowed brows. "It would do me no good to take a wife that was barren or unable to birth children. My clan's succession must be a healthy one. There'd be no point in my even *coming* here if I returned with a wife that couldn't fulfill her role."

"Well, house Argul is famous for our fecundity, so you needn't concern yourself with *that*."

She rose from her seat, came down from her throne, and placed an arm around his shoulders. If he hadn't shown himself so arrogant, she would've provided him with a *true* Argul for his bride. As it was, he could have the weakling's spawn. It wasn't as if she could annex such distant lands, anyway. She'd have to keep the girl's sire out of the boy's sight while he was at the keep to ensure he didn't see the resemblance and realize she was offering him defective stock, but that would be easy enough.

"I'm convinced you're worthy of a daughter of my house. Come, I have just the wife for you." She removed her mask and led him out of her audience chamber.

* * *

Rothas followed Lady Argul to the family quarters of her keep. Her topaz eyes were unusual, but he supposed others might find his own clan's family trait odd. They soon arrived in a sitting room. A girl sat on a couch, reading a book.

"I'd like you to meet my youngest daughter, Sia. Sia! Come here. I want you to meet Rothas Moraven."

The girl rose from the couch and walked over to them. He eyed her as discretely as he could and decided his grandfather would have no complaints about *her* hips. She had a figure that set his blood afire. He raised his eyes to her face. That was beautiful, too. She was a golden blonde with an exotic tilt to her eyes, which were a rich gold that matched her hair. Even her skin had a warm, golden tone to it.

She extended her hand, and he raised it to his lips with a bow. "Pleased to meet you."

"Likewise." Sia's voice was soft and had a lilting quality to it.

"Rothas here has come looking for a wife."

Sia's brows rose. "Have you?"

He nodded. "I was told your clan is powerful, and I have need of a connection to a powerful house."

"When he told me what he needs in a wife, my first thought was of you." Olva turned towards Rothas. "Sia will be sixteen this autumn and is ripe for marriage. I'd been wondering who I should choose for her husband and you arrived just in time to be the one."

He smiled at the girl. "I count myself fortunate then."

"As you are your clan's heir, I expect you're expected to wed in your own house's stronghold. Are you not?"

He nodded. "Yes, but that shouldn't be an issue. I can arrange for a transport to bring us back to my enclave."

The Argul clan leader sighed. "There's just one problem with that. *My* clan has a tradition when we wed. We normally do this when the bride and groom retire to the nuptial bed, but since you won't be here for that, we'll need to handle it differently."

Sia looked at her mother. "I'm willing to forgo the ritual."

Olva shook her head. "No, it *must* be done." She turned towards Rothas. "There is a clan superstition that doing this ritual ensures marital harmony."

Rothas raised his brows. "Harmony is important in my family. When papa married mama, he had a mistress, and the two became heart-sisters in order to have harmony in the household. Mama always said harmony can live with love, but not hate, resentment, or jealousy."

Sia beamed at him. "That's *beautiful.*"

He nodded. "I'm willing to do anything to have marital harmony. What does this ritual require?"

Olva smiled. "There's a drink that's made from a special family recipe. We simply call it nectar. We *could* let you take it with you when you leave, but we're not willing to risk it being misused, so you'll need to drink it here. Unfortunately, this drink works as a powerful aphrodisiac, so it's important that you bed Sia after drinking it or the consequences could be dire. I'm sure you realize why it's normally drunk just before retiring to the nuptial bed."

He blinked. "Are you saying I'd be bedding Sia *be*fore our wedding?"

"In order for the ritual to be completed properly, yes. You'll have to."

He frowned. "Ain't that a risk? Since I live far from here, you have no guarantee that the wedding itself would occur afterwards. It's hard to find a husband for a woman once she's no longer a maiden."

Olva chuckled. "*Trust* me; once you've shared a nectar enhanced bedding, you won't want to wed any other maiden."

He turned to Sia again. "Are you truly willing to be bedded before our wedding? I've never heard of such a thing happening in any clan."

Her eyes met his. "I believe I can trust you."

* * *

Late Summer Y1062

Rothas spent two weeks in Argul keep, getting to know

Sia, while Lady Argul prepared for the ritual bedding. He felt uncomfortable bedding a clanswoman this way, and only Sia's continued assurances of her trust in him convinced him to go through with it. When it was time, the two of them donned wedding wreaths as if they were truly entering the nuptial bed after a marriage ceremony. Lady Argul handed each of them a tiny cup, which barely contained enough of the drink for them to taste, and made sure they both drank. Lady Olva then ushered them into a bedchamber and locked the door behind them.

Sia immediately undressed, and he followed suit.

"You'll have to tell me what I'm supposed to do."

She lay down on the bed. "Come to bed with me."

He shivered, feeling chilled, but wherever he touched *her,* it was pleasantly warm. When he kissed her, he felt an urgency he hadn't expected. As her maidenhead broke, he apologized.

"I'm sorry," he murmured in her ear. "I know that was too quick."

"It's all right. I love you and you love me."

The warmth of love for her flooded his very being. "Yes. I love you."

"Say what I said. 'I love you and you love me.' It's important you say those exact words."

"I love you and you love me," he repeated obediently.

"Yes! I love you and you love me." She kissed him ardently, then put her mouth to his ear. "Now I'm going to tell you something very important. For the rest of this night until sunrise, only repeat the words, 'I love you and you love me.' Do you understand?"

He opened his mouth to say 'yes,' but what came out was, "I love you and you love me." Startled, he tried to say something else, but only repeated, "I love you and you love me." A shiver ran down his spine as fear filled his heart.

"Shh. Don't be afraid. I'd never hurt you. I love you and you love me. It's the nectar. It's ok for you to have drunk it tonight, but you must *never* drink it again. Do you understand?"

He felt his fear melt away and nodded. "I love you and you love me," he whispered in her ear.

"Good. If you ever taste the slightest hint of nectar again, it'll make you feel very sick, so sick you'll vomit. Nectar can make you feel and do things you wouldn't normally feel and do. It's fine and good for you to love your wife, but I don't want it to change you in any other way. You're a good man and I want you to stay true to yourself. I love you and you love me. I think I loved you when we first met and you told us what your mama said about harmony."

She kissed him again.

"You must tell no one else what I've told you tonight. Understand? While many know that it's an aphrodisiac, what nectar does to the mind is a family secret, and I can't allow anyone else to know the secrets of my clan. Nor do I dare allow my clan to know I've revealed this secret to you."

He nodded again and kissed her. "I love you and you love me."

She sighed. "I've already told you everything I know about nectar now, so you won't need to ask me any further questions about it. It would be dangerous to do so anyway. We don't want anyone else to know I've told you *anything*, but as long as we don't say a word about what I said tonight, we'll be safe. I love you and you love me."

Fear rose within him once more, this time though; it was not because of what she was doing to him. He was sure she loved him as much as he loved her and trusted that she'd do nothing to harm him. No, this was a fear that someone else would find out she'd told him what she had about the nectar.

"Shh. Relax. They can't know I've told you anything. I love you and you love me."

Relief washed over him, but she hadn't told him *not* to be afraid, so the fear didn't go away completely. "I love you and you love me."

She repeated the words back to him. For the rest of the night, whenever either of them spoke, they just repeated those words to each other, and at each repeat, his love for her grew.

***

It was late the next morning when they awoke, and he greeted her with a kiss. She smiled up at him. "I *love* you."

"I love you too," he replied, feeling giddy that he hadn't

said 'I love you and you love me,' again. "I never imagined coupling could be like it was last night."

She kissed him. "That was at least partially because of the nectar," she whispered in his ear. "I don't know if it'll be that way the next time or not. I've neither coupled nor drunk nectar before. Mama had to tell me what to expect in the nuptial bed."

He smiled at her. "Want to find out? We can have our 'next time' right now."

She laughed. "I would *love* to."

When they finally dressed and emerged from the room where they'd spent the night, he still felt a need to touch her frequently. She responded in kind.

Lady Argul smiled at the sight of them. "Welcome back to the real world. You can return to your clan's enclave whenever you please."

He nodded. "I want to return home and marry Sia as soon as possible. If we can leave today, that would be wonderful."

"You can certainly do so if that's your wish. There's a transport dock about fifteen miles east of the keep. I'm giving you a full company of guards as a wedding present. I allowed Sia to pick them out herself before we held the bedding ritual. They can protect you and also help with that war you told me about."

"Thank you. That would be wonderful."

***

Upon arriving back home, Rothas brought Sia to see his father. He wrapped his arms around her and smiled at Korander. "I had the greatest of luck. I found the love of my life in house Argul." He kissed her cheek.

Korander smiled at the girl warmly. "Welcome to house Moraven."

"Thank you. I'm sure I'll be happy here."

"We need to marry as soon as possible. I *must* make her truly mine."

"Your grandpapa will have to give the say so for that to happen," Korander replied dryly. "Why don't you take her to see him now?"

Rothas nodded. "Grandpapa can have no complaint about

Sia's figure." He sighed. "I don't think any woman could have more perfect proportions."

When they arrived at his grandfather's room, Rothas tapped with confidence.

"Come," called a voice from within.

He opened the door and ushered Sia inside.

"Grandpapa, this is Sia Argul. We need to marry as soon as possible."

"Do you, now?" the old man asked irritably. "Well, come here, girl; let me have a look at you."

Sia walked to the chair where he sat and stood beside it. "Hello."

He scrutinized her. "Well, you got a splendid figure all right." He turned towards Rothas. "It looks like you chose a good one, boy."

Rothas wrapped his arms around her and nibbled on her ear. "Her clan sent a company of guards as a wedding gift."

"Did they, now?"

Sia nodded. "Mama ordered them to protect me and my husband. Of course, Rothas will need to actually *marry* me before he qualifies as my husband."

Saerthan smiled slyly, nodding. "Clever. I see you've bedded her."

Rothas blinked. "How did you know?"

The old man snorted. "It's written all over you two. A man don't touch a woman like you've been touching her unless he knows her intimately. I suppose the reason for rushing the marriage is that she's already pregnant?"

Rothas pursed his lips. "I guess it's possible. Lady Argul said her clan is fecund."

"Are you, now?" Saerthan asked Sia.

She shrugged. "Twins are common in my family. I had a twin brother and several of my older siblings were also twins. It makes it easy to repopulate the clan should we suffer losses, though there *are* issues when twins are in the line of succession."

The old man cackled. "I'd say you found yourself an excellent bride boy. Prepare for the wedding at the earliest possible time. Now get out of here. You tire me."

Rothas brought Sia back to talk to Korander. "Grandpapa

says we can hold the wedding immediately."

"Very well," Korander said. "It'll take at least a week to prepare for a full clan wedding. During that time, Sia will need a place to sleep. I'm thinking she can share Lasria's room."

Rothas frowned. "I have a better idea. Sia can move into *my* room, and I'll bunk with Sere until after the wedding. That way, there'll be less disruption once we're actually married."

"You've really thought this through, ain't you?"

Rothas nodded. "I like the thought of Sia in my bed, even if I won't be sharing it with her until after the wedding." He wrapped his arms around her and nuzzled her neck.

Sia smiled and ran her fingers through his hair. "I like that thought too," she murmured, kissing his cheek.

Korander sighed. "Very well. Why don't you go introduce her to your siblings while the household staff unpacks her things?"

Rothas took Sia's hand and gave it a tug. "Come, I want you to love my family, too."

***

The first of Rothas's siblings that Sia met was Serelaf.

"Sere," Rothas said. "I'd like you to meet my wife-to-be. Sia Argul. Sia, this is my big brother Serelaf."

Sia frowned, her brows creased. "Your *big* brother? I thought *you* were the clan heir."

Serelaf smiled. "He is. *My* mama was papa's mistress."

She blinked. "I don't understand."

"Sere is a clan bastard," Rothas said. "Seven of my siblings are bastards. Remember how I told you mama became heart-sisters with papa's mistress?"

Sia nodded. "Oh. I see. Your clan treats bastards as if they belong to the house?"

Rothas shrugged. "More or less. Does your clan treat them differently?"

"In my house, there *are* no clan bastards. My uncle sired one, and the clan mocked him mercilessly because of it. He finally went and killed the boy."

Both men gaped at her for a long moment. Finally, Rothas found his tongue.

"That's horrible! That poor boy, killed by his own papa?"

She shrugged. "It happened before I was born. All I know of it is what's still said in my family. To this day, mama berates Uncle Garlos about his bastard."

"Well, in *my* clan, we celebrate our bastards. Sere and I have been best friends for as long as I can remember. I hope you'll love him as much as I do."

She leaned against him. "If *you* love your brother, how can I not? It's just foreign to me and it'll take me time to get used to the values your clan holds, that mine don't. Remember my clan's reputation."

Rothas smiled at her. "I've taken you far away from your clan and you're still young. You can learn our ways, so you fit in with us."

She nodded. "And I *want* to fit in. Please help me learn."

***

"I need to speak to the guards mama gave us as a wedding gift," Sia told Rothas as they were parting to retire for the night after the evening meal. "There are behaviors that *my* clan considers acceptable that *your* clan does not. I need to instruct them on what they may do and what they may not."

"Certainly. I'm sure you can use the audience chamber. We'll meet them there and you can tell them whatever you need to."

She shook her head. "I need to talk to them with no one from your clan present. There are things I don't want to say in front of you. Clan secrets."

He drew a sharp breath, his eyes widening.

She pressed his hand. "Not *that* secret, but things that, after what I've learned about your clan today, cause me to feel ashamed of mine. I don't want to hurt you with my shame."

He nodded, relaxing. "I understand. I'll arrange for you to meet with them privately."

She smiled. "Thank you."

***

Sia looked sternly at the people her mother had given her. She'd chosen each of them herself. She was grateful her mother had allowed her to pick several whose families served the clan her brother Lakor's wife belonged to. Those should fit in with house Moraven better than the ones that had served

Argul from the start would. She stood on the dais in front of the clan leader's throne.

"I have something very important to tell all of you. House Moraven differs from Argul. Those familiar with the customs house Shamaze practiced will find the customs of house Moraven more familiar than those who've only served Argul will."

She looked around and met as many of their eyes as she could. "If you can't follow the rules of house Moraven, I'll discard you. I want you to understand that. We need to fit into our new home. I want each of you to find a mentor among the Moraven folk and seek to learn what rules their clan requires followers to obey and accept that *those* are the rules you must follow from now on. I've learned, for example, they forbid vishing. This includes slum folk, not just clan followers, and there's nothing here that even *remotely* resembles the pens."

She again scanned the people in the room. "They also honor clan bastards. From what I've seen so far, Moraven treats its bastards as if they had nearly the same status as full clan. Understand this and accept it. I'm sure there are other differences that I ain't yet discovered. We must all learn these differences and *embrace* them. If you don't feel you can do this, leave now. We're far from Argul, and you won't find support if you desire to continue behaving as if you were still serving that house."

***

Rothas took part in the plans for his upcoming marriage with all his heart and soul. Having already made love to Sia, it was almost painful to not have her in his bed. He suspected this might be a side effect of the nectar Sia had given him and wondered just how long the need would linger. From what Sia had told him, he knew the other effects of the drug would be permanent, but he loved her so much he couldn't resent that. Besides, *she'd* taken it too. He'd talked to her, and she'd told him she found sleeping alone as difficult as he did.

Finally, the preparations were complete, and the day arrived for the wedding. His kin from both clans attended the ceremony. When he saw his Uncles Dasver and Foshi, he winked at them. They smiled back in approval. When he and

Sia could finally retire to the nuptial chamber, they were so hungry for each other they practically ripped their clothing off, barely making it onto the bed itself before they consummated their union.

***

Autumn Y1062

Lasria stood between Korander and the dining hall door, her arms folded across her chest and a frown on her face. "It's my birthday today. I'm fifteen now. You said I could marry Sere when I turned fifteen. We've both been very good and have done as you required. I'm *tired* of being good. I want to be tupped again and I don't think it was fair that Rothas got to be married before Sere."

He looked her up and down, sighing. She was nearly as tall as Lenoma now. "Very well. As long as Sere still wants you, I'll start the arrangements for the two of you to marry."

She smiled. "Sere will be *happy* to marry me."

"You're awfully sure of yourself," he commented dryly as he turned to call for his son to come over.

***

Serelaf and Lasria's wedding was a much smaller event than Rothas and Sia's had been and didn't require as much advance preparation. Saerthan would not countenance a full clan wedding for a pair of bastards and only immediate family attended.

As Korander watched the happy couple retire to the nuptial chamber, Sia and Rothas came up to him.

Rothas had a huge grin on his face. "Papa, Sia thinks she may be pregnant." He gave his wife a hug.

Korander stared at them. He wasn't sure he was ready to be a grandfather. "That's... good news."

Sia smiled at him serenely. "Twins run in my family, but I'm hoping my first child is a single."

"'Twins'," he repeated.

She nodded. "My clan has a tendency to produce twins. I, myself, had a twin brother, as had my mama."

He gave her a strained smile. "Then I certainly hope you achieve your desire. Even with a wet nurse to assist, caring for twins would be difficult."

***

"Ma," Diphar said. "Dint you say we swore to house Firain because of Fizran and his Argul eye?"

"Yes, dear, we didn't want to continue living in the slum with him. What of it?"

"There was a woman I served at the dinner table tonight that has *two* Argul eyes. The Firain folks were saying she's married to their kin from house Moraven. There's a party 'cause she's gonna have a baby."

Diphar's mother's jaw dropped as she turned towards her and her father looked up from where he was sharpening his sword.

"Are you sure?"

Diphar nodded. "Her eyes are gold like her hair."

"I'll look into it," her father said.

Her mother twisted her fingers together. "Maybe some other clan can have eyes like that."

Her father sighed. "I hope so. If Argul has made a connection here, we can't stay."

***

Moze spread the map on the table. "This map shows the full extent of the Torust holdings."

Korander examined the map thoughtfully. "Tell me about their clan."

"Their clan leader is Lady Malida Torust. She had an accident early in her marriage while she was pregnant that caused her to lose her fertility. The child, a son, survived the birth but was sickly and died this summer. Her brother, Tylen Torust, became her heir then. He's unwed." He pointed to a section of the map bordering on Moraven. "A younger brother, one Ballic Torust, a widower who's next in their line of succession, oversees this part of their holdings. It was undoubtedly a patrol from *his* holding that attacked you as you were heading towards Browarg that day. When the war starts, I recommend attacking here first. It's not only closest to us; a bit of wasteland separates the holding from their main enclave."

Korander nodded. "I see. Yes. We can take that portion of

their lands relatively easily and have a base from which to launch further attacks. I wish papa would let us start the war without having to wait for him to die."

Moze shrugged. "At least we have plenty of time to prepare. Torust can't *possibly* know of our plans to go to war with them."

***

"Come," Diphar's mother told her. "We're taking your pa his midday meal. Hurry now."

Diphar dutifully followed her mother to the gate, where her father stood guard. She enjoyed bringing her father his meal when he stood guard at the gate. They could sit outside the walls and look at the river while her father ate. When they arrived at the gate, they stepped outside and moved down the wall a bit like they usually did, but when she tried to stop at the place where they normally sat to eat, her mother pulled on her hand and they continued moving along the wall.

"Where we going?" she asked.

In answer, her father took off his coat and dropped it on the ground, then picked her up and set her on his shoulders. "We're going back to the slum."

Her mother handed him the basket they'd brought and shed her own coat.

"Rothas Moraven traveled south and took an Argul bride. They say he did this deliberately, seeking their protection against his pa's wife's kin."

"Who'll protect him from *his* wife's kin?" her mother asked. "And how did he even know to search them out?"

Her father gave a short laugh. "It was *our* fault. We were the ones who told them about Argul. Our fear that Firain might have a connection drove us to carelessness. We told them enough about Argul to give them the idea to send their kinsman south."

***

Rema sat on her makeshift throne, eying the small family that stood before her. "Why have *you* come crawling back? I thought you'd found a new home with another clan."

"*We* thought so as well," the husband replied. "Unfortunately, in our determination to avoid house Argul, we allowed house Firain to know of their existence... and *they* thought it was a fine idea to send one of their kinsmen south to take a bride. We've seen this bride. She and her husband behave the same way Lady Rosara and *her* husband did after *they* wed."

Rema's boredom vanished, and she sat up straight. "Argul is *here*?"

The man nodded. "I'm afraid so. The wife looks young, but she's accompanied by guards who, while the clan symbols they display are those of house Moraven, wear them on the red and black coats of Argul."

"Why would the fools choose to ally with a house such as *Argul*?"

The man looked decidedly ill. "I was told house Firain felt being connected to Argul would provide their kinsman with protection from the clan of his pa's new wife, whose house apparently has a similar reputation. They're also planning to go to war and want more troops to assist in that effort. This was why they recruited *us*."

Rema's eyes narrowed. "Who are they warring against?"

"A house Torust. It seems they wait only for the current Lord Moraven to die before they make their attack, and he's said to be a sick old man."

Rema tapped her fingers on the arm of her throne. "Perhaps we should warn house Torust of their enemy's intentions. If houses Firain and Moraven connected to Argul, then they're *my* enemies as well."

***

The gate guard looked down her nose at the slum beggars. "What do *you* want?"

The men who'd come to the gate where she was on duty looked at each other, shuffling their feet.

"We have some information your clan would find worth knowing," one of them finally said.

"And what is that?"

The beggars looked at each other again before one of them stepped forward.

"House Firain recruited me. I'd be with them still if they hadn't allied with a clan that's the enemy of my birth clan.

While I was serving their house, I learned that they and their ally, house Moraven, are planning to declare war on house Torust. They're joined in this by house Eldragon."

The guard frowned. While his admitted treachery made his story suspect, they couldn't ignore the man's words.

"Wait here. I'll send for someone with more authority to speak to you."

$* * *$

Malida sat on the throne in her audience chamber, drumming her fingers on the arm as she listened to the slum beggars speak.

"So," she said to the man who'd had the most to say. "You served Firain willingly until the Moraven boy married an Argul?"

He nodded. "My first loyalty is to my birth clan. Argul *destroyed* house Falynx. I won't serve any clan that would ally with them."

"And they're planning to go to war against *us*?"

"Yes. It's said there was an incident between your clan and Moraven. The Moraven heir's wife and mistress died in the attack. He's now determined to go to war and waits only for the death of the current Lord. Reports say he won't go to war over a wife that had served her purpose. Naturally, house Firain feels differently since the wife had been one of their own."

Behind her mask, Malida's brows drew together. "And you offer this information freely to us?"

He nodded. "Our slum boss thought you'd find the information of interest. Our entire slum is now hostile towards Firain, Moraven, and Eldragon because of the connection to Argul."

Malida clasped her hands. "We are hostile towards Moraven, but it hasn't escalated into war. If your information is accurate, there are preparations we need to make. I won't tell you my plans. You may feel you had cause to betray Firain, but you'd still sworn to serve them. I can't trust a traitor, regardless of the circumstances. I *will* reward you for your information, however, even though you offered it freely." She turned to her brother Tylen. "Give them a basket of supplies to take back to the slum with them."

***

Malida frowned at the map her spymaster placed on the table in her map room. It showed all the holdings that belonged to her clan. She pointed at a section that was separate from the main enclave and shared a border with Moraven.

"If the information of the slum folk was accurate, that will probably be the first target our enemies will hit. Send a messenger to warn my brother Ballic and tell him to prepare an escape from his manor house. We'll prepare an escape from the keep here as well. We'll prepare for war with Moraven." She pointed at a bay to the north. "We'll build fortifications in a line, starting at the keep and running north to the shore on the bay here so we can defend our holdings on the peninsula."

"My Lady, are we to wait for *them* to attack?"

She nodded. "It's possible the traitor lied. I ain't willing to bet one way or the other that the information he gave was accurate. What he said made sense and I can't ignore it, but I also can't place full trust in the words of an admitted traitor."

***

Winter Y1062

Korander looked out the window at the latest winter storm. There wasn't much he could do to prepare for the coming war during winter, especially when the weather was as bad as it was today. He was running out of things he could do, anyway. He knew what his first target would be and where he would go from there. Firain was busy producing weapons and ammo and Eldragon was still recruiting more troops from all the nearby slums, but his father's refusal to approve the actual war stymied him. He turned from the window and looked out over those celebrating the winter Solstice. His wife sat beside her sister, their son in her arms.

He had to smile as he thought of how surprised Lenoma had been when she'd healed enough from her surgery to return to his bed and he coupled with her once more. She'd apparently thought he'd lose interest once she could no longer have children and had seemed pleased when he'd assured her that wasn't the case.

He wondered what the two women were discussing so intently. Lasria had become pregnant soon after she'd married Serelaf, so perhaps that was it. Lenoma was still obsessed with babies, though she prioritized her son. The thought of becoming a grandfather while his last child was still in nappies was unsettling, and now *both* of his sons' wives were pregnant.

***

Lasria asked her sister if it bothered her that the issues Lenoma had suffered didn't plague *her* pregnancy. Guilt wracked her because she was having an easier time than her much loved sister had experienced.

Lenoma sighed. "I'm torn. I'm jealous that you're having no problems, but I'm sure I'll love your baby too. Not as much as Quinn, of course, but I'm sure I'll still love your baby."

Lasria frowned. "I've been thinking maybe I should ask the doctor to cut me open too, even if I don't need it, and make me barren so I'll only have one baby, same as you. I can tell him I'm worried I might have some of the same troubles you had when it's time for my baby to be born."

"Are you sure? I like the idea and think it would be great for us to share this in that way, but you can always just start taking preventive again. I know you don't enjoy being hurt, and being cut open *does* hurt."

Lasria nodded. "Yes, I'm sure. It will only hurt until it finishes healing and you're more important than *me,* anyway."

Lenoma hugged her tight. "You're the best sister I could ever have. I love you so much."

***

Ballic Torust led the way down the stairs into the manor basement. "We've made a great deal of progress with the tunnel. It's still a long way from being finished, but I thought you should know where to go should you need to use it."

They reached the bottom of the stairs, where he showed them the trick to opening the hidden door to the tunnel.

"As you can see, there's a staging area before the tunnel itself starts." He pointed around at the shelves that lined the room. "I've arranged for supplies to be stored here as emergency packs. Should the time come, you need to simply take one of these packs and head down the tunnel."

Lirin examined the packs, then walked to the tunnel itself, holding her bastard on one of her hips. "How far does it go?"

He sighed. "Right now, it barely reaches the edge of the manor walls. I'm hoping to extend it south into the wastes and build a proper exit, but we've made preparations in case the attack comes before we can complete it. We're storing explosives at the far end of the tunnel. In an emergency, the explosives can blow a hole in the tunnel's roof so those using it can get out. Fortunately, we can continue working on the tunnel no matter the weather."

"When's the attack expected?"

He shrugged. "We don't even know if it's really going to happen. An admitted traitor provided us with the information we have. He could very well have lied in order to advance some unknown personal agenda. We've been at odds with Moraven for a long time without the hostilities erupting into a full out war. We're only building the tunnel because we don't dare ignore the possibility that our informant was telling the truth. Make no mistake; if they're planning to call for war with both Firain and Eldragon as allies, we'll lose. We have no allies as powerful as Eldragon, who'd come to our aid. We'd have a good chance if it was just Moraven, and we'd still have a chance even if it was Moraven and Firain, but against Eldragon, we have no hope. That house is powerful enough they alone could crush us. The other two clans are overkill."

Lirin stared at him soberly, hugging her son.

* * *

The alpha male turned his head. One of the pack's humans had brought a small human he'd not yet met to the kennel. He rose and walked over to sit in front of them.

The larger human handed the small one a biscuit. "Feed the doggie."

The little human put the biscuit in its mouth.

"*No*. Give it to the *doggie*, son."

The little one looked up at the larger one, then held its hand out towards the alpha male. "Goggie."

The alpha male accepted the half eaten treat and shoved

his nose against the small one's chest, drawing in a deep whiff, his tail wagging. He would remember *this* one's scent always. This was a deeper bond than he normally had with the humans that belonged to the pack. It was a bond similar to those shared by scouting teams. *This* human hadn't just offered him food. It had shared its *own* food *with* him.

The alpha female came and sat beside him, looking at the small human expectantly.

The larger human handed the small one another biscuit. "Feed the other doggie, son."

Once again, the small human took a bite out of the biscuit.

"Give it to the *doggie*."

The large human pushed the small one towards the alpha female and it held its hand out with the treat. The alpha female accepted the food and sniffed the small human to seal the new bond.

The small human wrapped its arms as far around her neck as it could reach. "Goggie!"

Tail wagging; she lay down while it climbed on top of her.

Another human came to the kennel gate and looked inside. "Getting the urfren to accept your son?"

The larger of the two humans inside the kennel turned, exhaling noisily. "Yes. I thought it would be best to get this done *now* rather than waiting until he's old enough to work with them, just in case. He put the biscuits in his mouth and nibbled before he fed them, though. He puts *everything* in his mouth."

The other human made the pleased sound. "It'll be all right as long as the urfren ate their treats. They don't care if he takes a bite first."

* * *

Early Spring Y1063

"Eldragon continues to recruit troops," Spymaster Yalima reported.

"As if they didn't already have enough people to defeat any other single clan in the region," Malida cried, her dark eyes flashing. "What of the other two?"

"Firain has sent several caravans to Moraven. My guess is Firain's working on weapons and ammo. They have several skilled craftsmen. Moraven has simply been strengthening their defenses, training their troops, and storing what Firain's been sending them. All of this agrees with what the traitor told us. I know you weren't sure whether you should trust his words, but so far, our investigations confirm them."

"And our own measures?"

"The fortifications from here to the northern bay are nearly complete. We've taken down the walls around our holdings on the peninsula to use in their construction. Your brother Ballic reports that the escape tunnel from his manor house is now well within the wastes. The slum where the traitor lives is less than ten miles from where he plans to have it exit. Here at the keep, we've made a series of smaller tunnels that connect several buildings, with the last section emerging well away from the walls of the outer holding. I've stationed a team of scouts inside that tunnel to guard the exit."

Malida closed her eyes briefly. "I suppose I should be grateful that at least *we* have something Moraven and his allies *don't*."

Yalima nodded. "Yes. My spies discovered Moraven tried to get some urfren, but wouldn't pay the cost."

"Thank the gods for small favors." Malida sighed. "Send an envoy to one of the nearby slums. The one the traitor came from would likely be best, as they're already hostile towards Moraven and their allies. Arrange for our surviving people to be accepted there once we've lost. Oh, and pass the word among our troops that I've pre-authorized permission if they wish to have children. It will probably be too little too late, but we can hope. I've already sent out heralds to inform the non-combatants in the clan that they may migrate to frontiers if they wish."

"We *are* going to fight, then?"

Malida nodded. "We have no choice. We must at least try if we don't want to be wiped out completely. I plan to ensure that at least *some* of our people survive." Her voice hardened. "I intend to make this war last as long as I can. We'll do as much damage to our enemies as possible before I accept defeat."

"Do you want to try recruiting people from any of the slums?"

Malida shook her head. "Against Eldragon, our defeat is inevitable. Who would swear service if they knew?"

***

Mid-Spring Y1063

Sia rested in bed, nursing her new daughter. The child had been a single birth, as she'd hoped. She doubted house Moraven would resort to the tactics Argul used when the heir was a twin, but was happy she didn't need to put her belief to the test. Rothas sat by her side, beaming.

The door opened, and Korander came into the room and smiled at his granddaughter. "What's the child's name?"

She gave him a tired smile. "Her name is Shula."

Rothas grinned at his father. "She has eyes like her mama."

Korander looked more closely at the infant, noting the baby's golden eyes. "So she does."

***

Zavi and her cohorts stood before the slum boss. "This is our Lady's proposal. We fully intend to fight as long as we can, but we know our defeat is inevitable. Our clan needs a place where we can retreat and take refuge. We've been told this slum is already hostile towards our enemies, so we've chosen to seek asylum here."

Sesh leaned back in his chair. "Only *one* clan that has taken refuge here is hostile towards your enemies." He shrugged. "Though I suppose a second such clan among us wouldn't make much difference."

Rema stood. "Are you *really* going to allow them to come here? There are already more people here than the slum can support. Make them go somewhere *else*!"

The slum boss regarded Rema calmly. "You may have higher social status than I do by clan standards, but *I* am still boss of this slum, not you. Torust will come with goods and supplies. I'm sure they'll start delivering those well before their war starts." He turned back to Zavi. "Am I not right?"

Zavi nodded. "My cohorts and I will first need to prepare a storage area. Once that's complete, we'll periodically send caravans to deliver and store supplies from our enclave. We intend to leave as little behind to benefit our enemies as we can."

Sesh nodded. "It's as I thought. You'll be welcome. Pay no heed to Rema. She thinks *she* should be boss of this slum because she's a clan bastard, but *I* was boss here before she and her people arrived and I will *continue* being boss as long as I can perform the function." He eyed Rema cynically. "Clan blood means *nothing* in a slum."

***

Zavi followed the slum watcher Sesh had assigned as her liaison through the buildings he'd chosen for their use. The buildings he'd selected were less deteriorated than some others in the slum, but would still need many repairs. That would be her first order of business. After she'd decided what needed to be done, she fetched labor parties from the nearest Torust holdings and set them to work. They'd leave the exterior of the buildings as close to how they originally looked as possible.

She was standing in front of the largest of the new storehouses, directing the workers, when a man stopped by her right side and stood watching the renovation. She glanced at him. He was a man with refined features, dark, tousled hair and honey gold skin, wearing a clan coat that bore the same symbol as the woman who'd objected to house Torust being allowed into the slum.

"Do you want something?"

He glanced at her out of the corner of his eye; it had an exotic tilt to it and was a rich golden color. She'd seen no one with eyes like that before. *His eyes are probably a family trait.*

"I was just curious and wanted to see what you were doing."

"Your Lady don't want us here. Are you of the same mind?"

He shrugged. "It don't matter to *me* and Rema ain't a Lady, she's just a clan bastard."

Zavi had to smile at that. "You don't seem all that impressed with her."

"Yeah, well, being a clan bastard ain't as great a thing as she'd have folks think."

She cocked her head. "You sound like a man who knows what he's talking about."

He shrugged again. "I wouldn't claim that."

Her eyes narrowed. "But you *could*, couldn't you?"

"Some think I could, but I won't."

"Because being a clan bastard ain't a great thing?"

He nodded. "Being a clan bastard can get you killed. Even Rema knows that. Ask her about her brother Rasim sometime… if you can get her to talk to you."

She extended her hand. "My name's Zavi, by the way."

He turned towards her and shook it. "I'm Fizran."

Zavi raised a brow. A scar ran down the right side of his face, from his temple to his jaw, crossing through his eye, which, unlike the eye on the left side of his face, was milky white.

"Were you a guard at one time?" She motioned towards the scar. "That must have been a terrible wound."

"No, my family was farm workers. Though it was indeed a terrible wound. My ma initially thought it had killed me."

"How did it happen then? It looks like a sword cut."

"My memories of the event ain't clear. I think I was around five or six years old. All I really know about it is what ma told me afterwards."

"Oh? Did it happen during the war that destroyed your clan?"

He shook his head. "No, and a merger destroyed Shamaze, not a war."

Zavi nodded. "Ah. Was the dominant clan culling the clan bastards then? I can certainly see where you'd not care to be known as a bastard after that."

"Oh no. This was years before the merger was even a possibility."

Zavi frowned. "Then I'm stumped. I can't think of any other reason someone would try to kill such a young child. You said your ma told you what happened? What did she tell you?"

He lifted a brow. "Do you *really* want to know?"

"Yes. You've aroused my curiosity."

"Ma's lover tried to kill me. I won't call him pa. I'm no man's son. Ma actually dug a grave for me and didn't realize I was still alive until she picked me up to carry me to it."

A shiver ran down Zavi's spine as her words to Akaha came to her mind. Fizran had both a scar *and* a tragic history. "I'm sorry. Had he gone insane?"

"I'd *like* to think so, but can't bring myself to believe it. *Ma* does though. She told me that after he thought I was dead, he knelt on the floor of the house we'd been living in and wept before ordering her to leave and never return. She contacted her family. They all forswore themselves that night and sought service with Shamaze."

"What clan did *he* belong to?"

"Argul."

"Ain't that the clan Moraven's connected to?"

He gave her a twisted smile. "My family came north with Rema, not because we're faithful to her, but because she was moving away from Argul territory. It seems we can't escape their presence even here." He glanced at her sideways, out of his good eye. "Ironically, those who'd taken service with Firain had done so because they were unhappy about sharing the slum with *me*."

"Why would they be unhappy about sharing the slum with *you*?"

He gave a bitter laugh. "I believe they're bothered by my eye."

"It don't look *that* bad. *I* think your scar is attractive."

"I wasn't referring to my *blind* eye."

***

Late Spring - Summer Y1063

Over the next several weeks, Zavi came to know Fizran well. He didn't come by every day, but when he did, he'd stay by her side, watching the renovation with great interest. They spoke at length, and she learned how his family served Shamaze during his childhood and what he'd done since he'd become a slum dweller. He introduced her to his family, and she told him how bandits had killed hers, leaving her with no living kin.

As time passed, she started having him do small errands for her, which led to the other guards calling him her pet slummy and her friend Akaha teasing that she'd found her impossible man. Eventually, however, their friendship also came to the notice of the other Shamaze folk, and one day, a group of them confronted her.

"You shouldn't let Fizran spend so much time in your presence," their leader said.

She eyed them coldly. "I'll spend time with whomever I please."

The Shamaze women looked at each other. "He has Argul eyes... well, *an* Argul eye. He wouldn't have that if he wasn't one of them. Argul ain't to be trusted. Insanity runs in their house. He could become unhinged and go on a murderous rampage. Rema only allows him to continue living among us because she needs as many people who recognize her status as possible."

Zavi glared at them. "I've seen no signs of what you suggest since the day I met him. He's old enough that if he *were,* as you say, there'd surely be *some* hint of it by now."

"When he strangles you, don't say we didn't warn you."

The next time Zavi saw Fizran, she told him she'd been warned not to be friends with him. "I think I can decide for *myself* who I'll spend time with, though, and I *enjoy* being in your company."

He smiled at her words. "There've been others that listened to the warnings. I'm glad you won't. I enjoy spending time in *your* company, too."

"They told me some nonsensical tale. I suppose some would pay heed, but I've known you long enough now that I recognize it for the foolishness it is." She sighed. "Unfortunately, we're done repairing the storehouses and from now on we'll simply be delivering supplies to be stored here. That means I'll only be here once every other week at most, though I *will* stay overnight when I come. Also, I'm scheduled to serve at Ballic's holding this spring so I won't be here at all during that season, although that's closer to here than the holding where the keep is."

He nodded. "I understand."

"I can come by on my free time while I'm at Ballic's Holding, but I know you have tasks you need to do yourself and won't always be available to spend time with me."

He shrugged. "I mostly go begging at holding gates. This,"

he pointed at his scarred face, "seems to arouse a bit of sympathy from most guards. I've yet to come away empty-handed."

She laughed. "They probably think you'd been a guard yourself, as *I* initially did. They may even think your clan discarded rather than disenfranchised you. Guards care about their own and would treat you the way they'd wish to be treated in that situation."

***

Autumn - Winter Solstice Y1063

A shipment arrived in the slum on the eve of the winter Solstice. Since they were there during the holiday, they brought a feast with enough food for the entire slum. When Zavi saw Fizran that night, she walked over and kissed him on his right cheek.

"Happy Solstice." She smiled at him.

He whirled around to see who'd come up on his blind side. The wariness on his face fading as he recognized her. "You startled me."

"Sorry. I should probably have put a bit more effort in and approached your other side. Like this." She kissed him on his other cheek.

He blinked at her. "You're kissing me?"

She laughed. "Of *course*. It's a custom here at this time of year. Don't your clan do this?"

"We do." He pointed at a couple wearing Shamaze coats that were embracing passionately.

She sighed, her shoulders slumping. "Oh. Do you mean you prefer men?" She gestured towards a pair of male guards doing the same thing.

He shook his head. "No. It's just…"

Her lower jaw jutted out, her tusks fully exposed. "It's just *what*?" *Have I made a mistake? Is he going to reject me now?*

"No woman has ever shown that kind of interest in me before."

That was unexpected. "Why not? You're an attractive man. Aside from your eyes, you look a lot like your uncle and *he's* married."

"I believe they're *bothered* by my eye."

Her eyes narrowed. "*Their* loss. *I've* been looking forward to this holiday more and more since we first met."

She put her arms around his neck and kissed him directly on the lips. He hesitated a moment, then put his arms around her and kissed back.

He sighed as they separated. "I have to admit that I've never fully appreciated this custom before."

Zavi smiled at him. *Akaha's right, I* have *found my impossible man.* "*That* was just the beginning. Where do you sleep?"

"Where do I sleep?"

She took his hand; her smile deepening. "Yes. Take me to where you sleep."

***

Winter Y1063

Korander knocked on the door to his father's sitting room and waited. A minute passed. He frowned and knocked again, louder this time. Another minute passed.

He looked at the guards stationed just outside. "I'm going in. Something may have happened to him."

The guards nodded, and one opened the door, following him inside.

Inside the room, Korander found his father lying on the floor by his chair. Saerthan still breathed, so they took him to the infirmary.

***

Korander entered the infirmary room where his father rested and stood, gazing at where the old man lay on the bed. One side of Saerthan's face appeared normal, the other side sagged as if it had melted, presenting a startling contrast.

"Come closer, boy," the old man muttered, his words spoken with a distinct slur. "The healers say I ain't long for this world. I suppose that makes you happy."

Korander sighed as he sat beside the bed. "I don't wish you dead, papa. I would much rather you simply approved the war against Torust. Firain and Eldragon are both ready and only wait for my signal before they attack."

"Well, I *ain't* approving it," Saerthan grumbled, "and I

may be bedridden now, but I'm still in charge of the clan. You'll have time enough for your petty war when I'm dead and gone."

"I don't want to wait that long. Eldragon may back out by then. They have no stake in this."

Saerthan gave a wheezing laugh. "You don't know them well, do you, boy? Eldragon won't *ever* back out of a war. They *live* for bloodshed."

***

Tollot stopped a short distance from his father and waited to be recognized. Tylen Torust finished issuing orders before turning to acknowledge him. When he did, Tollot moved to stand beside him.

"Papa? May I make a request?"

"What is it?"

"I wish to be sent to Uncle Ballic's holding."

"We're stripping all the people we can from there. Not sending more troops. We expect that part of the enclave to be the first hit and the first lost. We need all we can, *here* guarding the primary holdings."

"Please? I can take the place of someone who would otherwise have had to stay."

"No. You're needed here. Your desire to serve in the most dangerous station is commendable, but unnecessary."

"I know we're rotating the troops stationed there. Can you at least add me to the rotation for a season?"

Tylen eyed him through narrowed eyes. "Why is this so important to you?"

"I have a lover there and she's borne me a son. I rarely get to see her as it is and they could kill her when the attack comes."

"I suppose we can station you there for a season." Tylen called the captain of the guard over and requested she bump the guards scheduled to serve in the distant holding that spring and send Tollot instead. "Whoever you bump can serve there during the summer."

Captain Marda nodded. "I'll get right on that."

As she left, Tylen grabbed Tollot's wrist and squeezed. "Don't think you have me fooled. I *know* who your lover is.

So does Ballic. *He's* known almost from the beginning."

The blood drained from Tollot's face.

"Oh, we won't call for your execution. You *are* still my son and Ballic treats his daughter with more indulgence than I think proper, but this will be the last time you're allowed anywhere near her. If we weren't preparing for a war we expect to lose, I wouldn't allow you to return to the holding at all."

Tollot's head drooped. "I'd marry her if I could."

"Put *that* out of your mind. It will *never* happen."

***

Zavi greeted Fizran with a kiss. "They ain't sending me to serve at Ballic's holding this spring after all."

"What happened?"

She laughed. "It seems one of the clan bastards has a lover in the holding and convinced his pa to station him there for a season, so I got bumped to summer. It'll be three more months before I'm stationed there myself. I ain't sure whether to be happy or sad about it. I'll be coming with supply caravans for another three months, but Ballic's Holding is closer to here than the keep, and we would've been able to meet more often."

***

Spring Y1064

Serelaf handed the report to his father. "We just got another shipment from house Firain."

Korander accepted the papers, then looked up at Serelaf and smiled. "Is that a new assistant you have there?" He gestured towards the baby his son was carrying.

Serelaf blushed. "Lassie's been leaving Arra alone in her crib when she don't need changing or feeding. That don't seem right to me, so I figured I'd keep her with me and take her to her mama when she needs feeding."

"It don't sound like she's a good mama."

Serelaf sighed. "She'd rather help Leni take care of Quinn. I guess it's just as well she can't have any more babies." He gave his daughter a kiss on her cheek. "I don't mind keeping Arra with me. I love Lassie, but I ain't sure I want my daughter learning her morals from her."

"That *is* a frightening thought."

"How's grandpapa doing?"

"He's been growing weaker, but he's still alert and his mind is sharp."

"So, we still need to wait before we can make Torust pay for what they did?"

Korander nodded. "It shouldn't be much longer, though." He looked at the table on which they'd laid out a map of the region with the Torust holdings clearly marked out. "It shouldn't be long at all."

***

Zavi smiled up at Fizran. "I have something to tell you. *I'm* happy about it, but I ain't sure how *you'll* feel."

He kissed her. "Well, if *you're* happy about it, how can I not?"

She laughed. "Oh, I don't know. Some men get funny notions when told they're going to be a pa."

"'Going to be…'" He blinked. "You're pregnant? With *my* child?"

She nodded. "Lady Malida gave orders granting all guards permission to have children without needing to make a special request when she was told about the coming war, and, well, you're the only lover I've had since then."

He stared at her. "I… don't know what to say."

"Say what you feel."

"I don't suppose your Lady would allow you to marry a slum beggar?"

"Do you want to marry me because I'm pregnant or because you want to be my husband?"

"Well, *both* actually." He kissed her again. "Your pregnancy just gave me the courage to bring it up. If you're willing to bear my child, I thought… I hoped… you might *also* be willing to be my wife."

She smiled at him. "In that case, I'll ask."

He took her hand. "Come, I'd like to tell ma. It should brighten her day. She's had little to be happy about for several years now."

They found Fizran's mother Erla cleaning some edible

roots in the section of the slum Rema had claimed for herself and her followers.

Fizran sat and assisted her. "Ma? Zavi has some news she'd like to share."

Erla looked up at the younger woman. "Yes?"

Zavi sat between Fizran and Erla and joined in with the chore. "You know Fiz and I have become lovers?"

Erla nodded.

"Well, you're going to be a grandma. I'm pregnant. The baby's due in late autumn, or, perhaps, early winter."

Erla pulled Zavi into her arms and hugged her. "Oh, I wish we could let Garlos know!"

Zavi felt Fizran stiffen on her other side.

"Garlos?"

"Fiz's pa. He'd be so proud to know he's going to be a grandpa."

"Ma, he *ain't* my pa. I refuse to recognize him. He tried to *kill* me."

"They *forced* him to do that. Argul is an evil, wicked clan. They tortured him and did something to his mind. He couldn't help himself." She looked down and drew a shaky breath. "He resisted a little, though. He *knew* the blow he'd struck hadn't been fatal." She looked directly into Fizran's eyes. "Garlos *loves* you. That's why he told me to leave. He *knew* you were still alive, and he wanted me to take you somewhere you'd be safe."

She turned to Zavi. "So I took Fiz, got the rest of my family, and we all went to Shamaze, where they allowed us to swear allegiance." She sniffed. "And if I hadn't stood there like a ninny while he got on his horse and rode away, he'd be here with us right *now*! I'm *stronger* than he is, and the torture had left him weaker than usual. I could have *forced* him to come."

"How can you be so sure he knew Fiz was still alive?"

"Garlos and I were together nearly seven years. During those years, I came to know him very well. He's a changeling. If he didn't have the eyes, you'd never know he was an Argul. He's a gentle, loving man. At night, he'd sometimes have nightmares of his clan finding out about us. He'd wake up in a cold sweat and check to be sure I was all right, then go check on Fiz. A man like that don't become a homicidal maniac between one visit and the next. *They* did that to him."

Fizran glanced over at Zavi. "He gave her something when he forced her to be his mistress. It messed up her mind, made her delusional."

Erla frowned at her son. "All it did was calm me down. I fell in love with him the minute I saw his eyes. If ma hadn't acted crazy over him taking me away from the dance, he wouldn't have even *needed* it."

Fizran rolled his eyes. "The rest of the family knows better, but because of that drug, ma always defends him."

"He's a good man! Why won't you *listen*?"

"Maybe I'd be able to see things the way you do if I weren't *half-blind*!"

Zavi touched Erla's wrist. "I don't want to cause trouble between you and Fiz. This should be a joyous time. Fiz asked me to marry him. I plan to request permission when I return to the keep."

***

Lady Malida Torust sighed as Marda finished speaking. "How can one of our guards want to marry a slum beggar?"

Captain Marda shrugged. "I'd placed her in charge of renovating the storehouses the slum boss gave us and she's accompanied caravans of supplies that we've been storing there. Apparently, they became lovers at winter Solstice. She told me she's pregnant with his child. Wanting to marry the man, however, goes far beyond what you've approved."

"What clan does he follow?"

"He belongs to the same clan as the traitor who warned you that Moraven is planning on starting a war."

Malida shook her head. "Tell her I'm sorry, but I can't approve of such a marriage. She'll have to be content to just be his lover."

***

Summer Solstice Y1064

Fizran made his way across the wasteland between the slum and Ballic's Holding. He'd started out at the crack of dawn as the walk took three and a half hours to complete.

When he arrived, he stood to one side, unsure of his reception. He'd never come to this gate to beg before, but Zavi had told him she'd be here.

As he watched, servants set up a table outside the gate and laid out a Solstice feast on it. His mouth watered as the breeze wafted the scent of food in his direction. The guards stationed at the gate came out and filled plates to eat on their breaks. He sat on his heels and continued to watch. The guards knew he was there. He'd seen some of them glance his way. They should invite him to take what he wanted from the table once they'd eaten their fill. He could wait.

It was late in the afternoon when Zavi came out of the gate and filled a plate from the table. She spotted him as she was doing so and came to sit beside him.

"Lady Malida refused to give permission for us to wed."

He sighed. "I figured as much when you didn't return to the slum."

She offered him her plate, and he accepted it. "We expect to lose this war. Once that happens, and we've taken refuge in the slum with you, I'll no longer be bound by her command."

He kissed her cheek. "I'll come by every day while you're here."

She leaned against him and sighed. "I'll be waiting."

***

Early to Mid-Summer Y1064

Lirin led her son's nurse to the hidden door to the secret cellar. "Now the tunnel's complete, we'll need as many as possible that know the route."

"Won't you and Master Ballic be leading us though?"

Lirin shook her head. "No. Papa plans to fight alongside the guards. He don't know it yet, but I'll be fighting *with* him. If he wanted me to obediently go with the non-combatants, he shouldn't have allowed me to take weapons' training. I expect you to take my son to safety when it becomes necessary."

She led the way down the stairs to the staging room and showed the older woman how to open the door to the tunnel. Once Lisdra knew the trick, she picked up a small leather case. "This is important. In here are the records of my son's birth and parentage. They need to be brought to my Aunt Malida."

She looked soberly at Lisdra. "These are the originals and there are no copies. Papa's been hesitant to let his sister know I took a lover and gave birth to a bastard. Keep them safe."

Lisdra nodded. "You have my promise, mistress."

Lirin set the case back on the shelf, lit a candle, and led the way into the tunnel itself. "The tunnel ends in a natural cave," she said as they headed into the darkness. "When the miners broke into it, papa thought it best to keep that part of the route as natural looking as possible. We've moved the holding's pack of urfren to the cave and ordered them to guard it." An urfren lying in the tunnel rose and came to nudge her hand with its nose. She scratched the animal's ears. "You'll need to memorize the landmarks outside so you can return to empty the storage room. We expect to have more supplies there than we can carry out in one trip."

"Surely, there are enough non-combatants in the holding to take all that's there?"

"I'm sure there are, but most won't have access to the tunnel. Only those who live in the manor itself can use it. The others will have to escape as best they can, and we're sending as many of them as possible to the keep. We have permission to take refuge in a nearby slum. The road north of the tunnel exit goes directly to it. The extra supplies stored in the hidden room are, in part, for any outside the manor house who gets out. Once we've lost the war, we'll need all the supplies we can get."

"Are we so sure we'll lose the war?"

Lirin sighed. "I'm afraid so. Eldragon alone could overwhelm us with sheer numbers. Add to them Firain and Moraven's weapons and devices and it's a recipe for disaster. If I knew who it was that escalated the hostilities between Moraven and us, I would strangle them myself. With my bare hands."

***

Korander visited his father every evening before heading to bed. Saerthan had deteriorated noticeably in the weeks since summer Solstice. On this night, when he entered his father's room, he found him lying on his back, his breathing labored. A couple times his father seemed to stop breathing, but then started again with a gasp. He sat beside the bed and just watched. His father had been doing this for a while now, and the healers told him there was nothing they could do about it.

Suddenly, the old man sat bolt upright, his eyes bulging. "Chazrel!" he shrieked. Then he fell back on the bed and lay still.

Korander went to the door and called for a healer, but the old man was dead.

***

Korander sat on his throne, looking around the audience chamber at the assembled clan folk. It felt strange to be wearing the mask of a clan Lord. When he was sure as many of his kin had arrived as could come on such short notice, he rose to his feet.

"Lord Saerthan Moraven is dead. *I* am now Lord of the clan. It's time for us to go to war. We attack Torust this very night!"

***

Homelands: Mid-Summer Y1064

Heavy booms rent the silence of the night, awakening the inhabitants of the manor house at Ballic's Holding. Lisdra dressed quickly and grabbed the bag of spare clothing she had ready, emerging from her room to absolute chaos. The house servants were running about in panic. She grabbed one by the arm and shook her.

"Get dressed and go to the basement. We've prepared for this."

She headed upstairs to Lirin's room. When she arrived, she found her mistress already dressed and trying to dress her son. Lirin looked up as Lisdra entered the room.

"Oh, good." She shoved the boy into her arms. "Take over. I need to join papa in battle. Remember the papers I showed you, and if you should see Tollot... tell him I love him."

Lisdra nodded and took the child. "Come son. You need to be dressed. It's cold in the wastes."

The boy glared at her. "Don't *wanna*."

She patted his bottom. "Well, you're *gonna*."

* * *

Fizran frowned as the walls surrounding Ballic's Holding came into sight. Something was wrong. He'd been making this trip daily since summer Solstice. The gatehouse should be visible now, but the familiar towers just weren't there. He broke into a run.

When he arrived at the place where the gate should have been, all that remained of it was a hole in the walls. Both gatehouse towers had fallen and rubble from both walls and towers had scattered everywhere. He searched frantically but found only the dead. He saw one female guard lying with a sizable block of rubble resting directly on her head. His heart thudded in his chest as he approached where she lay. When he got close, he sank to his knees and uttered a prayer of gratitude. Zavi was visibly pregnant now. This guard was thinner than her.

He turned towards the towers. Zavi had told him the guards slept inside them. One tower was so badly damaged he couldn't enter, but the door to the other tower provided enough of an opening for him to squeeze inside.

The lower floor of this tower was still fairly open. There was a lot of rubble, but at least *some* inhabitants had gotten out.

"Zavi?" he called softly.

"I'm here." Zavi's voice came from a pile of rubble by the outer wall.

He pulled the blocks and stones off the pile until he'd cleared enough that he could see her. "How badly are you hurt?"

"I think my legs broke. Other than that, I'm just bruised and battered."

He continued clearing the rubble away from her until the only piece left was a block of stone that rested directly on her lower legs. He examined it.

"I think I can use a lever to pry it off you. Do you think you could pull yourself out from under it?"

"My arms still work." She lay there, holding them protectively over her abdomen.

He searched until he found a spear he could use for a lever, then set a smaller block beside the one pinning Zavi's legs and worked the end of the spear into position.

"Ready?"

She nodded, and he pressed down as hard as he could on the spear shaft. The block lifted and Zavi scrabbled with her arms, pulling herself out from under it. Once she was clear, he released it and it dropped with a crash.

He scooped her up in his arms. "Let's get you out of here."

The easiest route appeared to be over the rubble that had trapped her and out through a hole in the tower's side.

Since Zavi was only wearing a thin nightshirt, Fizran collected blankets from the cots that had had escaped being crushed under the rubble and wrapped her in them. Then he searched for medical supplies, eventually finding what he needed to tend her injuries. He set her legs, wrapped splints on them, then sealed both legs in a casing that hardened into a cast.

"Are there any other survivors? My friend Akaha? Anybody?"

He shook his head. "Everyone else I found was dead." He gestured towards the other tower. "If there are any other survivors here, they must be in there and I couldn't find a way in."

Tears filled her eyes as she nodded. "I understand."

He scrounged through the wreckage and gathered everything he could find that might be of use, then constructed a travois and strapped her to it.

"Time to head to the slum. I'll have to drag you through the wastes. The going should be easier once we reach the road, though."

He piled all the useful items he'd found around her and fastened the entire burden firmly to the frame before picking up the handles and setting out. It was full dark by the time they reached the slum. He brought her into the first usable building they came across and they spent the rest of the night there.

In the morning, he set out to find a healer to come care for her. An hour later, he returned with his mother and a woman he introduced as Wisia.

Zavi frowned at the woman. "Why are *you* here?"

Wisia regarded her calmly. "I'm a healer. It's my duty to

care for the sick and injured. A duty I take seriously. *I* will not refuse my services to *any*."

"*Drop* it," Fizran told her.

"No. I will *not* drop it." She turned back to Zavi. "Followers of your clan arrived here late last night, seeking refuge. They've moved into the storehouses you worked on and refuse to share any of the supplies inside, not even the things we'd scrounged for ourselves. When he told them about you, they said he lied. That he was just trying to steal that which had they'd brought for *their* use." She turned towards Fizran. "Show her your face. Show her how her clan treats those who come to them in need."

Zavi looked directly at Fizran for the first time since he'd returned with the two women. "Fiz?"

Sighing, he turned so she could see him fully. Bruises covered his face. He had a split lip, and could barely see through his good eye. "It's nothing."

"'Nothing'?" Wisia demanded. "Sesh himself had to come intervene or they would have beaten you to death."

Zavi's eyes widened, then narrowed. "I guess it's a good thing you couldn't find my clan coat. If they'd do that to someone seeking aid for me, then I consider myself discarded." She held her hand out towards him. "There's nothing now to bar our marriage."

Conflict
Homelands: Summer Y1056

Yadrac leaned forward, his attention focused on what Lerali was saying. The woman paced back and forth, shadowed by her beast, her long black hair flowing freely around her shoulders.

"For the next three months, you will sleep, eat, bathe, and even *breathe* with your urfren. Your beast will be by your side at all times." She directed a stern gaze at the youngsters, her gray eyes gleaming. "The position of scout requires a special quality. Not all of you will pass the test. It is no shame to fail. The clan requires both guards and scouts."

Marrasi nudged Yadrac. "*You* can forget passing," she whispered.

Yadrac bit his cheek to keep from rising to her taunt. He was the youngest in the group and had barely qualified for this year's class, a fact Marrasi brought up at every opportunity. If he got kicked out of training, he wouldn't get a second chance.

"Ok. Who's ready to meet their beasts?"

Every hand shot up.

Lerali smiled at them. "Right then. Line up over there." She pointed towards the gate to the kennel where they'd brought the older pups. "When an urfren accepts a treat from you, take it by the collar and lead it through the far gate."

177

Marrasi pushed Yadrac behind her as they took their places. He closed his eyes, fighting to keep his temper. Marrasi was a clan bastard while he was just a crèche orphan. She'd get preferential treatment. He muttered a mean spirited wish that she'd fail the test. The wish had barely left his lips when he regretted it. He glanced around, worried that someone might have overheard him, but the others were lining up and paying no attention to him.

He reached the gate, and a scout gave him a handful of biscuits before allowing him to pass through. The young urfren were playing in the center of the enclosure. Successful trainees exited through a gate on the far side with their beasts. He held out a biscuit. "Here puppy. Here puppy." The words had barely left his lips when his cheeks started burning. *I hope no one heard me calling an* urfren *'puppy'*.

One of the urfren pranced over to him and snatched a biscuit from his hand, licking his face after eating it. Dutifully, he grabbed the animal's collar and led the beast to the far side, where he passed through to join the other successful trainees who were lining up to collect food dishes for their new companions. The server who handed him a dish for his urfren smiled.

"We'll be measuring the amount of food your urfren eats. Feed it from this dish. From now on, you're to be the only person who feeds your urfren. Just use this first day getting to know your beast and give it a name."

He nodded and led his urfren to one side of the courtyard, where a tree provided a little shade. He offered the food the server had given him to it. "Here puppy. Eat up."

The urfren gulped the meat and licked his face. He wasn't sure how he was supposed to treat the animal, so he petted it as if it were an ordinary dog, scratching it behind its ears.

Marrasi came over to where he sat, her own beast following at her heels. "So you passed the first test. What did you get? *Mine* is a dog."

He frowned at her. "I ain't looked."

She snapped her fingers at his urfren. "Beg!" The animal sat up on its haunches, tongue lolling from its open mouth, its forefeet folded in front of its chest. "You got a bitch. Bitches don't pass scout training. Bitches are just for breeding." She strutted away, laughing.

He glared at her. His fingers itched to grab one of her long, black braids and *pull*. "*You're* a bitch," he muttered. "Does that mean *you're* just for breeding?" He hugged his beast, giving her one of the remaining biscuits. "Don't let her bother you. We'll *both* pass the training. I *know* it. We'll be a *great* team some day." He sat under the tree and scratched the animal behind her ears. "What name should I give you? I can't keep calling you 'puppy'. That wouldn't be respectful. I know. I'll call you Kiko. How would you like *that*?"

The urfren tilted her head and barked.

"Ok, Kiko it is."

At dinnertime, the successful trainees filed into the dining hall assigned to them. Lerali stood at the front of the room. "Remember, your urfren is to stay by your side at all times. It will sit by your side when you eat. It will sleep in your room by your bed. When you need to use a chamber pot, it will be there."

Yadrac waited until Marrasi had collected her meal and sat at a table before joining the chow line. He sat as far from the girl as possible. Kiko nudged his arm as he took a bite. He glanced around. No one was looking his way. He slipped her a piece of meat from his plate.

The next morning, training began. As the days passed, Yadrac got into the habit of slipping Kiko bits of food from his plate. She started leaving food in her dish, preferring to eat from his plate. The servers who doled out the food he was supposed to feed her raised a brow when he returned her dish with food still in it, but said nothing. He feared Kiko might not be getting enough to eat, so he picked meat heavy foods and loaded up his plate when he collected his own meals. She ate less and less from her dish, eventually eating entirely from his and leaving the food in hers untouched.

Towards the end of the second week, Marrasi spotted him feeding Kiko from his plate. She called for Lerali and told her what he'd been doing. His cheeks burned.

Lerali eyed him sternly. "How long have you been giving your urfren food off your plate?"

He hung his head, his dark hair falling over his face, hiding it from view as he made his admission of guilt. "Since the first day."

"You know we need to keep track of how much each urfren eats."

He swallowed. "Kiko likes *my* food better than *hers*."

"I see." She shook her head. "I'm afraid you'll have to eat in a separate room from the other trainees. We need to keep track of how much food Kiko eats. If you're feeding her from your plate, then we need to measure *your* food."

After that, Yadrac and Kiko had to eat in a private room separate from the rest of the trainees. The server shook his head as he doled out their food.

He hugged Kiko. "They ain't kicked me out yet. When the time comes, we'll pass the test. You're my best friend. We can't fail." She licked his face.

Marrasi sneered at him for feeding Kiko at the table. "Wolf sits quietly at my side while *I* eat. He *never* tries to beg at the table and always eats *everything* in his own dish."

The day arrived when it was time for the ultimate test. This would determine whether the trainees had what it took to become scouts. Lerali stood and paced in front of the class.

"We'll start holding the tests this afternoon. Those who fail will return their urfren to the kennels once the testing is over." She looked around at the youths seated with their urfren. "Be aware that we have *never* had a perfect class. There've been years when we've only gotten one out of the entire batch. However, I have high hopes for this class." Her eyes twinkled. "That means I have cause to believe that nearly *half* of you will succeed." She scratched her urfren behind the ears. "We'll place your names in a bowl and draw them at random." Her eyes focused on Marrasi. "There is no favoritism in who goes when. There's also no shame in failing." She gestured towards the door. "Come. It's time for you to see the testing field."

Lerali led the way to an arena. On one side was a dummy target. On the other side was a stand built of real wood. The instructor pointed at it. "Each of you will stand on the landing at the top of this drop box. It's designed to drop you at an unexpected moment. When it does, paddles will strike your legs underneath."

"Your job is to command your urfren to attack the training

dummy and continue attacking after you fall and the paddles strike you. Once the test is over, healers will enter the arena, pull you out of the box, place you on a stretcher, and take you to the infirmary. Regardless of how the test has gone at that point, you are to act incapacitated while the healers carry you out."

"Your urfren must perform properly during the entire session." She eyed the trainees through lowered lids. "Be aware that the paddles *will* hurt and they *have* injured trainees during the test. You must bear the pain as best you can. This test simulates a battle in which you order your urfren to attack *one* target while a different enemy attacks *you*."

Marrasi smirked at Yadrac. "Wolf will perform to perfection. Good luck getting *your* little bitch to do her job."

He closed his eyes and bit his lip, draping his arm around Kiko's neck and hugging her. "I *know* you'll do this *right, girl*."

Lerali drew the first name for the trainees in the audience section. The named trainee strutted into the arena and climbed onto the drop box. The assistants retreated, and Lerali gave the command to start. Two tests passed without incident. On the third test, the trainee ordered his urfren to attack, but when the trapdoor dropped him to be hit with paddles, his beast ignored its orders and abandoned the dummy, destroying the box and curling around its partner. Lerali called a halt to the proceedings and healers rushed in to carry the boy off the field.

Yadrac gasped at the massive cost of the failure. *Why didn't they make the stand out of metal?*

Lerali turned to the class. "All right everyone. You can take a break now while we restore the arena. Be back in half an hour."

The tests continued. Two more urfren abandoned their attack on the target dummies before Marrasi had her turn towards the end of the day. When the healers released her, she gloated over Yadrac. "Did you see how Wolf destroyed that dummy? *Your* little bitch won't even *try* to attack it. She'll just curl around the box and go to sleep."

Halfway through the second day of the trials, they drew Yadrac's name. At the door to the arena, a scout stationed there offered Kiko a biscuit. She turned her nose up at the treat. The scout eyed Yadrac sternly.

"What's your name, boy?"

His cheeks burned as he replied. The scout wrote his name on a notepad before letting him through.

"I'll be *watching* you, boy."

He swallowed hard before moving out onto the field. One girl had broken her leg when her urfren abandoned its attack on the dummy and destroyed the box. His heart in his throat, he climbed up onto the box and ordered Kiko to attack. When the trapdoor gave way underneath him, he let out a yelp. The paddles did indeed hurt, but what tore his heart the most was seeing Kiko charging towards him from the target.

"No!" He pointed at the dummy. "Kill!" She ignored his orders and ripped the box into kindling.

As she curled around him, he cried into her fur. He'd failed. He lay limp when the healers came into the arena and loaded him onto a stretcher to take him to the infirmary. Kiko stayed at his side through the entire process while the healers examined him. He had bruised shins and there were breaks in the skin that had to be bandaged before the healers released him.

When the trials started again, he sat beside the girl with the broken leg in a section set aside for those whose urfren hadn't obeyed their orders. The girl had shaved her head, so she was completely bald. The girl sighed, hugging her urfren. "So far, over half have gotten through the test without their urfren breaking orders."

He nodded.

Marrasi walked past them, sneering. "What a bunch of losers. You can bet you're gonna be paying for those stands the rest of your lives."

Yadrac closed his eyes and hugged Kiko. He'd have to return her to the kennels once the trials were over and he'd probably never see her again.

The girl offered him her hand, her green eyes grave. "I'm Verda. I guess we'll be serving together on the clan guard."

He shook it. "I guess so. I'm Yadrac."

She smiled at him, her teeth flashing white against her warm brown skin. "We *all* know who *you* are. You were the first of us to be sent out of the trainee dining hall to eat in isolation."

He blinked. "There were *others*?"

She nodded, pointing at two other trainees. "I don't know if there were more after *me*, but *those* two did it, too."

He laughed, hugging Kiko's neck. "I don't feel so bad about it then. At least I ain't alone."

A blond boy on Verda's other side leaned forward to speak to Yadrac. "There were five in all that got sent out of the dining hall." He grinned. "Not all of us got caught." He looked around, his face sobering. "So far, all the ones that got caught are failing."

The morning after the last trainee completed their trial, the class assembled on the trainee grounds for the last time. Lerali strode to the front of the class and beamed at them. "Well done all! This is the most trainees to pass the test since I became scout mistress." She held up a document. "Would the following trainees please come to the front of the room?" She read a list of nine names.

Yadrac sighed, turning to Verda, who sat beside him. "Looks like the failures are being called out first. Want help to get up?"

Verda smiled at him. "Thank you. I'd appreciate that."

He helped her up, and they made their way to the front of the room.

Once the nine trainees had assembled at the front of the room, Lerali faced the rest of the class. "The rest of you are to take your urfren back to the kennels. I want to remind you it's no shame to fail the test. The clan still needs guards, and all of you have done well in your guard training."

Marrasi stood, frozen in place and staring at Yadrac, her mouth agape. She shook her head. "No! *I'm* supposed to be made a scout!" She stamped her foot.

Lerali frowned at the girl. "Mistress Marrasi, you do not have the qualities needed for a scout. There is no shame in becoming a guard. It's rare that we find a candidate that can pass the test. Few guards can even *take* scout training. Count that as a privilege. Now please, take your urfren to the kennels and turn him over to the kennel master."

Verda hugged Yadrac, her eyes bright. "We *did* it! *We*

passed. It was everyone *else* that failed."

He stared at her, his eyes wide. He turned and hugged Kiko's neck.

Once the last of the failed trainees had left, Lerali turned to the nine who remained. "All right then. Is everyone ready to start your *real* training?"

One trainee raised a hand. "Mistress Lerali? I thought we failed. Our urfren didn't obey us."

Lerali smiled. "We deceived you. The *actual* test was when a scout offered your urfren biscuits before you entered the arena." She nodded towards Yadrac. "The reason we isolate those trainees whose urfren stop eating from their own dishes and only eat from their partner's plate is because we want the bond to develop naturally. If the trainees knew that was a positive sign, there would be those who deliberately fed their urfren from their plates, just so they'll pass the test."

Verda frowned. "But... wouldn't that be a *good* thing? You could have a class where *everyone* passed."

Lerali shook her head. "Yes, everyone would pass, but not all would have proper bonds. Many, if not most, would have one-way bonds. *You* need to bond with your urfren just as much as your urfren needs to bond with you."

***

Homelands: Early Spring Y1061

Hathan climbed the tree. Something had damaged it at one point and the trunk bent halfway up, creating a place where he could sit. He looked around. *This would be a* great *place to build a house*! Close to the tree, he spotted the foundations of a building. *Looks like someone else had the same idea. I wonder why they abandoned the site.*

Movement at the corner of his eye caught his attention, and he turned to peer more closely. A girl with reddish brown hair worn in twin braids was walking along a path a short distance from the tree, carrying a large basket. He swung down from the tree and ran over to her, bowing.

"Good afternoon Mistress Sylda. May I carry your basket for you?"

She grinned up at him and giggled, her blue eyes shining. "Why thank you, kind sir. I'd appreciate that."

***

The senior scout stood at the side of the practice field and blew a whistle. Once he had everyone's attention, he made his announcement. "New assignments, everyone. The following scouts are to report to the main office for deployment orders." He read a list of names.

Yadrac turned to Verda. "Well, it's been fun training with you. Maybe I'll see you around sometime."

She smiled back at him. "I wonder when I'll get *my* assignment."

"It shouldn't be long. The first ones from our class got *their* assignments just last week."

When he arrived at the main office, his escort introduced him to a pair of older scouts.

Once the introductions were over, the senior scout addressed him. "Your new team mates will continue your training in the field. The assignment is bandit hunting. Good luck."

Yadrac followed his new teammates as they led the way to the guards' lounge. There, they introduced him to the captain of the squad they'd be working with. Captain Zavi was a wiry woman with coarse features, a narrow face, cropped sandy brown hair, and green eyes. As she shook his hand, she nodded towards Kiko. "Your urfren is smaller than the others?"

He shrugged. "I just finished my training last month. This is our first assignment."

She smiled warmly, revealing oversized canines in her lower jaw. "Welcome to the club. This is *my* first assignment too. I think it's as much a training mission as anything else." She glanced down. "It's personal for *me,* though. The bandits killed my ma. I'm the only one left in my family."

He pressed her hand. "We'll *get* them. You can be *sure* of that."

***

Spring Y1062

Hathan turned the wheel, and the water gushed through the opening into the field. He wiped his brow, brushing his light brown hair off his forehead. "That's it. We've irrigated the field. We're done for the day."

Kuren dropped to the ground and took a swig from his canteen. Sweat soaked his blond locks. After drinking, he passed the canteen to his friend. "Are you planning to go to the dance tonight?"

Hathan nodded as he drank from the canteen. "I'm going to ask Sylda to marry me."

Kuren grinned. "You know, I'd be courting her *myself* if you hadn't already swept her off her feet."

"You'll find someone of your own someday."

Kuren stood. "Maybe."

"Hey, don't sound so doubtful." He wrapped an arm around Kuren's neck and waved his free arm. "You just got to *look*."

At the dance, Hathan pulled Sylda to one side of the barn where the celebration was being held and proposed. She stared at him.

"I don't know what to say."

"Say 'yes'."

She beamed at him. "Yes!"

He pulled her into his arms and kissed her.

"We need permission from my parents and the holder."

He nodded. "We'll ask your parents *now*."

Her mother hugged her. "You're too *young*."

"Ma! I'm fifteen. *You* were my age when you married pa."

"Fifteen? You *can't* be. It was just a few years ago that you were born. You're still a little girl."

Her father turned a stern gaze on Hathan. "I'm willing to give permission, but you need your own home. I don't want my daughter to live in cramped quarters. When I married her ma, we lived with my parents until I could build a home for her. That's no kind of life for a newlywed."

Hathan nodded. "I'll ask the holder for permission to build a home when we request permission to marry. I have the perfect location in mind."

On the next court day, Hathan and Sylda went before the holder. When their turn came to make their petition, they stepped forward. Hathan bowed.

"Sir? I have two requests."

"Yes?"

"First," Hathan smiled at Sylda, "we wish permission to marry."

The holder nodded. "Very well. What are your names?"

"My name is Hathan."

"My name is Sylda."

"And your second request?"

Hathan took a step forward. "Sylda's parents want me to have a house before we wed. I would like permission to build such a house. I have a building site in mind."

"And what site is that?"

He explained exactly where he meant.

The holder nodded. "Permission granted. That site has been empty for *far* too long. However, you mustn't neglect your assigned tasks. You may only work on your house during your free time."

Hathan nodded. "Thank you, sir."

***

Summer Equinox Y1062

Kuren grinned at his friend. "Are you *seriously* going to work on a *holiday*?"

"I can only work on the house when I have free time. All I've been able to do so far is to clean up the site. I'm free *all day* today. I hope to get some proper work done."

The youths reached Hathan's building site and surveyed the area.

Kuren sighed and picked up a rock. "Well, let's get started."

"You don't have to help."

"Hey! Your pa's too old to help, you ain't got any brothers-in-law, and your brothers are too little. Besides, what *else* are best friends for?"

***

Late Autumn Y1062

"Hey! Yadrac!"

He turned, his eyes lighting up as he recognized Verda's distinctive shaved head. "Hey! How *are* you?"

She made a face. "Nia's nursing puppies, so I'm sidelined until they're weaned."

He laughed. "Same here. Both of my teammates had dogs, and Kiko mated with one of them. I didn't even realize she was in heat. Then she started gaining weight. Apparently, they can't assign me to work with *either* of them again, since we don't know which dog she mated with."

Verda linked her arm with his. "I know which dog *Nia* mated with. I caught them in the act."

He smiled at their linked arms, admiring how her darker skin complimented his lighter tones. "Care to join me at the Solstice eve festivities?"

"I would be *delighted* to."

***

Early Spring Y1063

Yadrac smiled at Verda as he waved the paper with directions to the location of their new assignment. "This should be an easy duty. Standing guard in an emergency escape tunnel? We could do *that* in our sleep."

She smiled back, linking her fingers with his. "I hadn't even known the clan *had* an escape tunnel."

***

Winter Solstice Y1063

Yadrac pulled Verda into his arms and kissed her. "Happy Solstice."

She wrapped her arms around his neck and kissed *him*. "I was wondering when you'd make a move. How many years has it been that we've known each other?"

"Too many and not enough."

She laughed. "*That* sounds suspiciously like a marriage proposal."

He gazed into her eyes. "It is if you *want* it to be."

***

Summer Y1064

Verda rushed to Yadrac and threw her arms around him. "We're at *war*!"

His eyes widened, and he stared at her, mouth agape. "What? Who are we at war *with*?"

"*Moraven*. Apparently, our Lady expected this. That was why they gave us blanket permission to have children if we want them. I was told they're going to pull all the scouts off tunnel duty and send them out to battle. They'll replace the scouts with regular guards teamed with urfren that just have basic bonds."

His hands went to her waist. "Do they expect you to go to war *pregnant*?"

She shook her head. "*I'm* to report to the crèche and will serve there until our child is weaned while *you* are off fighting somewhere." She kissed him. "Oh Yadrac, be *careful*!"

* * *

Autumn Y1064

Hathan led the way through the finished house. He held his chin high as Sylda's parents exclaimed over the work he and Kuren had done. It had taken long enough. They'd worked on it for over two years before the work satisfied him. Sylda's parents couldn't say *this* was a cramped house.

"Well? Do you think it's good enough for Sylda?"

Her father beamed at him. "I'd say it's good enough for the *holder*."

Her mother laughed. "It might be a little *small* for a holder's house."

"Perhaps, but it would make a nice guest cottage for the holder."

"So, how soon can Sylda and I get married?"

"As soon as it's furnished." Her father eyed him sternly. "I won't have my daughter sleeping on the floor or eating off the counter."

Hathan nodded. "I should finish furnishing it by the end of winter."

Her father placed an arm around his shoulders. "We'll plan on that for the wedding then."

* * *

Winter Y1064

Hathan and Sylda stood in front of the priest, surrounded by their friends and family.

The priest bowed and turned to Sylda. "Please state your name and extend your left arm."

Sylda smiled up at Hathan as she held out her arm. "Sylda."

The priest bound her wrist with a blue ribbon and turned to Hathan. "Please state your name and extend your left arm."

He beamed down at her as he extended his arm. "Hathan." His heart swelled in his breast as the priest bound their lives together.

After the ceremony, Kuren came and kissed Sylda on the cheek. He winked at Hathan. "If you ever tire of this big lug, just say the word and we'll run away together."

Sylda laughed, turning to her new husband. "As if I'd *ever* tire of Hathan."

***

Autumn Y1065

Hathan lifted his head. The midwife stood in the door. "You have a son."

"Sylda?"

She smiled at him. "She's fine."

He jumped up and rushed into the room. His wife sat in the bed, holding an infant to her breast. He sat beside her and kissed her forehead. "Congratulations on a job well done."

She smiled tiredly up at him. "I've named him Brock. I hope you approve."

"A fine name for a fine son." He extended a finger and touched a tiny hand, counting fingers. The baby grasped it. He grinned at her. "He has quite a grip."

She smiled at him. "Just like his pa."

***

Hathan slung an axe on his back and climbed the tree. He straddled a branch and chopped at the trunk just past where it bent.

"What are you *doing* up there?"

He looked down. Kuren stood at the base of the tree. "I'm going to build a tree house. Brock will enjoy having a place of

190

his own where he can play away from everyone else."

Kuren laughed. "Ain't it a little early to start work on it? He's just a baby."

"That just means I have plenty of time. I'm only getting the base of the platform ready now. We can always mix the wood in with the fuel for the cook fire." He cut through the trunk and the top of the tree toppled to the ground. "Watch out below!"

Every afternoon, until the autumn storms began, he worked on the platform that would serve as the base of the tree house.

***

Summer Y1066

Kiko's head came up and her ears pricked forward as she sniffed the air. Yadrac placed his hand on her shoulder.

"What *is* it, girl?"

Her tail gave a half wag.

He smiled, waving in the direction Kiko had pointed out. "Bring them in, girl."

The urfren darted out into the brush, returning a short time later. At her side was another urfren. Yadrac recognized the beast.

"Verda?"

The scout following Nia rushed up, throwing her arms around him. "Yadrac! I was afraid I'd never *see* you again." She kissed him full on the lips.

After Verda's band had settled in the camp, the two sat, talking.

Verda smiled at Yadrac. "You have a daughter. I named her Mohara."

"That's wonderful news, but where've you *been*? I spend my winters at the keep. The crèche was empty and no one could tell me where you were."

Her eyes blazed. "Communication with the rank and file is nonexistent. They moved the crèche to the slum while I was still pregnant. I doubt they even *considered* that the children's parents might want to know that."

***

Mid-Autumn Y1067

Verda slumped in the saddle and slid off her horse. Yadrac hopped off his horse and rushed to her side, only to pull up short. Nia was there before him, growling. The beast eyed him, her eyes blazing fiery blue. A shiver ran down his spine. The urfren sniffed at an arrow that pierced Verda's chest, nosed the woman's face, then raised her head to test the air before slinking off into the brush.

Yadrac motioned in the direction Nia had gone. "Hunt." Kiko followed her pack mate. He dropped to his knees at Verda's side, but Nia's actions told him there was nothing he could do. His throat hurt and tears welled up in his eyes. He gathered her in his arms and wept silently, rocking back and forth.

***

Shoulders slumped; Yadrac rode into the slum, heading to the building that was being used as an infirmary. Kiko limped by his side. Leaving his horse at the door, he stepped inside and hailed a healer. "My urfren has a hurt leg. Can you patch her up?"

The woman nodded, grabbing a medical kit. "What happened?"

He grimaced. "They have archers. We didn't even know they were there until we started dropping." He stroked his beast's flank. "We lost two teams." *Will Mohara be a crèche orphan like I was?*

When he left the infirmary, he strode aimlessly through the streets, Kiko at his side. He draped an arm around her neck. "We'll have to be more careful in the future. There's a little girl in the crèche who lost her ma and depends on us."

He looked around at the bustle as the healers tended injured guards. There'd been many changes since the last time he'd been here. He didn't know what housing was available and without Verda, they wouldn't allow him to bunk at the crèche.

He touched the arm of a pregnant slum woman who was walking by, a small dark-haired girl in tow. "Excuse me, mistress. I need to find a place to stay until I can go back out onto the field. Could you tell me where I can go?"

192

She turned, and he gaped at her.

"Zavi? What are *you* doing wearing the coat of a slum clan?"

Zavi shrugged. "Moraven wiped out my company in the first battle. I'm discarded now. I've married and my husband's clan has accepted me."

He closed his eyes, his thoughts going again to Verda. Too many had died. "I'm sorry."

She smiled at him. "You're welcome to stay with my husband and me, though. We can talk of old times." She rested an arm on her swollen abdomen. "You don't need to fear being poisoned. My husband's ma does the cooking."

At Zavi's home, she introduced him to her husband and his family. He smiled at them. "Thank you for taking me in. I was afraid I'd have to sleep in the rough." He patted Kiko's back. "Though Kiko here would keep me warm."

Zavi's mother-in-law offered him a bowl of soup. "Will you be staying for the winter? The year is getting late and the storms have already started."

He nodded. "There's a ceasefire during the winter storms. We take that time to regroup. It's the main reason we've been able to keep the war going this long."

"I see. Well, we have plenty of room in here for you and your animal." She eyed Kiko warily. "Does it eat a lot?"

He scratched Kiko behind her ears. "The clan provides her food. I'd appreciate it if you'd cook it for me, though. We eat together. She won't touch food unless I share it with her and I ain't fond of raw meat." He glanced around at the others in the room. "Since you're providing me with sleeping quarters, I can request enough to share with you."

The woman smiled at him. "We'd appreciate that."

As they were retiring for the night, he stopped Zavi. "I can't believe they discarded you for losing your company. We need all the fighters we can get."

She looked away. "They didn't. It's complicated. I don't want to talk about it." She smiled at him. "It seems so long since we were bandit hunting."

He nodded. "The other scouts that were assigned to your squad when we were bandit hunting were both killed. I'm the only one left." He lowered his gaze. "The entire war is senseless! What *reason* did they have for attacking in the first place?"

She shrugged. "I heard some of our people attacked their *current* Lord while he was traveling with his wife and mistress. I don't know how much truth there is to that." She pressed his hand. "It's good to still have a friend in the clan."

He smiled wryly. "Some of '*our*' people? So you still feel you belong to Torust?"

She gave a short laugh. "I gave most of my *life* to Torust. I think I'll *always* feel a part of it."

***

Winter Y1068

Hathan smiled at the infant in Sylda's arms. "What's her name?"

"Nisa."

"Welcome to the family, Nisa."

***

Autumn Y1069

Hathan brought Brock to the tree house he'd built. He showed his son how to climb the ladder and followed behind him. He smiled at the boy's expression when they went inside. "How do you like it?"

"This is *gweat* pa."

"If you like, I can come up with you to play here sometimes." He showed the boy a box on one side of the room. "You can keep some of your toys here."

"Wow!" Brock pulled rocks out of his pockets and put them inside the box. He hugged his father. "I keep my *wocks* here."

Hathan chuckled, returning the hug. "I think your ma will like that."

***

Winter Y1069

Hathan sat beside Kuren, his arms folded across his chest, and his brow furrowed. "So now they want *farm workers* to go to war?"

Kuren shrugged, nodding. "I guess they're running out of guards."

The speaker looked around the room. "Weapons' training will start immediately. You'll all ship out in the spring. Are there any question?"

Hathan stood. "How long are we going to be out fighting? I have a wife and two children. Are they supposed to just wait for the war to be over before we see each other again?"

"We'll allow those of you who are married to return on furlough during the winter to visit with your families. The storms make combat too difficult then, and we can get by with fewer troops."

Kuren grunted. "That leaves *me* out."

Hathan sat back down. "Sylda ain't going to be happy to have me gone so long."

***

Early Spring Y1070

Brock saw his father sitting on the front steps. He sat beside him. "Whatcha doin pa?"

His father smiled at him. "I'm waiting, son. Your ma told me to wait out here while she got ready to say goodbye."

"Oh." He looked at his feet. "You gonna be gone long?"

His father put an arm around him. "I'll be back for the winter. You can bet on that."

"I gonna miss you, pa. Ma won't go into the tree house with me."

"I know, son." He patted his side. "Hey, where's my satchel? I have a present for you in it."

"You leave it inside?"

"I must have. Will you get it for me? Your ma don't want me in her house until she's ready to see me off."

"Ok."

Brock went inside the house. His mother sat at the table, her face in her hands, her shoulders shaking. He put his hand on her arm. "Ma? What's wrong?"

She lifted her head and smiled at him through her tears. "I just don't want your pa to go away. That's all. Don't tell him I was crying."

"I won't. Pa wants his satchel."

She sniffed, pointing at where it hung on the wall. "It's over there."

He carried the satchel to his father, who opened it and pulled out a rag doll. "Here, your grandma made this when I was your age. She made one for each of us." He pointed at the doll's coat. "She used scraps from my clothes to make it and took a lock of my hair for its head." He smiled. "I thought this could sit in my place at the table while I'm gone and you could pretend I'm eating with you."

"A *doll*? Pa, I ain't a *girl*. You sure this ain't for *Nisa*?"

"You don't have to play with it. Just leave it at the table."

Brock hung his head. "Ok."

His father reached out and lifted his chin. "Cheer up. I'll be back. I'll *always* come back, I promise. Tell you what, when I come home again, I'll bring you a rock from the battlefield."

Brock smiled. "Thanks. That's way better than a *doll*."

"Why don't you take the doll and put it in my place at the table?"

"Ok."

***

Late Summer Y1070

Yadrac slipped through the brush. One benefit of fighting on destroyed holding ground was that the fertile soil supported concealing vegetation. He'd tracked a band of fighters to the ruins of a farmhouse that had once been home to holding workers. There was no way to know if they were friend or foe until he could see their coats. He crept around the perimeter of their campsite. If they were friendly, they might have urfren. If an urfren caught his scent, it would alert its partner.

He reached a spot from which he could see the people in the camp. They were wearing enemy coats. His eyes narrowed. There were too many of them for him to take on by himself, even *with* Kiko's help.

He ordered Kiko to hide and found a place where he could spy on the entire camp. He'd find the nearest company and report on the enemy's presence. They had a prisoner, a dark woman wearing the *Torust* coat. He watched as an enemy guard led her to the corner of a broken wall and allowed her to relieve herself. She limped as she walked and favored her right arm. He bit his lip. They needed *every* fighter. If he could slip in and free her, it would be worth the effort.

He observed as she was bound to a tree on one side of the camp. The men in the camp argued. They shouted, and one of them pointed at her. Others stood between him and her, shoving him back. The man glared at his fellow soldiers.

Yadrac's lip curled. "Filthy pig," he muttered.

He waited, half dozing, until late night when the enemy camp was still before creeping through it to the prisoner.

Silently, he made his way to where a guard stood watch over the sleeping woman. He came up behind the man and took him out, dragging the body back into the brush and looting the man's weapons before slipping to the woman's side. He covered her mouth with his hand, and she stiffened.

"Shh. I'm here to get you out," he whispered. "Let me see your hands."

Moments later, she was free.

He passed her the weapons he'd taken from the guard he'd killed. "Ok, let's get out of here."

She nodded.

They'd just left the tree when a man came towards where the prisoner had been sleeping. "Hey Delor," he called softly. "Be a sport and let me have one little go at her."

Yadrac pushed the woman towards the brush. "Go! *I'll* take care of him."

She slipped into the shadows as the man came closer and Yadrac stalked him. Just as he was ready to pounce, she leaped out of the bushes and plunged the sword he'd given her into the man's body. Yadrac shut his eyes and sighed as the man let out a yelp and the camp came alive.

"Kiko! To me!"

The woman gasped, turning. "Yadrac?"

His head jerked towards her. "What?"

"It's me, Marrasi." She gulped. "I'm sorry I spoiled the kill. He'd been trying to get at me since they caught me. I couldn't *bear* it any longer."

"Well, it's too late for 'sorry' now. Get going. Kiko and I will delay them. We can escape more easily than you could."

"Thank you." She fled.

* * *

Kuren was the first to reach the spot where the cry had come from. A man lay on the ground near where the prisoner had been bound. The woman was nowhere to be seen. He moved forward.

"Kill!"

The very ground seemed to rise in front of him as a monstrous beast leaped out of the bushes. The animal clamped its teeth on his sword arm, shearing the limb completely off. Crunching noises followed as the beast ate the severed arm. He fell to the ground, screaming. He heard his squad mates running towards him.

"Kill!"

The beast left him where he'd fallen and leaped on another guard.

He heard Hathan shouting. "Someone's giving it orders! There! *I'll* get him."

"Kill!"

He sank into darkness.

When he came to, he lay in a bedroll. He groaned. He had no energy, and his shoulder ached and throbbed.

A hand touched his good shoulder. "Hey soldier. How you doing?"

"What happened?" His voice was barely audible, but it was too much effort to speak louder.

"The prisoner escaped. We lost nearly a dozen guards. Three more have severe injuries, including you. We'll be retreating as soon as we can. Count yourself lucky to be alive."

He swallowed. "How many *were* there?"

"Just one man and an urfren. Hathan killed the man. When he did that, the beast went berserk and tore him to pieces before turning on the rest of us. We barely killed it."

He choked, his chin trembling. "Hathan's dead?"

"I'm afraid so."

Kuren shut his eyes, and the tears spilled over. "He wanted to bring a rock from the battlefield to his son."

"I'll pass the word around. Rest now. We nearly lost you, too." The healer sighed. "We found Bithin near where we'd tied the prisoner. Delor's body was in the bushes. I think

Bithin interrupted a rescue. I'll bet anything that if Bithin hadn't been thinking with his wrong head, we probably would have only lost Delor."

***

Marrasi hesitated at the door to the guards' crèche. She closed her eyes briefly before stepping inside. A caretaker came forward. "May I help you?"

"I heard Yadrac had a child in here."

The other woman nodded. "Yes. He has a daughter." She pointed at a little girl with warm brown skin, dark brown curly hair, and bright green eyes. "Her name is Mohara."

"What of the child's mama?"

The caretaker shook her head. "Verda died when Mohara was a toddler."

Marrasi bit her lip. "They killed Yadrac a few weeks ago. His daughter is an orphan."

The other woman sighed. "*Most* of the children here are orphans. Thank you for letting us know about Yadrac."

"He saved my life. I'd like to become his daughter's guardian. I don't want her to grow up as a crèche orphan."

"Are you *sure* of that? It's an enormous responsibility."

Marrasi nodded. "I'd like to take her with me now. She looks to be old enough to start guard training."

"It's a little early for her to start guard training. She's not quite six."

"These ain't normal times."

***

Early Autumn Y1070

"Brock? Come here, please." His mother's voice sounded odd.

He came into the front room. His mother sat on the couch holding his sister, tears running down her face. His father's friend Kuren stood in front of her, head hanging, his hair grown long and tied back in a ponytail. One of his sleeves hung empty. A knot tied off the loose end.

He eyed the two adults. "Yes, ma?"

His mother turned to him, her chin trembling. "Your pa died. He ain't coming home."

He stared at her, shaking his head. "No!"

"I'm sorry. He wanted you to have these." Kuren held a bag towards him.

Brock slapped the bag from his hand and turned, running to the table, where he grabbed the doll. He picked the doll up by one of its legs and slammed it against the table. "Pa *promised me*!" He slammed the doll against the table over and over until its head burst open. Then he dropped the doll and ran outside to the tree house. He climbed the ladder and sat beside the box his father had made for him, sobbing.

When he went back inside the house, his mother was mending the doll, his sister on a blanket at her feet. He retreated to his room.

***

Summer Y1071

Brock stomped around the house and stopped short. A strange man sat on the front steps, gazing at a carriage by the gate to the yard. He stomped over to him and stood glaring. "What *you* doin here?"

The man blinked at him. "I-I'm waiting."

"What you waiting for?"

"I d-don't know. Sh-she said to w-wait out here." He stared blankly into the distance.

Brock frowned and sat on the step beside him.

After several minutes, the man stuck a finger inside one of his boots and ran it around the top, then patted himself and turned to him. "Where's m-my satchel? I h-had a satchel. D-didn't I?"

Brock shrugged. "Maybe you left it somewhere."

"Oh." The man hung his head. "I have a p-present for y-you in it."

The hair on the back of Brock's neck stood on end. He stared at the man. "What?"

"I-I have a present for y-you in m-my satchel." He frowned. "Or d-did I already give it t-to you? I d-don't remember."

"Pa? Is that you? You came *back*?"

The man smiled at him. "Of c-course it's m-me. Who d-did you think it w-was? Did you think I w-wouldn't come b-back? I *always* come b-back. You *know* that. I-I've gone away b-before."

Brock burst into tears and threw himself at the man, wrapping his arms around him. The stranger was very thin and had silver hair with gold eyes and skin. He looked *nothing* like Brock's father, but how *else* could he have known about the present in the satchel?

"Oh pa, they said you were *dead*!"

The man nodded. "Y-yes. I r-remember. There w-was a grave." He hugged Brock. "I m-missed you. It's b-been so l-long."

The door behind them opened, and Brock heard his mother gasp. "Brock! Get away from that man right *now*!"

He turned. His mother stood in the doorway with a strange woman. He looked back at the man. "But…"

His mother grabbed his arm and pulled him away from the man. She turned to the strange woman. "Get him *out* of here. *Now*! I can't have a crazy man around my children."

The strange woman huffed and held her hand towards the man. "Come on. We'll try somewhere else."

The man turned and stared at Brock. "B-but…"

"Come *on*." The woman pressed her lips together into a straight line and grabbed the man's hand, jerking him to his feet and pulling him after her.

As the strangers were walking towards the carriage by the gate in front of the house, Brock's mother hugged him. "Did he hurt you?"

Brock frowned at her, pointing at the man. "Ma! That's pa come back."

She shook her head. "Don't be silly. That ain't your pa. He don't look anything *like* your pa. He's a crazy man Mistress Sia asked me to care for. I told her we can't have him here."

He stared at her, then turned towards where the woman was pulling the man towards the carriage. The man was stumbling after the woman, dragging his feet and staring back with a bewildered look on his face. Brock's throat hurt. Tears ran down his cheeks.

"Pa's *inside* him. He *talked* to me. He said things only *pa* knew."

"What?"

He sniffed, turning back to her. "Pa's come *back* and you're sending him *away*!" He pulled out of her arms and fled to the tree house, where he threw himself on the floor by the box his father had made for him.

It was dusk when he climbed down from the tree house. His chin trembled as he trudged to the house, opened the door, and stepped inside. The strange man sat on the couch, staring blankly at the fire. Brock froze.

His mother came up behind him and wrapped her arms around him. "Brock, this is Master Gary. He's a sick old man who needs someone to take care of him. I told Mistress Sia that we could *try* taking care of him for a little while and see how it goes." She turned him around and knelt to look into his face. "Master Gary lost his little boy many years ago, and that makes him very sad. Sometimes he hurts himself. Mistress Sia don't think he'll try to hurt *us*, but if he ever does *anything* that scares you, you come and *tell* me. Understand?"

He nodded.

"Ok then. Why don't you go talk to him?"

Aftermath
Homelands: Early Spring Y1072

An explosive blasted a hole in the holding's wall that surrounded the Moraven keep, and the last battle of the war had begun. The Torust forces fought their way to the keep wall and scaled it. Tylen, along with his two remaining companions, Lisha and Faro, had already dropped into the garden when the enemy engaged the bulk of their forces.

Tylen looked up towards the sounds of battle coming from the top of the wall. "We must go on. The others will hold the enemy off." His companions nodded, and the three moved on, deeper into the keep grounds.

As they continued through the garden, the trio stumbled upon a pair of sentries and they exchanged shots. One bullet hit the explosives Lisha had on her person and all of them went off at once, splattering everyone in range with bits of bone and gore. Tylen felt a blow strike his side, but downed one sentry. He turned towards the other one, but Faro had already taken that one out.

"Let's go," he hissed at his remaining companion, but the other man sank to his knees, coughing blood.

Tylen grabbed Faro by the shoulders of his coat and dragged him to the nearest wall. Faro opened and closed his mouth a couple times as if he were trying to speak before he became still, but all that came out was blood. Tylen closed his eyes for a moment and rubbed his signet ring. He was alone now and wounded. Methodically, he stripped the ammo and explosives from Faro's body and added them to his own arsenal. It was up to *him* now. He set his kinsman against the wall in a seated position with his gun at his side and gave him a salute of respect before setting off to find a hiding place from which he could assess his remaining options.

***

Korander followed Moze to the site of the last battle.

"As far as we can tell," the spymaster said. "All were clan, either full blood or bastards. It was a suicide mission. They must have known they couldn't do anything against us. We'd already defeated them before they even *started* their attack."

They reached the site and Korander stood frozen, staring at the bodies the guards had laid out for viewing. Many of them were children, and some of *those* were smaller than his youngest son. His gorge rose in his throat.

"Did we take any prisoners?"

"We captured two of the younger children alive. They're both injured, and we took them to the infirmary. Every other Torust is dead."

"Why would they *do* this? They could have hidden in a slum and we'd never have known."

"They did it to save their followers. You're connected to house Eldragon. If any Torust lived, your wife's clan would seek until they found the slum where they'd taken refuge and burn it to the ground to ensure the last of them was dead. By sacrificing themselves this way, house Torust has ensured that their disenfranchised followers will survive."

Korander closed his eyes. "Treat them with respect and bury them." He regretted the children's deaths, but couldn't think of anything he could have done differently that would have changed this.

A guard came running up and saluted. "Sir! Some of them got into the keep gardens."

In the gardens, they found the bodies of a pair of sentries who'd been on patrol. One sentry still lived, but the other was dead. Korander ordered the survivor taken to the infirmary and tended to. A third body lay nearby, damaged so badly that it would take a thorough exam in order to even tell if it was a man or a woman. From the condition of the corpse, a massive explosion had caused the death. Moze pointed to a trail of blood that led towards the wall.

At the end of the blood trail, they found another body wearing a Torust clan coat. This was a man, and he sat against the wall with his head hanging as if he was asleep. Moze prodded him with a stick and he fell over. A closer exam revealed that someone had stripped him of everything but his gun and even that didn't have any ammo.

"There must be at least one more," Moze said grimly.

"We'll see if the surviving sentry can tell us anything."

In the infirmary, Korander waited with his honor guard and spymaster for the healers to finish tending the surviving sentry. Finally, the door opened.

"She's awake and able to speak," the senior healer said.

Korander led the way into the room and sat beside the bed. "What can you tell us about your attackers?"

"There were three of them," she whispered. "When we shot, one of them exploded. I don't know what happened to the other two."

He gently pressed her hand. "Thank you. We found one of the other attackers. Your information tells us that there may only be one still out there."

She smiled and closed her eyes.

"She needs to rest," the healer said.

Korander nodded. "I think I need to talk to the prisoners. Would that be possible?"

"They're this way."

The healer led the way through the infirmary hallways to another room. Inside the room were two beds, which were occupied by a pair of young boys. Korander eyed them thoughtfully. One was barely more than a toddler. Even the larger of the two was smaller than his youngest son. The smaller boy's eyelids fluttered open, and he stared at Korander. Tears welled up in his pale blue eyes and spilled onto his dusky cheeks. The healer knelt beside the bed and brushed the hair off his forehead.

"Hush. It's all right. You're *safe* here."

"I want my ma."

"I'm sorry. I don't know where she is."

Moze glanced at Korander out of the corner of his eye. "You wanted to talk to them." He gestured at the tiny figures on the beds. "There they are."

Korander drew a deep breath. "How badly are they injured?"

The healer turned towards him. "The older boy has a head injury and ain't yet awoken. This one has multiple, lesser injuries."

"Do we know if they're full clan?"

"Each member of the Torust forces had their name embroidered on their coats and satchels. These two are Podero and Sazad."

"No clan name?"

Moze shook his head. "All the evidence we've found suggests that they're both clan bastards."

Korander sighed. "Once they're recovered from their injuries, send them to a crèche. Do your best to convince them to switch allegiance to house Moraven." He gripped Moze's shoulder. "I'll leave *which* crèche up to your discretion."

***

Korander looked up from his dinner. "You have something to report?"

Moze nodded, gesturing towards the woman by his side. "Trika discovered something when we took Torust keep."

Korander motioned for Trika to speak. I suppose it was too much to hope Moze caught the last Torust.

"Sir, we found urfren kennels in the keep. We await your orders before we proceed further."

"Urfren?"

She nodded. "There are pups in the kennels. We should be able to salvage more than enough to start our own pack."

Korander stood. "I'll come myself. I want to see them. We'll take a transport." He turned to Moze. "You stay here and continue searching for the Torust in the gardens."

Moze nodded.

Upon arriving at Torust keep, Trika led the way to a large enclosure, which contained nearly forty urfren, the biggest of which was the size of a large dog.

Korander frowned at the beasts. "I thought urfren were bigger than that."

"We believe they're pups, sir. The smallest of the ones we faced out in the fields were at least twice the size of the largest of these. There are also more kennels in that building." She pointed.

"Show me."

Trika nodded, and they proceeded into a building with several large runs, three of which held urfren bitches with young pups. Korander stopped in front of one and stared at the bitch inside.

"*This* is more like it."

He placed a hand on the door to the run, and the bitch charged, growling. He stepped back.

"Can they get out?"

Trika shook her head. "You don't want to get too close though, sir. The bitches are all vicious."

Korander examined the door. "Have you been able to feed them?"

"We can feed most of the pups in the big enclosure out front. The bitches in here are too aggressive, though. We tried tossing bits of meat through the bars in the doors, but the bitches just pushed the food back out when we moved away."

He walked along the row of runs, looking inside each one. Each urfren bitch had a litter of pups, and all three reacted with hostility towards his presence.

"Do we have anyone who knows anything about handling urfren?"

"We have dog handlers, sir, but that's it."

"Are there any documents about urfren in the Torust records?"

Trika shrugged. "We ain't found anything, but we ain't been here long. We only took this place yesterday."

Korander headed out of the building. "Get some archivists here. I want the keep records searched thoroughly. If they had *any* written information, get it. I want to salvage as many of the pack as possible for myself."

"Yes, sir."

* * *

"My Lord?"

Korander looked up from the stack of records he'd been reading. "Yes?"

"An urfren bitch killed and ate one of her pups."

He frowned. "Did you try feeding her?"

"Yes, sir. We'd actually offered her food just before she killed the pup, but she refused it. She's the smallest of the bitches and only has three pups. Well, two now."

He sighed. "Kill her. In fact, kill all three bitches. As much as I'd love to, I think we can forget about taming any of them. If the pups need to nurse, we'll feed them by hand. We ain't found anything in the records on the care and handling of the beasts."

The guard nodded and left.

Korander turned to the archivists sitting at the table who were going through the records. "Keep searching. If there's anything here on urfren, I want it brought to Moraven keep."

"Yes, sir."

He strode out of the room, heading to the large enclosure that held the smaller urfren. When he reached it, he found a trio of guards just outside the gate, playing with a pair of the animals. He stood, watching, until one of them noticed him.

The guard came to attention and saluted. "Your Lordship!"

He gestured towards the enclosure. "Are *all* of them this friendly?"

"Well, the largest ones are aggressive. We pulled those out and caged them away from the others." The guard pointed at a row of cages by the wall on one side of the courtyard.

"Have you been able to feed any of those?"

The guards shook their heads.

"Only the smaller ones like this one will accept food from us." The guard who'd spoken reached down and patted the urfren closest to him. The beast's shoulders came to just above the man's knee.

Korander drew his brows together as he regarded the young urfren. "Are all the ones you've been able to feed as friendly as these?"

The guards nodded.

"Bring all of them to Moraven. I'm on my way back to the

keep myself. I'll order kennels built to house the urfren." He looked again at the urfren in the cages by the wall. "Keep trying to tame those other ones, but if we can't, we can't."

"Yes, sir."

***

Mid-Spring Y1072

Captain Trika paced in front of the group assembled before her. Her eyes darted around the assembly hall. The recruits barely filled the seats directly in front of the dais. *His Lordship has ambitious plans for this unit.* "We ain't been able to find any documents on urfren among the Torust records." She grimaced. "Our Lord gave me this assignment solely because I was the one who informed Moze of the urfren we found in Torust keep. We chose each of you because you either have experience with dogs or survived an encounter with urfren."

One young man raised his hand. Trika nodded at him. "Your name is?"

"My name is Vemus ma'am."

"You may speak, Vemus."

"Um. Ma'am, I'm just a farm worker that was recruited to fight at the end of the war. I've only worked with farm dogs. I thought I was supposed to go back to my family's farm after the war was over."

"Well, Vemus, we lost a *lot* of guards during the war, and they need to be replaced. Any farm workers recruited for the war that showed skill in battle will remain guards." She smiled at him. He was a handsome man with black hair and blue eyes. A newly healed scar crossed his left eye. He was lucky he hadn't lost it. "Your status has increased permanently. If you wish to visit your family, you may do so when you have free time, but you can expect to spend the rest of your life as a guard. As for your experience with farm dogs, that's more experience than most natal guards have. It's more than *I* have."

He shook his head. "I don't *want* to be a guard. My family has a farm that I'd prefer to return to. I've got a sweetheart in my home holding. She's been waiting two years for me to return so we can get married."

Trika's smile faded. "Well, I'm sure his Lordship will allow you to marry if you wish to do so. As a guard, you may request your betrothed brought here, so you'll have her with you." She waved towards a door at the back of the hall that led to the kennels. "This will be your station so you can work with the urfren. Our unit will have our own crèche. If you wish to marry a holding worker, we can assign her to work there. Crèche staff ain't required to be guards."

* * *

Marsa dropped her bag on the first available bunk in the crèche dorm and looked around. *Is the paint on the walls still wet?* She stepped to the wall at the head of her bunk and pressed it with the tip of her finger. It was dry, but her finger left a dent in the painted plaster. She snorted. *Almost.*

She returned to where she'd dropped her bag and set to work unpacking her things.

Once she'd settled into her new quarters, she left the dorm room to explore. There weren't many children in the crèche yet, so there wasn't much to do. She familiarized herself with the layout of the rooms and left the crèche in search of her mother.

She entered the main barracks section of the building and reached the entry into a lounge area. She stopped in the opening. A pair of young men, one blond, the other with dark hair, both of whom appeared to be engrossed in writing letters, sat on couches. She entered the room.

"Excuse me, could one of you tell me where I could find Captain Trika?"

The dark-haired man glanced up. He was an attractive young man, and the scar across his left eye did nothing to detract from his good looks. "I think she's in the kennels."

"Ah." Marsa smiled at him and shrugged. "I just arrived. I don't know where the kennels are."

He pointed at a door on the far wall before returning his attention to his letter. "It's through there."

She nodded. "Thanks."

She glanced over her shoulder at the door and caught the blond staring at her. Her eyes met his, and she winked. The color rose in his cheeks and he buried his nose in his letter.

She chuckled and exited the room.

On the other side of the door, she faced three large kennel runs. Through the barred doors, she could see a wolf-like animal, about the size of a mastiff in each run. A woman with a baby on her back knelt in front of one door, her attention on the beast inside.

Marsa took a step forward. "Hello."

The woman stood and turned. Marsa recognized her. It was Yakara, an old friend of hers. She rushed forward and embraced her. "Kara! What are *you* doing here?"

Yakara grimaced. "They assigned me to the crèche."

Marsa laughed. "Me too." She peered at the baby on her friend's back. "Is the baby *yours*?"

Her friend nodded. "I'm *married* too." She pulled a blue wedding ribbon from her satchel and waved it at Marsa. "He's one of the holding recruits they assigned here to work with the urfren." She laughed. "He didn't feel comfortable just being lovers."

"You carry that around?"

Yakara smiled tenderly at the ribbon. "I never dreamed I'd *feel* this way. I always thought I'd take lover after lover like ma did, but I'm *proud* to be his wife. We've made a commitment to each other for the rest of our lives. That *means* something."

"So what's his name?"

"His name is Derrath. We've been together for nearly a year and a half now." Yakara tucked the ribbon back into her satchel. "But enough about me. I take it *you're* here because your ma's in charge of the unit?"

Marsa nodded. "It's my first assignment." She wrinkled her nose. "I wasn't *quite* old enough to be sent to fight during the war."

"Well, you just missed your ma."

"Where did she go?"

"She went to the other kennel." Yakara linked arms with Marsa. "I'll show you."

After Marsa checked in with her mother, Yakara offered to give her a tour of the building. The two young women were still together when it was time for the noon meal. Yakara led the way to the dining hall. They were filling their plates from the sideboard when a blond man came up behind them and kissed Yakara on the back of her neck.

"Hey beautiful, where've you been all my life?"

Yakara shot a stern glance over her shoulder. "You know I'm married, don't you?"

He grinned at her as he pulled the baby out of the pack. "What a coincidence." He kissed the baby on the cheek. "So am *I*!"

Yakara laughed. "Marsa, this big goof is my husband." She waved at Marsa. "Derrath, Marsa here is a friend of mine from the crèche where I grew up. She arrived today."

Marsa offered him her hand. "I'm assigned to the crèche here."

"Glad to meet you." He shook her hand.

"Have you gotten your food yet?"

He nodded. "I'm over there." He pointed at a table. "Come join me after you fill your plates." He kissed the baby's cheek again. "I'll take Sisca."

"Ok. We'll be right there." Yakara kissed him on the lips and he headed for the table.

When Marsa and Yakara joined Derrath at the table, he gestured towards a man seated beside him. "Marsa, this is Vemus, a friend of mine. We call him Vee."

Vemus was the man with the scarred face that Marsa had seen in the lounge area by the kennels. She smiled at him as she extended her hand. "Hello, I believe we've already met."

He scrambled to his feet and shook her hand. "Yeah, I was writing a letter."

"Who was the other man with you?"

"That would be Anrin. He's seated over there." He pointed at one of the other tables.

Marsa turned to look at the table he'd pointed at and caught Anrin staring at her. She waved. His face turned bright red, contrasting with his pale hair. He waved hesitantly back. She giggled as she sat.

As they took their seats, Derrath turned to Vemus. "I think there's just something we ain't figured out. We got all of them safely into the runs. There's no need to take extreme measures. They ain't full grown yet after all."

Vemus shook his head. "They ain't full grown yet, sure,

but that's the only reason we've been able to control them. We can't tame them. What do you think will happen once they *are* full grown? I seen a man get his *head* bit off. I spent time in the infirmary with another that got his arm bit off. They're *dangerous*. We've got plenty of the younger ones. We don't *need* the ones we can't tame."

Marsa raised a brow. "What are you talking about?"

Derrath sighed. "Some urfren we found at Torust keep are actively hostile. Vemus thinks we should just kill them."

Vemus snorted. "We've only been able to feed them by putting live rabbits and chickens in the runs with them. If someone hadn't figured *that* out, they would've already starved to death."

Yakara took the baby from her husband and offered her a breast. "They're talking about the urfren that are kept in individual runs. Everyone's supposed to try feeding them. Our leaders think if we can get them to eat, they'll allow themselves to be tamed. It's why I was in the kennel when you arrived."

***

That night, after the evening meal, Marsa joined Yakara and the two men in a lounge. During the evening, Yakara and Derrath slipped away, leaving Marsa alone with Vemus. She turned towards him with a smile.

"It looks like they abandoned us."

He drained his mug. "Yeah."

"So," she tipped her head to one side, "tell me more about why you think those urfren are so dangerous."

He set his mug on the table where they sat. "All right then. I grew up as a holding farm worker. I *know* dogs. We use them to handle our livestock. Dogs that act like those urfren have to be put down. They're vicious and untamable."

"You sound very sure of yourself, but Derrath disagrees."

"I'll *prove* it." He rose to his feet. "Follow me."

The two of them left the lounge and went to the kennels, where he uncovered a light globe. He gestured towards the nearest run. The urfren inside was solid black with white paws and a white spot over each eye. It paced back and forth in the run, growling.

Marsa knelt in front of the door. Vemus grasped her by the shoulder.

"Don't get too close."

"Ain't we supposed to try feeding them?"

"Yeah. They think if we can get them to take food, we'll somehow tame them and they'll become friendly. We've been feeding them live rabbits and chickens though, and it ain't made any difference."

She extracted a bag of jerky from her satchel. "Let's see if *I* can succeed." She tossed a small piece through the bars of the door into the run. The urfren inside dodged the treat as if it were a venomous snake.

"See?" Vemus gestured at the beast. "They *all* do that."

"Maybe they think we're trying to poison them. Ain't urfren supposed to be super smart?"

He snorted. "Even the *smartest* dog is still just a dog, and that's all they are, big dogs."

Marsa pulled a larger piece of jerky from the bag and held it up. "I know with children, sometimes you have to show them that strange food is good." She waved the piece of jerky back and forth. "Look dog. I have good food." She took a bite. "Yum, yum."

Vemus snorted. "You really think that'll work?"

"It can't hurt."

She took another bite and tossed the rest into the run. The urfren caught it in mid-air and gulped it down.

"It ate it!"

"What?"

She pointed at the urfren in the run. It rooted among the straw in its run and ate the first piece of jerky she'd tossed in. Then it came to the door, where it shoved its nose through the bars, whining. She reached towards it. Vemus's hand tightened on her shoulder.

"Don't."

Her finger touched the tip of the animal's nose and it licked her hand through the bars. She looked up at Vemus. He'd covered his eyes with his free hand.

"It seems friendly enough *now*." She pulled out of his grasp and inched closer to the door so she could stick her hand through the bars to scratch the urfren's ears. The animal wagged its tail furiously as it pressed against the bars of the door.

"I don't *believe* it!"

She glanced up at him again. He was now staring at the urfren. She laughed.

"I guess even someone who knows a lot about dogs can learn something new."

He stepped closer to the door to the run. The urfren turned towards him, baring its teeth and growling. He stepped back.

"Well, you seem to have gotten it to accept *you*, but not anyone else."

"Be *nice*," she scolded the beast. It whined again and licked her hand. She turned towards Vemus. "Maybe *you* need to give it some food now. If it accepted food from *me*, it should accept some from you too. Shouldn't it?" She offered him the bag of jerky.

"Could you move back while I try this?"

She nodded and rose to her feet, stepping away from the run. Vemus pulled a piece of jerky from the bag and tossed it through the bars. The urfren dodged away from it. He pulled out a larger piece and took a bite, tossing the rest into the run. This time, the urfren not only dodged the piece, it bristled and barked furiously as it pawed and bit at the bars of the door. He backed away from the run.

"Wow! None of them have ever reacted *that* way before."

Marsa frowned. "*Bad* dog! No! Stop that. Be *nice*." It turned towards her and dropped to the floor of the run, rolling onto its back. It swished its tail back and forth, its eyes on her face. A giggle escaped her and the beast leapt to its feet. It whirled in a circle beside the door, barking excitedly. It ended its antics crouched on its front legs, its bottom high in the air with its tail wagging furiously, still barking.

"I think we should tell the captain about this."

Marsa turned towards him. "You're right. I expect she's in her room now."

He looked over his shoulder at the door to the barracks. "Eh, maybe it can wait until morning."

She shook her head. "No. This is important." She grabbed his hand and pulled him after her as she headed through the door.

215

"What if she's... not alone?"

"Then she'll put her personal business aside to deal with what we just discovered."

She dragged him through the building to her mother's office and opened the door. It was unoccupied, but she could see light under the inner door. Marsa pointed. "She's still awake." She released his hand to tap on the door. Her mother opened it. She wore a robe over a nightshirt.

"Yes?"

"I got one of the urfren to eat food from my hand." Marsa peered through the door. Her father stood by a table, dressed similarly to her mother. She waved at him. He nodded back at her.

Trika embraced her. "That's *wonderful* dear! Give us a minute to get dressed and we'll come see."

When they returned to the kennel, Marsa went directly to the run with the urfren who'd accepted food from her and reached inside. It leaned against the door so she could scratch its ears. "See? It's *friendly* now."

Vemus shook his head. "It's only friendly to *her*. It reacted violently when *I* tried to give it food."

Marsa's father narrowed his eyes. "What did you do?" He knelt beside her.

"I just gave it some jerky after taking a couple bites, like we do for children that are reluctant to eat new foods."

"Show me."

She pointed at Vemus. "Vee has my bag of jerky."

Her father rose to his feet and faced the younger man. "Ok then. *He* can show me what you did."

Vemus gulped. "Yes, sir." He pulled a large piece of jerky from the bag. "Ah, which one should I offer it to? I already tried this with Marsa's urfren and it went into a fury."

Marsa's father smiled, his teeth gleaming under his thick mustache. He made a grand gesture that included every run in the building. "*Pick* one."

Vemus nodded and moved to the run to the right of the one that housed Marsa's urfren. He held up the piece of jerky to ensure the beast inside saw it and took a bite. He tossed the rest of the piece inside. The urfren caught it in mid-air and ate it. Its ears perked up, and it pressed against the door. As if in a dream, Vemus moved forward and reached inside to scratch the animal behind the ears.

Trika turned to Marsa's father. "Moze? What do we do now?"

He glanced at Marsa. "I'll have to talk to his Lordship about this before we take any further action. Ain't Marsa assigned to the crèche?"

"Yes. Ilith is the matron." She grimaced. "She won't be happy to lose one of her subordinates."

"Marsa must stay in the crèche. She can split her time between working with the urfren and tending to her assigned duties. It would be best *not* to place her under your direct command."

Trika nodded, turning to Marsa and Vemus. "Don't feed any other urfren. If they only become tame for one person, we want each of them to have a different handler." She took Moze's hand. "I want to see both of you in my office first thing in the morning."

After Marsa's parents had left, Vemus turned to her, his eyes wide. "Do you know who that *was*?"

She nodded. "Of *course* I do." She reached inside her urfren's run and gave it a last pat. "I think we should retire for the night. It's getting late and we'll need to get up early tomorrow if we're going to see the captain before breakfast."

"You're awful calm about interrupting Captain Trika and Spymaster Moze."

She laughed. "Why *shouldn't* I be? We had important news they needed to hear." She grabbed his hand and pulled. "Come on, we need to head to bed."

The color rose in his cheeks. "Goodnight then." He kissed the back of her hand. "I guess I'll see you tomorrow."

Her eyes twinkled. "I'm assigned to the crèche. There are guest rooms. You could spend the night."

He extracted his hand from hers and handed her the bag of jerky. "No."

"No?"

"No." His chin firmed. "I'm betrothed. I ain't spending the night with another woman."

She nodded. "Very well, I can respect that." She waved at him. "See you in the morning, then."

***

Late Spring Y1072

Anrin stopped. Someone had pinned a notice to the door of the dining hall. '*All squad members are to go to the assembly hall after lunch,*' the notice said. He glanced at Nabak, who'd come up behind him.

"We have an assembly after lunch."

The other man nodded. "Wonder what this one's about."

Anrin shrugged. "I guess we'll see when we get there." He opened the door and entered the dining hall. Once inside, he glanced around the room. Derrath and his wife sat at a table. The pretty, dark-haired girl sat beside Yakara. She hadn't been present at breakfast. He stared at her. All the other women here were older than him and/or involved with another man. The girl's dark eyes were bright as she laughed at something.

Would they mind if I joined them?

He filled a plate at the sideboard, but when he turned around, Vemus had sat by the girl's side. *He* hadn't been present at breakfast either. Anrin ground his teeth. Every time he'd seen the girl, she'd been with Vemus.

Ain't Vee betrothed? Is he planning on making the girl his side lover? Who does he think he is anyway, a clansman? He slunk to a different table and stole glances at the girl throughout lunch.

When he entered the assembly hall, his eyes widened. Spymaster Moze sat at a desk in the room's front. Anrin bit his lip. Spymaster Moze was the most powerful commoner in the enclave. He could change your assignment and override orders issued by anyone who wasn't clan. Moze could assign whatever punishment he pleased for any infraction and, supposedly, he made up infractions at whim. He could even assassinate someone and get away with it. The others entering the room took seats as far from the man as possible.

The girl entered the room and walked right to the desk, where she exchanged words with Moze. He pointed towards the side benches near the door to the kennels, and she took a seat near the back. Anrin lifted his chin. If he copied the others and sat as far from Moze as possible, he'd look like a coward to her. He deliberately sat in the center of the front bench by

Moze's desk. Not quite the closest seat to where Moze was, but not as far from the man as possible, either. He glanced over his shoulder just as Vemus sat on the bench beside the girl. He scowled as he turned back to face the front.

Captain Trika took her place in front of the dais and clapped her hands for attention. "Everyone listen up. We've learned what we need to do in order to tame the urfren that we've had to keep separate from the others. Unfortunately, these urfren only become tame towards one person." She smiled as she surveyed the assembled guards. "Still, this is better than their current status." She made a beckoning motion. "We've duplicated the initial taming."

Behind Anrin, a door opened and shut, followed by the click of claws on the floor. He turned to look over his shoulder. Vemus and the girl were walking towards the front of the room, accompanied by two of the urfren that had been in runs by themselves.

Trika motioned for the two to stand on either side of her with their urfren. "As you can see, these urfren are quite tame now, at least regarding their handlers."

She made another gesture, and a pair of senior guards wheeled a cage to the open space in front of the dais. Inside the cage, one of the urfren raged, biting and pawing at the bars. "I would like a volunteer to come forward for a demonstration of the taming process."

Anrin's hand shot up. *This* should earn him the girl's admiration. Trika nodded at him.

"You may come forward."

His mouth dried up as he moved to the front of the cage. Captain Trika came to his side.

"Your name is?"

He swallowed. "My name is Anrin, ma'am."

"All right then, Anrin, here is what you need to do." She handed him a piece of jerky. "Make sure the urfren sees this. Once you have its attention, take a bite and give it what's left of the piece. Be sure it sees you eat a piece of the jerky. Do you understand?"

"Yes, ma'am." He knelt within arm's reach of the cage door and held up the piece of jerky. He waved it to get the animal's attention.

"Hello pup. I have some food for you." The beast's eyes focused on him and he took a bite. He gulped the piece down and glanced at the girl. She was watching him with a smile on her face. He abruptly thrust the hand that held the rest of the jerky through the bars into the cage. He squeezed his eyes tightly shut and held his breath.

The urfren pulled the jerky from his fingers. A whine emerged from the beast and its tongue swiped his hand. He gasped and his eyes flew open. The urfren continued licking his hand.

"You should be able to release it from the cage now."

Anrin slowly opened the door to the cage and the urfren inside rushed out and knocked him over. It stood on top of him and licked his face while it wagged its tail.

Trika stepped past him. "We need volunteers for the remaining problematic urfren. If there are more volunteers than urfren, we'll draw names."

"That was very brave of you, sticking your hand inside the cage like that."

Anrin pushed the urfren's head away from his face and looked up. The girl had come to his side and was leaning over him with a smile on her face. His heart swelled in his breast and his cheeks burned. "Ain't that what I was *supposed* to do?"

She laughed. "*I* just tossed the jerky through the bars in the door. I didn't dare touch *my* urfren until *after* it started acting friendly." She patted her beast and offered him her other hand. "I'm Marsa, by the way."

He accepted the extended hand, and she helped him to his feet. Her touch left him lightheaded. "Thanks." He spent the rest of the assembly standing by her side. The warmth of her presence drove everything else out of his mind.

That night, the kitchen staff served dinner on the recreation patio, as all the recruits celebrated. The servants set out a serving table where the recruits collected their food. Marsa insisted Anrin join her when she went to fill her plate. He couldn't believe his luck. His spirits fell, however, when she led the way to the table Vemus and Derrath had claimed. He drank deeply as they feasted.

At one point, he noticed that Vemus, Marsa, and he were

the only ones left on the patio. Vemus stood.

"We need to head to bed. It's getting late."

Anrin stood as well. "Right."

He swayed and grabbed the table to keep from falling. Marsa put her arm around his waist. She giggled. "Take it easy. I think you had too much to drink."

He hiccoughed. "The floor is rocking."

She pulled his arm around her shoulders. "Come on, I'll get you to bed."

Vemus frowned. "Maybe *I* should take him."

She shook her head. "I've got him. You go on to your own bunk."

He stumbled as she pulled him towards the nearest door leading off the patio. Vemus came to his other side.

"Are you sure you don't need my help with him? I don't think he can handle the stairs."

Marsa laughed. "We'll be fine. I'll just put him down in one of the guest rooms." The door opened onto a lounge and she pointed towards the far exit. "See? They ain't that far. I can get him there by myself. Go to bed."

Vemus sighed. "All right then." He lifted her free hand and kissed it before heading to the door that led to the assembly hall.

Marsa smiled at Anrin. "All right, big guy. Come on. Let's get you to bed."

"Right." He turned his face towards hers and their lips met. The world spun around him.

* * *

Marsa giggled as the kiss ended. "Naughty boy! Are you faking being drunk?" He went limp and his full weight pulled her towards the floor. She barely got him onto a couch before she had to let go. She sighed. "I guess you *ain't* faking." She patted his face. "Wake up and come to bed."

The door to one of the guest rooms opened, and Derrath and Yakara emerged. They rushed to her side.

Derrath frowned at Anrin. "Is he all right? What happened?"

Marsa looked up at him. "He drank too much tonight and passed out." She pouted at Anrin. "We were just going to one of the guest rooms, too."

Yakara sighed. "Marsa, he's one of the holding recruits."

She raised a brow at her friend. "What does *that* have to do with it?"

"I told you about Derrath and me. He wouldn't do more than *kiss* me until after we were married. Anrin likely feels the same."

Marsa sighed. "Are *all* the recruits here from holdings?"

"Almost all. There are a handful of natal guards."

"Phooey!"

Derrath frowned at his wife. "What's the problem?"

"They assigned Marsa as a crèche worker. She planned to spend the night in the guest room with Anrin."

Marsa nodded. "I was so excited to be assigned to the crèche. I ain't been able to take a lover because of the war and now I have open permission to have a baby. The first night I was here, I asked Vee, but he said he's betrothed. Then Anrin kissed me... only to pass out before we could get to the guest room, let alone to the bed."

"Whoa there!" Derrath slapped his forehead.

Yakara frowned. "You can't take him to bed when he's this drunk. You'd be vishing him."

Marsa's shoulders drooped. "I know. I'm just disappointed. That's all."

"Well, let's get him to bed and tuck him in." Derrath picked the younger man up and slung him over his shoulder. "He can spend the night in the room Kara and I used."

***

Anrin groaned. His head pounded and his mouth was dry. He cracked open his eyes. A hooded globe leaked just enough light that he could see he lay on a bed in a strange room. He didn't remember entering the room or getting into the bed. He sat up. All he was wearing was his shirt. Something crinkled as he placed one hand on the pillow. He picked it up. It was a piece of paper, folded into a square. Slowly, he opened it.

It was a note that read: '*Hey sweetie, don't drink so much next time. I want you awake for the fun part. Marsa.*'

His mouth went dry. *What happened last night?* He stared at his surroundings. Someone had folded the rest of his clothes and left them on a chair beside the bed. He dressed hurriedly and left the room. As the door closed behind him, he glanced around. He knew where he was. He'd spent the night in one of the small rooms by the main entry to the lounge beside the assembly hall.

He scurried through the room to the assembly hall door and peered through it. It was empty. He slipped through the door and scrambled across that room to the stairs. The stair door opened as he was reaching for the handle. Theli and Nabak emerged into the assembly hall. They stopped in front of the doorway, staring at him. Nabak eyed Anrin up and down.

"Where have *you* been?"

"Uh, I drank too much at the celebration last night and slept it off in one of the guest rooms."

Theli reached out and plucked something off his shoulder. She held it up. It was a long, black hair. "Who *was* she?" She ran the strand through her fingers. "Was it," she sniffed the hair, "*Marsa*?"

The blood drained from Anrin's face.

"It *was*, wasn't it?" Theli giggled. "I think she's assigned to the crèche. She don't sleep in the women's dorm, anyway. You have a good time?"

Nabak raised a brow. "Is there a special meaning to Marsa being assigned to the crèche?"

Theli nodded. "Crèche workers don't have to ask permission to get pregnant since they wouldn't have to take more than a few days off." She patted Anrin's cheek. "Think we can look forward to a little Anrin in about nine months?"

Anrin snatched the strand of hair from Theli's grasp. "That's none of your business." He pushed past the pair. Her laughter followed him up the stairs.

By the time Anrin reached the dining hall, Marsa had finished eating and was heading out. She came over as he was filling his plate and kissed his cheek.

"Hey sweetie, I have special duties in the crèche today. I'll see you later. Take care."

He stared after her as she passed through the door. *Some*thing happened last night, but *what*? Had he *really* slept with Marsa as Theli implied?

***

Ilith brought two small boys to the front of the room and turned to face the assembled crèche workers. She nodded at the smaller boy. "This is Podero. He broke his left leg, and it didn't heal right, leaving him with a limp." She drew the older boy forward. "This is Sazad. He suffered a head injury and has fits. He needs constant supervision. Since each of them has special needs, we'll house them in the large room at the end of the hall in the crèche infirmary." She eyed the assembled women sternly.

"His Lordship wishes these boys made to feel at home here. Moze believes that since we're a small crèche and ain't likely to have many children in our care, this is the best place for them to be." She knelt between the boys and hugged both of them. "You are all expected to spend time with Podero and Sazad and get to know them today."

Marsa raised her hand. Ilith nodded at her. "You may speak."

"Ma'am, I'm responsible for an urfren now. I have to tend to it. I'm supposed to divide my time between the crèche and caring for my urfren."

The crèche matron smiled at her. "That's an excellent idea. I'll assign you to be Podero and Sazad's primary caretaker. You'll bring your beast here to the crèche. I'm sure it'll make the boys feel more at home."

Yakara covered her mouth. Her shoulders shook as she peeked at Marsa out of the corner of her eyes. Marsa grimaced at her friend.

***

Anrin surveyed the dining hall. Marsa wasn't present. Her urfren had been missing from its run when he'd dropped his own off before coming to the dining hall for lunch. Derrath was there with his wife. He stopped beside the other man before going to the end of the line.

"Um, I was hoping to talk to Marsa. Do you know if she'll be here later?"

Derrath's wife turned to him. "I'm sorry, Anrin. Marsa has a new assignment in the crèche. She'll be eating there for the foreseeable future. You'll have to wait until she has free time

before you can see her again. She asked me to give you this."
She handed him a piece of paper folded into a square.

Numbly, Anrin accepted the note. "Thanks." He tucked it into his satchel.

Derrath smiled at him. "Come to our table after you fill your plate. We'll save you a seat."

After lunch, Anrin cleaned his urfren's run and spread fresh straw over the floor. He made a pile in one corner where he sat with his beast at his feet and pulled Marsa's note out of his satchel.

'*Hey sweetie*,' the note said, '*I'm sorry I missed having breakfast with you this morning. I really want to see you again. I should have free time next week. There's something important we need to talk about. Marsa.*'

He stared at the note. There's something important we need to talk about? It's looking more and more like I slept with Marsa last night. Yesterday was the first time I even spoke to her! Could she really be pregnant with my child? Is that what she wants to talk to me about?

Someone tapped on the door to his urfren's run. He looked up. It was Brabeo, another guard who'd become a handler for the problem urfren.

"Hey Anrin, get moving. We're supposed to take our urfren to the exercise grounds."

Anrin nodded. "I'll be right there." He stood, calling for his urfren to come as he headed out of the run.

When he arrived on the exercise grounds, a trio of the others stood by the door to the kennel. They grinned at him as he came out the door.

"Hey lover boy," one called mockingly. "I hear you've adopted guard mores. Have fun last night?"

Blood rushed to his cheeks. Brabeo frowned at the three.

"What are you jokers *talking* about?"

"Nabak told us Anrin spent last night with Marsa. He said Theli told him Marsa's trying to get pregnant."

Brabeo's frown deepened. "So? It's an *honor* for a man to be chosen to sire a guardswoman's child." He shook his head. "Honestly, you lot are acting like you ain't left the crèche." He clapped Anrin on the shoulder. "Come on Anrin. Let's take our places on the grounds."

By lunch time, everyone in the group knew the rumor about Anrin and Marsa. Brabeo was the only one who didn't seem to care. All the others were holding recruits, and either found the tale amusing, shocking, or both. After they'd returned their urfren to the runs and washed up for lunch, Vemus pulled Anrin aside, his face thunderous.

"What's this I hear about you and Marsa? What happened after I left last night?"

Anrin gulped. "I don't *know*. The last thing I remember was her kissing me. I woke up on a bed in one of those little rooms by the lounge entrance this morning." He pulled out the note Derrath's wife had given him. "She sent me this note."

Vemus frowned as he read the missive. "Well, it don't *look* like you forced yourself on her."

The blood drained from Anrin's cheeks. "It never occurred to me I might have done that. Gods, what should I *do*?"

Vemus sighed. "Well, *first*, you need to talk to her." He returned Marsa's note to Anrin. "I can't help but wonder what your ma would say if she knew what you were up to. Marsa's just a kid."

"She looks to be around *my* age!" relief tempered Anrin's annoyance. If Vemus thought of Marsa as a kid, he *couldn't* be romantically interested in her.

Vemus wrapped an arm around Anrin's neck and knuckled his forehead. "Well, *you're* just a kid yourself."

Anrin sputtered. "Like *you're* all that much older!"

Vemus drew himself to his full height. "Not only am I *years* older than you, I'm betrothed. Jasya should be here soon. I hope to be married by the end of the month."

When they arrived at the dining hall, Vemus dragged Anrin to the table where Derrath sat with his wife. He frowned at his friend as they sat.

"Have you heard the rumor going around about Anrin and Marsa?"

Derrath frowned. "What rumor?"

"Nabak is telling everyone they slept together."

Derrath stared at Vemus. "He's saying *what*?"

Anrin stared at his plate. "The last thing I remember is her kissing me. I woke up this morning in one of those little guest rooms off the lounge by the assembly hall. I bumped into

Nabak and Theli by the stairs. They guessed I'd been with Marsa and Theli said Marsa's trying to get pregnant."

Derrath shook his head. "I'll have a talk with Nabak. He has no business spreading such tales."

Yakara nodded. "And *I'll* have a talk with Theli. Captain Trika won't look kindly on such gossip."

Vemus raised a brow. "You seem awfully calm about this. When *I* heard the rumor, I was ready to rip Anrin a new one."

"Anrin did nothing wrong." Derrath frowned at Anrin. "Neither did Marsa, so don't let *that* thought get in your head."

***

Marsa brought the children in from the play yard. Sazad was feeling faint. She set the boy on a couch in the lounge and told Podero he could play with her urfren while his friend rested. She fetched Sazad a glass of water and sat beside him while he drank. The door opened and Ilith entered with a woman Marsa didn't know. She smiled at the stranger.

"Hello. Have they assigned you to the crèche, too?"

Ilith nodded. "This is Jasya. She's a holding worker who's betrothed to a recruit. Jasya, this is Marsa."

Jasya had dark red hair and green eyes. Her face was pale and blotchy. She extended her hand, and they shook. "Hello."

"Since Jasya's new to crèche life, she'll assist you in caring for the boys." Ilith turned to Jasya. "Come with me for now and I'll show you to your dorm. You'll return here after you've settled in."

When Jasya returned, she sat beside Marsa. "Matron Ilith told me that both these boys have special needs."

Marsa nodded. "Sazad here," she pointed at the boy who was now lying down on the couch, "suffered a head injury and has fits." She waved a hand at the younger boy. "Podero has a bad leg. Aside from any other considerations, their special needs mean that neither of them will ever be guard material."

Jasya stared at the urfren. "Why is a dog in here?"

"She ain't a dog. She's an urfren. Her name is Dancer." Marsa called Dancer to her and directed the beast's attention to Jasya. "Dancer, this is Jasya. Be *nice* to her."

***

Anrin headed for the dining hall early. It had been a week now and Marsa should have free time today. At last, they'd have the very important talk she'd mentioned in her note.

Marsa arrived at the dining hall accompanied by Derrath's wife and a redheaded woman. Her urfren pranced by her side. When Vemus saw the redhead, he rushed over and grabbed her, pulling her into his arms for a kiss.

"Gods Jasy, I've *missed* you."

Jasya smiled tremulously. "Oh Vee, I'm *so* glad to see you." She raised a hand to his temple. "What happened to your face?"

He shrugged. "An enemy cut me in battle. It's nothing. Let's get our food. We can talk at the table."

Jasya nodded and followed the others to the sideboard to collect her breakfast.

Marsa piled eggs and ham on her plate before sitting at the table. Derrath raised a brow.

"You sure you can eat that much?"

Yakara laughed.

Marsa grimaced. "Dancer ain't left my side since I brought her to the crèche. She insists on eating from my plate now." She tossed her urfren a slice of ham. "I have to get enough for both of us."

Anrin bit his lip as he sat beside her. "Hey Marsa. Your note said you wanted to talk to me about something important?"

"Yes!" She kissed his cheek. "I would have asked you to come to the crèche and talk to me there, but Kara thought that might not be a good idea. They've assigned me a special job."

Jasya scowled. "Someone should give those boys a p*roper* home. Not keep them in a crèche."

Vemus wrapped his arm around Jasya. "What boys?"

She turned towards him. "They're the most adorable little ones, but they're both broken. Sazad has fits and Podero limps. I'm *sure* they'd do better in an actual home than in the crèche. It must be hard for them to know that they can never become guards like the other children. They don't even have their parents around to care for them."

Marsa smiled at the other woman. "Podero has really taken to you. I think you remind him of his ma. I heard him call you that when we put them to bed last night."

Jasya nodded. "He's such a sweet little boy. It must be hard for him to have lost his ma. He needs a proper home even more than Podero."

Vemus frowned. "How long have you been here?"

"I arrived yesterday. Matron Ilith assigned me to be Marsa's assistant in caring for the boys. I could only come to the dining hall with Marsa for breakfast today so I could see you. From now on, we'll have staggered free days, so the boys always have one or the other of us with them."

After breakfast, Vemus accompanied Jasya back to the crèche while Marsa pulled Anrin to the garden so they could talk privately. The two of them sat in the gazebo. Anrin stared at his feet as Marsa sat beside him.

"What did you want to talk to me about?"

She smiled at him. "You like me, don't you?"

He gulped. "Um, yeah."

"That kiss we shared was sweet." She kissed his cheek.

"Um… a guardswomen said…"

She laughed. "Kara told me about the gossip. I would never *do* that to you. I like you too." She laid her head on his shoulder. "You passed out. Derrath and Kara had been in one of the guest rooms, so we put you to bed in there. It was a good thing they showed up. I would have had to leave you on the couch otherwise."

His head came up. "So we didn't?"

"Of course not. You deserve to be awake for it when we do."

"*When* we do?"

She nodded. "I'm assigned to the crèche. I like you more than any of the others I've met here, and would *love* to have your child."

He blanched. "I *couldn't*. Ma would *kill* me if I had a child with a woman I ain't married to!"

She sighed. "Kara warned me you might feel that way. It's ok. I'm just sixteen. We can get to know each other better before we decide on anything." She tweaked his nose. "Who knows? You may change your mind. Or we may decide to get married. Kara thinks marriage is great."

"Would you agree to marry me?"

She shrugged. "It's for life, ain't it?"

He nodded.

"I'd have to think about it. I ain't been able to take a lover yet and my parents never thought marriage was necessary."

"I could court you. That's how it normally works." He bit his lip. "That would mean you can't take a lover, though. Not while we're courting."

She sighed. "I *guess* I can do that. Will you mind if I'm still a maiden?"

He grinned at her. "Of *course* not! I'd actually prefer it that way." He pulled her into his arms and kissed her on the lips. Afterwards, she sat, resting in his embrace.

"Are you sure you don't want to do the fun part right now?"

His arms tightened around her. "Yes. I want to wait for that until *after* I'm married. I'd like you to meet my parents, though, and I think I should meet yours."

She giggled. "You've *already* met my parents."

"I *have*?"

She nodded. "Captain Trika is my ma and Spymaster Moze is my pa. Don't tell anyone else, though. I ain't supposed to get special treatment. That's why I didn't move out of the crèche when I got Dancer." She reached over to scratch her urfren's ears.

The blood drained from his face and he felt faint. "What?" His voice was barely a whisper.

Marsa patted his cheek. "Are you ok?"

"Spymaster Moze is your *pa*?"

"Well, yes. Is that a problem?"

"They say he could assassinate *anyone*, even *clan*, and nobody would ever know."

She snuggled against him. "Well, I'm sure he wouldn't do that to my lover."

***

Captain Trika leaned back in her chair. "You may take a seat."

Vemus pulled a chair to the front of the desk and sat. "Permission to speak, ma'am."

"Permission granted."

"My betrothed has arrived. I would like to marry her as soon as possible."

"Are there any special arrangements you need for your marriage?"

"Um, well, Jasya ain't comfortable living in the crèche. It would help if she had the support of her parents. It would be ideal if *both* our parents were here to attend the wedding."

"Write them. We'll plan for your wedding as soon as they can arrive."

"Thank you, ma'am."

She waved him away. "You're dismissed."

After Vemus left, Trika leaned back in her seat. There were others among the holding recruits who had requested permission to marry. Vemus was merely the first. Still others already had wives. The crèche wasn't big enough to house them all, and holding women would be useless as guards. She sighed and pulled out a notebook. She'd have to come up with a solution before the situation got out of hand. Vemus's betrothed wasn't comfortable living in the dorms, was she? Where *would* she feel comfortable living? Was she typical of the holding women?

She went to her office door and stuck her head out to ask her assistant to fetch the girl. What was her name? Jasya.

When Jasya arrived, Trika leaned forward in her seat. "I just had an interview with your betrothed. He told me you ain't happy in the crèche dorms."

Jasya clasped her hands in her lap and stared at them. "No ma'am. I ain't happy to live in a dorm with other women. I should look forward to my wedding with anticipation, instead I'm dreading it. The thought of sneaking around any time I want to be alone with my husband, appalls me."

Trika sucked on her lip. "I see." She drew a deep breath. "You understand that Vemus's status has increased permanently, do you not?"

Jasya sniffed. "It don't *feel* like that. It feels like we *lost* status. We'd planned on living with my parents until we could get our own home. Now we ain't got that option." She raised her head and her eyes met Trika's. "I'm a *holding worker*, not a *house servant*. House servants live in dorms. Holding workers have p*roper* homes."

"I see." Trika leaned back. "So you would prefer a cottage rather than live in a dorm?"

"Of course! I also want to raise my children *myself*, in a home of my *own*, not send them to a crèche."

"Hmm. You're but the first of many women from holdings that I expect to come here. Vemus ain't the only betrothed guard. Some of the holding recruits already have wives. Do you think the other women will feel the same way?"

"Of course! Especially if they already *had* homes. What woman would want to have her circumstances reduced?" Her eyes hardened. "You may say Vee's status has increased all you like, but a dorm room ain't in the same class as a cottage. Even a two-room shack is better than a dorm."

Trika rubbed her face. "You present me with a problem no guard unit has ever faced. Guards don't normally marry and when we do, it ain't to holding workers. The crèche don't have enough beds to house all of you. I had thought of having a new dorm built on the land attached to the barracks, but if you think that would still feel like a decrease in status, perhaps a different solution is in order."

"If you have space for a dorm building, could you make a row of cottages instead?"

"Cottages would take up too much space. The fertile soil needs to be used. Right now, it's serving as grazing grounds for his Lordship's herds."

Jasya perked up. "The cottages wouldn't need to have very much space between them. They could even have shared walls. How many other holding women do you expect to arrive?"

Trika shrugged. "I expect thirty so far, but some recruits also have children. There may be more in the future."

"If the cottages have two or more floors and share walls, could you build them in the same area you thought would work for a dorm building?"

"That *might* be possible. I'd have to consult with an architect."

"Some cottages could share kitchens."

Trika's eyes lit up. "What if *all* the cottages shared the same kitchen and washing space? You'd have bedrooms and a lounge room for each unit, but each family would do their washing and cooking in shared areas. We could even assign house servants to help with those chores so the mothers could spend more time with their children. Would that be acceptable?"

Jasya nodded. "Speaking of children... there are two little boys in the crèche. They're both orphans and neither will ever be able to become a guard. Would it be possible for me to take them into my home with me once it's ready for me to move in?"

"What are their names?"

"Podero and Sazad."

Trika regarded Jasya searchingly. "Those boys are prisoners of war. They're Torust clan bastards. I don't have the authority to allow you to take them into your home, but I *can* pass your request on to his Lordship. Do you understand the responsibility you'd be taking on if his Lordship agrees?"

***

Summer Solstice Y1072

Marsa sat on the bench beside Anrin, her eyes sparkling. "I've never been to a wedding before." She put her arm around him and rested her head on his shoulder.

He gazed around the room. Captain Trika was present, but Spymaster Moze was not. He breathed a sigh of relief. He shot another glance at the captain and caught her eying him sternly. Anrin squirmed inwardly. Of *all* the girls he could have fallen for, he *had* to pick one whose parents had the power to crush him like a bug.

Marsa sighed as Vemus and Jasya's wedding progressed. When the priest bound the couple's wrists together, she turned to Anrin.

"Tell me what the priest is doing with the ribbon."

He bit his lip. "Well, you know Jasya embroidered their names on the ends of the ribbon, right?"

She nodded. "Jasy showed it to us when she made it. I've seen Kara's ribbon too."

"Ok, well, when the priest binds their wrists, he tucks their names together in the middle so they touch the veins on their wrists. The veins in the wrists see the names on the ribbon and whisper them to their hearts."

"Oh… I *like* that!"

He hugged her. "After the bride and groom's hearts know each other's names, the couple retires to the nuptial bed to consummate the union. It makes coupling extra special when your heart knows the name of your love."

She turned and kissed him. "*Now* I understand why you want to marry before the fun part."

When the ceremony was over, Captain Trika stepped forward and held up her hands. Once she had everyone's attention, she spoke. "If you would all come out back to the construction site where housing for the wives of married recruits is being built. The first unit is complete. His Lordship provided the furnishings himself." She smiled at Vemus and Jasya. "As the first couple attached to the urfren squad to marry, the unit is yours. Since the rest of the structure is not yet complete, you will continue eating here in the barracks, but you now have your own living quarters. Congratulations."

***

Early Summer Y1072

"Hey Anrin, Captain Trika wants to see you in her office."

Anrin turned. "Right *now*?"

The other recruit nodded.

Anrin's heart felt like lead in his breast as he put his urfren in its run and hurried through the building to Captain Trika's office. When he arrived, he tapped on the door.

"Come."

He opened the door and stepped inside. Spymaster Moze sat on a couch against the near wall. Captain Trika was at her desk at the far end of the room. She pointed at a chair.

"Sit."

Gingerly, he took a seat in the chair. Behind him came the rhythmic sounds of a blade being sharpened. The hair on the back of his neck stood on end and sweat beaded on his brow.

For what seemed like an eternity, Captain Trika regarded him.

"You've been spending a lot of time in the company of Marsa during recent weeks."

"I've been courting her. We care for each other." He swallowed. "A lot."

Trika shuffled the papers on her desk. "Marsa informed me she's told you she's our daughter."

He gulped and nodded. Sweat trickled down his back. The snick, snick of the blade stilled for a moment, then resumed.

"You are not to share that information with *anyone*."

"No ma'am."

Trika leaned back in her chair. "She also told me you have some holding worker hang-up about becoming lovers."

"Um, ma'am, my ma would kill me if I had children with a woman I ain't married to." He straightened up in his seat. "I care for Marsa a lot, but we ain't really known each other long enough to be sure we want to make that commitment yet. Once we *have* known each other long enough, if we've come to truly love one another, I swear I'll make her the happiest bride in the world."

"*Will* you, now?"

He nodded. "You can *bet* on that."

* * *

After the boy had left her office, Trika turned to Moze and stood at attention. "Spymaster Moze, sir!"

He rose and moved to stand in front of her. "You may speak."

"Permission to try for another child, sir!"

He smiled. "Permission granted." He took her in his arms and kissed her. She rested her head on his shoulder.

"Mmm, Moze? How long have we been together?"

He ran his fingers through her hair. "Since you were a recruit, fresh out of the crèche and I was an up and coming young assassin."

"Do you think we've known each other long enough to make a commitment for life?"

His fingers stilled. "Are you asking me to marry you?"

"I think so, yes. The recruits here who are married seem to be happier than those I've known who just take lovers."

"That's a serious commitment. Are you sure you want to take that step?"

She nuzzled his neck. "All my life, I've never wanted another man. I've been faithful to you for twenty years now. I think it's time we tied it up with a ribbon."

"Then my answer is 'yes'." He kissed the top of her head. "I'll see that Marsa has competition for the world's happiest bride."

She chuckled. "Do you *really* think she'll marry that boy?"

"If she don't, it won't be for a lack of trying on *his* part. He showed he has a spine in here. Tougher men than him have crumpled in my presence without my having to say a word. I know all the rumors about me." He laughed. "I *should*. I've *started* some of them."

***

Mid-Summer Y1072

Anrin stopped at the door to the dining hall. Someone had pinned a notice to it. '*All recruits report to the assembly hall immediately after breakfast,*' it said.

He groaned. Both he and Marsa had free time today, and he'd planned on spending it with her. Behind him, Nabak tapped his shoulder.

"Hey, lover boy. What's it say?"

"Assembly immediately after breakfast."

Nabak nodded. "Right then. Let's go eat. The sooner everyone arrives in the assembly hall, the sooner it'll be over." He pushed past Anrin and entered the dining hall.

Anrin collected his breakfast and joined Marsa at her usual table. He leaned over to kiss her as he sat. "I have to go to the assembly hall after breakfast."

She smiled at him. "It must be important. Everyone from the crèche is supposed to go there too, even the children."

He grinned at her. "Well, in that case, we can sit together for it."

When they arrived at the assembly hall, Spymaster Moze sat at a desk in the room's front. Anrin froze, his heart thudding in his chest. Marsa walked directly to him and they exchanged words. She then bounced over to Anrin and pulled him to sit on the bench beside Moze's desk. He forced himself to face forward and his breath caught in his throat. Seated on the chair on the dais was a man who wore a blue mask with black designs painted on its surface. He could only be one man. Captain Trika *never* sat in that seat. Anrin turned to Marsa and pointed at the masked man.

"That's…"

Her eyes were enormous. "This must be even *more* important than I thought."

Vemus and Derrath joined them with their wives. Jasya had a pair of small boys with her. She sat beside Marsa with the boys between her and Vemus, her eyes fastened on the masked man.

Captain Trika moved to the front of the dais and smiled at the assembly. "Welcome. Today is a day of celebration." She made a beckoning motion and Moze came to her side. "I believe you all recognize Spymaster Moze." She took his hand and surveyed the people gathered before her. "Moze and I have been lovers for twenty years now. We've had children together." She made another gesture, and a priest came to stand beside her. "Today, Moze and I will wed."

Marsa threw her arms around Anrin and planted a kiss on his lips.

Trika smiled. "All the happily married couples under my command have impressed me. You've inspired me to want that for myself, so I asked Moze to marry me and he agreed." She turned and bowed to the man seated on the dais chair. "We requested permission and his Lordship was gracious enough to grant it."

After the ceremony, Trika and Moze retreated to her quarters and the members of the urfren squad filed out of the assembly hall. Jasya stood and led the two boys towards the dais. She stood in the open area in front of the dais and curtseyed.

"Your Lordship, I have a request."

"You may speak."

She pulled the two boys forward, so they stood in front of her. "I'm one of the crèche workers assigned to care for these children." She lifted her head. "The crèche is not the best place for them. They need a p*roper* home. Captain Trika has provided my husband and me with private quarters. I wish to be given full custody of these boys. I'll take them into my home and care for them as if they were my offspring." She knelt to hug the smaller boy. "Podero already calls me 'ma'."

Lord Korander Moraven leaned forward in his seat. "You are Jasya, wife of Vemus, are you not?"

Jasya nodded.

"Captain Trika has made your request known to me. Where is your husband?"

Jasya rose to her feet and extended her hand behind her. Vemus came to her side, and they clasped hands.

"I am here."

"The boys your wife wishes to take into your home are Torust bastards. Do you agree with her request?"

Vemus placed his hand on the shoulder of the older boy. "Yes, my Lord. I support my wife in her desire to give these children a home. If you grant our petition, I will treat the boys as if they were my own sons. They deserve to be given as close to a normal life as is possible."

"The two of you make a convincing argument. I have no wish to see children suffer. I grant your petition with one caveat. You will provide Captain Trika with monthly reports on the boys' status. In addition, Matron Ilith will visit your home to check on the boys. You will keep custody of them as long as they prosper."

Jasya beamed. "Thank you, your Lordship. I assure you, we will give these boys the very best of care."

***

Jasya opened the door. "This is your new bedroom."

Podero limped into the room and looked around.

"Where we gonna play?"

"You can play in the front room." She turned him around and pointed back out the door. "You can also go outside and play in the yard." She hugged him. "There'll be other children living in these homes. You'll be able to play with *them,* too."

Sazad walked to one bed and sat. He glanced up at Jasya. "How long we gonna live *here*?"

"You're going to live here permanently. You heard his Lordship. This will *always* be your home."

He lifted his chin, his dark eyes smoldering. "He ain't *our* Lord. We ain't s'posed to *be* here. We were s'posed to die with the *others*."

She knelt beside the bed and pulled him into her arms.

"No. Your ma shouldn't have allowed you to be sent to die. She should have kept you with her. There was no reason for your clan to sacrifice you."

He turned his face away from her, his body stiff. "We owe it to the followers, so you'll leave em alone."

"You don't have to die for us to leave them alone." She hugged his small, rigid body. "We're leaving them alone *now*. I *love* you, Saz. *Vee* loves you, too. We're going to give you the best home we can. We want you to be *happy* here."

Vemus carried the boys' belongings into the room, his urfren at his heels.

"Let's get your things put away."

Secrets
Homelands: Mid-Summer Y1072

Alius Moraven led the way up the stairs from the road to the manor house. Talora followed close behind him, holding Lyna's hand, while the rest of their children trailed after her. When they reached the door, Alius turned to her. "What do you think?"

"It looks… very military."

"We stationed troops here during the war. We can make it homier." The family entered the manor, and he pointed at the stairs to the second floor. "For now, let's get settled in our new quarters."

***

Nerhar yawned as he left the dining room. *Why did we have to move* here*? This place is boring.* He scuffed his feet on the floor as he walked. Maybe there was something more interesting outside. He headed for the manor entrance.

Outside, one path led north to a groundskeeper's cottage. A narrower path led south along the side of the manor itself, while the wide stair they'd climbed the night before curved down the hill to the road. He couldn't see where the path to the south went, so he took that first. The path ended at a wrought-iron fence with an open gate. The fence closed off a nook made by the walls of the manor house itself.

He stepped into the enclosure. Tucked into the northern end was a shelter large enough to house at least one horse. He looked inside. A layer of moldy straw covered the floor. *Must be some kind of animal pen.*

He returned to the manor entry and took the stairs that wound down the hill where his new home stood. When he reached the bottom of the stairs, he found a statue. He'd glimpsed it when they'd arrived, but hadn't had a chance to really examine it. The figure on the plinth was that of a monstrous wolf-like beast. The animal was crouched with teeth bared in a snarl. Between its forefeet lay a small child. He couldn't tell if the child depicted was supposed to be dead or asleep. The child was life-sized. If the artist also intended the beast to be life-sized, the child was just big enough to provide it with a snack. He laughed at his morbid thought and crossed to the other side of the road, where a path led to the northeast.

This path wandered through a grove of fruit trees until it ended at the guards' practice grounds. As he emerged from the grove, a rabbit burst from a clump of grass beside the path and dashed off through the trees.

His steps quickened. Weapons' practice would at least occupy his time.

***

Thalion stepped out of the dining room and looked up and down the hall. To his right was the manor entry. To the left were the audience chamber and a hallway that he'd been told led to the guards' lounge. The quickest route from the family quarters to the main floor passed through the audience chamber. They'd discovered that last night when they'd arrived. He turned left and headed in that direction.

"Thal? Where you going?"

He glanced down. Barlion had come up beside him. He smiled at his little brother. "I'm going to explore the manor."

"Kin I come?"

He nodded. "Sure."

From behind him, Lyna tugged at his shirt. "Kin I come too?"

CLAN

"You bet." He picked his baby sister up and set her on his shoulders.

***

Nerhar dropped to the ground in the shade of the fruit trees and grinned up at the youth who'd been his sparring partner. "So, is there anything to do around here other than work and weapons' practice?"

The other boy sat beside him and took a long drink from a canteen. "Not much so far, but I've only been here a couple of months. I arrived with the workers." He offered Nerhar the canteen. "I understand the holding sat fallow during the war. There was no one but guards here then."

Nerhar wrinkled his nose as he took a drink. "Did you even have a party for the Solstice?"

"Oh sure, but the workers have been busy getting the fields planted and stuff. They had little time to do that since the war just ended this spring."

Nerhar sighed. "So, there's nothing to do for fun?"

The other boy eyed him with a smirk on his lips. "Oh *sure*, there is. We just have to be creative."

"So what do you do?"

"Well, for one, we tell scary stories to each other. Anyone told you about the urfren statue?"

"Urfren statue?"

The other boy nodded. "By the stairs to the manor house entry."

"Oh. That thing. What about it?"

"At midnight, it comes alive, eats the child at its feet. Then it sets out hunting for another child to take its place. The beast can walk through walls to get at naughty children."

Nerhar rolled his eyes. "You jest."

The boy shrugged. "The little children believe it. We tell them it can't get them if they behave. It sounds scarier if you tell the story in the dark. Especially if you have someone hiding with an urfren skin ready to jump out at the right moment."

"Where would you get an urfren skin?"

"Lots of guards have them. They skinned a bunch of the urfren they killed during the war. My ma has one. She had the head mounted on the skull so it looks almost alive. At least the head does, anyway."

Nerhar perked up. "For *real*?"

The other boy nodded.

***

When Nerhar entered the dining hall for dinner that night, he hesitated in the door. Seated at the table was the clan spymaster. *What's* Moze *doing here*? He eyed the man warily as he took his seat.

Thalion entered the room, walked up to Moze and shook his hand. "What brings *you* here? I thought Uncle Kor had you stationed at the keep."

The man's teeth gleamed beneath his thick mustache as he smiled. "My job requires me to travel throughout the enclave. Right now, I need to spend some time here."

"Will you be here for my birthday?"

"I can certainly stay for it."

Thalion grinned. "That would be great."

Nerhar grimaced. Of course, *Thalion* would be happy to see Moze. Thalion was *flawless*. *He* never got into trouble for *anything*.

***

After dinner, they sent Nerhar with the younger children to the sitting room his parents had designated as the nursery while Thalion stayed with the adults. Nerhar ground his teeth.

I'm fifteen. *That's old enough to join the adults like Thal does*.

His lips pressed together, he eyed his siblings through narrowed eyes. He stalked to the windows and stared out at the scenery. The urfren statue was visible from here.

He smirked, turning towards where his younger siblings were playing with their toys. "Hey, come here and look out the window."

Tiari came to his side and peered out.

He pointed at the statue that sat in the pooling shadows beside the road at the base of the hill where they'd built the manor house. "See that statue?"

She nodded. The other two joined them at the window to see what he was talking about.

"That's a statue of an urfren. It's life-size."

Tiari shook her head. "No, it ain't. I seen the urfren Uncle Kor had brought to the keep. They're smaller than that."

"Those are just babies. That statue is of an adult urfren." Nerhar wasn't sure if he was right, but their uncle *had* said the urfren they'd found at Torust keep were all young.

The three younger children stared out the window at the statue down below.

Nerhar leaned down to whisper to them. "At midnight, the statue comes alive. There's a child under it. It eats that child and then goes searching the holding for another child to take its place."

Tiari frowned at him. "No, it don't. It ain't real. It's just a statue. You're trying to scare us." Tiari was a sober little girl who didn't tolerate frivolities.

"It is *so* real. I made a new friend today. His name is Kerith, and he told me all about it. The statue is magic. It comes alive at midnight to hunt for a new child to take the place of the one it ate and it can walk through walls to hunt."

Lyna burst into tears. "It's gonna *eat* us!"

Barlion hugged her. "It's ok. Nerhar's here. He won't *let* it." The boy looked up at his older brother, tears in his own eyes. "You *won't*, will you?"

"Oh, I'm sure it won't come after any of *us*." Nerhar leaned on the windowsill, peering outside. "Wait a minute. Did it just move?"

Tiari's face turned white as the two younger children shrieked and ran out of the nursery.

* * *

Nerhar hunched his shoulders as his father berated him.

Alius paced back and forth by the desk in his new office. "You say you want to be treated like an adult and then you pull a stunt like this. Both Barlion and Lyna are afraid to sleep in their rooms now."

"It was just a joke."

"One of these days, your 'just a joke' will cause someone to get hurt. *Then* what will you have to say for yourself?"

"I'm sorry. Okay? I didn't hurt anyone. They're just a little scared. That's all."

As he left his father's office and passed through the main room of his parents' suite, his mother glanced up from her seat by the fireplace, where she was comforting his youngest siblings. His cheeks burned as she regarded him solemnly, her eyes following him out the door.

***

The next day, when Nerhar arrived at the practice field, Kerith waved at him from the far side. He joined the other boy, choosing a practice sword from the rack to use for sparring.

Kerith squinted at him. "I brought ma's urfren skin with me today. You said you wanted to see it."

His eyes lit up. "Yeah."

The other boy led the way to a shed on the opposite side of the field from the fruit trees. Inside, he opened a chest and pulled out a fur rug.

Nerhar's eyes widened. "That thing is *huge*."

Kerith held up the head. They'd mounted it on the skull with the mouth open in a snarl. "Ma told me *this* urfren bit a guardsman's arm clean off."

Nerhar eyed the head narrowly. "That statue by the road is life-sized. Ain't it?"

Kerith nodded. "I think urfren are about the same size as bears. Maybe even a little bigger."

"I want to show this to my siblings. Can you bring it into the manor house?"

Kerith shrugged. "Sure. I can't bring it to the top floor, though. I ain't allowed to go there."

"And if *I* brought it there, my parents would want to know what it was and what I was doing with it." Nerhar frowned. "Is there a room you could hide it in?"

"Well, I could hide it in a storeroom."

"Wouldn't a servant notice it?"

"Not if I put it in the cellar storeroom."

"What cellar storeroom?"

Kerith grinned. "You ain't seen the secret cellar?"

Nerhar's eyes widened. "A *secret* cellar?"

"Yeah. There's a secret door to it in the audience chamber. The servants don't go down there much."

"*Show* me."

***

Nerhar led the way to the audience chamber. He'd only been able to convince Barlion to come, but Tiari would probably tattle to their parents anyway, and it was no doubt best not to scare Lyna again. Barlion would be ok.

He pressed the knob on the wall, and the secret door swung open. "See? There's a secret room."

"Wow!" Barlion's eyes were wide.

"Come on. Let's see what's down there." He stepped through the opening, his little brother at his back. A single globe at the top of the stairs provided the only light. He and Kerith had taken all the light globes out of the fixtures in the cellar itself. He pulled a portlight from his satchel and pointed it at the steps.

When they reached the bottom, he shone the light towards the center of the room, where Kerith was crouched under the urfren skin. The head came up with a growl. The light glittered off the glass eyes mounted in the eye sockets. For a moment, he almost thought the beast was alive himself.

Barlion screamed and ran back up the stairs.

Kerith dropped to the floor, laughing. Nerhar pulled the urfren skin off his friend.

***

Barlion ran to the guard lounge. Thalion would be there. *He'd* know what to do. When he reached his oldest brother, he couldn't get the words out. He could only repeat his other brother's name.

Thalion rose from his seat. "Show me."

Barlion led the way to the audience chamber and pointed at the still open door to the room Nerhar had brought him to.

***

Thalion's eyes narrowed as he made his way down the stairs. The room below was dimly lit. When he reached the foot of the stairs, he saw Nerhar and a youth he didn't know lying on top of an animal skin, laughing. A portlight lay on the floor near the two boys, providing the only illumination. He pressed his lips together and stepped into the room.

"What the *hell* did you *do* Nerry? Barli's scared out of his wits."

Nerhar glared up at him. "It was just a joke."

The other boy jumped to his feet.

Thalion bent over to grab the fur. "What *is* this?"

The stranger hung his head. "It's an urfren skin. It belongs to my ma."

"Well, take it back to her right now."

"Yes, sir." The boy folded the fur and pulled a chest out from under the stairs to put it in.

Thalion turned to his brother. "Papa's going to tan your hide. He should have done that last night instead of just scolding you for telling that stupid story to the little kids." He picked up the portlight and checked out the room. Empty light fixtures lined the walls. He shone the light at one of them. "Where are the light globes?"

"In a bag under the stairs."

"Well, get them out and put them where they belong."

"*You* do it! You ain't papa. I don't have to do anything you tell me." Nerhar grabbed the handle at one end of the chest the other boy had stuffed the fur into. "Come on Kerith. I'll help you take your mama's fur back to her."

After the other boys had left the cellar, Thalion looked under the stairs. There was the bag with the light globes. He pulled the bag out, set the portlight on a table by the stairs, and circled the room, shoving the globes into the fixture sockets with more force than necessary.

Damn *Nerhar. He's* so *irresponsible.*

He reached the last wall. He'd nearly finished now. Two more to go. He ground his teeth as he shoved yet another globe into its place. With a soft click, the wall beside the fixture shifted, leaving a small gap between its surface and the next wall panel. He froze, staring at the crack. Slowly, he reached out and pushed the loose panel. The wall swung like a door into a darkened space, swinging back with enough force to close with another soft click. A musty, animal odor wafted into the room as the wall sealed shut.

Absentmindedly, he restored the remaining globe to its socket, then pressed down on the previous globe. The wall shifted open with a soft click. Thalion grabbed the portlight and pushed the wall open again, stepping through into the space beyond. The wall closed behind him.

***

A soft click woke the sentries. Their heads came up, nostrils flaring as they sniffed the air. Light briefly spilled into the tunnel as a section of wall swung into the passage and then swung shut. Unfamiliar scents flooded the passageway, including the scent of strange humans. Fur bristling, the female lunged to her feet, the male only a fraction of a second behind. Their task of guarding this end of the tunnel had become interesting.

***

Barlion sat in the audience chamber, staring at the door to the cellar. He'd wait for Thalion to come back up. Nerhar and a strange boy came up the stairs first, bringing a large chest with them.

Nerhar glanced at him. "It was just a joke. There ain't anything to be afraid of down there."

Barlion hunched his shoulders. "I ain't talking to you."

"Suit yourself."

The two older boys left.

Barlion was still sitting in the audience chamber when it was time for dinner.

His father came into the room. "Hey Barli, it's time to eat."

Barlion pointed at the still open door. "I'm waiting for Thal to come out."

"I'll go get him." His father went down the stairs, but returned shortly, shutting the door behind him. "There's no one there. Come on. It's time for dinner."

"But Thal went down there and dint come back out."

"He must have. There's no one there. It's just a storeroom."

***

Nerhar sat at the table in the cellar storeroom, eying the walls. *Barlion* insists *that Thal never left this room.* He rose and walked around the room. *Thal must have put the light globes back in their sockets.* He examined the fixtures. One globe on the stretch of bare wall beside the stairs sat a little higher in its socket than the others. He pushed it into place. With a soft click, the wall beside the fixture shifted, leaving a slight gap between it and the rest of the wall. He stared. There was a *second* secret door. One that led *out* of this room.

His eyes gleamed as he pushed against the wall. It swung away from him into a dimly lit space beyond. He stepped through the opening and the wall sealed shut behind him.

***

Mid-Autumn Y1072

Barlion left the nursery and headed towards the stairs to the next floor. The door to Nerhar's room was ajar. Soft sobs issued through the opening. He peeked inside. His mother sat on Nerhar's bed, crying into her hands.

He entered the room and touched her shoulder. "Mama? Are you ok?"

She pulled him into her arms and hugged him tightly. "I'm just missing your brothers, sweetie. Today's Nerhar's birthday. I wish he and Thal would come home."

"They ain't never coming home. The monster in the cellar ate them."

She sighed. "There's no monster in the cellar, dear. It was just an animal skin. Kerith's mama made him tell us about the trick he and Nerhar played on you."

"Yes, there is. It ate them both. It's gonna eat *all* of us." He shivered in her arms.

She leaned back and looked him directly in the face. "Tell you what. I need to go through the pictures that the guards found here when they first moved in and see if we want to keep any of them. I've been putting that off. Would you like to help me?"

He nodded. "Okay."

His mother took his hand and led the way to the second floor of the manor house, where she opened the door to a triangular room. Inside, stacks of pictures leaned against the walls. "Why don't you look and see if there is any picture in here that you might like to have in your room?"

"Okay." He walked over to one wall and turned a picture around so he could see the painted canvass. His mother went through the stack next to the one he was looking at. She glanced over at him as he discarded painting after painting.

He finished each stack and moved on to the next, hardly noticing the images. Suddenly, he froze. The picture he'd just turned over depicted a little girl with a pair of wolf-like dogs seated beside her. One animal was black with a frosting of white in its fur, while the other was white with a dusting of black.

His mother came to his side. "Do you like that picture? The little girl is pretty, ain't she?"

He started and focused on the girl. She had jet-black hair that hung around her shoulders in loose curls. Her eyes were as black as her hair and she was beaming, her teeth gleaming white against her dusky skin. She had her arms around the animals' necks and was hugging them.

"Barli? Do you want this picture for your room?"

"I don't like *them*." He pointed at the dogs. "Why's she *hugging* them? They'll *eat* her."

"They *won't* eat her. I think they're her pets." She rubbed the label at the bottom of the frame and examined it. "It says this is Lirin Torust at age ten. It's dated seventeen years ago."

"They ate her. They got real big and ate her." His chin trembled. "They got big and turned into monsters, then they ate her."

"They didn't sweetie. Let's see if we can find more pictures of her. I'm sure she was ok."

Tears filled his eyes. "Where *is* she then?"

"She would have died in the war, honey. Every Torust did."

"The monsters ate her." He ran out of the room.

After dinner that night, his mother pulled him aside. "I have something for you." She handed him a wrapped painting. "Open it."

He bit his lip and took the wrapping off the picture. It depicted a couple with their arms around each other. The woman smiled warmly at the man, who was kissing her hand as he gazed back at her. Both of the people in the picture had matching black hair and eyes with dusky skin. The woman's skin was a shade or two darker than the man's.

His mother pointed at the label. "See what it says there?"

"Lirin and Tollot."

"That's right. See the date? They painted it just a few months before the war started. This must be their wedding picture. Monsters did not eat Lirin. She grew up and married a man she loved." She sighed. "And then they would both have died during the war. Would you like to have *this* picture to hang in your room?"

He nodded.

***

Winter Y1072

Barlion patted the painting that hung over his bed. "Lirin grew up and only died in the war. The monsters *did not* eat her," he whispered to himself.

He dressed for breakfast and left his room. When he reached the second floor of the manor house, he left the room where the stairs to the family quarters were and headed to the upper level of the guard lounge. He frowned. There were no guards sitting at the tables. Usually, there'd be at least a few guards in the lounge area. He shivered as he took the stairs to the first floor. The lower level of the guard lounge was empty as well. He quickened his steps as he made his way through the manor.

When he reached the dining hall, his father wasn't there. His mother sat in his father's usual place at the table, holding a child younger than Lyna. Her face was pale and there were lines around her eyes. The child's dark coloring made her look extra white. Tiari and Lyna had already taken their places. They'd used the route through the audience chamber. It was only a matter of time before the monsters ate them. He'd warned them of the danger, but they insisted on taking the shorter route.

He took his seat at the table. "Mama? Where's papa?"

She smiled at him, but there was a tightness about her face and the smile didn't quite reach her eyes. "He's gone hunting, sweetie. The storm packed snow against the holding walls and beasts from the wastes got inside and attacked the workers' livestock." She hugged the child in her arms. "Little Myla here couldn't stay home, so we're going to take care of her for a while. She'll go with you to the nursery after breakfast."

In the nursery, their nanny took Myla and told the rest of them that there would be no lessons. Barlion sat beside a window and peered out at the statue by the foot of the stairs that wound down the side of the hill to the road. The snow had stopped falling, but drifts covered the ground and the wind whipped up sprays of snow that whirled around, first concealing, then revealing the landscape.

A snow spray hid the statue and his heart beat faster. It appeared again, but it looked different. Hadn't there been snow on the statue? He furrowed his brow. The animal's head turned. Another one appeared beside it. The wind dropped and the swirling snow fell to the ground. Now a trio of the monstrous beasts stood around the snow-covered statue. One raised a reddened muzzle and sniffed the air. A second one shook itself like a dog. Then the three beasts were gone, trotting through the snow towards the grove of fruit trees between the manor and the guards' practice grounds. Barlion's heartbeat quickened, and he shivered.

It was lunchtime before Barlion's father returned to the manor house. His mother gripped his arm. "Was your hunt successful?"

He shook his head. "They got out over the walls. I sent patrols to clear the drifts outside the holding. They won't get back in." He chucked Myla under her chin. "Hello Myla. You're going to live here with *us* from now on."

***

Spring Y1073

Barlion stared at the dark boy his father had brought to the dining room. Something about the stranger seemed familiar. The boy was only wearing a shirt and trousers. His shoes had holes in them. Didn't he have a coat?

"Everyone, this is Lason. He'll be doing whatever work he can for us." He glanced at Barlion. "Barli? I thought you might want another boy to keep you company." He turned to Lason. "Barli don't like to go outside, so he spends little time with the children of the guard and the children of the workers don't come to the manor at all, so he has no one to play with but his sisters."

Lason stood stiffly beside Barlion's father and stared

directly at Barlion. "You want me to play *nursemaid*?"

"Barli will turn nine this summer. I was thinking you'd play the role of companion rather than nursemaid. It would mean that I'd allow you to go to the top floor."

"I ain't staying the night. I can come in the morning, but I need to go home to ma for dinner and I won't come every day."

Barlion's father nodded. "That's all right. Technically, Barli ain't permitted to have a proper companion anyway, since I ain't the heir and he ain't even my eldest. In the meantime, please join us for lunch. You can get to know my son during the meal." He gestured towards a seat beside Barlion.

Throughout the meal, Lason's eyes darted around the room as he ate. He responded to Barlion's overtures with monosyllabic replies. Barlion turned towards where his father sat at the head of the table. Wasn't he and Lason supposed to be getting to know each other? How could they do that if they didn't talk to each other? He felt reassured when he saw his father was regarding Lason steadily, turning his gaze towards his plate whenever Lason glanced in his direction. He looked back at Lason. The other boy was slipping food from the serving bowls under his shirt.

Barlion's eyes widened, and he turned towards his father again, catching the man's eye. His father shook his head slightly and briefly held a finger to his lips.

After lunch, Barlion turned to Lason. "What do you want to do?"

Lason gazed at him coldly out of jet-black eyes. "It don't matter. You're the boss."

"Well, would you like me to show you around the manor house?"

Lason shrugged. "Sure. Why not?" He didn't sound very enthused.

Barlion sighed. Lason wouldn't be much of a companion if he was going to act that way. Weren't companions supposed to be friends?

He led the way through the entry to the guard lounge. A pair of guards were wrestling in the pit while others looked on. "Most of the guards spend their free time here." He pointed at the opening in the ceiling. "Or upstairs." He turned, but Lason had left his side and was leaning on a table, smiling at a guardswoman. What was he *doing*?

"Hello there. Do you come here often? Would you like to go somewhere more private? Maybe a room with a bed?"

The woman turned her attention from the pit to eye Lason. "Ain't you a little young to be coming on to women?"

Lason's dusky cheeks flushed darker still. "I ain't *that* young."

"How old *are* you?"

Lason's head drooped. "Thirteen," he mumbled.

The guardswoman pinched his chin. "Look me up in about four or five years. Until then, enjoy your childhood. You only get to be a child once." She rose and moved to a different table.

Lason glared at her. "I *ain't* a child. Not anymore."

After dinner that night, Barlion tugged on his father's sleeve. "Papa? I don't want Lason to be my companion. He's odd."

His father tousled his hair. "Lason's a slum brat. What did he do you thought was odd?"

"He asked a guardswoman to go with him to a room with a bed."

His father paled and swallowed visibly. "Okay, and what did she say to him?"

"She asked how old he was and he told her he's thirteen. Then she told him to be a child, and he said he *ain't* a child. What did he mean by that?"

"Living in a slum is hard. Slum brats grow up fast. That's all. I'll have a talk with him before the two of you spend any more time together. Everything will be all right."

When Barlion went to bed that night, he lay gazing at the picture of Lirin and Tollot that hung over his bed. There were few shadows in his room. He kept his light globe uncovered, and it shone brightly all night long. The picture comforted him. The couple looked happy. Lirin had grown up and married. She'd died in the war. The monsters didn't eat her. His mother had assured him of that. He frowned and sat up in bed, staring at the picture. Tollot's expression was identical to how Lason had looked at the guardswoman.

***
Summer Y1073

Barlion left the nursery. Lason would eat lunch with them today. The older boy always set him on edge. The way Lason approached any woman he hadn't met before made Barlion's skin crawl.

He reached the lower level of the guard lounge and frowned as he turned the corner into the hallway and glanced to his left. Lason stood by the door to the audience chamber. The blood drained from his face as Lason opened the door and went inside. He had to warn the other boy of the danger. He raced down the hall and entered the audience chamber himself just in time to see the door to the cellar stair close behind Lason.

He bit his lip as he opened the door and crept down the stairs. He hadn't gone to the secret cellar since Nerhar had shown it to him. When he reached the foot of the stairs, he saw Lason standing with his hand on the wall next to a table. Unlike the first time he'd come here, the room was well lit. Suddenly, a monster shoved its head through the wall beside Lason's hand. Lason's hand dropped to his side, and he took a step back. With a whine, the beast shoved its head further into the room. Barlion gasped. Nerhar had been right! The monsters *could* walk through walls.

Lason turned, and their eyes met. "Hide."

Hide? Yes, he *would* hide. Lason's command roused him from the paralysis that had gripped him at the sight of the animal's head. Barlion turned and fled up the stairs. When he reached his room, he crawled under the bed and lay there, trembling. Tears filled his eyes and ran down his face. Lason made him uncomfortable, but he hadn't wanted the other boy to be eaten by monsters, and Lason had saved him from being eaten, too.

He didn't know how long he'd been hiding under his bed when the door to his room opened. He cowered in his hiding place.

"Barli? Are you in here?" It was his mother.

He crawled out from under his bed and rushed into her arms, sobbing.

"What's wrong sweetie? The guards said you ran through their lounge."

"Lason!"

"What about Lason, dear? Did he do something that upset you?"

"Monsters ate him."

She sighed. "There *are* no monsters. Lason is sitting at the table waiting for lunch to be served. Now *come*. It's time to eat." She took his hand and pulled him after her, taking the route through the audience chamber.

***

Barlion's feet dragged on the way to the nursery. He snuck peeks at Lason as they walked through the manor. How had Lason escaped the monster and why hadn't he said anything about it to anyone? He bit his lip. "Why were you in the cellar?"

Lason glanced at him out of the corner of his eyes. "What cellar? I ain't seen any cellar here."

"The secret cellar under the audience chamber."

Lason snorted. "Well, if it's secret, no wonder I never seen it."

"You were *there*! I *saw* you!"

"You must have dreamed it."

"You were standing by the wall and a monster stuck its head through. How did you get away from it?"

"That's *proof* you dreamed it. It ain't possible. I never been in your secret cellar and there ain't no monsters. Your pa told me you make up stories about monsters. I been *wondering* when you'd try it with me."

Tears filled Barlion's eyes. "No one believes me, but they're *real*. I seen them outside once. They were by the statue."

"You sure?"

"Yes. There were three of them. They appeared by the statue, then ran off. My brother said the statue comes to life, but it just sat there."

Lason raised a brow. "I didn't know you had a brother. I thought you just had sisters."

"I used to have two brothers, Thal and Nerry. They're both

dead now. The monsters ate them. Mama and papa say they ran away, but Thal wouldn't have done that. His birthday was the week after he disappeared. Even if he *wanted* to run off, he would've stayed for *that*."

***

Autumn Y1073

Barlion patted the painting that hung over his bed. The frame was becoming shiny from his ritual. He yawned as he dressed. Storm winds had howled outside the manor house that night and he hadn't slept well. Winter was coming. In the hallway, he glanced out a window. The winds had died down, but the rain was so heavy it obscured the view of the land outside. He shivered. It wouldn't be long before the rain turned to snow.

When he reached the dining room, his parents and sisters were already eating their breakfast. His mother glanced up as he sat in his place. Her brows had a crease between them and there were lines around her eyes.

After breakfast, his feet dragged as he made his way to the nursery. On a day like this, he couldn't even count on the dubious company of Lason. There was no way the other boy would come to the manor in *this* weather.

His mind drifted during his lessons, and the nanny scolded him.

At mid-day, he took his usual route to the lower guard lounge. He glanced towards the doors to the audience chamber as he rounded the corner, then resolutely turned his back on that part of the manor and walked along the hall by the side of the wrestling pit towards the entrance.

He was halfway across the entry when the outer door opened, and Lason stepped inside. The storm had soaked older boy to the skin and water dripped from his hair. Lason's dark eyes glittered as he looked directly at Barlion. He laughed.

"You look like you seen a ghost."

"I dint expect you to come today. It's nasty outside."

Lason wrung some of the water out of his shirt. "It's just wet and windy." He headed towards the door to the north hallway. "I'm hungry. Let's get some lunch."

When the two boys entered the dining hall, however,

Barlion's mother marched Lason up the stairs to the washroom on the second floor of the manor. She insisted the boy take a hot bath and change into dry clothes before he ate.

"We'll wash and dry the clothes you normally wear. You'll be staying here until the storm is over. I don't care if your mama will worry. I ain't letting you go out in that weather again."

Lason leered at Barlion's mother. "You want to wash me?"

She sighed. "You're old enough to wash yourself." She pointed through the door. "Hop to it."

The rain continued throughout the day and by the time Lason would normally leave; the wind picked up. Barlion's mother came to the nursery.

"Lason, you'll be spending the night here in the manor."

He looked towards the windows. "But…"

She shook her head. "No 'buts'. We've already locked the outer doors for the night. If you'll follow me, I'll show you where you'll be sleeping. Dinner is in one hour."

They gave Lason one of the tower rooms just down the hall from Barlion's. When he pointed that out, the other boy just shrugged.

"So what? You want me to tuck you in like a baby when you go to bed?"

"Papa said you're supposed to act like a companion for me. You ain't *ever* acted like a companion. You ignore me when we're in the nursery and just cuddle Myla. Companions are supposed to be friends."

"You gonna tell your pa you don't want me here then? I'm ok with that."

Barlion hung his head. "I told papa you ain't a good companion when you first came. He said you had a hard life and I should give you a chance. I *gived* you a chance. I *been* giving you a chance since spring."

Lason sighed. "What do you want to do, then?"

"We could maybe tell each other stories before we go to bed."

"All right. I'll tuck you in and tell you stories."

After dinner, Barlion led the way to his room, where he changed into a nightshirt.

Lason stood in the doorway. "Where did you get *that*?"

His voice sounded strange.

Barlion glanced back at the older boy. Lason was pointing at the painting of Lirin and Tollot, his other hand clenched in a fist at his side.

"It was in a storeroom. Mama told me I could have it. I like it." He pointed at the woman. "She's pretty and they look so happy together." He blinked. Lason looked even more like Tollot than he'd realized.

"Ain't you afraid of ghosts?"

"Ghosts?"

"Yeah. You're afraid of monsters, but you ain't afraid of being haunted by ghosts?"

"Why would ghosts haunt *me*?"

"Why *wouldn't* they? You murdered every Torust and stole their things. You think their ghosts ain't mad about that?"

Barlion dropped onto his bed. His heart raced, and he felt lightheaded. "*I* ain't murdered *anyone*! I'm just a little boy."

Lason sat on the bed and wrapped an arm around him, hugging him tight. "Maybe they *won't* come after you. If you take good care of their picture and don't let any harm come to it. *Maybe* they'll let you off the hook. Since you're just a little boy."

Barlion raised his eyes to Lason's face. "Do you think the monsters could be ghosts?"

Lason shrugged. "I ain't thought about that. Maybe they *are*. You said you saw one stick its head through a wall?"

Barlion nodded.

"Well, ghosts can walk through walls. I see ghosts in the slum sometimes. They don't bother *us* cause they died long before we moved there. Maybe when you thought you saw me in that secret cellar, it was really a ghost."

"If that was a ghost I saw in the cellar, who do you think it was? It looked just like you. It even wore the same clothes."

Lason shrugged. "Maybe it was the ghost of a relative of mine. Someone from the slum may have tried to steal from the manor. Maybe someone killed him, and he became a ghost. Besides, all slum rags look the same."

"Do you really think so?"

"Yes."

"You know a lot about ghosts. Don't you?"

Lason nodded.

"What else do you know about ghosts?"

***

Barlion looked up at the painting over his bed. There was something different about it. He frowned. The painting was in shadow. His entire room was dim and full of shadows. He glanced at his light globe. He'd left it uncovered, but now it emitted a muted red glow. As he watched, the light grew dimmer still. That shouldn't happen. Light globes shone brightly unless you broke them or covered them up so the light didn't leak out. He tried to sit up, but couldn't move.

A clatter from the wall over his bed drew his attention back to the painting. The people in the picture had turned into skeletons and were staring down at him through empty eye sockets. The skeleton that had been Tollot pointed at him.

He screamed and sat up.

Everything in his room was as it was supposed to be. The light globe shone as bright as it had when Lason left his room and he'd lain down to sleep. His heart in his throat, he peered up at the painting. Lirin and Tollot gazed into each other's eyes as they always had before.

***

Winter Y1073

Barlion sat up in bed. The wind was howling outside. He shivered and patted the painting over his bed. "Please don't haunt me. I'll take good care of the painting. I won't let anything hurt it."

He dressed and headed to breakfast, glancing out a window as he hurried down the hallway. Besides the howling winds, it was snowing outside. A lump filled his throat and his mouth felt dry.

When he reached the dining hall, both his parents sat at the table. His father had dressed for the outdoors and lines had appeared on his pale face.

"Papa? Are you going out in the storm?"

His father shook his head. "I was going to, but I'll have to wait until it ends."

His mother smiled at him. Her eyes were too bright. "It's Myla's birthday today. We're going to have a party."

Tiari sat up straight in her seat. "How old is she, mama?"

Their father reached over and patted the little girl on her head. "The records say she's three now."

Barlion stared at Myla. "Are her parents coming? I bet she misses them."

His parents exchanged a look, and his father coughed. "I'm afraid not."

Barlion frowned. "Why not? Don't they love her anymore?"

"They *can't* come. Myla is part of *our* family now."

"They're dead. *Ain't* they? Monsters ate them." Barlion hung his head, tears filling his eyes.

His mother came to his seat and hugged him. "Yes. I'm afraid they *are* dead. Do you remember how beasts from the wastes got over the wall last winter?"

Barlion nodded. It had happened more than once. He'd only seen the monsters that first time, though.

"Well, the beasts killed Myla's parents when they tried to save their livestock. They're just animals, though. Animals, not monsters."

He sniffed. "I seen them that day. Out the window. There were three of them by the statue. They're monsters."

* * *

The children's nanny told them they could spend the day playing for Myla's birthday. The party would last all day long. Barlion sat by a window and stared out. The sky cleared up after a couple of hours. He watched as his father left the manor with several guards and they all rode towards the nearest gate.

It was nearly time for lunch when he spotted a lone figure struggling through the snow. He gasped. It could only be Lason. He stared intently as Lason made his way through the snow towards the manor until movement in the distance along the other boy's back trail caught his eye. Monsters were following Lason! They moved faster through the snow than he did. Barlion held his breath. Lason reached the top of the stairs to the road, trudged up the manor steps, and vanished from Barlion's view. The monsters stopped beside the statue and lifted their heads to look at the manor. He turned away from the window and ran out of the room. The nanny called after him.

"Barli? Where are you going?"

He hesitated at the door. "I saw Lason outside."

She nodded. "Very well." She turned to the girls. "Why don't we *all* go to the dining hall?"

***

Spring Y1074

Moze and Lason entered the dining hall together as Barlion was taking his seat. His father greeted the spymaster as Lason went to his place at the table.

After lunch, Moze turned to Barlion. "I'm afraid I'll be stealing Lason from you for the next couple of months. He'll get training from me. I think he has qualities that would be useful for one of my staff."

Barlion gaped at the man. "I thought he was supposed to be my companion."

Barlion's father shook his head. "Barli, you ain't the clan heir. If Moze has a better use for Lason than as your playmate, you'll have to accept that."

Moze smiled at him. "It's ok, Barli. It will only be for a couple months, and during that time, your uncle and his wife will be here with Quinn. You can spend time with your cousin while Lason is training."

***

Winter Y1076

Barlion stared out the window in the nursery. Lason hadn't come to the manor for weeks. Maybe he'd come today. His father had gone out early that morning with workers and guards, clearing the snow from the road. The monsters only came over the wall when there were drifts outside the holding, and his father had workers clear those too, so it would be safe for Lason to come. He bit his lip. *But what if the monsters get Lason before he reaches the gate?* In all the years Lason had been coming, it was the first time the thought had crossed his mind. He shook his head. *Lason never had a problem getting here before. He can take care of himself.* The nanny called his name, and he turned his attention back to his lesson.

At lunch time, he headed towards the dining hall. He had just opened the door to the entry when the outer door opened and a guard came in with Lason on her arm. Lason had a large bundle on his back and was coughing. He dropped to his hands and knees just inside the outer door, and the guard knelt by his side. The guard looked up as Barlion stared at them.

"Go fetch a healer. Quick."

Barlion took off running.

Hours later, Barlion sat beside the bed in the room reserved for Lason whenever he spent the night at the manor, watching over the older boy. The bundle on his back had proven to be a small child who was also sick. Barlion's mother had taken the little one to the master suite.

A healer entered the room carrying a tray. "I'll take it from here. You go get something to eat."

He nodded and left the room.

In the morning, a ruckus in the hall outside his room awakened Barlion. He stumbled to the door, yawning and rubbing his eyes. Lason was in the hallway, struggling against the healers who were trying to get him to return to bed. He fastened fever-bright eyes on Barlion. His face had a grayish tinge to it.

"Where. Is. *Oca*?" He coughed between each word.

Barlion blinked. "Oca?"

On the other side of the hall, the door to Barlion's parents' room opened and his mother stepped out.

"My *daughter*!"

Barlion's mother gasped, and her face turned white. "She's in here."

Lason turned towards her. "Let me see her."

Barlion's mother nodded to the healers and stepped back in the doorway to allow Lason to enter the room.

Barlion followed the others into his parents' room. His mother led the way to the fireplace in the main room, where they'd set up a cot for the little girl. Lason sat on the edge of the cot and stroked his daughter's forehead.

Barlion's mother fetched a blanket from the closet and draped it around Lason. Then, taking a seat beside the cot, she placed a hand on his knee.

"Lason? How old is your daughter?"

He sniffed. "She's three." He broke into a coughing fit. When he got his breath back, he looked directly at Barlion's mother. "Three and a half."

Barlion's father stepped forward. "*You* have a daughter that's three and a half? Where is the child's mother?"

Barlion stared at his father. The man was trembling and his voice had a rough edge to it.

"She's dead. She got sick and died last week." Lason sniffed. "Everyone in the slum is sick. There's no heat. We only have enough fuel for cooking. When Oca took sick, I had to bring her here where it's warm. I don't want to lose her." He coughed again and raised his head to look at Barlion's father. "I figured if you won't let *me* go out when the weather's bad, you'd help care for *her*." His head sank again as another coughing fit overcame him.

"You thought right. Neither of you is leaving here." Barlion's father turned and headed for the closet. "I'll arrange for supplies to be taken to the slum. We have fuel to spare. We can send bedding and food, too."

Lason's head came up again, his eyes wide. "They won't deal with you. The slum is hostile to Moraven."

Barlion's mother's eyes lit on him, and she nodded in his direction. A healer bundled him out of his parents' room, ushered him into his own room, and instructed him to get ready for breakfast.

***

Barlion didn't see Lason or either of his parents again until that evening, when he went to the dining hall for dinner. His parents were at the table as usual when he arrived for the meal. "Papa? Were you able to help the people in the slum?"

His father smiled at him, nodding. "We disguised ourselves as Browarg. They'll never know it was us that helped them."

"How are Lason and Oca?"

His mother sighed. "Oca is doing well, but Lason is very sick. Would you like to visit with him after dinner?"

He nodded.

The fire there made Lason's room so hot, Barlion felt he was suffocating. He took his coat off and unbuttoned his shirt. Lason lay bundled in the bed, staring at the flames moodily; his eyes fever bright. On a table beside the bed sat a stack of clean handkerchiefs, while a basket underneath the table waited for used ones.

Barlion sat on the chair beside the table. "You gonna be ok?"

Lason sniffed. "I don't know. I'm sick."

"Mama says Oca ain't as sick as you are."

"That's good."

***

Spring Y1077

After lunch, Lason suggested that all the children join him in the fruit grove. "We can play hide and seek. The weather's nice and we can get some fresh air."

Barlion bit his lip. The snow was gone, and he didn't think the monsters would be loose in the holding, but still. Play *outside*? He *never* went outside if he could help it. He didn't even go into the garden.

"I don't know..."

Lason hugged him, ruffling his hair. "Come *on*. Take a chance for once."

"Oh, all right."

When they reached the grove, Lason turned to them, holding Oca's hand. "Ok. Here's what we do. I'll be 'it' first. All of you hide while I count to ten. Then I'll come looking for you. If I find you, then *you'll* be 'it' and *I'll* hide while *you* count to ten. When it's time to go inside, if anyone didn't get found, they're the winner. Otherwise, the winner is whoever got found the fewest number of times."

Tiari pointed at Oca. "Is Oca gonna play too?"

"Oca's too young to hide by herself. She'll stay with me. We'll be 'it' together and hide together."

"Ok."

Barlion ran as far from the start as he could during the count, climbed a tree, and hid in the branches. The scent of the blossoms soothed his mind. Monsters couldn't *possibly* come out on a day as nice as this one was. He was staring out over the blossoming trees when Myla called out from below.

"I *found* you! You're it!"

He laughed. This *was* a fun game. He climbed down from the tree and covered his eyes. "Ok. *You* hide now."

When he'd counted to ten, he set out, looking for the others. He spotted something blue on the ground and went to check it out. It was the little coat his mother had made for Oca. He frowned, picking it up. Why was it laying on the ground? He continued in the same direction he'd been going when he'd found it and came out of the fruit grove. From there, he could see Lason sitting on the wall with Oca on his back. The older boy gripped the top of the wall and swung over to drop to the ground on the far side.

Barlion raced to the wall and stared at it. The wall's surface was rough with plenty of handholds. He stood, staring up at the top of the wall. Then he drew a deep breath and began climbing. When he reached the top, he could see Lason in the distance, heading south. He swallowed and climbed down the other side.

The ground in the wastes south of the holding weren't really flat, and he lost sight of Lason. The other boy had been going south though, so he continued south. At dusk, he came to a road. He stopped, straining his eyes as shadows continued to spread. Which way was home? He whirled around, but it had grown so dark he couldn't make anything out. He sniffed, sobbing as tears welled up in his eyes.

Gravel pattered on the ground a short distance away.

"Lason?"

In the dim light, a dark shape loomed over him.

"Lason? Is that you? I'm lost."

The dark shape charged him, knocking him to the ground. He stared up into the gaping mouth and lolling tongue of a monster. A dollop of drool landed on his forehead. His heart seemed to stop as the beast's rank breath filled his nostrils and he knew no more.

Barlion awoke beside the holding wall. He looked around, but he was alone. He swallowed convulsively and climbed back over the wall. As far as he could tell, he was at the place where he and Lason had climbed out earlier.

When he reached the manor entry, a guard grabbed him by

the arm and hauled him to where his mother sat in his parents' suite. Upon sight of him, his mother pulled him into her arms and held him tight. Sobs shook her body. .

"Oh, Barli, I was afraid we'd lost you. Where *were* you?"

He swallowed. "I saw Lason climb over the wall with Oca and followed them."

"Where *are* they?"

Barlion shook his head. "He was so far ahead of me, I lost sight of where he went. Then a monster came, and I fell asleep. When I woke up, I was by the wall, so I climbed back over and came home."

His mother turned to the guard. "Please pass the word that Barli is safe at home. It's no doubt a lost cause to continue looking for Lason and Oca. When Alius returns to the manor, please send him here."

The guard bowed. "I'll see to it, madam."

Barlion's mother ran her hand over his coat. "What did you get *into*?" She sniffed at him, wrinkling her nose. "You need a bath. Right *now*."

*** *** ***

Summer Solstice Y1077

Barlion watched, wide eyed, as a guard escorted Lason into the dining hall during the Solstice feast. The guard looked down his nose at the older boy.

"Look who came back."

Barlion's mother jumped to her feet, ran to Lason, and embraced him. "We've been so worried about you. Where have you *been*, and where is little Oca?"

He shrugged. "I took Oca home to ma. I ain't leaving her here with you." He turned to look directly at Barlion's father. "I can come in the morning, but I go home to ma for dinner and I ain't coming every day. I ain't sworn to you, and don't owe you nothing."

Barlion's father closed his eyes and let his head drop with an audible sigh. "Very well."

Barlion's mother shook her head at her husband. "No! That's *not* acceptable." She faced Lason again. "We *love* Oca. We want to help care for her."

Lason stiffened. "She's *my* daughter. You can't *have* her. I only brought her here because she was sick. She's staying with ma from now on."

"Talora…"

Barlion's mother glanced over her shoulder at her husband.

"We don't have any right to Oca."

Her face crumpled, and she broke into tears. "But I *love* her." She turned back to Lason. "Could you at least bring her to visit sometimes? I worry she won't have warm clothes or enough to eat."

He shrugged. "Maybe. I ain't making any promises."

Over the next few weeks, Lason resumed his previous routine. Moze arrived as he had each summer for the last four years. This time, however, instead of occupying Lason with training, he had the youth brought to the meeting room on the second floor. After meeting with Moze, Lason went to sit in the garden, staring at the pond. Barlion joined him.

"Is something wrong?"

Lason tossed some food to the fish in the pond. "Moze said if I want to continue training, I have to swear service to Moraven. He said I could start advanced training, but only if I swear service."

Barlion stared at the fish swimming in the pond. "So *are* you?"

"I don't know. I wouldn't be able to go back to the slum every night if I did, and I'd only be able to see ma and Oca when I have free time."

"Would you have to go live in the keep?"

Lason shook his head. "Moze said I'd live here, but I'd have to sleep here every night unless I had free time. He said he'd send a new teacher here to work with me when he was busy elsewhere in the enclave."

"So, what are you going to do?"

"I don't know. I have to think about it."

At lunch a week later, Lason told Moze that he'd swear service to Moraven.

***

Early Summer Y1077

Barlion's mother told them all to dress in their very best after breakfast. "Your Uncle Kor is coming to swear Lason into service today. He'll hold court too, since he'll be here himself."

Barlion felt his heart sink. They'd all have to attend court if his Uncle Kor was handling it. That meant he'd have to sit in the audience chamber while it was in session.

Lason's swearing service to Moraven was the first business dealt with. Barlion's Uncle Kor then opened the proceedings up to any other business. Barlion's father stood before his brother first. He bowed.

"My Lord, my daughter Tiari is now fifteen. She's of an age to think of marriage. There is no one in the holding that would make a suitable husband for her, however."

Kor regarded his brother through the eyeholes of his mask. "Very well. She will return to the keep with me. Young men of other clans visit the keep every year. She'll spend spring and summer at the keep until she's found a husband."

Barlion's father bowed. "Thank you, my Lord."

* * *

Autumn Y1079

Barlion's parents ushered him and his sisters into the carriage.

"Is everyone in? Did you pack all you'll need?" his mother asked.

His father patted her hand. "It'll be all right. If anyone forgot anything, we can replace it when we arrive at the keep. Even gifts."

"I wish she'd found someone who *wasn't* the heir to his clan." She sobbed. "She's going so far away."

"We still have Barli, Lyna, and Myla at home."

She buried her face in her hands. "For how long? They're all growing up so fast. Barli's already fifteen. We'll lose *him* next."

Barlion sat by a window and stared out as the carriage traveled to the keep. Would he see a monster as they traveled? Every spring and summer, his father had work done on the walls. Still, when winter came, the monsters got inside. He'd seen them outside the manor house almost every winter. They were always out in the wastes, though.

At the keep, their carriage joined others traveling to the

transport docks. Barlion had never ridden a transport before. As his family entered the transport, the Casand ambassador and a crewmember greeted them. The ambassador gestured towards the crewmember, who bowed.

"If you'll follow me, I'll show you to the passenger compartment."

Barlion's father tapped the top of his head. "Don't stare. It ain't polite."

Barlion flushed and looked down. The crewmember looked so strange. He'd seen no one who looked like that before. Were crewmembers even human? He snuck peeks all the way to the passenger room.

Upon arriving at their destination, they disembarked, and the ambassador instructed them to follow his carriage. The dock stood beside a river, which they crossed. Once they were all on the other side, they headed northeast. The rocking of the carriage lulled Barlion to sleep.

A hand on his shoulder startled him awake. They had arrived at the Casand keep.

Barlion found the wedding boring. His mother cried and hugged Tiari, and his father shook everyone's hand. Then it was back to the transport and home.

On the transport, Barlion talked to a crewmember.

"Every crewman I've seen looks alike."

The crewmember smirked at him. "What makes you think I'm male?"

Barlion's cheeks burned. "I'm sorry. So you're a woman?"

"That would be telling now. Wouldn't it?" The crewmember pointed at a pod. "You need to enter your pod for the journey. Please get inside."

By the time they arrived back at the manor, Barlion was tired of riding in a carriage. He headed to his room on the third floor, his mind absorbed by the mystery of the transport crew. What *were* they really?

He was halfway from the top of the stairs to his room when a door further down the hall opened. He glanced down the hallway.

Lason stepped into the hall from his room, followed by a woman. Once in the hallway, he pulled her into his arms and stood on his toes to kiss her. "Come back anytime."

The woman giggled and danced towards the stairs.

Barlion frowned at Lason. Lason had been bringing women to his room ever since he'd sworn service to Moraven and moved into the manor permanently.

"If papa catches you keeping the housemaids from their work again, he's going to make you move into the barracks with the guards."

Lason snorted. "She had free time. We *both* did."

Barlion rolled his eyes at Lason and entered his room. Just inside the door, he froze, staring at the wall above his bed. The blood drained from his face. "*NO!*"

Lason poked his head in. "What's wrong?"

He pointed at the wall above his bed. Lason looked at where he was pointing.

"What?"

"My painting! My picture of Lirin and Tollot. Where *is* it?"

"Maybe a servant took it to clean and just ain't brought it back yet."

Barlion shook his head. "They know better. I've told them not to touch it."

"Maybe it was someone new."

He stumbled to his bed and dropped onto it, covering his face in his hands. "If anything's happened to it, their ghosts will come for me."

Lason sat beside him and put an arm around him. "Barli? Those ghost stories I told you. They ain't true. They're just stories. There ain't really any ghosts."

"Yes, there are. I *saw* them. They came to me one night. They appeared as skeletons and Tollot pointed right at me. It was a warning. They'll come for me if their picture gets damaged. I have to keep it safe."

* * *

Barlion's father ordered the manor searched from top to bottom for the missing painting. At dinner each evening, the seneschal reported on the progress of the search.

His mother tried to comfort him. "It has to be inside the manor. It's too big to carry out past the guards at the entry." She patted his shoulder. "Would you like to move into Tiari's old room? You have the right to that room now. Since your brothers ain't here anymore and Tiari had to move to Kyomar's enclave, you're in line to take over running the holding after your papa. That room has a key, so you can lock it when you ain't there."

He gulped and nodded.

Finally, after nearly two weeks, someone found the painting. A servant brought it to his room.

"We found this in the cellar storeroom. It was underneath the stairs."

***

Spring Y1080

Barlion frowned at his father. "I don't *want* to go to the keep. The last time I left the manor, my painting went missing. We still don't know who took it or why they hid it in the cellar."

"Take it with you."

He shook his head. "And risk it getting damaged in travel? No."

His father sighed. "You're nearly sixteen. You should start thinking about marriage. How are you going to find a spouse if you don't meet anyone?"

He hunched his shoulders. "They can come *here* to meet me."

Myla grinned at him, her teeth shining white against her dusky skin. "It's ok, Barli. Since I ain't your sister, you can marry *me*."

"Sorry Myla. You're too young. Besides, you're a commoner."

Barlion grinned back at Myla. "I can wait until she grows up. Besides, didn't Uncle Kor want to marry his mistress? Wasn't *she* a commoner?"

Barlion's mother gripped her husband's hand tightly. "I think that's a *wonderful* idea. If Barli marries Myla when she's old enough, it would be the perfect answer to what *her* future should be. She's lived with us so long she ain't really suited to living as a commoner anymore, and it won't hurt Barli to wait for her to grow up."

"And what if they change their minds, then?"

"If that happens, we can discuss what to do about it then. There's no need for Barli to rush into marriage."

Barlion's father sighed. "Very well." He eyed his son with a jaundiced eye. "You and Myla can consider yourselves engaged to be wed. I expect you to treat her as your betrothed. You are to spend every moment of your free time in her presence." His lip curled in a smirk. "We'll *see* how much you want her to become your wife after spending a few months as her swain."

"You mean a few *years*." Barlion winked at Myla. "I already care about her. I'm sure we can come to love each other as a husband and wife *should* by the time she's old enough for us to marry."

***

Winter Y1080

Barlion sat staring out a window in the nursery. Storms had locked them in the manor house for three days. The weather had been clear for less than an hour. If the monsters were going to get inside, *now* would be the time. He hugged Myla tightly as he strained his eyes. Movement by the path to the fruit grove caught his eye.

"Look." He pointed through the window. "The monsters are inside the holding."

She peered through the window where he'd pointed, her dark eyes sparkling. "Those are just wolves."

"Wait until they get near the statue. They're bigger than wolves. I've seen them every winter since we arrived here. The first year I saw them was the year you came to live with us." He swallowed convulsively. "They killed your parents. That's why we took you in and made you part of our family."

"If you see them every year, why ain't you showed them to me before?"

"I didn't want to scare you when you were so little, and we didn't spend all our free time together then."

Myla hugged his neck. "Well, we're safe in here. They can't get inside the manor."

He closed his eyes. "No. No, they can't get inside."

***

Spring Y1081

Barlion sat looking out the nursery window with Myla on his lap.

She sighed, leaning against him. "I *enjoy* being engaged to you. How much longer do you think we'll have to wait to get married?"

"Oh, at least another five or six years. You're still a little girl."

"I heard some girls get married at twelve or thirteen. Couldn't we get married when I'm that old? That wouldn't be so long."

He shook his head. "Those are child brides. I don't want a child bride."

"Why not?"

He chuckled and kissed the top of her head. "You'll have to move into my room and sleep in my bed with me once we're married. If you do, you could get pregnant. If you get pregnant when you're too young, it could hurt you. I don't want you hurt." He closed his eyes. "You know how Lason brought his daughter here that winter when they were both sick?"

She nodded. "I wish he'd bring her back for a visit. He said he might, but he ain't yet."

"Do you know how old *Lason* is?"

"How old *is* he?"

"He's twenty-one now. Do you know how old his *daughter* is?"

"How old?"

"Well, she should be eight on her birthday this year. She was three when he brought her here. He was only sixteen then, so how old do you think that made him when she was born?"

She sat up straight and glared at him. "That's a *math* problem."

He laughed. "I had to figure it out myself. He was only thirteen when she was born. I think her birthday is in the summer and Lason's birthday is in the spring, so he would have only been twelve when her mama got pregnant with her."

Myla wrinkled her forehead. "Do you mean *Lason* was a child bride?"

"He wouldn't have been a bride cause he was a boy, and I don't think he married Oca's mama, anyway. It hurt him, though. I think that's why mama and papa let him get away with things they'd punish *us* for."

"Like when housemaids go into his room with him?"

"Yeah. Like that. I ain't allowed in your room and if you came into *my* room, they'd punish both of us and papa might say we can't get married after all. He might even send you away." He tapped her nose with a finger. "So we just have to wait until you're the right age. Meanwhile, we can do everything *else* married people do."

"Like what?"

"Like we can give each other gifts. We can sit together like this and cuddle while we talk. We can sit beside each other at meals. I can fetch you treats on holidays. We can go for walks. We can play together. That sort of things."

She frowned. "We *been* doing those things and most of the time *you* do things for *me*. That don't seem fair."

"There's something very *special* you'll do for me once we're married that will more than make up for all I do for you."

"What's that?"

"I'll tell you after we're married."

She sniffed and turned to gaze out the window. "Someone's coming." She pointed.

He looked out the window. A carriage, surrounded by guards, was coming from the direction of the gate. He sat up straight. "That looks like Uncle Kor's carriage."

***

At dinner that evening, Barlion's uncle sat in the place his father usually occupied. Moze was present at the table too. Lason sat in his usual seat, stiff as a board.

Kor smiled at the family. His smile looked forced. "I suppose your youngsters are wondering why I'm here."

Barlion leaned forward. "Why *are* you here, Uncle Kor?"

"Your cousin Quinn is moving to Vellisan. I'm visiting each holding to find people to go with him."

Barlion's eyes widened, and he turned to his father. "Papa? Do we have enough people that we can spare anyone?"

"Your uncle will only take a few people from here." Barlion's father nodded towards Lason. "One person who will go is Lason."

"I ain't been back to the slum since last *year*!" Lason glared at Kor. "Will I at least have time to visit my friends and family there before we leave for Vellisan?"

Kor shook his head. "I'm afraid not. We're working on loading the transport now. We expect it to depart for Vellisan the day after the Solstice. You'll be returning to the keep with me."

***

Spring Y1082

When Barlion escorted Myla into the dining hall, he stopped short just inside the door, staring at the table. Lason sat in his old place.

He walked over to the man with his hand out. "Lason! I didn't expect to ever see you again. What brings you here?"

Lason smiled as they shook hands. "Lord Sequinne needs more people. I'm here to recruit from the slums in the region."

"Have you had much luck?"

Lason nodded. "I convinced an entire slum to return to Vellisan with me. I'm here because we need handcarts for their belongings." His eyes flicked to Myla. "Greetings Myla. You're looking well today."

Myla grinned at him. "I enjoy being engaged to Barli." Her eyes shifted to Barlion's father. "I can't wait until we can get married, but papa says I ain't old enough yet."

Barlion's father grimaced. "It'll be years before that day arrives. You're still a little girl."

"Only three or four more years." She turned back to Lason. "Lyna is at the keep this year, being courted by a bajillion clansmen."

Lason laughed.

Barlion pulled out a chair so Myla could sit and took his own seat between her and Lason. "What's it like in Vellisan?"

"Everything is green. There are dense forests both north and south of Lord Sequinne's keep. Game animals run wild."

Myla grinned. "That sounds nice. I wish we could come visit you sometime."

"I'm sure Lord Sequinne would welcome you with open arms."

Barlion's mother smiled at Lason. "You'll be spending the night. You can take the carts to the slum in the morning."

He nodded. "If you could have a wagon loaded with carts, I'll take them to the slum and return the wagon afterwards. Lord Sequinne has provided me with the means to pay for the transport, so all we need from you are the carts themselves."

***

Summer Y1083

"I can't be with you this morning."

Barlion raised a brow. "Why not?"

Myla smiled at him. "I'm making your birthday present myself. I want it to be a surprise, so go off and do weapons' practice or something."

He laughed and kissed her on the forehead. "All right, I'll go do weapons' practice until lunch."

At the practice field, he sighed as he chose a practice weapon. Even when it *wasn't* winter, he avoided going outside as much as possible, so he wasn't very skilled with *any* weapon. He worked on stances for an hour before accepting a sparring partner.

They had barely begun exchanging blows when his partner struck his hand. He dropped the practice sword.

His partner gasped. "I'm *so* sorry, sir. I didn't mean to do that."

He grimaced. "It's ok. I ain't any good at this." He examined his hand. The skin across his knuckles had broken and blood was dripping on the ground.

"Let's get you to a healer and get that bandaged."

He nodded. So much for spending the morning at weapons' practice.

When he left the healer, he headed back to the manor and made his way to the nursery. Myla wasn't there. He sighed. She was probably working on her present for him. He checked the sitting room the adults normally used. The doors to the ballroom were open, and he heard his mother's voice issuing through the opening. He stuck his head inside.

"Where's Myla?"

His mother turned. "I sent her to collect some decorations."

"She told me she was making me a birthday gift. Did she finish that?"

His mother nodded.

"I'll go help her bring the decorations here, then. Where is she?"

"I sent her to the cellar storeroom."

Barlion felt the blood drain from his face. He'd given up on warning his sisters years ago and had *never* told Myla about the monster in the cellar. "Where?"

"The cellar storeroom."

He turned and rushed out of the room, running to the stairs. He took the steps two at a time. When he reached the second floor, he hesitated a moment, biting his lip. He'd have to go to the audience chamber anyway, so he fought back his fear and opened the door to the stairwell where the spiral staircases led down to the audience chamber.

It took much too long to find the knob that needed to be pressed to open the door to the cellar stairs, but he finally found it and charged down them.

The cellar storeroom was empty.

He stared around the room wildly. Was Myla safe? Had he just missed her? Had she left here before he'd arrived? He dropped into a chair beside the table, panting. A crate sat on top of the table. He stared at it blindly. Slowly, he reached out and pulled it to him.

It contained party decorations.

He buried his face in his hands. "No."

A soft click sounded on his left. He turned his head and stared as the wall beside him shifted and then swung out into an open space beyond. Myla stumbled into the room, holding a grimy portlight. When she saw him, she threw herself into his arms, sobbing. Behind her, the wall sealed shut.

***

Barlion sat with Myla on a couch in the adults' sitting room on the top floor of the manor, his arms around her. She pressed her face against his shoulder, sobbing. His mother sat beside them, stroking Myla's hair.

They'd spent an hour in silence when the door to the hall opened and Barlion's father entered the room. His shoulders slumped, and he looked tired.

"The secret door opens onto a tunnel. I sent a squad of guards to see how long it is. I didn't go past the bones myself. There are two skeletons. From the remains of the clothing we found with them, they must be all that's left of Thal and Nerry." He drew a shuddering breath. "I'll have the tunnel sealed off. No one else will die in there."

Barlion's mother raised her head, her face dead white. "What killed them?"

"Something gnawed on their bones and there's animal scat as far as I could see. We'll know more when the guards return from exploring the tunnel."

***

Winter Y1086

Barlion placed a wedding wreath on Myla's head. He smiled at her. "Did you think this day would ever arrive?"

She shook her head as she placed *his* wreath on *his* head. "I'd thought it would never come. We've waited so long."

"Are you sure you still want to go through with it?"

She nodded. "Are you?"

He embraced her. "I ain't had any doubts since that day you came out of the secret tunnel and ran into my arms."

Characters

Inheritance	Description
Aybrim	A Guard. Hulos's friend.
Barza	Sulwin's first wife.
Burzock	Drill instructor.
Chianne	A doxy from the Irclaw tavern
Ciarus	A Guard. Hulos's friend.
Dracna	Kirtu's Wife.
Dulgo	A Guard. Hulos's friend.
Edreal	Kirtu & Dracna's son.
Grukor	A Guard. Hulos's friend.
Hulos	Sulwin & Nemed's son
Kirtu Rastag	A Rastag clansman.
Miawa	Kirtu & Dracna's daughter.
Nemed Starblossom	Sulwin's second wife.
Norris	Hulos's son.
Rilva	Grimwolf seneschal.

Serrin	Sulwin & Chianne's daughter.
Shade	A child.
Sila	Serrin's nursemaid.
Sulsi	A Guard. Shade's mother.
Sulwin Grimwolf	Lord Grimwolf.
Tharula	Hulos's tutor.
Ulson	A Guard. Hulos's friend.

Ascension	Description
Aelan	A senior Grimwolf servant.
Alith	Grimwolf artist.
Burk	Nevia & Ricco's son.
Digen	Grimwolf kennel master.
Dinsil	Captain of the guard.
Drogan	Hulos's son. Kip's father.
Grukor	One of Hulos's honor guard.
Hane	Norris's foster brother.
Hulos Grimwolf	Lord Grimwolf.
Jenna	Dinsil's daughter.
Kadan	Norris's foster brother.
Kalida	Norris & Shade's daughter.
Kip	Drogan & Tekla's son.
Miawa Rastag	Hulos's wife.
Mora	Nevia & Ricco's daughter.
Navry	Norris's foster brother.
Nene	A Guard. Shade's friend.
Nevia	Norris's foster sister.

Norris	Hulos's son. Shade's husband.
Quia Splitskull	Drogan's wife.
Rafin	Norris's foster father.
Ricco	Nevia's husband.
Serrin	Hulos's half-sister.
Shade	A guard. Norris's wife.
Sulsi	A guard. Shade's mother.
Tavar	Norris & Shade's son.
Tekla	Kip's mother.
Tisha	Norris's foster mother.
Ulfan	Grimwolf horse wrangler.

Escalation	Description
Akaha	A guard. Zavi's friend.
Arra	Serelaf's daughter.
Ballic	Malida's youngest brother.
Dasver	Rothas's uncle.
Davia (1)	Korander's mistress.
Davia (2)	Korander's daughter.
Diphar	A child.
Erla	Fizran's mother.
Fizran	A slum beggar.
Foshi	Rothas's uncle.
Galar	Lenoma's brother.
Garlos Argul	Sia's uncle.
Korander	Saerthan's son. Moraven heir.
Lasria	Lenoma's bastard half sister.

Lenoma Eldragon	Korander's second wife.
Lirin	Ballic's daughter.
Lisdra	Lirin's son's nurse.
Malida Torust	Lady Torust.
Marda	Torust Captain of the guard.
Maya	Korander's daughter.
Moze	Moraven spymaster.
Nes	A servant.
Olva Argul	Lady Argul.
Rema	A slum dweller.
Rothas	Korander's son & heir.
Saerthan Moraven	Lord Moraven.
Sequinne	Korander's youngest son.
Serelaf	Korander's son.
Sesh	Slum boss.
Shula	Rothas & Sia's daughter.
Sia	Olva's youngest daughter.
Sythda Firain	Korander's first wife.
Tollot	A clan bastard. Lirin's lover.
Tylen	Malida's younger brother.
Wisia	Slum healer
Yadrac	A scout.
Yalima	Torust spymistress.
Zavi	A guard.

Conflict	Description
Bithin	A guard.

Brock	Hathan & Sylda's son.
Delor	A guard.
Gary	Mentally broken man.
Hathan	A farmer.
Kuren	Hathan's friend.
Lerali	Scout trainer.
Marrasi	A clan bastard.
Mohara	Yadrac & Verda's daughter.
Nisa	Hathan & Sylda's daughter.
Sia	A clanswoman.
Sylda	Hathan's wife.
Verda	A scout. Yadrac's wife.
Yadrac	A scout. Verda's husband.
Zavi	A guard.

Aftermath	Description
Anrin	Moraven guard
Brabeo	Moraven guard.
Derrath	Moraven guard.
Faro	Tylen's companion.
Ilith	Crèche Matron.
Jasya	A holding worker.
Korander Moraven	Lord Moraven
Lisha	Tylen's companion.
Marsa	A crèche worker
Moze	Moraven spymaster.
Nabak	Moraven guard

Podero	Prisoner of war. Torust bastard.
Sazad	Prisoner of war. Torust bastard.
Sisca	Yakara and Darrath's daughter.
Theli	Moraven guard.
Trika	Captain of the urfren unit.
Tylen Torust	Torust clansman.
Vemus	Moraven guard
Yakara / Kara	A crèche worker. Marsa's friend.

Secrets	Description
Alius Moraven	Korander Moraven's brother.
Barlion	Alius & Talora's son.
Kerith	A guard in training.
Kor	Lord Korander Moraven.
Kyomar Casand	Casand heir. Marries Tiari.
Lason	A slum brat.
Lirin Torust	Girl in painting. Deceased.
Lyna	Alius & Talora's daughter.
Moze	Moraven spymaster.
Myla	Orphaned child.
Nerhar	Alius & Talora's son.
Oca	Lason's daughter.
Sequinne	Korander's son.
Talora	Alius's wife.
Thalion	Alius & Talora's son.
Tiari	Alius & Talora's daughter.
Tollot	Man in painting. Deceased.

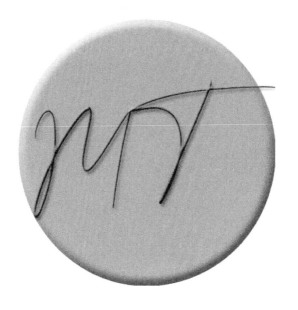

Made in the USA
Middletown, DE
08 May 2022

65511978R00166